The "Jimmy" Trilogy

novels by the same author

Mon cheval pour un royaume
Jimmy
Le coeur de la baleine bleue
Faites de beaux rêves (winner of Le Prix La Presse)
Les grandes marées (winner of the Governor-General's Award)

THE JIMMY TRILOGY
JACQUES POULIN

TRANSLATED BY SHEILA FISCHMAN

MY HORSE
FOR A
KINGDOM

JIMMY

THE HEART
OF THE
BLUE WHALE

Anansi   Toronto

These three novels were first published in French in Montréal by Les Editions du Jour.

The publisher and translator would like to thank the Canada Council and the Ontario Arts Council for their assistance.

Made in Canada for the
House of Anansi Press Limited
35 Britain Street
Toronto, Ontario M5A 1R7

Cover Design: Joss Maclennan
Photo of Sheila Fischman: François Rivard
Photo of Jacques Poulin: Denys Arcand
Typesetting: Video Text Inc.
Printed by The Hunter Rose Company

Canadian Cataloguing in Publication Data

Poulin, Jacques, 1938-
  [Jimmy.   English]
  The "Jimmy" trilogy

(Anansi fiction series ; AF 39)

Translations of Jimmy, Le coeur de la baleine bleue, and Mon cheval pour un royaume.

ISBN 0-88784-074-4 pa.

I. Title.

PS8531.083J5413   C843'.5'4   C79-094057-4
PQ3919.2.P59J5413

Contents

Introduction

In Quebec City several years ago, there was a big celebration to honour the city's writers. When Jacques Poulin appeared at the door he was asked for his official card. Jacques Poulin didn't have one.

"You aren't allowed in without a card."

"Literature is well guarded here," the writer replied.

He remembered then that he did have his tennis club membership card—and while the literature of Quebec was being celebrated, Jacques Poulin was playing tennis, like an illiterate zouave.

That's the sort of man he is. A free man who pays the same scrupulous attention to a page of writing as to a tennis match. I should add, too, that for the past few years he has been living on the shores of the St. Lawrence River, that royal road to dreams.

If you look for adventures when you read, read Jacques Poulin's novels. If you think that a book represents a serious game between reader and writer, read Jacques Poulin. Catch hold of the ball he sends bouncing from the life of reality to the life of dreams, from one novel to another, from memory to the future. It doesn't matter how you return the ball: it will always come back to you in some unexpected way. For this game is no futile exercise, but an assiduous search by a writer who has become a child again in order to explore his life as a man.

The writer, then, sees things for the first time, catching a glimpse of death—inevitable—on the horizon; like a child, the writer is filled with curiosity as he contemplates a world unwilling to be understood, and filled with tender affection for a world unwilling to be loved.

If one must live in this solitude, how much better to be surrounded by friends who share the same experience. And so Hemingway appears, that image of paternal strength, along with the solitary cowboy from old movies, a racing-car driver—and a cat. As he seeks what might be the world of reality, the "guinea pig" may stop for a moment before familiar signs that identify some of the things he desires. And in a moment of intimacy the "carapace" (a word the narrator is fond of) opens. Reality is no longer strange.

Don't expect Jacques Poulin to present a sociological post-card of Quebec: although his novels are strongly rooted in time and space, they open onto "a galaxy of signifiers, not a structure of that which is signified," to quote Roland Barthes. Poulin's writing is not falsely accessible: the reader must tame the characters as, discreetly, they flee and metamorphose. He must pay attention to the signals they send out.

Jacques Poulin is a writer. What can I add to his message? Anything that I, his friend, might try to say is far less interesting than a single sentence by Jacques Poulin, whose fresh, spontaneous writing is the result of painstaking work and a deep knowledge of language.

When you read Jacques Poulin, try to become once more the sad child who abandoned himself to dreams when the world was very big and you were very small.

Roch Carrier/translated by
Sheila Fischman

My Horse for a Kingdom

My kingdom for a horse!
Shakespeare, *Richard III*

It seemed like a stone, heading for ecstasy.
Henri Bosco, *Malicroix*

Mon cheval pour un royaume *was first published in 1967 by Editions du Jour in Montréal.*

Prologue

If only we had memories!
But who has memories?
Rainer Maria Rilke

So I said that it all seemed rather strange. Let me explain. Would you be kind enough to give me a cigarette? It's about this window. You're very kind.

Until then the window had seemed natural, honest, totally lacking in originality. I didn't know how to interpret the signs. Does my negligence surprise you? Don't protest: for so long you've seen me as a careful observer. Besides, as you told me, that's why I was chosen as a guinea pig for your experiments.

Are you writing down everything I'm saying? Good. I very much appreciate your concern for accuracy. I thought it was an ordinary window. It happened this morning, around six o'clock. Be very scrupulous, make a note of everything.

But still, I've been using this room for some time now; no matter how far back I go into my past I don't remember having had another, nor do I remember living in any place but this strange hotel. To tell you the truth, I've forgotten all my old memories. By the way, one thing here surprises me. Have you noticed? All the employees wear black uniforms with gold buttons. I think you're the only one who wears a long white smock. It suits you; you're right; white isolates you, confers a certain majesty on you.

I was telling you about this window.

This morning, it was raining. As it happened, I was looking out the window; I've always liked the rain. I was standing up, sir; all the windows here are too high. That was just a comment—I'm not complaining. They're too small too.

It was around six o'clock and it was pleasant to watch the rain. That's not always the case: the rain is a woman, so it's constantly changing. The rain was blue this morning, a very rare phenomenon of course, and one that forebodes some strange happening: it was a sign. But I wasn't paying attention. Don't smile. I was dreaming.

I'm usually cautious. I think there's something vulgar about any kind of surprise and I can say in all modesty that I'm very rarely caught off guard. When the rain is blue, sir, when the rain's a gentle, blue woman, you must be ready for anything.

Suddenly, there was a vision: I no longer recognized the window, I could see very clearly—as though in a flash of light—the courtyard of the prison, the cobblestones of a prison courtyard, four grey walls hugging them close; the rain stopped and everything was tense, glowing, blinding. And at the same time I felt a hideous burning sensation under my clenched fingers: iron bars!

Then the vision vanished. Everything became normal again. It was raining. I had a slight headache. The rain was grey.

I was lying.

No, everything wasn't normal. In fact I can still feel the bars whenever I want to, feel them under my fingers; they're cold now. The vision disappeared, but the bars are still there.

I'm too fond of normal life, you understand. I must find some way to justify the existence of these bars at my window; once they become plausible, perhaps one day they'll disappear. Who could go on living this way, in my place?

I've thought it over carefully.

I'm going to replace my lost memories. I'm going to construct a past for myself that can make the presence of the bars legitimate. I have no choice: I'm a guinea pig who enjoys a normal life.

1

Once I've arrived here I walk more slowly. A kind of lingering respect. According to the calèche driver, this street, rue de la Fabrique, is the only one in Quebec City that's really a woman. (A hell of a beautiful high society woman.)

In any case, I'm a good half hour early. Quebec is so pleasant in the morning; people are getting on the bus, going to work, the sparrows are eating horse dung. Everything is disciplined. You can feel life. I wonder if the delegate from the Front is interested in the sex of streets the way the calèche driver is.

(This street offers itself with great generosity, but with great dignity too. Look: you go down this gentle, inviting slope. You glide past delicate articles of clothing, perfumes, porcelain, glass, jewels; and the Empire Cinema, right in the middle, where you go for pleasure. . . .)

In the past I used to go down this street as the calèche driver did; some days I felt like slowly sliding down it on my stomach.

And here I am once more at the bottom of the hill, like a stone, and I haven't tasted its charms.

I wonder if the delegate. . . Not likely.

A man in his thirties, I imagine; at least I hope he's older than I am. Projected onto a wall: the enlarged shadow of man delegate standing behind table thin single low lamp.

Gently. The sun puts you right out of it. My shirt's sticking to my skin; the day's going to be very humid. For the past week it's been like the same day over and over again.

Another fifteen minutes before the meeting on rue Couillard. I have time to walk to the Porte Saint-Jean. For a long time now my carapace has been almost hermetic.

[The sun seemed to have set on rue Saint-Jean. I guessed that something was coming along in the middle of the unbearable heat.

I switched sidewalks.

Sweat was pouring into my eyes. The thing, whatever it was, was coming from the people. Their eyes. I was out of breath. People stood right in front of me and looked through me. Their eyes were hollow.

I began to run, charging at them.

And now they started to have ants in their eyes. They climbed up my legs. Some were on my stomach. I ran like a madman as the ants crawled over me.]

2

Rue Couillard.

It's the right number. The house, a fairly old one, stands at the corner of rue Saint-Flavien, leaning a little against its neighbour on the left.

The stairs creak, which is normal. (At the top, turn left; then just follow the old red carpet—brownish as a matter of fact, but it's hard to see—the door at the back: that's it. *Salut.*) I knock. A gentle voice answers.

I open the door. He's sitting at a table, arms folded, watching me.

He looks like a civil servant.

He's sitting across from me and looking at me (will he never speak?). He looks at me and his face is elongated, thin, rather greyish, practically the same colour as his jacket and tie. I wait, motionless, inside the silence which is as hard and dense as my skin.

I am inside my carapace.

A light stirs inside the hollows of the man's eyes. The fire moves gradually to the thing which has once again become me.

The man motions with his hand.

"There's a chair," he says simply.

It's as though he had created the chair. As though things were coming back to life. I sit down. The room is shabby: an iron bed, a chest of drawers, the table between us, dirty walls.

The delegate says in his soft voice, "It's all arranged."

"Good."

"The boss agrees."

" . . . ."

"He already had a plan for the monument; your proposal came at the right time."

I tell him I'm glad. His thin face looks satisfied too.

"I didn't have any trouble persuading him," he adds.

After a moment of silence: "I've read your novel. Your hero has some interesting ideas about the Quiet Revolution. Very interesting."

"That's got nothing to do with it, *Monsieur le Délégué.*"

"Ah."

He sits there with his mouth open. I feel awkward; I'd rather his face became grey and impassive again. The hole in his face seems to be asking for explanations, which are impossible for me to supply.

"Your hero has a political ideal. That's become rare, you know."

"That has nothing to do with it either, *Monsieur le Délégué*," I say, forcing myself to smile this time so as not to annoy him.

"Ah."

That hole again; my fault. The delegate thinks I'm a revolutionary. In his place I'd think the same thing.

He gets up, shrugs slightly. "You're an intellectual: the goal of the Front du Québec requires the participation . . ."

He pursues his thought, pacing, hands behind his back, seeming cautiously to follow a line on the floor. I won't tell him I have no social preoccupations, and no political ones either. The delegate sees me in a certain way and I just have to conform to the image he's created.

I wait for him to stop speaking. Then I ask, "So, when does it happen?"

He must have noted all the information, taking all the necessary precautions, like a good civil servant.

He's read my mind.

"It's fair play, if you don't find an old British expression out of place."

I don't think it's out of place. I simply think that I don't even understand myself; that I won't ask any more questions, that I'll wait for his orders.

Finally, in the same tone: "Tomorrow night, ten o'clock, Parc Jeanne d'Arc. A man will give you a parcel and the instructions."

Rue Couillard is grey and dark. It seems as though it's permanently damp. When you turn the corner onto de la Fabrique it's light again, so soft you feel as though it's just been born.

3

[I finally stepped onto Place d'Armes and recognized the Château.

Sitting sideways on a bench, knees drawn up to my chin, I cried a little, I think, like the fountain, and I didn't see that it was beautiful.

I smelled a strong odour of horse. I looked up: a man was standing in front of me and the smell came from his clothing.

"Would you like a calèche ride?"

I nod.

"Get in then. You can call me Simon."

"I'm Pierre. Pierre Delisle," I pronounce, not stammering too much, but with a slight hesitation.

"And this is Plato," said the calèche driver, getting into his seat after he'd helped me up. He picked up the reins and leaned towards his horse.

"Pierre Delisle," he said slowly rather loudly, as though the horse were somewhat hard of hearing. Then he turned to me.

"This is a very proper horse," he added sententiously.

Simon clicked his tongue, then turned the calèche around in front of the Château and started down the street. At the bottom the horse assumed a suitable trot and turned left by himself. . . . The images become muddled there. But at the end of a little tree-shrouded street we entered an enormous park furrowed with roads. "The Plains," said the calèche driver, and in my eyes banks of fog clung to the hills and rows of flowers sprang up at every turn. Simon spoke in a low, muffled voice, strangely monotonous, and like a magician he mixed together flowers, fog, seaweed and sea. I understood little and felt confused, at the threshold of a world that was mysterious, unknown and marvellous, where my ants might be not completely out of place.

"Come back whenever you feel like it."

We were near the Château again. I was asleep. It was already dusk.]

4

"Another coffee?"

"Yes, Nathalie. You're very kind."

Her eyes become sad.

I know, it's idiotic to tell her that. In fact those aren't the words I really said in the depths of myself. "Yes Nathalie, and I love you." That's what I said inside; but the only thing that came out, that was dragged outside my carapace of stones, was the ridiculous remark: "You're very kind." Absolutely idiotic. That's why I don't talk to Nathalie very much and why we say only ordinary things to one another.

"Forgive me, Nathalie, I'm a zouave; and light the candle, will you please?"

"It's all right, I like the kind of zouave you are." She smiles and her eyes become as bright as they were before when we were eating, almost in silence. She puts the old Grand Marnier bottle on the table, with red candle stub in it. "Besides, it was a good day," she adds, pouring the coffee. "I met Simon at noon. He invited us to go for a ride after supper."

She is happy and asks me if I've had a good day too.

"Yes."

"Don't drink till the candle's lit, and pour the cognac now."

I take a second bottle from the cupboard and pour a little cognac into each cup.

After my morning appointment I just walked through the streets. I walked all day long, inside the old walls; I haven't gone outside them for a month. I feel as though something has changed, as though the walls were closing in around the old city.

She bows her serious face over the candle; the long black hair on either side of her face comes together under her chin. All sorts of colours have burned in this bottle. Green, blue, red and white drips have hardened on its bulge.

Nathalie holds the trembling yellow flame of a match to the candle.

Nathalie, you experience things with the softness and the patience of your hands; you know what's at the heart of things. Whereas I slide over the surface; with my writer's words I have the fragile knowledge of the wind.

Nathalie holds her breath. She knows that the candle has a sense of drama, that it can refuse the fire. The hand that holds the flame is the same one that has delayed the hardening of my carapace. It's a patient hand; the candle finally agrees to accept a very small flame. Then it abandons all resistance and the fire shakes its head, takes up a little more space, starts to breathe. No mistake. The candle burns, tall, clean, upright.

I drain my cup in one gulp and I can feel the warmth of the coffee and the cognac flowing inside me.

Unconcerned about the untidy bedroom, the open door, Nathalie goes down the stairs ahead of me. She walks silently, with feline suppleness; her hair drifts about her shoulders.

Rue Sainte-Anne is already covered in shadows.

On rue Sainte-Anne a stranger could easily find out by himself where the calèche drivers stay; whether he goes in one direction or the other, horse dung will inevitably lead him to Place d'Armes or to the Esplanade off rue d'Auteuil.

Simon's calèche is parked at Place d'Armes.

American tourists with dark glasses, cameras at their belly-buttons and advertising brochures on their backsides stroll around the fountain, assailed by the calèche drivers' vigorous "buggy rides."

Simon is standing with his back against a tree. A broad smile splits his fine round sunburned face.

"I proclaim that my day is over," he tells us gaily. "Now if the lady and gentleman would be kind enough to get in."

As the calèche driver lifts Nathalie up and helps her sit down she wraps her arms around his neck, gives him a long kiss. I sit close to her. Simon takes his place in front and the calèche sets off.

"You just reminded me of something," Simon says, turning towards Nathalie.

". . . ."

"Something I have to do right now."

I look at Nathalie but there is nothing to indicate what it's about. I don't see anything, except that she's as pretty as ever, that her green eyes are sparkling as they always do. She and Simon understand each other almost without speaking; their ease amazes me.

The calèche leaves the old walls behind and goes past the Porte Saint-Louis, heading for the Plains.

"Driver, tell me how we met," Nathalie asks.

I've heard this story at least a dozen times; but the calèche driver keeps transforming it, and every time his meeting with Nathalie becomes a new story. Simon believes he must renew the past; he says it's necessary to "make it breathe some fresh air." But for the moment it's the present that interests me, because it escapes me a little and that's where you must begin.

The calèche driver coughs—it's a tradition—to clear his throat. "Well, it was a Friday."

"Friday the thirteenth," Nathalie specifies.

"It was Friday the thirteenth," the calèche driver begins again, "It was raining and it was spring. (He counts on his fingers.) That was seven years ago. In those days I didn't have all my illusions yet, but I was making encouraging progress. That's why I thought that every man's entitled to see a beautiful woman when he gets up in the morning.

"That particular morning I hadn't yet had the chance to satisfy this need. I was alone in my bed, just as I was when I went to sleep the night before as a matter of fact; but what bachelor doesn't harbour a secret wish to find a woman beside him when he emerges from a night that's been filled with dreams? I was alone. All I had to do was start looking for someone. I got up and went out. It was still early. As I said, it was raining."

"A soft, gentle rain," Nathalie adds.

"It was a soft gentle rain and I'd been careful not to eat breakfast, because it's a lot easier to find a woman pretty if you're fasting; your body's closer to your soul and it clears your vision. You must do everything to have luck on your side.

"So there I was at the corner of Saint-Jean and de la Fabrique, standing in the rain in front of the florist's shop. I stopped every woman who went past and offered her a flower. The ones with umbrellas didn't even answer, or else they said excuse me, which amounts to the same thing. They were in a hurry or indifferent. I thought they were particularly indifferent about themselves. If a woman's going to be beautiful, the first thing she has to do is accept the fact that she's beautiful; that morning there were lots of women who didn't accept it.

"After a while I was soaking wet and starting to get hungry and it was still raining. I sat down on a step to rest; I wasn't discouraged, only a little tired. But I just closed my eyes for a minute.

"Then suddenly I heard a voice very close to me."

"Monsieur, will you give me a flower?" Nathalie asks, on my left in the calèche.

"As you can see," the driver went on, "I'd just found what I was looking for. I was sure of it even before I looked. And when I looked up she was beautiful, no umbrella and her name was Nathalie; I called her 'tu' and 'vous' at the same time and she did the same. She was laughing."

She is laughing again as the calèche drives slowly across the Plains. The sun shines on us slantwise and the oval shadow of the wheels continues to tread the grass silently, like a ghostly reaper.

"A little patience, we're almost there."

Simon urges his horse on. He seems simultaneously mysterious and delighted, like a child about to reveal a secret. He whistles briskly as the horse climbs lazily to the top of a hill.

Simon pulls firmly on the reins and brings the calèche to a stop by the side of the road. Without a word, he jumps to the ground and takes Nathalie in his arms. As I get out on the right side I notice that the sun is hidden behind the high walls of the prison. But the calèche driver is pulling us in the opposite direction, and we follow him into a clump of trees beside the road. Simon walks briskly among the bushy trees; he seems to be following a path that I can't see.

In the distance I can see his back bending to avoid a branch. He straightens up, stops. We enter a clearing. Nathalie is a little winded. I have never been here before.

The clearing slopes rather steeply; at the bottom, the edge of the woods. Running, sliding, we rush down the hill until we come to a hollow in the ground that draws us abruptly to the right: before us there is a path, narrow and half hidden.

Simon has started to whistle again, very softly. Nathalie follows him. I bring up the rear.

The path, a very long one, keeps going down, a little at a time. Here there is peace or the void. An almost total absence of sound. A few insects; from time to time a cricket. Nathalie's legs before my eyes. Her hair dancing on her shoulders. We walk in a corridor of shadow. We have been walking for a long time. The shadows become denser. The trees are tall, narrow; the tallest touch the light of the sun. Above, through the clearings, I make out the occasional soaring flight of a gull.

One more step and I'd have run into Nathalie.

Simon has just stopped in front of an oak tree. He is breathing hard and seems strangely tired. The tree is grotesque. The trunk is swollen in places. The twisted black branches assume strange postures; they are like knotted arms. Nathalie has walked around the tree and gestures to me through the low branches. I go to her.

A rose bush climbs between two large roots, clasps the trunk and winds around the bottom branch. Right against the trunk, where a low, knotted branch begins, is a scarlet rose. As in the hollow of a shoulder.

It isn't a wild rose bush.

"This is a tree that has a little trouble surviving," says the calèche driver. "I wanted it to rock a rose in its arms on windy days."

5

No one spoke much during the trip back to Place d'Armes. There, Simon left the calèche. I thought it wasn't very prudent; he said he wanted to walk for a while.

We followed the usual route: rue des Remparts, d'Auteuil, Sainte-Geneviève and back, taking the walk on top of the walls as far as Porte Saint-Jean. I had the same impression again—that the triangle formed by the walls was squeezing tighter. And it seemed to me that the old city had started to die.

We walk up rue de la Fabrique, Nathalie between us; we stop across from the Basilica.

I look at Nathalie, who looks at me too. I think of the softness of her skin, the warmth of her bed. I don't know what she's thinking about, as I don't share her ability to read people's thoughts: I need a word, a sign. I wait.

Eventually I discover a kind of disorder in her eyes: the lashes are blinking slightly. She's patient and has probably been waiting for me to notice. Her blinking indicates to me that a third person has intruded between us; I turn towards Simon. He too was looking at Nathalie. It's never easy to know what the calèche driver is thinking but to me Nathalie's eyes reflect Simon's desire. We feel the same need, he and I.

It's not unpleasant. We share the same desire.

Spotlights cast greenish reflections on the façade of the Basilica. The colour spreads over our faces and hands as well. The calèche driver starts watching me. He seems to be gauging the strength of my desire; at least that's what occurs to me. He scrutinizes me easily, unperturbed. It's impossible for me to follow the course of his examination: I think it's better to trust him and wait. After a moment he seems satisfied and turns to Nathalie. I do the same.

Nathalie looks at Simon first. For a long time and very gently, it seems to me. I suppose it's about me; I can't check. My carapace.

Then everything happens more quickly. Nathalie bids me good night; I tell the calèche driver goodbye; together they go off towards rue Sainte-Anne.

And I head for rue d'Auteuil.

It could have ended differently; it's strange how our actions take place outside of us. Most often it's I who sleep with Nathalie and the calèche driver who goes home, alone, to his apartment on rue d'Auteuil. If it had ended differently I would have slept on rue Sainte-Anne.

(During the day we open the burlap curtains: a huge many-paned window appears, transforming the very ordinary apartment into a sort of large glassed-in gallery that looks onto an old fashioned park with a tangle of wild bushes and rank weeds among the mossy trees.)

A straw lampshade hanging from an electric cord surrounds a table and chair in the middle of the room with a circle of light. The calèche driver has left a notebook and a pencil for me on the table. He doesn't write himself; he did it especially for me.

In a life as empty as ours, where nothing happens behind the walls but the stories we tell, rituals are essential. I sit at the table. The circle of light envelops me, isolates me. I pick up the pencil, a large wooden one with a rounded tip. I sharpen it with my pocket knife. I draw some symbols on the paper, haphazardly and rather absentmindedly—circles, straight lines, curves. It's a strategy, a kind of idea-trap. The drawing, vague at first, gradually imposes a form. As predicted. I need only finish it. The result, most often, represents a woman.

I study the woman at length, hoping to catch her personality by surprise. A sketch of a story is drawn. My ideas start falling neatly into place; other characters are added; the story is filled in. I finally write a tale almost in one burst, then I throw myself into the calèche driver's bed. His bed is narrow, but comfortable.

6

[The city becomes liquid motion—the sun liquefies the last snow on the roofs, which drips onto the walls of houses and the sidewalks cars splatter with water passersby venturing out coatless cautiously watching where they step to avoid getting their dry feet too wet that's most important—even wet they're happy because of the new warmth of the sun they can sense through their clothes and say hello how are you to people they haven't greeted since the Carnival stop at street corners to chat to smoke to catch up on the news and turn around to watch a woman sailing past carried along by the current of spring—the current moves over me too but it flows above me as though I were a motionless stone at the bottom of a stream (lying on the beach on the Ile d'Orléans I let the tide come up until it was about to submerge me—my myopic mother shouted from the top of the cliff Pierre supper's ready) the current glides rapidly to the surface just barely perceptible around me inert round pressing heaving against the bottom—now I am sitting on a bench without the slightest desire to move impossible anyway might as well stay here with the weight of the old houses leaning against one another and the old wall with all its stones weighing on me as I sit here for all eternity not understanding exactly why for the first time spring is rejecting me and anyway what would be the use of understanding better to stay here think of nothing and wait but it's even harder to think of nothing you think of this and it's already something especially when you're supposed to be an intellectual an intellectual's something that thinks nothing is something so the ideas connect mechanically and the assembly line unwinds tirelessly around the stone at the bottom of the stream—the assembly line suddenly carries along a vague disturbing idea threatening not far from me the thing finally comes to rest somewhere in front of me becomes clear becomes a presence I guess something or someone that's a danger for me I feel a malaise a weight in my chest and I'm threatened by this presence that belongs to the same species as me attacked within my self my indivisibility by another of the same substance as I—I look up a man sitting in a broad armchair hands spread on his knees an energetic face framed by a full beard looks over my head straight ahead of him a monument carved from this grey stone granite and there's nothing opposite me really but this man sitting in his granite but the assembly line starts up again carries along the void the peaceful dark and my myopic mother shouts again supper's ready come on now.]

I'm hungry.
It's almost noon.
Nathalie must be expecting me for lunch.
Still the same hot humid day.
The same tourists, identically blissful and in the way, collect their final memories of these dying streets, prematurely shadowed by the multicolored signs: Rooms, Bath and Shower, Free Parking, French-Canadian Hospitality.

Ten o'clock, Parc Jeanne d'Arc. The time and the place; clear and easy to remember. You need only be on time and in the right place to avoid having things become muddled.
"Simon wasn't at Place d'Armes?"
"Didn't see."
In the hollow of her hand Nathalie picks up the breadcrumbs that had fallen onto the tablecloth and scatters them along the window ledge. She leans on her elbows and places her chin in the middle of a sort of hollow that she forms by bringing together her slightly curved hands. A ship washed upon the sand.

Simon could be on the Esplanade or at work; she knows as well as I do. No need to mention it.
"He was supposed to come for lunch," she emphasizes.
I have stayed at the table with my coffee after the usual

ceremony. I contemplate Nathalie in the mirror above the sink; it's my way of seeing her again as she was the first time. The mirror strips her of the habits with which I've clothed her in the meantime. It likely indicates an inability to see reality as it is, but behind every mirror there's another world, the only real one perhaps. And who can say which side of the mirror we are on?

"You just have to break the mirror."

I must have been thinking out loud. But it's not that easy, Nathalie; there's always another mirror. And the ones that don't break.

She says, "In this city one dog out of three is a man."

". . . ."

"It's easy to say absurd things."

". . . ."

"Simon was sad last night; that's what's important."

"I didn't notice."

She doesn't reproach me. She speaks gently. She is gentle. "I'm not reproaching you," she says.

There it is.

I say to her, "Tell me."

"He left around midnight. Because of his calèche, he said. He didn't want to sleep with me."

Someone knocks at the door. She leaves the rectangle of the mirror, walks past me dressed like the Nathalie of today. She opens the door.

"Inspector Mc . . . . . on. Provincial Police."

I was two seconds too late when I tried to recall the name, uttered in a sharp voice. A face moves through the door frame; it is round and reddish with very round glasses standing out against it. An English name, the last syllable reverberating in my head like a bell. The man twirls the hat he is holding in both hands, begins to cast a sidelong glance at my armchair; I invite him to sit down; I must have greeted him mechanically.

The man says he's sorry to disturb us, he wouldn't do so without a serious reason, he's been given the assignment because of his knowledge of psychology, he preferred the word intuition himself, he'd spent a good part of the night and all morning working on it, he'd made good progress and just wanted some additional information, it was mainly a question of personal satisfaction, once again he was very sorry to disturb us, he asked (Nathalie) if he could smoke his pipe, it was mainly a question of habit, he'd have gladly taken a cup of coffee but he didn't want to impose, besides he intended to get to the point right away, he asked if we'd be so kind as to take a quick look at a piece of paper.

I pick up the paper.

It is crumpled, one corner torn. The writing is familiar. Nathalie looks over my shoulder.

<blockquote>
won't make it over the hill
I'd set: turn forty tomorrow.
life and I'm happy;
there's a reason and it's
. . . is. Soon it would have been hard to
love her. I'm dropping the reins.
Everybody pays his own price. In my case,
it's my horse for a kingdom.
</blockquote>

Silently Nathalie turns back to the window.

The inspector removes a speck of dust from his hat. He's a young man, well dressed, fat. He must scrape his face every morning when he shaves that pimple on his chin. I see him at home in the evening, in a cosy house, filled with concern for his children. He quietly draws on his pipe. A nice guy.

He asks if I recognize the writing.

"Yes."

"Your friend the calèche driver?" he asks patiently.

"Yes . . . but the paper's torn."

". . . because of the pocket knife. The paper was stuck to a tree on Place d'Armes with a pocket knife. A taxi driver brought it to the station. Nothing too interesting so far, is there?"

"No."

His pipe has gone out. I hand him a match.

"Thank you. Besides, I was sleeping then; when nothing's happening I recuperate. (He strikes the match.) They woke me up around two this morning: calèche without driver on the bridge to the Ile d'Orléans. The driver of a car phoned."

The inspector just has time to light his pipe again before the flame burns his fingers.

"We've got a file on every calèche driver who's come for a licence. I looked in our records: the fingerprints on the paper correspond to your friend's. Then I was driven to the bridge to the Ile d'Orléans. The calèche was in the middle of the bridge; the horse was still there, not moving, head drooping. The night was so peaceful and calm I couldn't resist an urge to try an experiment: to bring the calèche back to the city myself; put myself in the driver's place, try to understand him. I let myself be rocked by the rhythm of the calèche and the city lights slowly came closer to me. I think I'd have enjoyed being a calèche driver. The trip was pleasant, but it didn't help me understand. No, you don't die that way when you're happy. I decided to go home and sleep."

He takes off his glasses, brings them to his mouth and exhales, a sort of sigh. A sheet of thin paper held between thumb and forefinger traces increasingly smaller circles on each lens.

"Early this morning I took up the investigation again. I asked questions, consulted files. (He takes a notebook from his pocket.) Came from the Gaspé or the North Shore. Studies philosophy at the university, teaches it at the Séminaire de Québec. Special note: gives students the portion of his salary that's above the country's average. Next, studies or travel, or both: France, United States, Mexico, South America, it's rather confused; this information comes from a restaurant, the Aquarium. I made a discovery at City Hall: a ten-year-old file where his name appears with the mention 'day labourer.' He was put in charge of the upkeep of the Plains. You know, cutting the grass, cleaning the grounds, trimming the shrubs. With the help of the file I even found one of the people he used to work with, who'd taken up a collection when your friend decided to become a calèche driver."

In the beginning there was a torn piece of paper. Then this man discovered events long forgotten. He shook the dust off them, cleaned them, made them like new again. He invented others that hadn't existed before and methodically fit the new facts to the old ones. One after another the pieces took their place in the set of gears and the well-oiled mechanism began to move. The man—mechanic or magician—had a marked advantage over me; he can make up an event so that all the facts follow logically. The same advantage as Simon.

He emptied his pipe by tapping it against the ashtray. The distinct sound chases the sparrows from the window where Nathalie is leaning. He says nothing more; his forehead has been creased for a moment. Then, in his sharp voice: "Two things still baffle me: first of all, the real motive; and then the reasoning that could have made a professor of philosophy become a calèche driver. Now, if you think you might be able to help me . . ."

In a grey city three and a half centuries old, whose walls close in a little more every day, a man with round glasses and a face like a ball has lost a friend. He has spent a whole night searching for him, wandering through the streets and over a bridge with the help of a message he deciphered like a map that shows where treasure is buried. By asking questions and searching in dusty places, he has found a trail that has led him finally only to two silent people without emotion.

"No further ahead than I am? Less perhaps? And you, Mad... (he stumbles over this word, between Madame and Mademoiselle). You aren't saying anything?"

Nathalie says nothing. The sparrows have come back.

"All the same. You lived with him, if my information is correct. It's true that for several years it hasn't been enough for you, apparently. (He glances in my direction.) Loving two men at the same time, another thing that . . ."

He is mistaken. He should stick to the mechanics of it.

I waved goodbye but I think he's already left.

He deserved more sympathy.

I could have used a trick I know; it's dishonest but it works. I start by closing my eyes to eliminate distractions and help me concentrate. I think of myself. After a minute or two I see myself as I really am, but removed from myself. Then this image of myself feels sad and starts to cry. I feel sympathy for this weeping person and I end up crying too, imitating myself: it's the only way.

7

They don't seem to realize.

They walk around in there as though everything were normal. AS THOUGH THEY WERE FREE. They even still have their free men's faces: mute and impassive. They don't know that they're all going down the same corridor. From Sainte-Foy, Sillery and Lower Town, the buses let them out and scatter them at the Carré d'Youville. They form a line, close ranks and then they're swallowed up inside the Porte Saint-Jean, all on the left-hand sidewalk. They all go along the same sidewalk down rue Saint-Jean, then turn right and go up rue de la Fabrique to the Basilica. Then they cross rue Buade and change sidewalks. Immediately, they slow down: the sidewalk splits. Some go to the right and make their way among the street artists on rue du Trésor; the others go along rue Buade and don't turn until rue du Fort. But the two branches meet again at the entry to the Terrasse. When they've walked enough from one end of the rectangle of parallel boards to the other—walking in twos and forming what is called a couple—they return to the same precise, narrow corridor, retracing their steps. They go out through Porte Saint-Jean not suspecting that the walls are closing in on them, pushing into a single corridor those who are walking trustingly through the old city. They walk there without suspicion. Something in the way their backs are bent becomes docility later, when the buses pick them up again at the Carré d'Youville.

I enter the corridor through the door that opens onto the Terrasse and let myself slip into the line of people getting off. The heat has reached its sultry mid-afternoon maximum; the grey sky seems almost to be leaning against the roofs of houses. The steeper slope of rue du Fort leads me to the branch that then turns onto Buade.

[It was lost in advance, but I wanted to try my luck again, try once again to defeat my old visual habit. Change the fold of vision. I moved closer, eyes shut, until my hands touched the iron railing that protects the store window under the old sign: Magasin des Arts du Vieux-Québec.

I opened my eyes.

Very bad start: I recorded the notion of quantity—as usual. A heap of objects, without enough space for the eyes to rest for a moment. The second stage is automatic then: a hovering glance, horizontally from left to right; the usual order. Bad beginning, bad ending; can't hope for anything from the rest. The rest, in fact, was classification, on the way to becoming traditional.

The dozen carvings in white, brown and black wood (two African statuettes). The three pairs of sealskin moccasins. The standing ashtray mounted on popsicle sticks. The agates scattered among the bracelets and letter-openers with Indian heads. The row of beer mugs. The period dolls. The RCMP. The two cuckoo clocks. The ivory chess set. Tired of looking. Ivory. Tired. . . . At last, the sailboat. A three-master, with decks, ladders, ropes and all the rigging suspended from the ceiling by chains, drifted above the jewellery and characters. Phantom ship. Coleridge. End of the line, everybody out. Once again the store window ended with Coleridge. What was forcing me always to see in the same way?]

The ones coming from rue du Trésor joined us and the corridor became clogged; the people kindly slowed down as long as necessary, then resumed their normal speed, pushed forward a little, pulled back a little. They are docile and so am I and I like order as much as they do because intellectuals are part of the world of order. There are still a few cracks in my carapace, and from them brief shafts of light sometimes slip out and I can't determine whether they come from inside me or outside. The rest of the time the carapace remains hermetically sealed around the kind of false lucidity that makes me think of a flame perpetually feeding on itself.

If necessary—the shafts of light are unpredictable—I can always put on my store dummy act; Holt Renfrew's window lends itself to it very well. It's a very clean window, an appropriate space, not too large, cooled by two fans. You stand there in well-cut Scottish tweeds, briefcase under your arm and carrying a cane, inert and impervious. People walk past on the surface.

8

Place d'Armes.
I open the newspaper on my knees.

TRAGEDY ON ILE D'ORLEANS
A man drowned in the St. Lawrence last night. Investigations are being carried out in an attempt to locate the body of the victim. An empty calèche was found in the middle of the Ile d'Orléans bridge and it is assumed that the tragedy occurred at that spot. The note reproduced opposite enabled police to identify the presumed victim as a forty-five-year-old calèche driver known as Simon. Inspector MacNaughton of the provincial police is in charge of the investigation.

PRAYER TO ST. JUDE
O glorious apostle St. Jude, faithful friend and servant of Jesus, the Church honours you and calls on you universally as the patron of hopeless causes. Pray for me in my misfortune. I beg you from the bottom of my heart to use your great privilege to bring speedy and visible help to those who call on you. Come to my aid and relieve my misery. Obtain for me the help and the grace of the good Lord and in particular (particular requests). Help me to become one of the chosen and obtain for me eternal salvation.

St Jude has a long white beard and he walks across the water. Under his arm he carries a halo the size of a life jacket, tied to his left hand by a cord. He is looking towards the bridge where the calèche driver, a biblical millstone about his neck, is being dragged into the void.
   "You're smiling?"
   "As you can see. Hello."
   "What are you doing this evening, Monsieur?"
   "I have an appointment."
   "An important appointment?"
   "Yes, I think so."
   "In that case, Monsieur, your appointment must certainly be with me."

She is standing on one leg in front of the fountain, head bent, hands behind her back. The young woman's smile is both mysterious and very gentle, but it's hard to know what she's really doing in the park at this strange castle where time itself seems to be lost in the endless corridors. One even wonders whether the young woman is really there among the enigmatic characters at Marienbad or whether it is, rather, last year.

"It is with you, Madame, in a way."

"I like your absentmindedness; it allows you to forget me. Then you can find me again; I like that."

"And whom does one find?"

"Me. Always me."

"And who are you, Madame?"

"I am the person whom you find."

Nathalie starts laughing and sits on my bench.

I ask the question abruptly: "You aren't sad about Simon?"

"No. You?"

"I'm not honest when I'm sad." Feeling that I am becoming ridiculous, and a little irritated at feeling that way, I add, "You obviously haven't read the paper."

"I'd rather that you address me formally this afternoon, if you would be so kind," Nathalie says with a smile.

"As you . . . as Madame wishes."

We can hear the trickling of the fountain and the cheeping of sparrows that have come there to drink. A calèche sets off with its cargo of tourists; the staccato clattering of hooves on the pavement moves slowly away down rue Sainte-Anne.

I feel vaguely that I'm becoming disagreeable.

"You want to put some distance between us?"

"No one can control that distance. I just want to let you be different with me. I'm going to have to change a little now . . . now that Simon won't be exactly the same any more."

"I don't think I understand you."

"That's not surprising," Nathalie remarks, with no irony.

"Explain, then."

[He covered the blackboard with symbols and figures, I asked him questions until the board was completely covered with white chalk and my head filled with white light, a light that placed me above the other students, I wanted to keep it prisoner, wall it within my head, I asked the teacher to explain even when I understood, I had the impression I was feeding the light the way you tend a fire.]

9

To go down into the belly of the old city and flee the air, heavy with rain that's been too long in coming, there are fourteen steps if you enter on the side of rue Desjardins (the same number as on the Ile d'Orléans). Fourteen steps, a corridor, an arch-shaped door flanked by leaded-glass windows which I enter, holding up two fingers: the bartender brings me two drafts. He greets me and slips the twenty-five cents into his pocket without handing me the change, as usual. (She used to like to repeat what my father said: he said you're ripping your eyes out.) La Chapelle is the most attractive tavern in the old city.

The only tavern located in a basement.

The rather rough comfort of the sturdy chairs and the heavy tables, the room's pleasant bareness, invite contemplation or relaxation, depending on whether there are many drinkers or a few. This evening there are rather a lot. Some are familiar to me, and they greet me with a wave or with their voices; my identity is progressively asserted as each one recognizes me. (The lighthouse at Sainte-Pétronille, which was lit, told me when it was time to go down to the cellar.) The calèche driver tells me he'd been in underground shelters in London during the bombing.

He also said that going down into a cellar or a basement is like descending into your own childhood. It was at La Chapelle, in any event, that my carapace experienced its finest weaknesses in the past. I hold up two fingers and the process begins again. On other occasions this ritual gesture, repeated a certain number of times, miraculously opened to me the gates of a boundless, liquid disorder. It's ruined this evening, I know that in advance, and it's only through the force of circumstances that the green and yellow cupola of the Price Building, silent and motionless against the black sky, still gives passersby a rough indication of this final fortification which is, in turn, being invaded by the closing in of the walls.

When I think of it it's rather sad.

I will no longer be able, as I could in the past, to transform La Chapelle, make it into a new place. Too bad. I used to think of myself in a bar at the Château Frontenac. My beer would take on the taste of champagne. The rough floor, the wooden chairs would change to deep carpets and velvety chairs. The people arguing noisily about freedom would become important persons. The sociology student I know very well, who is trying to stand up on a chair, would be an M.P. preparing to make a speech. He wouldn't have so much trouble hoisting himself up on the chair and making himself heard over the applause. He wouldn't vacillate so much as he shouts: "Freedom, Messieurs, is something you must choose; and you must make it as vast as you can stand it!" His improvised stage wouldn't collapse. He wouldn't roll foolishly under the table.

I'm unable now to change the décor, drown the old habits. There's something in me that defends me against myself. A second lucidity is keeping watch over my lucidity. A kind of grey eminence, similar to the embrace of the walls, protects me internally from any harm that I might bring on myself. The nature of this protection escapes my knowledge and control; so that I will be even better sheltered, I'm forbidden to know what it is in me that protects my lucidity. I just know that it's part of my carapace.

"Intellectual my ass!"

I recognize that voice.

"So you don't see your friends any more?"

That mocking voice. It's Pagé, editor of *l'Action Chrétienne*. Across from him, a photographer from the same newspaper: Cliche signals to me to join them and he seems as drunk as his colleague. I sit at their table, opposite the sociology student. Head thrown back, he stares at me; his open mouth surrounded by a coarse black beard forms a vaguely obscene hole.

"People don't know how to drink any more," says Cliche, pulling the student's beard. "This one doesn't react like a civilized man. This Pepsi generation of ours is a fine thing. The speeches about freedom are finished for the day."

"Let the dead bury the dead," says Pagé. "We have to drink to the health of our friend the intellectual."

"Waiter! Two glasses of absolute for this young writer!"

The two friends burst out laughing at the bartender's bewildered expression. Pagé slaps his thigh. The photographer punches my shoulder. Cliche's laughter is coarse, like a belly laugh. But at times when the photographer is catching his breath, the laughter is stuck on a clear note that makes his shoulders shake and seems to cause him some pain.

The student, sitting between them, looking lost, his mouth still open, continues to stare at me with his hollow eyes. He could be dead.

"Don't pay any attention to that man," says Cliche between two punches. "He isn't a man, he's an owl. Look at his eyes. I'm telling you that's an owl."

"So we have to rebaptize him," Pagé interrupts.

He picks up his drink and pours it over the student's head. "Owl, I baptize you in the name of the Father and the Son and the Holy Spirit."

"Amen," Cliche concludes, in a severe tone.

The laughter, contained during the ceremony, starts up again louder than ever. Twice as loud. I think my companions are mistaken. They can no longer tell the difference between what is only comical and what is truly funny. Because of the beer they aren't responsible; they're all making the same mistake. Pagé holds his stomach with both hands. A plump man with pendulous cheeks that shake in rhythm with his laughter. Beer is dripping into the student's eyes and bright yellow drops cling to his beard.

I drain my glass, ask for another beer, taking my time; only then do they stop laughing.

The drops in the student's beard have turned white. The others are no longer laughing. Disconcerted and suddenly sober, they look at one another. All jauntiness dissipated. The yellow liquid just had to turn white.

I don't know if they understand the sounds coming chaotically out of the black beard. Sobs, hiccups and words all tumble out in the jumble of an unintelligible rosary punctuated by sighs and tears. During a sigh we learn that a woman has left. He lets his head drop into the angle formed by his bent elbow on the table. His shoulders heave gently. On either side of him a man pats him on the back. Pagé says that the woman will come back; Cliche says that another one will take her place. They say whatever comes into their heads.

I mustn't start to smile.

It doesn't make sense. Other people's pain can make me laugh: it's a permanent risk. In my opinion it isn't a sadistic reaction, but rather a simple reflex by my carapace. I don't know in advance if pain will provoke laughter or pity. The risk is that, without my knowledge, a substitution will occur and instead of becoming sad I'll start to laugh. It isn't serious, just embarrassing. And the mere fact of thinking about it increases the risk.

Prudently, I drink. I force myself to think only of sad things. Simon folded hands his waxen face a black coffin four candles people saying the rosary kneeling on the purple carpet.

The more I drink it's strange how my world becomes clearer around me movements slow down as though to fix the limits of La Chapelle they come closer and every detail becomes clear in my head it's the same clarity as outside when I drink my lucidity is curtailed at the top of my head it grows round closes in on itself assumes the shape of a ball that squeezes my temples—the tide has risen and only the round polished head of a rock emerges—my lucidity is on the surface it becomes clear and intense increasingly the details of the tavern enter penetrate my head arrange themselves there in precise order and the stone ball is lit by a dazzling light objects stand out there illuminated and bare—my intelligence is a fiery stone my eyes burn my head aches I stumble towards the door I run onto rue Sainte-Anne with the obsessive idea of burying my head in the damp earth.

I need Nathalie.

10

Lying on our backs.

The white plaster has come away in places, furrowed by cracks. Vague shadows, hesitant lines, sketch powerful creatures on the ceiling. Creatures on the threshold of existence. They wait to take on a complete form, they wait for me to give them life.

From the ceiling I descend vertically to my feet. As I stare at my shoes, I also make out the indistinct profile on my left. I see clearly Nathalie's feet, bare, a little dirty, beautiful; the rest becomes less and less precise and I see nothing of the head. The head isn't there.

Nathalie starts to overflow. Here's what happens. Nathalie goes beyond her limits. As she lies inside her body, close to me in my carapace, she has started to go outside her two shores. She has transcended her body, she continues to stretch out slowly, everywhere at once, like a layer of water steadily advancing. She gains ground, makes progress towards the hollow in the bed, now she covers the space between us, she is going to reach me with this wave that comes from her self and reaches to the limit of my body, she continues inexorably to overflow; at any moment I will be invaded by the liquid substance that comes from her, flowing uniformly towards my carapace.

Abrupt thrust of the loins. I sit up.

Nathalie, eyes half-closed, lies there prudently, completely self-contained. She has recovered her body. She waits.

I raise my head, draw the blanket up to her shoulders. Her hair, black, stands out clearly against the white pillow, a reassuring stain, too visible to be dangerous. Overcome by the coolness of the pillow Nathalie sighs comfortably, wraps her arms around my neck as I bend over her; she makes herself heavy and I throw the sheets to the foot of the bed. She opens her eyes and feigns astonishment at every move I make; she likes to act out this little comedy every time.

According to the ritual I must now kneel by the bed.

I unfasten her blouse, starting at the top for the pleasure of seeing, after the second button, the opening of the hollow valley between her breasts.

"This is Nathalie," says Simon.

I look at this girl, at least fifteen years younger than he is. She lives with this man who is almost her father; she is faithful to him. He introduces her to me; I still don't understand that he's offering her to me. It always takes me a while to understand. I adapt words to my carapace.

She smiles at me and with my fingertips behind her back I unfasten the hooks on her brassiere and with the same motion I then pull it over her head along with the blouse. Hands crossed modestly, she hides her breasts which I must uncover by force, a slow force, not abrupt; disguised gentleness.

Nathalie prefers liberty to force. With me according to her desire, with Simon according to their need, she is faithful to herself, to events.

Nathalie's half-clothed body seems indecent to me; I can rarely resist this stupid notion. So then I sit Indian-fashion at the foot of the bed and draw the remaining garments towards me. She assumes a surprised expression and helps me a little, first by lifting herself up so that her skirt and pants slip off more easily, then raising her knees to free her feet. Naked, somewhat relieved of the suffocating heat, she seems comfortable, she spreads her arms and legs.

She is content to watch me then as I undress, according to the ceremony. Carefully I fold my clothes and put them on the chair; hers are strewn on the floor, as she wishes them to be.

I lie down beside her.

I must wait a while.

Wait. Long enough for body and soul to find each other. Simon has told me of a similar agreement between Nathalie and himself. She turns to me.

"You have to know one another physically first, that's more within our reach. Afterwards, if we know how to live, we can go further. But you have to start with what's easiest."

Troubled, I begin to reason with her: psychology, the common good and all. Invulnerable, intact, smiling as well, she replies, "Ask Simon, he's a wise man."

The wise man cautiously rolls a cigarette, strikes a match on his thumbnail, lights up, taking his time, leaning against his red and black calèche. Between two puffs you can always practise recognizing the passage of salmon up the rapids, the flowers that don't release their perfume till they've been crushed, the layers of water beneath the desert . . . but as far as the rest is concerned, all is lost in the smoke of obscure allusions and incomplete sentences. Pushed to the wall, he goes to the fountain, washes his hands, and rather sadly, says, "Ask Nathalie, she's direct."

She has given the name "meditation period" to these moments of waiting when she wants to give the mind time to catch up with the body. For me, it's the reverse: the carapace is always late. You must be patient with the carapace; in time, usually, it softens and grows warm. It starts to become flexible at the joints and then waves of warmth come from the head and spread down below.

My hands set off to find Nathalie. They discover her limits, trace her outlines, graze the slopes and search the secret entrances. Her skin becomes moist and eager.

My mouth, more sensitive than my hands, begins the ritual exchanges. On its tongue and lips it collects the desires that emerge from everywhere onto the surface of her skin; it redistributes all over the violent need that is clenched inside me to possess this body that trembles and stirs.

She moans Nathalie moves her knees rise and lower beneath me I crush Nathalie scratches my shoulders her nails furrow my sides the small of my back burns all distance between us the same warmth is contorted it's salty in my mouth Nathalie's neck her hair in my mouth on hers moans a long lament from her throat I enter her I hurt her I make her feel good—something someone is arriving is already there before me a boiling come into the world in the midst of me of her snake on the rock jazz Simon his music rises cunningly crawls onto my stomach wants to glide beneath the carapace at the level of his mouth Simon lifts the blue vase the candle inside it the movement of a priest at mass combines freedom anarchy his words my brothers jazz is born and human distress since Adam's exile the people in the Aquarium make fun of his words the marvellous anarchy of jazz freedom that breathes they laugh applauding the comical professor drunk in front of his philosophy students brings him back docile to Nathalie put on

Ella Fitzgerald These Are the Blues the voice becomes thin drawn out in a thread of water seeking the route to the sea Nathalie lets the water curl around her neck flow over her body the stream is drawn out serpent moan hear me crying I've got the blues the Saint Louis Blues invades Nathalie shudders moans the cool water on her skin whirls 'cause my man got a heart like a rock cast in the sea it swells it coils up the jazz bites into my stone the salty water retreats before the tide slaps the rocks the foam boiling on Nathalie shakes me three seconds clenched like the hand at ebb tide time grows broader calmer on the surface Nathalie stirs a little in the middle slowly now calms down slowly quiet drifting.

11

Bodies separated now, and lying on our backs again.

On the other side of Place d'Armes, through the frozen silhouettes of trees, the twilight of this stifling day illuminates the windows of the Château Frontenac with steel grey reflections.

I've pulled the covers up to our chins. All the covers, in spite of the intense heat. I light a cigarette for Nathalie, one for myself, a third for the calèche driver; this is our custom and when it's Simon's turn he lights a cigarette for me in the same way. The third cigarette burns until it goes out by itself.

I'm not by nature a sad man, not preoccupied, that is, by the future. But still, just now . . .

I know already what's going to happen even before my cigarette is finished, I've experienced it often, just as I know in advance all the useless precautions. My hands and feet start to feel cold. It seems to me that we could have the right not to become ourselves. It would be more orderly if we had a choice: that's the only comment I'll allow myself in my capacity as an ordinary observer. As the outcome was determined in advance, I consider that the struggle started here is, in a way, just as uneven and dishonest as the progressive stifling of the old city by the pressure of the walls.

But the cold is already invading my hands and feet; it brings with it a forgotten odour, the dry smell of stones. The cold enters my skin, stiffens my muscles, passes through my flesh, descends towards my bones and wanders through my blood. I feel all the warmth withdrawing from my limbs, and my skin hardens like a stone that is growing an inch at a time. Pushed back by the wall of stone, a mass of liquid warmth glides from my belly to my chest, beating a retreat towards my head: from feet to shoulders now I'm cold, dry and hard as stone. My carapace squeezes and chills me up to my neck.

My head remains.

A small flame still burned there, in spite of the great warm breath of love. But it was pale, unobtrusive, tolerable, the reflection of a lucidity that wanted to pass unnoticed.

The liquid mass down below bursts in my head. It creeps along the walls around the flame; the tide begins to rise in a series of small waves. The fire flickers, seeks its breath, folds back on itself, troubled, then moves, swells, rises again. Now it is burning tall and straight, with a flame that has burned white, a clear, blinding white like the reflection of an axe. The tide stops.

The mass of moist heat, pushed back against the walls, begins to smoke, with something like a sigh at first and then, when the fire spreads its dryness all around, a kind of whistling sound. The dampness escapes in mist and the mass along the burning walls begins to crack, split, harden. It becomes like baked clay.

The dry white fire has reconstructed a wall of baked clay around him.

My carapace is intact, hard and unfeeling around the lucidity that watches over the impeccably white interior and feeding on itself. The game had been played in advance. A barely perceptible odour of burned flesh wafts through the room. A few spirals of blue smoke from the partly extinguished butt of my cigarette drift up to the ceiling in the pale glow of the streetlight on rue Sainte-Anne. The cannon at the Citadel has just announced half-past nine. I am an intellectual and the time has come.

"You're leaving."

Three syllables in an even tone. It was a statement. I thought she was asleep. A statement, not a question. She wasn't sleeping. I was going to close the door again.

"Yes," I say, simply.

"You'll come back?"

". . . ."

"It's dark."

"Yes, Nathalie."

"It's late."

"It's late."

After a brief silence she begins again.

"It's good, making love."

"Yes."

"Am I good?"

I smile at her in the dark. I close the door silently. Yes, she's good.

12

There are flowers everywhere, nestling in the shadows. In the middle stands the traditional statue of the Maid of Orleans on horseback. It's almost the time we'd agreed upon.

I go slowly around the park, walking carefully down the paved laneway that follows the rectangular border; one by one my silent steps disperse the false disorder of the night. As objects are gradually replaced the park becomes symmetrical again. All the flowers are in the narrow border between the lane where I'm walking and the hedge that encircles the park, broken on either side by a stone staircase with a spotlight shining on the Maid. Benches are set out at regular intervals along the laneway. I sit on the one that seems most dimly lit.

A bum in a salon. The flowers, which I don't know too much about, worry me and their heavy perfume in the humid air makes me feel sick. Simon used to walk around them with me like a proprietor and call them all by their names, which he would pronounce fervently: tulip, pansy, carnation, violet, hyacinth, gladiolus, forget-me-not, primrose, convolvulus, snapdragon. He would fold back the petals, making the dragon's jaw snap open just for me.

I wish I hadn't started.

I didn't hear anyone walking: a narrow silhouette came and sat down silently, and without turning my head I shuddered in spite of myself.

Now I am silent. Certain that it's not up to me to speak first, I wait. It's easy when you're waiting for something specific. I think of Simon who used to say: "Maybe it's because of my age but my dreams are vertical, like trees, while you're like the wind, your dreams are horizontal." And I look up, telling myself as I have every day for a week that it's going to rain.

"The delegate appreciates your discretion very much."

I turn around, astonished: it's a woman. The gentle, musical voice rolls the r's slightly. I wasn't expecting a woman.

"Of course they've had me followed," I say, emphasizing "they."

"It's the rule."

She says r-r-r-rule. I begin to distinguish her features more clearly.

"Since yesterday morning?"

"Before that. Since your first contact with the Front."

A thin face, very short hair, brown or black, hard to see. A woman of thirty or forty, rather pretty.

"And I passed the test?"

"Yes, Pierre. And how about me?" she replies with a laugh.

"You don't look like a terrorist."

"Disappointed? You hoped to see La Passionara? Sorry."

"Don't apologize."

"Sshhh."

She puts a nervous hand on my arm, asking me to be quiet, comes closer to me and whispers, "Someone behind us."

Briskly I put my arm around her shoulder. Steps ring out in the laneway. Her mouth is dry and I wet it with my tongue. Someone passes on our left; slowly the steps move away towards the street that borders on the park.

"You're smiling," she says, moving away from me.

"I'm thinking of La Passionara."

"What you did? Classic and ridiculous."

"Maybe I went too far."

"Don't apologize."

"I enjoyed it."

"Thanks anyway! But it's better not to hang around here. Here are the orders: you're to be at the Palais station at two a.m.; the woman called Nathalie will be with you; with this key you'll be able to open a locker; there'll be a parcel and instructions."

"But I was supposed to be given the parcel here. Change of plans?"

"Just being careful."

". . . ."

She gets up. The scent of flowers isn't so strong.

"Come with me as far as the exit to the Plains."

"Your wish is my command, Madame."

I said this without irony. She explains.

"It was wise to lie to you: you could have been setting a trap for us."

"And now?"

She walks silently and I can scarcely feel her hand on my arm.

"Now, it's all right apparently."

"Basically you aren't very careful."

"We're just ordinary people."

She thinks: being ordinary people gives us our best chance. No, I'm the one who's thinking; she's just someone walking beside me. I also think the rare things always happen outside the walls. That's false. Or superficial at least. The walls seem insignificant and you let yourself get caught. I feel as though I'd like to explain that to the woman, who is thirty or forty years old, and is silent and soft as a shadow.

"The walls don't show anything."

"You must be careful."

"When we look at them they seem motionless."

"Because we don't see them moving."

"Even inside, everything seems normal."

"Normal as a habit."

"You must look behind the mannequins; that's where the concern is."

"In spite of the gates."

"The three Gates."

"Saint-Louis. Saint-Jean. And the Kent in between."

"Three breaches in the wall."

"Where you can go in or out as you wish."

"That's an illusion. Once we're inside the wall closes around us."

"Imperceptibly."

"It takes advantage of our absentmindedness, of the fact that we're busy elsewhere."

"Of the fact that we're busy living."

"It closes in around us like a carapace."

"The carapace is tightening around the Old Town."

"People gliding down the corridor."

"They see nothing."

"The old houses are piled up together, holding each other up."

"Some are crumbling."

"They're the oldest, the most tired."

"Some are burning."

"Like monks in Indochina. To protest."

But now there is no gentle hand on my arm; no one is walking or speaking close to me. For the past few minutes, perhaps, I've been alone across from the Porte Saint-Louis. I must believe that she doesn't live inside the walls.

I was speaking to myself, uselessly. It's through our skin that we understand each another, I and this town with our similar skins.

The key in my pocket feels hard; foolishly, I expected it to be soft and flexible.

She reminds me that I must advise Nathalie.

I leave Saint-Louis for rue d'Auteuil, d'Auteuil for Sainte-Anne and at the other end, near Place d'Armes, there is a light in Nathalie's window.

I can make out two silhouettes: Nathalie's is long and narrow; the other, heavy and square, has something both familiar and peculiar about it. Better telephone; the Aquarium is two steps away. The phone is in the vestibule.

Nathalie's voice is gay: fine, she'll be here in a minute, I should have a coffee while I'm waiting; she says I won't believe her, that she has a surprise for me. She laughs, hangs up.

The waitress brings my coffee to the back room.

"Thanks, Olga."

She smiles: the room is usually reserved for lovers.

"We don't see you any more, Monsieur Pierre."

The coffee is scalding hot. I make a face. She starts again.

"Are you still writing?"

"Yes."

"And is it going the way you want?"

I reply that yes, thanks, it's going well, because I don't know any better answer. If Olga weren't quite so fat she'd be pretty, but there's that strange moustache under her nose—no. Definitely not.

She bends over me.

"I wanted to tell you, about Simon, that hurt me. He was such a nice man. An inspector came and asked me a bunch of questions. Do you think the calèche driver really tried to. . . He loved the bridge to the Ile d'Orléans so much. It's unbelievable. I can't believe he'd try to . . ."

It's true that it's painful for Olga. I can see her brassiere, black, in the opening of her blouse. I try to smile at her: immediately her face freezes, as though I had wounded her, and she walks away muttering something about her work; she walks with her feet turned out somewhat, waddling like a duck.

The coffee is still hot.

Nathalie arrives with someone in tow.

I don't know the man and yet. . . Suddenly I don't feel well. Nathalie's happiness is so acute that she speaks without stopping for five minutes, she who is usually happy to be silent; I have trouble warding off the flood. His name is Mathieu or Simon, it's for me to decide. She herself has already chosen: an old friend she's met again, she realized how unlikely it was and she was quite right wasn't she to say that I wouldn't believe her, and she was right not to cry either, he had told her that people don't live completely don't die totally, they were Simon's words and his voice and his eyes in the same face, it was normal the police didn't find his body, there are some people you've always known without ever seeing them, she could see how surprised I was and agreed that I should take time to think, as far as she was concerned, she who was still so close to childhood, she had no trouble recognizing a childhood friend, Simon agreed, Mathieu too, differences would melt in the sunlight and people could say what they pleased.

The flood ended abruptly.

"Here's Simon."

I look at the man. My dizziness persists.

What's got into this man who looks so much like the calèche driver? He has the same general appearance, perhaps it's his age too, and most of all the same grey eyes set a little too far apart, filled with a softness that warms you. When you look at him in a certain way . . .

Nathalie always looks at people in a certain way. The carapace is inclined to delimit the past and the present; rooted in the moment it resists, tightens around me. What's most important is for Nathalie to be happy.

She is calm again and her joy has taken refuge in her eyes. They are sitting at my table, both of them across from me. Every time Nathalie looks at him her eyes are filled with a moist tenderness that I've seen somewhere before; perhaps in the eyes of dogs. It must be the gleam of fidelity. It's very pleasant, exactly as it is when Nathalie, taking a bath with me, perfumes the water with rich bubbles. Yes, what really matters is Nathalie's happiness.

Olga comes over to our table, asks what we want.

"The usual," Nathalie replies.

The waitress stops staring at the man who is with us and comes back in a moment with a coffee for Nathalie and a beer for Mathieu. She has stopped looking at me; she only has eyes for the man with Nathalie.

"I feel like a calèche ride," Nathalie says, putting four sugar cubes into her coffee at once. "All three of us will go. Simon?"

"The calèches are all inside; it's after eleven."

It was I who answered. She looks at Mathieu and says, "That's true. Sorry. Memory like a sieve!"

She laughs.

"Doesn't matter," says Mathieu. "Tomorrow, if you want?"

She nods, with a little comic grimace; her coffee is scalding; it even brings tears to her eyes. Mathieu lends her his handkerchief. It's a new one, impeccably white. Sitting side by side, they continue to talk and to show me, through their words and gestures, that everything is fine and there are no problems.

They act out their meeting, recreate their shared past, apparently by chance and with no precautions, but in fact they're experts and they act well. I am the spectator; I play the part of the mannequin in the window.

"Cigarette?"

Nathalie smokes Mathieu's cigarettes: they're her favorite brand. They speak a lot, confusing the essential and the secondary, as usual, but they make no mistakes about their habits. The calèche driver's skin fits Mathieu well, he fills it completely, just as he fills Nathalie's vision.

"How's the rose in your oak tree?" she asks, concerned.

"Fine, thanks."

"And you think a man of forty still has reason to hope?"

"Of course, as long as there's still one rose."

He assumes the vaguely absent expression of someone who is remembering, and inhales the cigarette which he holds between thumb and forefinger. Like workmen: of the three of us the calèche driver was the only one who smoked that way; but didn't he hold his cigarette in his left hand? I don't remember very well; likely I'm wrong. No past would resist Mathieu's confidence and I like him because he commits no errors. He is very attentive to Nathalie, whose eyes support him, help him to become Simon. I am present at this birth, guaranteed a certain objectivity behind my window: I find that Mathieu looks more and more like the calèche driver, perhaps for the simple reason that it's hard to distinguish between two people who have the same past.

"Let's go to your place," Nathalie suggests.

"Be my guests; today's my birthday."

They consult me. We leave.

In a corner of the room which we cross a man and a woman are playing chess: Mathieu holds the door open; I follow on Nathalie's heels and he smiles at me as I walk past him; he is wearing a dark grey sweater that reveals a white shirt collar, and black velvet trousers.

Outside the heat is still overwhelming.

"Look."

". . . ."

"The man."

"Yes."

Twenty paces away on the sidewalk on rue Sainte-Anne, the man begins to approach us.

"He's on his feet and walking," explains the calèche driver.

I see nothing surprising: most men walk on their feet, but everything always surprises him.

"And the air," he says, "you mustn't forget the air."

"What? The air?"

"It might be the same air that passed near a flowershop in Paris or a bathing girl in Tahiti. You go outside and the air hits you: and then anything can happen."

"It isn't likely."

"Everything's possible. Look."

"What now?"

He raises his head.

"The cupola."

". . . ."

"It's lit up."

"As it is every night."

"Every night, yes. The city's dreams keep it there, yellow and green, like a fantastic kingdom suspended between the black sky and our heads; and in return it protects us all."

With Nathalie between us we arrive at rue d'Auteuil where the tall trees seem eternal, waiting for something; it is hot and it takes time for the night to pass. Lovers walk very slowly, arms around necks and waists, scarcely more alive than the motionless silhouettes on the benches of the Esplanade.

Mathieu digs in his pockets; he is perspiring. Nathalie opens her bag, takes out a key. I walk ahead of them, turn the doorknob: the door opens by itself.

"That's silly," says Nathalie.

At my back I can hear their nervous uncontrollable laughter. Simon's door is never locked.

"I didn't have time to tidy up. Sorry."

Nathalie's friend goes directly to the fridge. He hasn't stopped laughing. He takes out two beers, puts them on the table. He takes off his sweater and it soars through the air to join the old pair of socks, the nylon stockings and the pyjamas scattered over the unmade bed.

He opens the cupboard, takes out the bag of coffee. While the water is heating on the electric hotplate, he carefully pours coffee beans into the grinder, then turns the handle; the strong salutary aroma of freshly ground coffee begins to spread through the room.

"No one makes coffee as well as you, Simon."

Nathalie watches him pull out the little wooden drawer, pour the powder into a filter, then fill it with boiling water and stir it gently. Elbows together on the table, hands on either side of her neck and fingers wandering through her hair, Nathalie doesn't take her eyes off Mathieu.

"Like a strange bird," he murmurs, "folding its long wings on its neck."

And to prevent her from moving he feeds her the coffee himself, small slow mouthfuls, holding the cup with both hands.

"Not too hot?"

"A little. Not too."

"Good?"

"Very!"

Around them, with words and abbreviated gestures, they construct a world of gentle gaiety and happy tenderness; for some time now they have been doing it on the bed.

I've drunk my beer, Mathieu his, Nathalie her coffee; all is in order. Except for the time, and I no longer have a very clear idea whether it's approaching the hour I'm waiting for, or moving back.

They are asleep.

He sleeps with his head on Nathalie's shoulder, arms around her neck, his left knee across her legs. I tap his shoulderblade with the tip of my index finger; a woodpecker on a tree trunk.

Nathalie opens her eyes first.

"I'd like you to come with me."

She frees herself from Mathieu's arms, sits on the edge of the bed. He wakes up.

". . . going on?"

She looks at me for a long time, looking up because I am standing before them. I read no question in her eyes, just a kind of gravity that reflects my own. She puts on her shoes, buttons her blouse, shakes her hair.

"I'm leaving with Pierre," she says.

He is on his back, arms folded under his head.

"Fine, Nathalie."

She bends over him, kisses him, while I say, "I'm sorry."

"Fine," he repeats.

"I'll be back," Nathalie says.

As we are going out she looks at me to find out when. I reply, "In the morning." She turns toward Mathieu and tells him, calling him Simon, that she'll be back in the morning; but he had understood before she repeated it, I think, because he was already nodding.

13

First we slip slowly onto rue d'Auteuil. Then, though we don't really notice it, a faster slide begins, which ends in an abrupt dive into the corridor of rue Saint-Jean.

"You know, I've become an anarchist."

No, I think that statement is too foolish; it would drop like a stone. Nathalie doesn't ask questions, she does nothing to help me. The words that would be appropriate escape me. And yet the Palais station is a good distance away and I'd have time to explain to her.

In the middle of the corridor and at a right angle, the Côte du Palais opens up. The street is deserted, except in front of the Victoria Hotel, and we both walk in silence, her arm under mine; we are obviously lovers. The abrupt, curved slope slyly precipitates us into the entry to that other world of Lower Town, through a breech in the wall between the Hôtel-Dieu and the Arsenal.

"I'm going to get a bomb."

Not a dazzling idea.

"I've made a decision."

There was no decision, just a coming into gear.

"Listen, Nathalie."

Ridiculous. That's all she does: no one is more ready than she is to listen, understand, approve. It's just that the words finally lose their meaning. Nothing is certain any more, unless it's the fact that the Palais station is looming ahead of us.

I look for the clock. Above the list of departures and arrivals it shows ten to one, standard time. So it's ten to two then. People on the wooden benches, alone or in small groups, are waiting.

Through the door that opens onto the platforms you can see the cars of a train going more and more slowly, finally coming to a stop with a squealing of brakes.

The key!

Briskly I turn my pockets inside out. The long row of metal lockers stretches out against the wall on the left.

We are standing in the middle of the waiting room.

"What are you looking for?" Nathalie murmurs.

I was no longer thinking of the key but of the time, of Nathalie and me; I'd forgotten the rest.

"That!"

"One sixty-three," she reads.

"This way."

While I lead Nathalie, compact groups of travellers coming from the platform surge into the room and surround us. We clear a passage and meet those who are already busy in front of the lockers.

Locker number one hundred and sixty-three.

I inserted the key. It won't turn. A man approaches the next locker. I try twice, three times, four . . .

"Nothing to be done."

"Give it to me."

She repeats the motions, with no more success. The man turns his back to us; he is wearing a military raincoat with the collar turned up and a brown hat.

"Wait."

I remove the key, examine it, compare the numbers: identical. The man in the raincoat turns around.

"Excuse me," he says.

He brings his hand up to his hat and, bowing with rather laboured gravity says:

"Mademoiselle."

The hooked nose in the face like a knife blade hangs comically over the too thin mouth. He shows his key, looking embarrassed.

"Doesn't work! You have the same problem? Forgive my indiscretion, but I told myself: perhaps the keys were . . . mixed up? Is that how you say?"

He holds out his hand.

"Allow me, Monsieur?"

We exchange keys. He waits politely while I try it; the key turns easily; he bends over me as I open the door: there is a small brown suitcase inside. I can feel the man breathing on my neck.

"You can't hear the ticking," he whispers.

"Ah."

"Take it, if you please."

Cautiously, I take out the suitcase, put it down at my feet.

"Synchronize your watch with mine, two eleven," he announces in a scholarly manner.

I adjust the minute hand. Nathalie is watching me. She is watching everything that is happening, attentively: I suppose she understands it all now. Her big green eyes, rather sad, but you have to be very careful to notice. The man looks around, gestures to me to pick up the suitcase and says, "Come."

We leave the station after the last travellers have gone. Outside, the dampness envelops us; he could lend Nathalie his raincoat if the rain . . . no, that wouldn't be prudent.

"Trust her," he said, as though he had just reached this conclusion.

"In any case . . ."

"I mean: she's the one who's doing the work."

"Of course."

"You're only an instrument."

"I know."

"Like me, for that matter."

He laughs silently, then adds, as though to himself:

"They're stronger than we are."

"What time will it be?"

"Four o'clock exactly. You know the place?"

"The monument on the Esplanade. Near the Porte Saint-Louis."

"Precisely. Put it on the plinth. You can choose the best moment yourself: you're free."

At the corner of rue Saint-Paul he stops suddenly.

"Your key, if you please."

I hand him the key. Then he turns to Nathalie and, raising his hat, murmurs:

"Goodbye, Nathalie."

Then he pats me on the back.

"Take care of her."

I pick up the suitcase. The raincoat is a stain, increasingly pale, in the night. He said to take care of her. She puts her arm under mine and we are two lovers, still.

The woman spins around with her white stole and her hand-bag swinging at arm's length and says in a piercing voice that the show was really cute, while on the same sidewalk, facing us, other people, no less drunk, are leaving Chez Gérard's nightclub and the man is pushing her into a taxi, his hands on her behind.

"Take it easy!"

Nathalie squeezes my arm. The driver laughs.

"Where are we going?"

"The Château Frontenac!"

"To Simon's?"

"It's safer."

"And closer to the monument."

"Why are you doing that?"

"I can't help it."

He lets go of her posterior, looking falsely contrite, but still helps her into the car and sits beside her.

"Forward march to the Château!"

The doors slam.

We're off, the two of us and the suitcase.

14

I shove the suitcase under the bed between Mathieu's legs; he is in pyjamas, his hair dishevelled, and he is rubbing his eyes. It's safe. So are we: through the doorway at the end of the corridor it's easy to watch what's happening around the monument.

I stand guard first.

Standing on his plinth, holding the flag, helmeted and stained with verdigris, the English soldier is in profile against the Porte Saint-Louis with its turrets and the stone wall that disappears into the shadows. At the intersection of d'Auteuil and Saint-Louis the law runs in neutral, red, green, yellow, red, now directing only silence.

At night the walls allow people and things to pass through only very parsimoniously: sometimes a taxi, a dog, a cat. My intellectual's carapace is just as impermeable; I feel no fear about what is to come, nor anger at the English soldier. At the very most, a vague regret at the thought that this man of stone, witness to the blood shed by Canadians for the Empire, will be reduced to bits: I suppose it's what is known as pity.

Nothing to report. I go back to the apartment. Three o'clock.

Mathieu is wearing pyjamas with vertical red stripes. The stripes are intersected at a right angle by Nathalie's arms, which form a brown belt across his back. The pyjamas cover everything but the two heads at the top, the belt in the middle, the four feet at the bottom and the brassiere lost somewhere between the legs. Their breathing, rather hoarse, overlaps.

When the switch clicks he moves and the bed creaks. I wanted to avoid noise, let them sleep, but he wakes up, turns his head towards me and starts laughing, a silent laugh that shakes his shoulders gently; then I see myself in front of the hotplate, holding the coffee pot and half crouching, grotesque. He sits on the bed, legs dangling, and I in turn laugh at the sight of him laughing, his hair wild, the suitcase between his red-striped legs.

Without a word, Nathalie's friend gets up and takes my place at the end of the corridor.

Nathalie seems to be lost in a personal fog and the sound of water in the coffee pot helps bring me back to reality; in a single slow, supple motion she slips out of bed and sits Indian-fashion near the hotplate. Her smooth black hair covers her blouse, which is open, and the light from the electric heater glows copper-coloured on her face and breasts. I lie down beside her, head between her knees that are still damp because she was warm a while ago and I remember a phrase: "Woman with seaweed sex and old candy."

There are books in a room, then, many books on the four walls of a small room, books piled on top of one another, stuck together, standing straight like menhirs, rows of books with no space between them, bound, cold and hard, accumulated patiently one stone at a time, shelves filled with books without a single crack and impenetrable as the grey stones of a wall.

The wall is impregnable and Nathalie's strong odour drifts to the surface.

She gets on her knees and takes my head in her hands. The skull is round as a ball, and full: there are no holes between the bones; the eyes, the mouth, the nose are filled with a hard white substance like marble. She contemplates it at arms' length, silent, not seeing the dry and lucid flame that burns behind the marble. The head itself is blind and knows only the appearances of Nathalie: the bearer of light does not see beyond the circle of brightness it projects or the wall of shadow it constructs.

She puts the head on a cushion, gets up: the coffee is ready, she pours it into cups, puts one on the floor near me and takes the other two to her friend at his observation post. The door to the corridor closes silently behind her; once the carapace is burst the slightest draft could extinguish the intellectual's false lucidity, more fragile now than a candle flame.

Holding his cup, he bursts out of the corridor, still in pyjamas. He comes directly towards me, shakes my hand and, stepping back out of the circle of brightness outlined by the lampshade in the middle of the room, he sits down.

He sits across from me on the floor, on the other side of the circle, and he speaks.

In the half light I see his lips move: he fabricates the words in his mouth and breathes them in my direction; the words cross the periphery, pass through the center and come to rest on me with the small soft sound of clumps of damp earth striking a wall.

It's hard for me to acknowledge that people prefer the company of animals to human company, because only the human voice is never bereft of warmth. Even if we don't understand the words. The words arrive, detached and damp and rather tepid, like life, that reveals the hidden presence of human warmth. Generally, only half attentive, we experience nothing more, but sometimes, eventually, the words take on a colour, yellow most often, they are naked, clothed or hairy, smell good or bad. It's of little importance to me, then, to try to understand everything he tells me, just as I'm indifferent to the name—Mathieu or Simon—of the man who is murmuring in the shadows outside the circle of light; besides, it's easy to imagine the meaning of the words.

"I'll take care of Nathalie if anything happens."

If anything happens. This condensed formula says a great deal but leaves things delicately in suspense; it would please Nathalie, who is fond of clichés: she says it's as though several people were speaking at once. For me, the future is unknown. I become aware of events as they occur. A man without a carapace would be alarmed and I would understand him without difficulty. If I were worried, Mathieu's words would no doubt comfort me. Hypothetically, I am reassured.

Creaking of the door, light gliding of bare feet: Nathalie's silhouette comes and sits in the silence. In a moment I'll take her place at the guard's station, but for now our shared presence here seems more important: it takes three people to make a world. We are the three people and each of us is sitting on the edge of the circle of light. It is half past three. We are sitting on the floor, the light in front of us, the darkness behind, and each of us forms a triangle of shadow that begins at the knees spread apart on the floor and stops at the crown of the head. Each triangle sits on its base exactly like the other two and is closed in the same way on its shadow and its silence.

On both sides, they lean their silence against me, weigh with the same constant weight, slowly draw me in; gradually I slip towards the centre; they hold me there in the middle under the light through the balanced force of their silence.

I close my eyes.

The strange light, still there, blinds me. It comes from the inside, from my carapace. It is within me; I surround it; the walls are around us. There is a sort of life that strangely resembles death. Here in this cell there is not a single rich grey corner of shadow that is left untouched by the sun.

The silence becomes less oppressive and the pressure of the triangle eases off. Slipping towards the back, I slowly return to my place on the rim of the circle.

In the shadows I am almost cold.

"It's very warm," she says.

"It will rain soon," he explains.

They speak of it in low voices.

When the swollen drops strike against my stones the calèche driver's rain bursts with a rumbling sound; it is a yellow rain, earthy and cold, and each drop, as it bursts, proves to me that I exist. Nathalie's rain touches me so gently that I have to admit I don't always hear it splashing delicately against my carapace; tepid and manifold, it caresses, fondles and finally goes to sleep in a scent of ancient moss and damp wood. I sit before the large fireplace in the old stone house and listen to the rain drumming on the roof, strong and gentle, earthy and sylvan, the hermaphroditic rain.

A raven's croaking drawn out by a kind of rattle:

"R-r-r-ready; it's now or never-r-r-r."

The rain, as though astonished, has stopped by itself.

15

From here he looks rather small.

The square is deserted. People in Quebec City sleep well every night, except on weekends; I've been able to observe that since I've been here. This is Wednesday. Awake, and therefore set apart, the man deserves special attention. It's hard to see through the trees; for the moment, a single impression: he seems short.

He is carrying something.

From this distance it's a formless thing, of average size and indeterminate colour; night transforms the bodies of objects, respecting only the soul. Pulled to one side by it, the man carries the object awkwardly, as though it doesn't belong to him or frightens him. It's only an impression; the night, the distance reduce me to it.

He must hear the mechanical heart.

Where he is now, he must certainly hear, even better than I, the muffled panting, like the breathing of a cardiac patient, that the traffic light, changing from one colour to another at the corner of d'Auteuil and Saint-Louis, emits spasmodically. Two long rattles, silence, two rattles, the heart stops, starts again, breathes laboriously all night long, and you can hear it beating as soon as the city is asleep, as though through a giant stethoscope. The man must hear it too, more distinctly than his own.

From close up, the man seems more and more ordinary.

Rigid like an ordinary man. I have often noticed this frozen, controlled attitude. Not controlled by will; by the habits of everyday life. One foot before the other, the body tense, paralyzed by the weight of the damp air: he is frozen in the posture of a man who is astonished—or waiting.

Now I see his face.

He keeps his impassive, rather hard face turned towards me; it has no wrinkles and no age; it is like a mask, his mannequin's face; no doubt he has his reasons. It's as though he doesn't see me: he looks beyond, farther into space; or time.

Perhaps because of his skin.

His skin is grey, furrowed with greenish streaks. I know the type very well; it's trustworthy and efficient: it's old, heavy, almost impregnable since childhood. I know what he must feel: nothing. He is sheltered from everything. Almost everything. In his carapace feelings, emotions automatically become ideas; they are at ease there, they form a space around themselves, come together and are knotted in a bright, pure, glowing flame. The light is rather blinding but it isn't serious. You get used to seeing poorly. It isn't serious. And true lucidity is so rare.

He makes me feel sorry for him.

The nighttime prowlers here are mostly dogs, free and concerned. He is not concerned, and certainly not free. He inspires in me not the bad kind of pity, but the good kind—sympathy for one's fellow creature. We resemble one another because of our carapace. And yet it sometimes happens that I want a naked man to cross the night of the Quartier Latin like a wild animal. Not a tortoise-man, a crocodile-man, a tattooed man. A man.

Perhaps he himself doesn't know what he wants.

Let him take his time. When you have a carapace you need a lot of time to recognize your own desires; lots of time and lots of patience. It's most important that he take his time. Often, in fact, you never arrive there: all that's left then is blind, gratuitous action. Let him be patient with himself.

The man is not patient.

He consults his watch.

Abruptly, he flings himself at me, pushes a dark suitcase between my legs and now I hear him running off towards the Porte Saint-Louis and . . .

16

A sort of whirlwind carries along in its circular movement the ground under my belly, the earth in my mouth, the staircase of the Porte Saint-Louis and the whole Quartier Latin, all jumbled up.

The first flash shot up from the earth and hurled me into the stone débris at the foot of the stairs, eardrums burst and head empty; more lightning flashes come from the sky now, bursting through a fine, close rain, but the thunder sounds almost pleasant, like the attenuated echo of the original detonation.

I lie flat on my stomach in the cool mud; the rain soothes the burns on my back. My left shoulder is particularly painful and bright red blood streams down my arm. I draw my knees up under me, propel my body forward: I manage to place my head on my arms. I lick my blood. The taste of blood, mixed in my mouth with the taste of earth, is heavy, full, and at the same time smooth and salty. It's been years since I've tasted my blood.

The staircase stops moving.

Never have I seen it from so close, touched it with my own hands, my face, my stomach; I had examined it with my feet and thought I knew it. Supporting myself on my elbows, pushing with my knees, I drag myself across the first steps. Take a breath: my shoulder. Fragments of stone débris, sharp and wet, stick into my cheek, which is pressed against the steps, prick the skin of my hands and belly.

The pieces are new, wet, not yet worn out, new stone; they were born quite recently. This isn't the staircase that I know.

One knee on the next step, an arm two steps higher, I advance a few degrees. The staircase scrapes my skin from head to feet;

turning over on my back I offer my sore stomach to the rain. My skin is striated with long abrasions where small strips reveal bleeding sores. Pieces of grey stone débris are mixed with chunks of skin; spots of mud are furrowed with reddish lines. My skin crumbles away, one small piece at a time; it takes on the colour of mud and blood.

Flat on my belly I drag myself, with a single effort this time, to the middle of the staircase. Forced to catch my breath again. (The old horse. One summer. The horse was old and out of breath: he had the strangles. Simon would invent historic sites, launch into long, fantastic explanations that the tourists listened to very patiently; the horse would rest. The calèche driver's air of false conviction as he described imaginary battles for the benefit of his old horse!) A belly laugh shakes me completely, for long minutes, until the image has vanished completely.

I feel better, able to stand up. It's done, but I've lost a shoe. Doesn't matter. In a single burst, broken by a brief pause, here I am at the top of the staircase, still half-smiling and very giddy, very pleased with myself: I've reached the tower on the Porte Saint-Louis.

All lit up and wide open, the kingdom is offered to me.

It is wide open on two sides, the other two forming a wall indented with irregular crenellations; a row of three turrets above the stone walls; the paved ground is black, gleaming and, in the corners, strewn with pieces of broken bottles. The people who walk on the walls of the fortifications, from Porte Saint-Jean to the Citadel, cross it. You stop there for a rest, a drink, a piss in the corner: the castle is open to all.

The rain has stopped. I am sitting in the middle of the enclosure, on the wet asphalt, my behind wet, my skin scraped, my shoulder opened by a pain that spreads through my entire body.

My castle is lit from inside and the walls around me reflect a greenish light. This soft, unreal light seems to well up from the stone itself, rise above the wall and spread to a certain point in the night. Born of the stone, it lives in an open castle, mingling freely with the night.

Something is released in me and moves, at ease, an old familiar accustomed thing, a creature coming out of a long sleep, looking around calmly, a light shining in the depths of its eyes, like the light that passes discreetly over the walls of the castle.

At first there was the squealing of brakes, the double slamming of the doors of a car, a brief gallop across the pavement, then other doors slamming and a car starting up rapidly; then calm was restored.

Now the noises increase and overlap. The squealing of tires becomes confused with a growing lament that seems at the same time to be climbing up rue d'Auteuil and down the Grande Allée. The roaring of motors is cut off by the distinct backfiring of a motorcycle. Farther away, in the heart of the Quartier Latin, the high-pitched voice of a siren tears through the resonant mass with a naked, strident cry whose steel blade is aimed directly at me. Nearby and hysterical, the cry drops off, dives, is choked into an increasingly muffled roar that rather regretfully yields to a new silence.

A silence already inhabited by the sound of footsteps. A raucous voice is raised, distributes a few staccato phrases; then the steps speed up, there is a furtive sliding to the right, the clattering of hobnailed boots and a metallic clanking to the left. The red beam of an intermittent searchlight sweeps the turrets of the castle. I hear the shrieking of stone débris scattered along the staircase.

Violence.

I was going down rue de la Fabrique the day before yesterday. A feminine street. The thing was inside me. Thing or creature.

Violence.

Like a stone, I was descending the most feminine street in Quebec City. The thing must have moved inside me and I didn't feel it.

Violence.

Let them come. My kingdom is open to all.

Epilogue

You'll have your docile guinea pig from the good old days again.

I was able to recreate this morning's experiment.

Up before dawn, I watched the daybreak: a dirty early morning that took its time. Usually the walls of my room change from black to white fairly quickly; they stayed grey: a sign of rain. I moved to the window so as to lose nothing. My window is too high and too small; I've said that already, I know.

It was an ordinary rain, I can swear to that under oath. But nevertheless I continued to watch it, having made up my mind to leave nothing to chance. I carefully watched the rain which was grey.

Suddenly, it was blue.

Attention is a fragile thing: I didn't notice but the rain changed from the grey to the blue colour it had been last month. Very excited, I paid more attention to it.

It finally stopped, late in the afternoon, as even a blue rain should do: the dreaded vision had not occurred. I left my observation post, head light and stomach empty; they had probably served my breakfast without disturbing me while I was at the window, and no doubt with the same tact later had removed it, cold and inedible. I've always been well treated here.

The experiment, carried out under highly satisfying conditions, seemed conclusive to me: no vision, no bars, no prison. So I shall resume the normal life to which you see me so strongly attached, in this rather strange hotel which is, all in all, fairly comfortable; and to catch up with the delay caused by this story, you will be able to take up with me the outcome of your own experiments.

You're not saying anything.

Your silence is pregnant and icy as a mirror.

Would the extent of the experiment be limited? Would some doubt remain? Of course no one knows the future. . . . Every time the rain is blue my safety may be threatened; even an ordinary rain will arouse some concern in me. My peace and freedom will always be only provisional.

You aren't speaking.

I appreciate and respect your silence, but if you have any advice for me, it seems to me that this is the time. So don't just reflect my own anguish. Talk to me, at least, of those mornings when the blue rain will start to fall.

You are the silent man.

It occurs to me to wonder if you really exist. You never say anything. Do you really exist or have I invented you as I invented my past? Or if you do exist, have I invented myself? Am I nothing but a creature of invention?

Jimmy

Evening becomes a ship you see
I am its master and its captain too
Come, sit close beside me
As peace spins its wool

Pierre Morency

Jimmy was first published in 1969 in Montréal
by Editions du Jour. The novel was re-issued
in 1978 by Les Editions Leméac.

I

Curled up on the half-moon shaped desk, Chanoine has fallen asleep.

The girl is lying on the couch. To tell you the truth I don't like all of them: I like the ones who tell stories.

Papou lights his cigarette and gives the signal to start: "Say whatever comes into your mind."

The girl closes her eyes like Chanoine, takes a deep breath and moves her legs apart.

"Once upon a time there was a miller, who left but little estate to his own three children, all of them boys, beyond his mill, his ass and his cat. To the eldest went the mill; to the second, the ass; to the youngest, this very cat."

And she told the rest of the story.

You don't move a hair, don't swing your legs or anything. You watch the whole business from behind the one-way window. Papou has stopped writing. He asks abruptly, "Why does Puss in Boots wear boots?"

A good question, but.

It's talking to the deaf. I mean I prefer the girl, to tell the truth. She just tells stories and doesn't answer questions. She goes back to her story. From behind the window you have a good view of everything that's going on. She's left them all alone—Papou between the arms of his half-moon, Chanoine asleep on the desk—and she's gone back to her story.

I and Papou, we both like stories. But he doesn't know I'm there. He puts out his cigarette, draws something in the ashtray with the butt, then suggests: "Tell me a dream."

Papou maintains that dreams put us in touch with the other side of ourselves, through the tunnel of the night. I mean, he says that all in one breath and he doesn't have to hunt for the words or anything.

The girl tells him.

There's a lot of water in her dream and the dream gets thrown into the sea. She's on the bank of a river, wearing her nightgown, and the riverbed's all white with ice. A man comes up to her, hovering between life and death, on the deck of the ferry that goes across to Lévis, and he says to her, "Listen to what's moving inside you: simply being alive makes life more acceptable than death." She looks at him without curiosity and starts to smile. Then she turns back to the river: the water and ice have completely disappeared and the riverbed is empty. Then the girl and the man set off along the streets beside the river, in search of the sea. They have a strange way of talking about it, as though it belonged to them. They say: "Our sea."

The girl smiles. Papou asks why.

"I'm thinking about my mother."

"Do you want to talk about her?"

"Stay like this, lying on your couch, not talking or thinking."

She travels by herself for a while; then Papou says to her, "The cat's boots mean servitude: he works for his master, the Marquis de Carabas. And Tom Thumb's signify power—the Seven League Boots!"

She has brought Chanoine. She said when she came in that she'd speak only in his presence. They're all weird, the girls who come to the clinic at the Hôtel-Dieu every week, and their stories are funny. What happens in a story is, you start to tell it and then you drift like a raft on the river and you haven't any idea where you're going to land.

She sits on the edge of the couch and shakes her hair.

"Goodbye!"

"Already?"

"I'll leave Chanoine."

"Thank you."

"I've decided to call you Puss in Boots."

"Puss in Boots!"

From here you can see very well that he isn't surprised, that he's pretending. The girl puts on her shoes and leaves without another word.

It's raining on the clinic, on the Quartier Latin, on Quebec. It's spring.

You feel as though Papou's Sunbeam Tiger knows we're going towards the river. It has trouble breathing in the Old City, where getting through the rush-hour traffic is hard work, and it purrs with pleasure when it turns the corner at rue d'Auteuil and springs eagerly onto the Grande-Allée. Across from station CJLR Papou turns left, towards the old Chemin Saint-Louis. Chanoine hops up on the dashboard and presses his nose against the windshield; he tries for a few moments to catch the wipers; then, resigned, he crouches there and starts to take an interest in the landscape.

We're sports car experts. I mean, Papou drives just like me, to tell the truth, with his hand on the gearshift, in third or fourth, and the Tiger waltzes to the left and right, weaving in between the rows of trees like a snake.

Cap-Rouge is a gulf. Papou shifts into second. You dive into a kind of gigantic funnel that winds down to the river, and up above your head there's a tiny train like a caterpillar going along a track that's hanging in the sky. Chanoine jumps onto my shoulder and rests his head against my neck.

The sun's out again, but.

The sun's hitting the river at an angle so the Plage Saint-Laurent's in the shadows, and what it looks like is the shadow's looming up right out of the cliff or something. And the guard on the way in, all he says is, "Speed limit fifteen miles an hour!" but he talks in this funny voice that sounds mechanical and female.

Papou stops the Tiger under a birch tree.

The cottage sits upon pilings, right at the end of a rocky point. At high tide it looks like a boat on legs; you can't help thinking of Mamie's song.

Papou climbs up the iron ladder and I follow him, carrying Chanoine and not holding onto the rungs or anything. Mamie's standing on the doorstep. She says, "Hello there."

"They call me Puss in Boots too," he interrupts.

"Since when?"

"Ask this little rascal."

She turns to the little rascal and repeats her question, adding that she thinks he looks very handsome. She's talking about Chanoine, to tell the truth. With Mamie, if you don't answer her she can repeat herself ten times. So I say, "This afternoon."

She asks Papou, "A new patient?"

"Yes, a lady! Ah, I must introduce the Canon."

"You're working too hard," she says.

She laughs as she says it. Chanoine slips between her legs and into the cottage. She's wearing her sky blue bikini. She's all wet and she stands there on the doorstep with a bath towel around her neck. She digs in her ear with a corner of the towel and you can easily see part of the white sailboat if you're a boat expert.

"I went swimming in the rain."

"You could have caught cold."

He laughs too as he says that, and puts his arm around Mamie's neck. They go inside.

"Shall I make you a fire?" he asks.

"No need, my friend."

"How about a cognac?"

"No thanks, your presence makes me warm."

"You're crazy!"

He kisses her right on the nose. The nose means treason, the forehead affection, the cheek is friendship, the mouth is love and the neck is passion. Then he jerks his chin in my direction.

"You should have a talk with him."

"What?"

"I said you should have a talk with the little rascal."

Chanoine, the rascal, pokes through all the rooms, his nose on the ground and his tail in the air, and I have to follow him wherever he goes. If you want Mamie to understand you have to speak clearly to her. So Papou says, "He was in the observation room again."

"Hard to believe."

"He comes there often."

"It's up to you to talk to him, isn't it?"

We scurry between them on our hands and knees at a hundred miles an hour, but Papou grabs Chanoine by the tail. Brake to avoid collision. Papou looks at me like Eliot Ness, then he lets go of Chanoine's tail and says, "I'm going to rub your back."

He picks up the big towel.

"You're awfully kind," says Mamie. She loves to have her back rubbed. She unties the strings of her bikini. The white sailboat on the towel falls down to her ankles. Papou rubs vigorously in every direction while Mamie bends over, feet spread because of the rolling and hands crossed on her chest so the two buoys won't swing to port and starboard. She moans dully, as though he was hurting her. Chanoine's fur stands up and his ears are flat against his head. Papou stops and takes away the towel. Her back's red, as though she has a sunburn. She's still moaning, but more softly now. Then Papou wraps her in the towel with the sailboat on it that's as big as a blanket, picks her up and sits with her in the big wooden rocking chair.

She seems very small, all curled up with her knees touching her chin and her head in the hollow of Papou's shoulder. Her hair's blonde and very short to tell the truth. She seems to be asleep, half sighing as though she can hear what he's murmuring in her ear, a song or the stories he's listened to that day.

Chanoine's finished exploring. Curiously or suspiciously,

he's examined every room in detail, underneath the furniture and everything: the library and the living room in front and the kitchen and both bedrooms at the back. Then he went up to Papou's attic. Now he's asleep in the living room, curled up in a ball in front of the fireplace. The rocking chair creaks and Chanoine purrs.

They'll likely even forget about supper.

After coffee Mamie went into her room.

She is sitting at her vanity table, staring into the mirror; her back is curved, her hands roaming in the drawer through the jars and creams and unguents and powders and perfumes. I sit beside her on the little bench.

The lips move in the mirror, the head shakes the pink plastic bag and the hose that hangs down her neck. Words, buried by the purring of the machine, keep tumbling gently out, the way her hair rollers tumble outside the plastic bag that fits over her skull. Her left hand comes out of the drawer and a threatening index finger is pointed at me.

The finger pushes a button.

"I had to tell you,"

The silence isn't silence, but the water in the river gently licking at the pilings. The tide is in. Mamie takes off her helmet, releases the rollers one by one and begins to brush her hair.

Chanoine bursts out from under the bed. She asks, "Did you understand?"

"Yes, but."

"But what?"

"Chanoine was scared."

"You won't go back, promise?"

"Catshit!"

I pick up Chanoine and lie on the bed. Mamie, still sitting before the mirror at her vanity table, has her hands in her hair and her elbows sticking out like the handles of a jug and the jug is full of questions.

"What was the story?"

"What story?"

"You're repeating, little parrot!"

"You're repeating, little parrot!"

I and Chanoine dive into the trench between the pillows: the hairbrush comes skimming over us and crashes down in the corner, onto the chamberpot which shatters into a thousand pieces. She'll box your ears for that! The chamberpot isn't broken—there isn't any chamberpot because this is Mamie's room. It's Mamie's voice that's shattering into a thousand laughing fragments. The pieces roll around the room, bounce off the walls, hit the corners and land on the bed.

"So, have we made up our mind?"

We make up our mind.

"It was the story of Puss in Boots."

"Come here, closer."

Mouth open, she looks at me.

I crawl under the bed to pick up the brush and move towards Mamie, staring at the round hole of her mouth. She looks me up and down.

"You fibber, I'll box your ears!"

She forbids you to go to the clinic but whenever you do go she makes you tell her the stories. Last time it was a father who worked in a room with his daughter every night to make an insect. She even believed me. And today it's the story of Puss in Boots and she says she'll box my ears. So then I say:

"Ask Papou."

That's the sentence that puts an end to her questions and my boxed ear and everything; you use it to get some peace. Mamie goes back to her vanity table and sticks her hands inside the drawers again, into the jars and creams and unguents and powders and perfumes. I come back and sit beside her. I put my hand behind her and gently, so she won't notice, I turn the big key to wind up the spring in the middle of her back. I'm the biggest liar in the city of Quebec.

Her arms start to work; they begin to move and all the rest is still. The hands come out of the drawer. The left one pours a layer of azulene blue milk—that's what's written on the jar—onto a round sponge and with the fingertips of her right hand she makes a kind of abbreviated sign of the cross, putting on her forehead and her cheeks and her chin and her nose a little bluish spot the same colour as the Milky Way, to tell the truth. Then the sponge follows exactly the same path, spreading everything out and making it even. The hands go back into the drawer.

Her still face shines like the full moon.

Mamie is sitting on the sofa, wearing a dressing gown or something, with her legs folded under her. Papou wraps a blanket around her shoulders and tucks the corners under her legs; all you can see of her is her head with the funny short hair, the round glasses she wears for reading, her hands and her cigarette. He kisses her on the nose and she says, "Thanks, my friend."

He lights the fire, gets himself a Molson and sits in his rocking chair with his newspaper.

"Lend me the comics," she asks.

"Sure, my friend."

I'm sitting on the real Australian wool rug. Papou tosses me the section with the comics and it lands on my head. With one hand I pick up Chanoine by the scruff of his neck, then I lie down on my back and lift up the comics with my moccasins, high enough so Mamie can take them without getting up.

"Thank you," she says.

"Catshit!"

As I regain my balance Chanoine escapes and slips under the sofa.

"Who dropped that?" Papou inquires reproachfully.

Mamie bursts out laughing like a loony and takes her legs out from under the blanket. He puts down his paper and looks at her; he waits, looking serious. Then he takes a big swig of Molson and picks up his paper again. After a moment he says, "Did you read this story?"

Mamie goes on laughing like a loony.

"It's about a farmer looking after his pigs. Heart attack, passes out. You won't believe it, but while he's lying on the ground the pigs start to eat him. A few hours later they find him swimming in his own blood and half eaten up."

Mamie's still laughing; her laughter hasn't even started going downhill. You don't know if she's laughing at Mutt and Jeff or at Papou's story. All day long Papou listens to stories behind his half-moon desk and then at night he reads stories or else he goes up to his attic and writes. You absolutely aren't allowed to go up to the attic and neither is Mamie. I roll across the rug, from Papou's sheepskin slippers to Mamie's toes. I've got some of Chanoine's fur in my mouth. If Papou got up to kiss Mamie I'd slide in between them and make myself as flat as a snake. That'd be the story of a flattened snake.

But nobody comes and kisses Mamie; Papou's still reading his paper. He's stuck to his rocking chair like some kind of zouave. Chanoine jumps onto the cushion, then up on the back, where he sniffs the smell of the milky way on Mamie's neck, and the shampoo in her hair. Then he climbs down the other side, lies between her knees with his head against her stomach and turns on his motor.

The flat snake crawls to the bottom of the trench along the sofa, cautiously threads his way under Mamie's legs, sticks his head under Tarzan and resurfaces on the other side of the paper; then it moves into the corner between Mamie and the back of the sofa. Mamie says I'm tickling and starts to laugh.

Papou drops his paper, yawns, stretches and makes up his mind: he comes and lies down on the sofa, head against Mamie's knees and a little bit against Chanoine too, to tell the truth. He takes a deep breath and closes his eyes; when he finishes breathing out and the end's in sight, a sound comes out of his mouth something like the one that Chanoine makes. Awake, Chanoine turns on his side and starts playing with Papou's hair with his paws. Papou's sound gets louder. He says, "That's nice, my friend."

"Tired, my friend?"

Mamie can read her stories and go on laughing and make Papou think she's stroking his hair and say exactly the right thing all at the same time. Papou and Chanoine purr, the fire's very small and underneath the cottage you can hear the lapping of the high tide.

"The high spring tides," Papou murmurs.

"You asleep already? You've got grey hair."

"I'm asleep."

"Is she pretty?"

"What did you say? I'm asleep. You smell good."

"Is your new patient pretty?"

"Ordinary."

"Do you like my hair? A little short, isn't it?"

"Eh?"

"I don't look like a little boy?"

"Who said that? You're crazy."

"Me."

"It's fine. You're crazy, let me sleep."

"I called Mamma."

"Eh?"

"Can I have a cigarette?"

"I'm asleep. In my shirt pocket—there."

"She's stopped using her crutches."

"Congratulations."

"She says our neighbours are coming at the end of the month. You know, I really think I look like a little boy. I asked Mamma."

". . . ."

"She said no, it was just. . . ."

"You see! Scratch my head some more."

"Scratch my head some more *please*."

"Please, kitten."

"You aren't going to sleep upstairs, I hope."

"I'm sleeping with you. You're crazy. The tide's in."

"I don't like to wake up alone at night. You can't imagine—the bed's as wide as the river. The ashtray, if you can. . . ."

"At high tide you sleep well and you dream better. I'm going to sleep downstairs; I like the sound of the water under the cottage. Remember last year?"

"What?"

"She was afraid the cottage would drift away!"

"You waken the dead!"

"She'd wake up at night and yell!"

"I wasn't really afraid, I was dreaming. If you go on like that I'll pull out your hair, I'll pull out all your grey hair!"

"The little girl got up because she was seasick."

"It was the high autumn tides."

"And she phoned her mother in the middle of the night."

"Anything else?"

"Mad at me?"

"You're making fun of me, you're mean."

"Come on, I was just teasing."

"Even last year you were mean."

"I was not. I kissed you and held you in my arms and rocked you."

"And you wanted me to go to the. . . ."

"If you'd listened to me back then. . . ."

"You'd leave me all alone and go up to the attic. Will you put that in the ashtray?"

"Of course. I just wanted a little laugh; you take everything seriously. Excuse me, all right?"

"All right, if you stop making fun of me."

"This year you're . . . happy, aren't you?"

"You mean am I cured?"

"Don't start that again, please. I'm going to sleep now. Just be quiet, all right? Let's not talk any more. Play with my hair."

"Are we going to sleep?"

"All right, we'll go to sleep."

"Are you going to give summer courses?"

"Eh?"

"I said are you going to give summer courses like last year?"

"Of course not, I'm staying here with you, you know that."

"Starting now?"

"You're crazy! During my holidays."

"When's that?"

"In July, as usual."

"But I'll get bored!"

"You will not. Come on now, be reasonable, you won't be all alone. The neighbours are coming soon, your mother said so. Don't waste your breath. I'll be here every night. Calm down. We're going to bed now. Listen to the tide."

"Don't you want something to eat?"

"What did you say?"

"I asked if . . ."

"Eh? You're always talking, my friend, try to sleep a little. Listen, it's raining. Didn't your mother tell you to go to bed early? She must have forgotten. Eat what, my friend?"

"Toasted home-made bread."

"Toast with maple butter, and some coffee."

The fire in the living room fireplace was consumed a long time ago and Tarzan's carrying me through the heart of the jungle from one vine to another, amid monkeys and parrots, above swamps where it's hard to tell the tree trunks from the crocodiles that cry like babies; then he puts me on my bed after forcibly unlocking my wrists from around his neck; and now Mamie's pulling the covers up to my chin as she tells him she could eat me up, and I think about cannibals and the pigs that ate a man in Papou's story.

She sleeps in on Saturday so you fix everything yourself. Chanoine laps hungrily at your bowl, and you have to hurry and eat your cornflakes while there's still some milk left.

"That isn't clean."

It's the first thing Papou's said this morning. I won the race. Chanoine finishes drinking by himself and you can see he's being careful not to dip his tail into Papou's coffee. Papou's wearing his yellow bathrobe with the C where his heart is, and the hair's standing up on his head. He yawns and says, "Your feet are dirty."

I wonder how he can tell without looking under the table or anything. And he asks, "I wonder how you can have dirty feet when you get up in the morning. Show me!"

I stick one foot on the table, between Chanoine and the quart of milk.

"That's disgusting."

He puts his glasses back in his pocket and takes a long swallow of coffee.

"Were you outside?" he asks.

"So was Chanoine."

"Since when?"

"Since the sun came up."

"And for what reason, if you please?"

"Exploring."

You could give just your name, rank and the number of your section: Geneva convention. But you answer all questions. You betray your homeland beneath Chanoine's contemptuous gaze; he, at least, won't speak. Papou doesn't trust anybody; he protests, "Chanoine hasn't got dirty feet."

"He was wearing his boots."

He scrutinizes Chanoine with an extremely suspicious eye. Chanoine remains impassive, licking his paws and starting to smooth his false whiskers. I'm prepared to tell everything, but I've never managed to really talk with somebody. I mean, you're all set to tell something, you put all the words on the ground and hold them by the tail for a minute and then you let go of them all at once and they go running off on their hands and knees in every direction. Then some zouave thing happens to you. Chanoine woke me up, to tell the truth; I looked out the window and saw a flock of seagulls on the beach. I wanted to walk in the water. I'm ready to start my story now, but Papou's got his head back, draining his cup of coffee. He runs his hand through his hair, mumbles something and heads for the attic stairs. In the middle of the stairs he opens the trap door and you can see that he's cut his neck, then a little farther he's cut off at the stomach and then the legs. His feet go up the last two steps all by themselves. I feel like going and getting Mamie.

I open the door.

The Marquis de Carabas takes off his sweater, drops it on the floor, unfastens his belt and lets his pants and the whole business fall in a heap on the shore of the river. He gives Puss in Boots a look that begs for encouragement, then he lifts off the blankets: Mamie's underneath, curled up in a ball. The Marquis de Carabas, careful not to slip on the round stones, slowly enters the water, arms crossed, sounding the unknown bottom with a cautious foot, while behind him Puss in Boots has already hidden the worn-out garments under a rock. The river bed gets deeper and the Marquis de Carabas gradually sinks into it, enjoying the pleasantly cool water and not suspecting that Puss in Boots is noisily scouring the countryside, shouting that his master is going to drown, and without knowing either that soon, inevitably, the King's carriage will pass that way.

Chanoine leaps onto the bed and starts his dance with the wool: back arched, tail erect, he buries his paws one by one in the blanket, all his claws out, slowly at first and rather absently, then speeding up to the accompaniment of louder and louder purring. He buries his nose in the wool and nibbles at it with obvious pleasure. Mamie takes Chanoine's head between her curved hands. He throws himself back, then straightens up, and very slowly his head slips and gradually emerges between her palms—the nose narrowed, the jaw extended, the eyes elongated—like the bare head of a snake. He takes a few steps across Mamie's chest, then lies down near her face; a little saliva comes out of his half-open mouth. Somewhat impatiently he stretches his head towards her and wildly rubs his moist nose against the warmth of her neck. She stirs, moans, rolls her head on the pillow, laughing nervously because of his whiskers; she lets him do as he wishes.

Now Chanoine is at the foot of the bed, crouching black velvet, his tail stuck to his flank, paws folded against his chest like a monk's hands hidden in homespun sleeves, a white star pasted between his half-closed eyes.

If you stroke Chanoine's head behind the ears he'll stretch his legs and spread his toes apart, just exactly like your own toes when you dig in the mud with your foot. I haven't got duck's feet. There aren't any ducks on the beach but there are gulls, except that the gulls are white, like tame ducks. Some gulls are grey. There's a birch tree near the cottage and just beside it there's a little post and sometimes a gull comes and sits on it. The post looks a little weird all by itself next to the tree, except when Papou sits on it and then he makes me think of a grey gull because of his grey hair. Papou sits on all kinds of things, with a book or nothing at all, and he can go for hours without saying a word, just reading or looking at the beach. He says it's a bank, not a beach. I opened the cottage door and hollered to him to come for a walk with me. He came down from the attic right to the middle of the stairs and then, with his hands in his pockets and staring into space like some kind of zouave he recited: "In Ketchum near Sun Valley, at the bar of the Christiana Motor League, Hemingway spots two F.B.I. agents where there are, in reality, only two travelling salesmen."

Papou really did say that all in one breath, without hunting for the words of anything, like he does every time he's acting like a zouave. Then he mumbled something else and finally he came down to lie on the beach and Mamie came too, looking at him with this funny expression. Papou puts a book over his head to protect himself from the sun and that makes me think of the roof that's over his head when he's in the attic. I tell him, "Your book makes a house."

He gets to his feet abruptly and the roof goes flying into the sand; he looks at you and he's got these creases in his forehead, as if he's surprised to see you there. His mouth's open and his eyes are big and you feel as though he's going to start yelling. But then he lies down on the sand again, closes his eyes and says lazily, "I'd like to have him see a . . ."

"No!" Mamie shouts.

She's all red but Papou isn't getting worked up. He opens his mouth and one eye, but all he does is look. Then she states, more quietly, "No, he's too young."

Papou opens his other eye. They look at each other and don't say anything more. There's an ant walking along Papou's leg, zigzagging because of the hair. A gull shrieks as it soars above us and then heads out to sea. Two barges cross in the channel and from here it looks as if they're going to collide, crash into each other without making any noise, come together , then apart in silence. Suddenly Papou and Mamie burst out laughing. Catshit! They were just pretending they were mad. Then Mamie gives the signal: I throw a big handful of sand on the ant and over Papou's legs. We stand on either side of him and take turns throwing handfuls of sand. He laughs and doesn't try to stop us. Now his legs have completely disappeared and we attack the rest. Mamie, still laughing, daintily pours a little heap of sand on his chest right where his heart is. It isn't going fast enough: I turn my back to Papou and then, bent over, feet spread apart, I throw the sand back between my legs like a dog digging a hole. Now the laughing turns to panting. All you can see of Papou is a handful of grey hair sticking out from under the roof-shaped book. Mamie tries to write something on the mountain of sand with strips of seaweed that smell bad.

Mémé told me the little sister was ready to come out, that

maybe it would be a little brother, from the size of the stomach. She'd taken Mamie's place in the house because Mamie had gone to the Hôtel-Dieu for a week; every week Mémé said that Mamie would be back the next week, with a little sister that might be a little brother. Then one day she said it was a little sister but she wasn't happy when she said it because she was crying. Mamie still hadn't come back from the Hôtel-Dieu. And when she did come back Papou had got in the habit of going up to the attic. Mamie'd learned how to laugh a lot and play with me, and she'd got thin.

It smells rotten in Papou's attic, like your finger when you take it out of your belly button. Papou asks Mamie not to go up there any more, but. When you ask Mamie something it's like talking to the deaf.

I help Mamie open the trap door. There's a big table lengthwise down the middle of the room, covered with books and messy papers, and a little bench without a back. There's an inch of dust on everything, to tell the truth, and balls of fluff that go flying whenever you run around the table. Mamie turns serious and says, "Be still!"

I slam on the brakes and examine the situation. Mamie looks at the ceiling.

"Papou says that. . . ."

She hesitates.

"What?"

"Something about the roof, the curve of the roof I think."

"Look at all the fluff!"

"Will you be still?"

"Can you see anything?"

She doesn't answer but reflects, still looking up at the ceiling. I'm standing there with one foot in the air; I ask permission to put it on the floor.

"Put it down," she says, without laughing or anything.

"Can I sit down?"

"You may. But please be quiet."

I sit on her left. Her fingers are playing the piano on the table. Then she puts one hand inside the other one and just when she whistles into the hole like a train coming into the station, the sparrow you can see through the window on the hydro wire drops a turd. I want to go out on Papou's Tiger and look, but Mamie asks,

"Don't you remember?"

"What?"

I don't like questions very much unless I'm the one who's asking them. She makes another train, a smaller one, then she says again, "When Papou was coming downstairs this morning he talked about the F.B.I. Then he said something else. Try to remember."

I look at the sparrow which isn't doing anything now and I try to remember the whole business. When Papou came down from the attic this morning he looked like a zouave. Chanoine was on the windowsill. Now it's coming back.

"He talked about the birds."

"What?"

"He said: 'There are birds that meow like cats.'"

"I'll box your ears for fibbing! Try to remember what he really said. It was something about the roof."

Mamie knows the names of all the birds, and in the fall when they migrate and come and sit in the trees all around she can name every one, even the ones you've never seen, I swear. She knows the names of all the flowers by heart, and perfumes too. In her room, where there's bottles everywhere, beside the dolls, she'll pretend she's blind. She'll close her eyes and move from one piece of furniture to the other. She'll grope around for every bottle, unscrew the top and breathe in the smell. Just like a magician she'll tell you the name of the perfume and then she'll ask you to check the label. If she makes a mistake she'll say you don't know how to read. Then there's a pillow fight on top of the bed and under it, in the corners and the closet, till you decide to play something else or Papou pounds on the attic floor with his heels so he can have some peace and quiet.

"COME DOWN OFF YOUR CLOUD AND HELP ME!"

Then I start yelling too:

"HE SAID: 'IDEAS FOLLOW THE CURVE OF THE ROOF!'"

"Fine! But why are you yelling?"

"Because!"

Last night I heard a noise; I got up and put my nose to the window. Out on the gallery there were two big huge raccoons. I went to get Chanoine to show him. He had his nose against the glass and his ears all flat; his fur was standing on end and his tail was all puffed up and he was growling. And then Papou, who'd come up behind us without making a sound, said:

"This isn't a cottage, it's Noah's Ark."

The iron ladder in front of the cottage has twenty rungs and it's sunk in the sand like the pilings. There are three rows of four pilings and it would be easy to do the multiplication, but. I mean, when you look at the pilings you don't feel like doing a multiplication, to tell the truth: you can't help thinking that the damn pilings are rotten. Papou says they would have rotted even faster in salt water. The water at Cap Rouge isn't salt; it starts to get salty at Les Eboulements. I went to Les Eboulements once. And I went to Sept-Iles and even as far as Moisie when we went to visit the dam at La Manic up north of Baie Comeau. We visited Manic 2 with Laurent, who works for Hydro-Québec. We didn't have permission to visit Manic 5, but Laurent said: "It isn't hard to imagine Manic 5, it's five times as big."

Every spring before we move to the cottage we come and see the pilings, I and Papou and Mamie and the Commodore who lives in the next cottage. We all put on our boots because of the mud and we make this sort of pilgrimage to the pilings. We talk about the whole business: you have to see what damage has been caused by the high autumn tides and the winter ice, and then you have to decide if the pilings can make it through another year. The Commodore's got the highest boots: he's the expert but he talks the least. I'm beginning to think that when you're an expert you should talk as little as possible. Papou walks around each piling and taps it with his axe, then he makes a little hole with his brace and bit. Finally he says it's red spruce and it'll last a lifetime. The Commodore nods and smokes his pipe and Mamie says, "That's what my father used to say." Mamie's father is dead. They start to talk about him, till they notice that Mamie's shivering and then they go up to the cottage and make a fire and drink *gros gin*. The heat from the fire gets rid of the musty smell. I and Mamie rummage in the cupboards, looking for mouse turds. They start talking about the days when the Commodore was a boat pilot like his son Thiers is today. Mamie really likes him: she calls him Thierry la Fronde. Catshit! We came for the pilings and now Papou and the Commodore are drifting down their memories like boats through the little islands and I and Mamie are stuck with the mouse turds. I say that to everybody and they stop then and there; they drop anchor and disembark. We go back down to look at the pilings under the cottage. This time it's the Commodore who picks up the axe and the brace and bit. Papou starts to say that the red spruce pilings made by Mamie's father who's dead aren't as good as they were back then, a little bit rotten, quite rotten, just good enough for one more season. Our boots are covered with mud.

There's a love story between I and Mamie: we both love Papou.

One of the things we like most about Papou is when he makes his scientific fire on the beach. He always starts by making a square with four logs four feet long. The beach is covered with logs that have been dropped by the schooners on their way up the North Shore, sailing towards the pulp mills in Quebec City and Trois-Rivières. You might think there's no connection between a gull and a schooner, even though a gull's a *goéland* and a schooner's a *goélette*. I mean if I asked you out of the blue, like the nun in school who points her finger at the back of the class and you have to get up and look silly and you're tempted to give Chanoine your tongue. Papou explained the similarity to me, and he told me the story of the schooners at the same time. It's very complicated, all about roots or something and if you want to remember it you have to start with the fact that the logs used to be trees and the trees had roots and then . . . catshit! I forgot the whole thing! But it was very scientific, I swear. Mamie said a bird and a boat were the same thing, and to prove it she sang her famous song: "Mamma, I see boats sailing past on the water. Do they have legs or do they have wings?" and everything; we laughed and slapped our thighs, all except Papou who said it wasn't scientific.

Papou starts with his four-foot logs. He leaves a space at the corners so the fire can breathe. He puts wads of paper and strips of birchbark in the middle of the square, then he puts down another layer of four four-foot logs, supports them against the middle of the first logs, with spaces so the fire can breathe. In his opinion it's very important for the fire to be able to breathe, and when I say scientific that's what I think of, and also of the way he stands a wigwam up in the middle of the square, on top of the wads of paper and strips of birchbark. It's made of long pieces of driftwood tied together at the top by a length of wire if necessary; it's necessary when there isn't a single piece of wood with a fork at the end to support the others, and my stones don't do anything. I throw stones at the wigwam and if it all falls down we have to start all over again and wrap a length of wire around the top. You've never, in your whole career, as Papou says, met anybody who's more patient than he is when it comes to doing something scientific.

He lights the fire at the four corners, in all the breathing holes. Then we sit down and talk.

They tell about how they met.

When it comes to lying, I'm the best one in the whole city of Quebec. When I tell something I start thinking about lots of other things that are more interesting than what's happened to me, and when you hear my stories you'd swear they'd really happened and I could even swear it myself. I've never been to Manic 2: they don't admit children. I never throw stones at the wigwam: all I do is blow as hard as I can and so does Mamie; she blows along with me as hard as she can.

They tell this story about how they met. I'm not saying they're liars and the whole story didn't happen, but. They tell the story every year and every time they change the whole thing, as though they didn't already know it.

"You preferred the 'Louis-Jolliet,'" Papou begins.

". . . ."

"You'd never set foot on the 'Bienville.' Wait, don't say anything."

Mamie doesn't say anything in any event and Papou pretends to find out why the catshit she never got on board the "Bienville."

"It was in July; there were stars. Wait, the 'Louis Jolliet' has a front deck for passengers and the 'Bienville' doesn't!"

"I always used to take the 'Louis-Jolliet,'" says Mamie. "It was the fourth of July."

"The American sailors! They were as drunk as skunks."

"They got off at Lévis."

"But you didn't get off at Lévis, you always came back to Quebec. You were leaning on the railing, near the chest where they store the lifejackets, and you seemed to be looking at the stars. You didn't even see me there."

"I was pretending. You'd been following me all evening, in the Quartier Latin, at the Riviera, at the Buffet de la Traverse, and then onto the 'Louis-Jolliet.'"

"It was your third trip."

"You dropped a paper cup in the river."

"I did it on purpose."

"The gulls came to see what was happening. You were carrying books and you had a long beard. I could see you very well. I even got a few drops in my face."

"I threw the cup in the air so you'd see it."

"Two or three drops."

"Seven-Up."

"You didn't say anything, you just sat there with your books in your lap."

"You were silhouetted against the moon. I kept sitting there so I could see you."

"On the fourth trip I turned around: there was nobody there! All right, he went for a glass of Seven-Up, maybe two glasses. The books are on the bench, he'll be back."

"It was a trap."

"He isn't coming back. But he hasn't jumped in the water, has he?"

"I'm coming back, you're sitting next to my books."

"The one on top had a pretty pink cover."

"I was trying to impress you. It was *The Psychoanalysis of Neuroses*."

"I asked if you could see the lighthouse at Sainte-Pétronille on the Ile d'Orléans, as I could. You didn't answer."

"I was fascinated. The ferry was heading straight for the lighthouse you were pointing to. I even wondered if the 'Louis-Jolliet' was obeying you."

"Your mouth was open. And when the siren sounded you jumped."

"I understood everything when I saw the barge. The ferry was taking a detour to avoid a black barge with lights at either end."

"Then all of a sudden you started talking a lot; you called me 'tu' and 'vous' at the same time. We decided it was our last trip."

I like stories about boats, but.

That one was a zouave story, with the moon and the Seven-Up and the lighthouse at Sainte-Pétronille and everything. It doesn't make sense to tell a person that one of the ferryboats heads straight for the Ile d'Orléans, unless it's in the winter. In the winter, it could be okay. With the ice and the wind, some of the ferries will end up there. Same thing for the canoes, on the last Sunday of Carnival; they're going to end up in the same place. Not the Lachance brothers, or most of the professionals either. But the amateurs, they head straight for Lévis when they leave the Bassin Louise instead of going along the Canada Steamship wharf, the Queen's wharf, the Riviera wharf, the Traverse wharf and everything, and then head for Lévis on an angle so they can take advantage of the tide. Then they'll finish really far away, down at that end.

Anyway, I like stories about boats.

When we went up to the North Shore to see La Manic, Laurent didn't just say Manic 5 was five times bigger than Manic 2; he said to go to Moisie and come back to Sept-Iles, to take the ferry. Anyway, when you get to Moisie you have to come back to Sept-Iles because the road ends there. If you want to go to Havre Saint-Pierre or Natashquan or Blanc Sablon, you have to get yourself a boat. The road makes a circle: it turns back on itself and the feeling you get, it's as if you've shrunk six inches. And you still feel that way till you come back to Sept-Iles and take the ferry. The ferry's called the "Gaspésien."

It should be a good boat story because Papou got seasick. I'm not saying I was glad he got seasick, but. I mean even before they sailed, the men were having trouble getting the cars on the "Gaspésien." They slid the two leather straps under the car, attached the cables on top, in the hook on the winch, and the men on the dock hollered that they could go. You'd think they were experts when you saw them with the straps and then taking the car out, but they still had to wait for a lull between two waves before they could take the car down into the hold of the "Gaspésien." They were nervous. I don't want to make a big fuss about this, I mean it really isn't any of my business, it's their job and everything. But the floodlights were shining on the wharf, it was around nine o'clock at night and you could see on their faces that they were nervous. It wasn't that there was anything in particular about their faces that was different; it's like when you punch somebody in the face with your fist, the whole face looks as if it's moved or something. The man on the wharf let out a big yell so the man in the winch cabin would lift up the car, and the man on the bridge, near the hold, let out a yell too so the man on the winch would let the car down all at once, in between two waves. I liked hearing them yell, to tell the truth. I really liked the whole business: the rain, the waves, the "Gaspésien's" moorings, the misshapen faces, the light from the floodlights, the reflections off the wet oilskins, the people shivering on the wharf, the outline of the man working the controls in the winch cabin—and through all that, the shouts that would bring the cars down to the bottom of the hold all at one go, in between two waves.

Papou had his damn seasickness half an hour after we sailed, and all night and part of the morning too, until the "Gaspésien" drew up at Sainte-Anne des Monts, and he looked zouave. I didn't get to visit Manic 2 because they didn't let children in, but when I talk about Papou's seasickness, it's true. At Manic 2, they told me to wait in the car. At Sainte-Anne des Monts, Papou was green. He swore he'd never set foot on a boat again for the rest of his goddamn life, not even the ferry between Quebec City and Lévis.

But me, I can tell you I wish I'd seen Noah's Ark.

You start a story beside the river at Cap Rouge, sitting around a scientific fire, and then you quietly set out to sea like the Marquis de Carabas, who goes farther and farther down the river; for a while your boat goes between Quebec City and Lévis and then because of a big black barge with lights at both ends it starts drifting to the Ile d'Orléans and even farther, to the North Shore and the Gaspé where the St Lawrence is so broad there are these big storms that make you seasick and people can drown like the Marquis de Carabas who slips and falls while Puss in Boots runs like a loony towards the King's carriage and you don't really know then where your boat is or where you are either, whether you're in your bed or in the bed of the river like the Maquis de Carabas or even if you're already asleep or if you're still sitting around the scientific fire with the others and the tide's coming in slowly in the dark and it's threatening to put out the fire and all the stories too.

There's another love story between I and Mamie: we both love cars.

It's a zouave story, but. Lots of weird things started when Mamie went to the Hôtel-Dieu: the perfumes and the dolls in her room, Papou's work up in the attic, my visits behind the window at the clinic, and this zouave story about cars.

Mamie had a room in the Hôtel-Dieu. She was convalescing or something and we could go for walks in the Quartier Latin. The Hôtel-Dieu's in the Quartier Latin, unless you're very strict about the definition of the Quartier Latin.

You go down rue des Remparts, for instance. We used to do that often. You can go down rue des Remparts starting at Côte de la Montagne as far as Côte du Palais and there's cars parked all along the street or just about. We didn't really like cars, to tell you the truth. I'm not saying we talked about the whole business and decided there were some things we really liked about cars and other things we didn't like at all. I mean, it wouldn't have made any difference to Mamie and me whether there were any cars on rue des Remparts at all, or even on rue de l'Université for instance, because it's pretty with the bridge in the shape of an arch and the entrance to rue Sainte-Famille. To tell you the truth, even if there weren't any cars in the whole Quartier Latin at all or even in the whole city of Quebec it wouldn't have made the slightest bit of difference to us. But you go down rue des Remparts, with the curves and the little terraces, the rows of cannons and the trees with branches that climb right over the walls, the old houses, the Hôtel Louis-Jolliet, the beautiful house at the corner of Sainte-Famille, the entrance to the Côte de la Canoterie, the view over the Bassin Louise, and Anglo Pulp, you look at those things as you go down and then just past the Hôtel Louis-Jolliet, let's say, at the straight part, all of a sudden you see an old Jag. I mean, there's nothing but ordinary cars and then all of a sudden there's this Jaguar, all scrunched down in the back as though it was getting ready to leap, with the fine lines of the radiator grill, the nice arrangement of the lights and the yellow fog lights on the front bumpers. You don't think about all that. You just think there's the old Jag and that's all, and then you go on walking down rue des Remparts.

You're at the part of the Hôtel-Dieu where there's cars on both sides, but the hospital's really too ugly to look at. It's a kind of big square box to tell the truth, and you look over the rampart, past rue Saint-Paul, over towards the big Canadian Import sign, where you can read, in green, how many degrees the temperature is and then all of a sudden you see a little Lotus. You think, there's the little Lotus, that's all.

Or else let's say Mamie's feeling fine. In the middle of rue des Remparts you turn left so you can go up rue Saint-Famille, slowly because Mamie's convalescing or something. When you get to the top you can walk in a sort of square that isn't bad at all: rue de la Fabrique, rue Chauveau, rue Sainte-Anne and rue Desjardins. Mamie and I went around that square in the direction I just explained, opposite to the hands of a watch. To tell you the truth, I should have put my watch down on the sidewalk so we could have a good look at it and then talk about the whole business. I mean we didn't even think about the whole question of the hands of a watch; we just went in the right direction without talking about the whole business at all. You can make that square any time you want, there's always cars everywhere. Then you go down rue Desjardins, let's say, you get to the bottom, you glance at the Empire theatre with the posters on either side. Then all of a sudden you see an Aston-Martin. I mean, on the Hôtel de Ville side, for instance, in between two ordinary cars, just by chance you see this Aston-Martin.

In nineteen hundred and fifty-nine, in the Vingt-Quatre Heures at
Le Mans, Carroll Shelby and his co-driver Roy Salvatori, in an
Aston-Martin, beat the Ferraris. But you don't think about that.
You think there's the old Aston-Martin and that's all.

Mamie managed very well with the MGs, the Triumphs, the
Sunbeams and the Austin-Healeys. You take ten people: nine times
out of ten they'll confuse a Midget and a Sprite. But not Mamie.
Just a glance at the grill or the trunk and she'd know exactly what it
was. To tell you the truth, I'd shown her the difference and all the
rest, on other cars too, but I didn't think she was going to become
an expert; she was convalescing at the Hôtel-Dieu and everything.
You go walking with Mamie when she's convalescing or something
and she tells you right off whether it's a Midget or a Sprite and she
doesn't even stop. It's strange: it's as if in the whole Quartier Latin
there was nothing but old Jags and little Lotuses or Aston-Martins,
or as if there weren't any cars at all, as I explained, but just trees
like the ones with their branches climbing over the wall on rue des
Remparts, or flowers like there are around the Parliament. The
strangest thing, to tell you the truth, when I and Mamie went for a
walk together on the days when she could leave the Hôtel-Dieu,
was the man who followed us everywhere from a certain distance.

I just discovered two things on the beach that were very clear.

I may seem zouave, but. To tell you the truth, I spend half my
time keeping things from getting all mixed up.

I was walking on the sand, through the rocks and the seaweed
and the garbage washed up on the beach by the tide. Chanoine was
following some distance behind me, sniffing around here and
there, acting as if he didn't know me at all. But as soon as I got too
far away he'd come running up at a hundred miles an hour. Then
all of a sudden I and Chanoine saw two things very clearly. I mean,
we really saw those things: when I closed my eyes they were still
clear in my head and everything. The things themselves are clear.
But catshit! The problem comes when you decide to explain it to
somebody. Your story goes drifting off and everything gets all
mixed up.

Papou's sitting on the little post that looks so weird beside the
birch tree. Gulls come and land on the post sometimes. Papou's got
a book on his head. Mamie's lying with her face in the sand. I start
the story by naming one of the two clear things:

"There's a black revolver."

I stop there because I'm out of breath from running a hundred miles an hour with Chanoine, and because I want to see if the book's going to fall down. I point to the place where I saw the revolver on the beach. The book falls, to tell the truth, right on Mamie's legs, just above her knees. Mamie's wearing her little sky blue bikini, as usual, with the bottom that always makes you think of a rabbit's ears because of the knots on her thighs. You'd think books are always falling on her legs: she doesn't move even one inch. One thing I like, she isn't too zouave. I mean, she isn't often *against* something. But she turns over on her back when Papou says, "Are you crazy? Where?"

Mamie's face is covered with sand. I answer without getting all upset or anything, "Beside her."

It really hits you, to tell the truth. Obviously, with suntan oil your face is always covered with sand. But it still hits you when you see it. On Friday night I saw that thing they call a beauty mask. I was sick, not really seasick but something, and I puked on the white Australian wool rug. Papou started getting upset.

"Beside her? Who?"

He isn't yelling, but. He's on his feet and he's getting all worked up. I name the second clear thing, "The blonde woman in the torn dress."

I get on my knees next to Mamie and I start taking the sand off her. She's blonde, but she's got very short hair. The sand sticks to my fingers because of the suntan oil. Sometimes she puts a big towel over her head and bends over the basin filled with boiling water and herbs. That's to have soft skin, and she can spend an eternity there. She has got soft skin, to tell the truth. I decide to take off the sand in little balls by rolling my finger over her skin. Suddenly I feel a firm hand on the seat of my pants. You've hardly started your work and you feel this hand on the seat of your pants.

"COME AND SHOW ME!"

He pulls me to my feet by the seat of my pants, I swear. He's all red. I pick up his book; he doesn't like it very much when things are left lying around. Chanoine and I decide to go and show them what we've seen on the beach.

Chanoine runs ahead, I follow him, then Papou comes with his book and Mamie brings up the rear. Papou doesn't like to play snake at all and we aren't really playing either, except that Mamie laughs a lot as she makes the line sway to the left when Chanoine goes off to the right, and far to the right when he goes left, even though we haven't really decided to play snake. If we stopped for a minute, if we talked about the whole business—we'll play or we won't—I'd be against it, to tell the truth. Just when it looks as though Papou's going to shout something, Chanoine stops. We're there.

I'm glad to see the two clear things again. I mean, I'm glad to see that everything's still the way I and Chanoine saw it: in there with the seaweed and the driftwood, the doll with its clothes all torn, its face smashed and the black plastic revolver beside her. The things haven't drifted away. When I say that the things are clear in themselves that's what I mean. But you start talking about a doll and a revolver and the tide starts to come in, like Papou when the blood rises to his head and he gets all worked up, the tide rises higher and higher till the anchor isn't touching bottom and the whole mess drifts away. You take a drowned man that's been in the water for a week: he gets bigger. That's what I'm trying to say: the doll can get bigger too, and your revolver; people get worked up, they grab you by the seat of your pants and you go off on a pilgrimage like some kind of zouave who doesn't want to make a snake along the way, till you find yourself wondering if everything hasn't drifted away, the way the cottage could do when the tides are high, and if you're going to discover a blonde woman with short hair, her face covered with sand because of the goddamn suntan oil and a real black revolver beside her.

I'm glad to see that things haven't drifted away, but Papou isn't. He doesn't say anything at all and he goes back and sits down with his book on the little post that looks weird beside the birch tree. The birch is the kind of tree I and Papou like best. I mean, we talked about the whole business once and we agreed about the birch tree. It was a good discussion: the branches, the leaves, the bark, the colour and even that thing they call "dying-off disease"; the birch trees in the Parc des Laurentides have caught it. They all died and all you can see on the side of the mountain is the tall white skeletons of the birch trees that finally rot and crumble to the ground. We talked about the whole business and it was a really good discussion.

We don't have discussions like we used to any more, to tell the truth. Let's say your feet are dirty; he tells you to go and wash them, but. He doesn't even seem to be looking at your feet and the first thing he says is to go and wash them. You take a bus driver: he tells you to move to the back and you can tell from his voice that the bus doesn't belong to him. That's what I mean about Papou: sometimes he talks as if I didn't belong to him or something like that. It's one of those funny things that started when Mamie was in the Hôtel-Dieu for a long time, back when I used to go for walks with her on the streets of the Quartier Latin and all that stuff about the cars I told you about. Now there's as many funny things as Chanoine has whiskers. I really did count the hairs and it's the same number. I'm the biggest liar in the whole city of Quebec.

Mamie's down on her hands and knees in the sand. She takes away the seaweed that's mixed in with the doll's blonde hair and blows the sand off the doll's face.

"I'm taking her up to my room," she says.

She examines the smashed face.

"A little Lepage's glue."

Mamie lifts up the torn dress; you can see a funny little pink slip and there's nothing under that at all.

She brings in the doll.

I pick up the black revolver.

II

Chanoine is clinging to the back of the sofa, his tail as big around as my arm, his nose against the window and his fur as stiff as a porcupine's.

We're being invaded, inundated, submerged, taken by storm. We've closed the front windows and the back ones. Papou's gone up to the attic with a case of Molson's and Mamie's shut herself in her room. The Commodore hadn't even got to his cottage before Trixie, Dixie and Flixie had jumped out the car window and took off at a hundred miles an hour as though their asses were on fire. They ran around their cottage twice, then made a mad dash for the beach and came and took us by storm. We've barricaded ourselves inside; we can hold out for a week with the food and everything.

They climb up the iron ladder and run along the gallery of our cottage, barking and crashing into one another; they come and stick their noses against the glass, standing up on their back feet with their tongues hanging out between yellow teeth, ears pointed, tails stiff, slobbering. Then they go away again, howling like the devil, jump down the ladder without touching a single rung and go back home, taking detours to avoid the trees and jumping in the air to catch butterflies. Chanoine buried himself under the sofa; I pulled him out by the tail, grabbed him by the scruff of his neck and sat him at the window to give him a detailed view of the invasion.

Every time the assault began again he'd start snarling and spitting.

I go out on the gallery with the helicopter. From Dufferin Terrace you get a good view of the helicopter taking off from the icebreaker "d'Iberville" and then flying over the river between Quebec and Lévis.

They come down the road and climb up the back stairs. I swoop down on them, propeller whirling. They've never seen a helicopter in their lives and they get the jitters; they retreat and I pursue them down the stairs and onto the road. I push my motor as far as it will go and with my propeller blades I swipe at the grasshoppers, horseflies, butterflies, grass, flowers and branches in my way. Trixie, Dixie and Flixie jump off the road, moaning plaintively, and scurry off across the fields with their bellies to the ground and their tails between their legs. Catshit! I just broke a blade on a tree and I'm crumpling into the ditch. The main blade, catshit, my rotor! It's fine to make a helicopter with a mop in front and a poker in the back, but then you break your rotor on a goddam spruce tree and you land in the ditch on your hands and knees, with your poker and half of the mop handle, head first in the mud, to tell the truth.

The pilot doesn't hear the dogs or anything; he's a bit stunned and he wonders if anybody's seen the whole business: his main blade that broke on the spruce tree and his helicopter that dived into it, and as a matter of fact somebody puts a hand on his shoulder.

"The dogs aren't bothering you too much?"

It's the Commodore. He's wearing his Commodore's cap and everything.

"We had enough rations for a week!"

"Did they attack you?"

"Took us by storm."

The Commodore sits on the edge of the ditch, pushes back his Commodore's cap and wipes his forehead on his sleeve.

"I see, you launched a counter-attack."

"No."

"No?"

"I tried to get out."

"I see. An accident?"

"Broke my rotor."

He whistles between his teeth and says, "The birch tree?"

"The goddamn spruce."

"A squall, I suppose?"

He stands, picks up the other half of the mop and examines it in silence, like an expert.

"No, I was flying low," I say.

"No way to fix your rotor. Anything else broken?"

"Fractured skull."

"Oh!"

"Could have been worse."

"Can you stand up?"

I manage to get to my feet. He holds out his red handkerchief so I can wipe the mud off my face. He examines the fracture thoroughly while I explain.

"It could have been worse, I could have landed in the river."

"You think you can walk?"

"No choice, with a broken propeller."

"Unless I lend you another rotor?"

"Thanks, I'll walk because of the fracture."

He extends his hand to help me out of the ditch. I watch him walk towards their cottage to unload the rest of the baggage from the trailer. He really would have lent me another propeller blade for my helicopter. Halfway there he turns around and says:

"All the same, you shouldn't fly over the river too often."

Mamie is half-lying in the living room, her head on a pillow, and Chanoine is stretched out on top of her.

The two comrades glance at the pilot just as he goes past them to hang the poker by the fireplace and put the broken mop away in the cupboard. They don't look directly at him; they simply give him a sideways glance and don't ask any questions. It's the pilot's favorite moment, to tell the truth. When he walks past them, he stops for a minute, puts down his propellers and takes the time to tie his shoelace so the comrades can get a better idea of the whole business: the broken blade, the fracture and everything. They pretend they aren't looking and don't feel like asking any questions. Out of discretion or something they act as if nothing has happened, and you'd do exactly the same thing in their place.

The pilot draws himself up before his comrades, whistles a few notes very softly, almost absentmindedly, picks up the little blade and the other one that was broken, staggers slightly because of the fracture, and goes to put his things away. That's discipline: the wounded pilot doesn't think of himself. The equipment comes first. All the comrades do the same when they return from a mission; they're well trained and they do what they have to do, mechanically, because discipline's stronger than being tired or hurt. The pilot hangs the poker on the nail to the right of the fireplace and puts the two halves of the mop in the kitchen cupboard between the broom and the dustpan. Everything in its place.

Only then does the pilot think of himself. He heads calmly for the bathroom, takes off his muddy, sweaty clothes, puts in the plug, turns on the water and pours in bath salts. The pilot checks the temperature of the water with the toes of his right foot, puts his other dirty foot in the tub and crouches down, almost stretched out. At the base of the falling water, perfumed foam bubbles up, spreading out as the tide rises.

Mamie opens the door.

She picks up the pilot's clothes, examines them and sticks them in the laundry basket without a word. Just then Chanoine comes in, swishing his tail from side to side; he jumps on the edge of the bathtub and stretches out his paw to catch the chain that's holding the plug. Mamie sits beside Chanoine.

"Want me to help you?"

"No."

I give two or three rapid orders—clear the decks for action, everybody down, close the hatch, periscope, and things like that; the submarine starts to dive and I put the washcloth over it. On the surface, the foam begins to disappear. The sea is calm. The submarine slides under the water. Mamie throws an underwater grenade; water sprays Chanoine in the face.

"Rub hard," she says.

I pursue her soap which slips between my fingers and down my back, then gets stuck between my legs just under the submarine. Mamie strokes Chanoine.

"Rub! Rub!"

I must look like a real Egyptian mummy in a sarcophagus. She made me put soap all over, even in my hair and ears. She's laughing like a loony. Then she asks, "Have you seen Thierry?"

"Soap in the eyes!"

She holds out the towel. You take your bath, wash your face— and you always get soap in your eyes. And you can't use the washcloth because of the submarine.

"Is that better?" Mamie asks.

"Twenty Thousand Leagues Under the Sea."

"Have you seen Thierry?"

"Captain Nemo doesn't answer questions."

She picks up the chain that holds the plug.

"Answer me or I'll pull it out!"

The river will empty, the submarine will run aground. I answer at a hundred miles an hour.

"Not seen Thiers!"

She drops the chain. Chanoine holds out a paw to pick it up. But I add, "I'm not sure."

"Explain."

"Amnesia or something."

All at once she pulls out the plug. The tide starts going out. I explain the whole business.

"Fractured skull!"

And as I dig my heel into the hole to stop the water I point to where I was hurt. Without even looking at the fracture she abruptly turns on the shower taps. A flood! Blinded, inundated, drowned, I capitulate, ask her to pardon me, stop playing.

"Catshit!"

With a jerk she turns off the shower. Everything's drifted away: soap, suds, sponge, washcloth. And the submarine's capsized, periscope pointing down. I want to answer everything, really lay it on, everything she wants to know.

"Did you or didn't you see Thierry?"

"No, I swear!"

"Is he coming?"

"Yes!"

"When? Who told you? The Commodore?"

"The Commodore brought Trixie, Dixie and Flixie and the baggage in the trailer and he said Thiers would be coming at a hundred miles an hour with the girls, he asked if you were better and how was Papou and if the pilings seemed to be holding up and he said not to fly over the river and he's going to give me a new propeller blade."

"A propeller blade?"

"I swear! Put the plug back, please."

She puts the plug in the hole. Chanoine took off when the flood began. She comes closer to examine the fractured skull; I replace the washcloth over the submarine which has straightened up, with the periscope pointing to the surface. It seems as if Papou hasn't come down from the attic or anything. Mamie runs her hand through my hair to take an account of the damage. I warn her, "The skull's split in two."

"Tell me what happened."

The wounded pilot tells the whole story: the assault, the

attempted getaway, the helicopter, the broken rotor, the Commodore.

Anyway, there's another love story between I and Mamie: we both love Thiers, the Commodore's son.

Thiers is a boat pilot. He pilots boats in the channel of the St Lawrence from Quebec to Les Escoumins and back. He just pilots boats, to tell the truth. I mean, I'm a pilot myself: helicopters, boats and racing cars. But he sticks to boats. He's the best boat pilot you've ever met in your whole life. You'd think he'd surveyed the channel at the bottom of the river in a diving suit and lead-soled boots with a waterproof electric lamp and an underwater camera, from Quebec to Les Escoumins and back. He's an expert and he's the one who gives me advice about everything that has to do with piloting boats. But after Les Escoumins you have to manage on your own if you feel like heading for the Gulf.

Every summer they all come and move into the cottage next door: the Commodore, Trixie, Dixie and Flixie, Thiers and the long-distance swimmer and their six daughters—Patsy, Ingrid, Kathy, Mary, Lucy and Jenny. I named them in descending order. Mary's the same age as me but she's smaller. She doesn't know one goddamn word of French. Neither does Thiers's wife. He met her in South Africa back in the days when he was in the Merchant Marine, in some kind of cottage at the Cape of Good Hope where they could see the Atlantic Ocean and the Indian Ocean at the same time. You might think that Thiers is as good a liar as me, but he isn't. Mamie calls him Thierry because he makes her think of Thierry la Fronde on television.

What I like about Mamie, she isn't too zouave. Most zouaves make you wash your ears, but not Mamie. Yesterday, though, she cleaned out Chanoine's ears with some cotton batting on a toothpick and when Chanoine started getting impatient she looked him in the eyes and said, "I know it's no fun, but. You can't go around with one ear dirty and one ear clean!"

For once she was zouave.

Papou bought it at Latulippe Surplus de Guerre and I always sleep in it.

It's khaki for camouflage, and inside it's white with red and blue flowers all over it. You could turn it inside out and put the flowers on the outside, but. I mean, I've tried everything and here's what I think about the whole business: the best thing to do is pull the zipper all the way up and pull down your pillow so your head doesn't stick out and go to sleep naked in the flowers, lying curled up with your feet on Chanoine who's at the bottom, purring, his eyes shining from time to time, yellow or green.

Today's the day they're coming.

I remember a long time before the Hôtel-Dieu, Mamie took me in a corner and asked me three questions.

"What's your mother's name? What's your father's name? What's your name?"

If you answered the three questions correctly she'd let you go, convinced you could go on living. I mean, you really felt as if you were going to die all of a sudden if you missed one answer.

They're coming today, Thiers and the whole family.

I pull down the zipper. Chanoine gets out of the sleeping bag as he does every morning and stretches. The fresh air envelops me; I turn over on my stomach and close my eyes for a second, but Chanoine comes and licks my cheeks and then, purring, he rubs his wet nose against my neck. Only one way to have any peace with Chanoine: you get up, give him his breakfast and open the cottage door for him.

I put on my jeans and my grey sweatshirt with the hood. I don't wear the hood very often, but. You like to know that the hood's there on your back. Sometimes I put Chanoine inside when I take him for a walk but he doesn't really like it, especially in the helicopter. I have to tie the cord around the hood otherwise he'll parachute down first chance he gets. He thinks he's a flying squirrel or something.

It's a problem, Chanoine's breakfast. You take one step, he brushes against your legs, you lift your feet really high so you won't step on his paws and you end up looking just like a ballet dancer; you look weird, to tell you the truth. He loves fish: his favorite breakfast is a dish of fish and a bowl of milk. I won't say anything about the milk but I've tasted his fish a few times: usually I go and spit it down the john at a hundred miles an hour. Mamie's tasted it, I swear, and she spit it out too, in the same place. Good thing the john didn't decide to spit it out too.

The floor's cold. I almost forgot my moccasins. If you forget your moccasins in the morning you can hurt yourself on the bamboo points.

It's an old story. You've been shipwrecked, you grab hold of some flotsam and all the rest and you end up on a desert island in the Pacific. You don't know it's deserted yet, to tell the truth; you land there in the pitch dark with just enough moonlight so you can make out the jungle with the monkeys and the parrots and the vines and the bamboo. With your bone-handled hunting knife you cut one-foot long bamboo stems with the ends pointed like an arrow and you stick them deep in the sand with the point on top, in circles that get broader and broader. You lie down in the middle under the stars, protected by your circles of pointed bamboo. You've hollowed out a little hole in the sand for your hips that they call the camper's hole and you fall asleep thinking it would have been a good idea to paint the bamboo points with curare. You're safe from wild animals though: even if a black panther was attracted by your smell during the night he'd have to leap over the bamboo points and he'd hurt himself and stay there all night long, moaning. In the morning you could approach him slowly, give him something to drink, take the pointed stems out of his paws, look after his sores and feed him something; he'd get his strength back and he'd end up being your friend, as gentle and faithful as Chanoine.

It's an old story, the one about the chief scout whose totem is the Tiger; the tame panther saves his life when he's stealthily attacked by a real tiger in the jungle and he finally dies in a circus, fighting against an elephant that's furious because some zouave put a lighted cigarette up his trunk.

I put on my moccasins and give Chanoine his breakfast so I'll have some peace. I put the can of Puss 'n Boots on the kitchen floor and start to take off the top with the can-opener. We're both down on our hands and knees. The fish smell gets stronger. Chanoine rubs his chin against the edge of the can, then he licks my fingers, weaves between my legs, jumps up on my back and sticks his tail right in my face, purring like a helicopter that's about to take off. I fill his pink plastic dish with fish and his yellow bowl with milk. The milk's in a cardboard carton but I prefer glass bottles because of the sound they make when you knock them together like the milkmen do early in the morning when they put them down on your steps; they do it on purpose, the milkmen, to let you know the day's begun. It's a signal, like the beadle who rings the church bells.

Chanoine crouches down, eyes closed, to attack his fish, and you'd think he hadn't eaten for a week. I go out, propping the cottage door open with an empty pint cream bottle so Chanoine can go out too. When he's got his fish down he races out at a hundred miles an hour and nobody inside the cottage has any peace till he's outside.

The Commodore's walking along the beach by himself, with his hands behind and his pipe in front. He's wearing his

Commodore's cap and he's put on his great white sweater with the kind of Indian totem on the back.

I yell at him:

"Ship ahoy!"

He isn't really in a ship, but. To tell you the truth I just wanted to see the Indian heads. He turns towards me.

"Ahoy young man!"

You can clearly see Hawk Eye and Sitting Bull on either side of the zipper, with their feathers and war paint and everything, exactly the way you wanted to see them.

"They coming today?"

"At noon," the Commodore replies. "How's the helicopter?"

"Catshit on the helicopter!"

"That bad?"

"Chanoine's coming. We sleep in the flowers. He ate his fish."

"I see."

"You should have a talk with the dogs."

Without taking out his pipe or anything the Commodore spits on a rock. I spit too, two rocks closer. He's luckier because he's bigger; if he got down on his knees we'd probably spit on the same rock. I ask him if he wants to try.

"Okay young mate."

He gets down in the sand on one knee and I come closer so I'm on exactly the same line as he is. I say "un deux trois go" and I spit first: my spit takes off and disappears in a hole between two rocks. Then he spits, in exactly the same hole, I swear. I wipe off my chin. Apparently if you've got a stitch in your side from running too much you just have to lift a stone, spit in the hole, put the stone back on top of it and your stitch is gone. The Commodore gets up, tries to light his pipe and says:

"Don't you like dogs?"

"Yes, but Chanoine doesn't. Do you like raccoons?"

"Of course."

"I don't like dogs when I'm flying in my helicopter."

"You can have the new propeller whenever you want."

He tries again to light his pipe; he puts his lighter flame in a little shelter made by curving his hands so they form a hut. If Papou smoked a pipe he'd shield his flame with a book. Papou doesn't smoke a pipe.

"You should ask if Mamie's better."

"Why?"

"Because."

"Is Mamie feeling better?"

"She's very well, thanks. She nearly drowned me."

"In the river?"

"In the bathtub. Do you have to be able to swim to be a good boat pilot?"

"Not necessary."

"You should ask about Papou."

"How is he?"

"Don't know, he spends all his time in the attic."

"Sick?"

"No, he's writing or something. You should ask if the pilings seem to be holding out."

"Why?"

"Because."

He takes off his Commodore's cap with one hand and with the other he scratches his ideas with the tips of his fingers. The two Indians turn towards me.

"They aren't holding out?"

"Don't know, they're rotten."

"Let's go have a look."

One thing I like about the Commodore is his great white sweater with the totem on the back and the two Indian heads on the chest, on either side of the zipper like on either side of a river, Hawk Eye and Sitting Bull. I mean, you get out of your sleeping bag with the little red and blue flowers, you put on your jeans and your grey sweatshirt with the hood, and your moccasins so you won't hurt yourself on the bamboo points, you give Chanoine his Puss 'n Boots to get some peace, you go outside and there's the Commodore with his sweater like I explained, and right away he's ready to come and see if the pilings seem to be holding out.

He walked around the twelve pilings, taking a long time to look at each one of them. He knocked his pipe against the last one to empty it. We sat down in the sand with our backs against a piling and I asked him, "Do you know the song?"

"The song?"

I start singing him Mamie's song: "Mamma, I see boats sailing past in the water. Do they have legs or do they have wings?"

I take away a stone that was digging into my bum and I sing all the verses right to the end. The Commodore declares coldly, "I know all the sailor songs that are sung on every sea in every port in the world."

"You're talking through your hat!"

"'Valparaiso,' for instance."

"Sing it and see."

He unscrews his pipe and then, with his head cocked to one side, he blows hard into the stem. Good thing he turned his head: all the puke would have landed on his legs. Finally he answers, "You ask Thiers, he sings better than me."

"They get here at noon?"

"Yes. Didn't you already ask me?"

"Time?"

He looks at the sun above Saint-Nicholas.

"Nine o'clock."

"And the pilings?" I ask.

The Commodore doesn't answer. His eyebrows are grey and I swear they're an inch thick. He's got grey eyes, too, with wrinkles in the corners whenever he's thinking like an expert. Finally he asks, "You worried about them?"

I frown like him and I scrunch up my left eye by twisting my mouth on that side. I'm not an expert when it comes to pilings. I'm an expert in racing cars, boats and helicopters; I'm also an expert at making up stories and I'm the best liar in the whole city. But pilings, that's beyond me. The Commodore's the only expert in that area. At first you might not think there's any similarity between a pilot and a piling, but the Commodore used to be a pilot and he's an expert in pilings. He's the only expert on pilings but he doesn't say anything.

Jimmy Clark won the World Driving Championship in nineteen hundred and sixty-three and sixty-five in a Lotus and he missed the Championship by a hair in sixty-four because of the goddam Grand Prix race in Mexico. I mean, CATSHIT, WHEN YOU KNOW SOMETHING YOU SAY IT! Jimmy won more Grands Prix than Fangio, the best driver of all time. A zouave idea goes through your head: maybe it isn't just the pilings that are rotten. What comes out of the Commodore's pipe when he unscrews it and blows in the stem isn't very pretty. What I mean is, catshit—maybe the cottage is rotten too!

AND GODDAMMIT WHEN SOMETHING'S ROTTEN I GET FURIOUS!

I climb up the iron ladder at a hundred miles an hour. Jimmy leaps into his Lotus, makes the motor roar and the single-seater charges onto the first curve of the Monaco Grand Prix. When it comes out of the curve, the Lotus is leading and the driver steps on the accelerator, right down to the floor, and outstrips the compact class—the midnight blue Eagle, the green and orange BMW, the bright red Ferrari, the green Cooper-Maserati with white stripes, the green and bronze Brabham, the Japanese Honda and the rest of the Formula Ones that are desperately trying to stick with their class. Jim Clark's still in the lead after one lap and he's widening the gap! The throbbing of the motors operating at top capacity reverberates off the walls of the houses, the gearboxes and brakes moan as they go into each turn, the tires squeal and a revolting smell of burned oil spreads through the air and gets in your throat in spite of the handkerchief protecting your mouth and nose. All along the streets, behind the barricades and at the windows of the houses, the spectators' faces rush past at a frantic rate. It's a hell of a course and when you drive it you have to keep switching from the accelerator to the brake and step on the clutch every three seconds. But the other cars are coming closer, they gain a few seconds at every lap and now Jimmy's starting to feel the red Ferrari breathing hotly on his neck. Suddenly the yellow-striped red flags snap out: oil on the track! The driver lets up on the accelerator a little and starts to slow down, one eye on the rear-view mirror to check whether the other competitors are doing the same thing. They're slowing down. Jimmy Clark looks over the track carefully.

Standing on the gallery near the door that goes into the cottage, strangely wrapped up in his long yellow bathrobe with the letter C where his heart is, Papou is standing, motionless. Mamie's beside him.

Jimmy applies the brakes, brings the good old Lotus to a stop with its oval nose and its long yellow band, breaks the contact.

The Commodore, leaning against the railing, takes his old pipe and his tobacco pouch out of his pocket. Mamie and Papou, frozen in the persistent smell of burned oil, watch Jim Clark—nicknamed the Flying Scot—slowly extract himself from the cockpit and push his rubber goggles over the visor of his protective helmet.

Papou's wearing glasses on the end of his nose and carrying a book. He asks, "May I know what's going on here?"

The Flying Scot feels as though he's all wet. It's hard to explain; I mean, you get out of the cockpit where you were half lying between the gas tanks, an overheated gearbox and a boiling motor and it can be over a hundred inside your bloody fireproof coverall that you're wrapped in from heels to neck, but it isn't that. Jimmy feels soft and wet and a little bit sticky.

The Commodore pushes back his Commodore's cap with his

pipe and explains, "We came to have a look at the pilings. How are you?"

Mamie smiles without saying a word. Her arms are folded. She's barefoot.

"Fine, thanks," says Papou. "How about you?"

"Not too bad."

"And the pilings?"

The Commodore shakes his head, sucks on his pipe and mutters, "Hard to say."

"We'll have to take a good look at them. You're an earlybird!"

The Commodore jerks his chin towards Jimmy.

"We ran into each other on the beach."

The burnt oil smell's been replaced by tobacco and the driver feels a little bit zouave; he isn't really in the mood for talking, to tell the truth. He's in another world, in his long white coverall with the red stripes that sticks to him from the ankles to the neck, with the various zippers encrusted in the fabric, the white silk handkerchief over his mouth and nose like the cowboys in the Far West and the black helmet with the white visor. Thoughts go whirling around under his helmet like the multicoloured single-seaters following each other at a wild speed down the streets of Monaco.

Mamie's happy just to walk around the Hôtel-Dieu. She's convalescing or something. It's a good day: we've just seen a little Lotus on rue des Remparts. She walks slowly, looking at everything, She says, "The Quartier Latin has a soul."

"Why?"

"Because it's old."

"So I don't have a soul then."

"Why?"

I'm talking to the deaf, obviously. Must speak to the Commodore about it. What's a soul anyway? I mean, I and the Commodore will have to take sometime and sit on a rock; he'll be wearing his great sweater with the Indian heads and we'll have a serious talk about the whole business. I'll start with the pilings.

"They're rotten—yes or no?"

"Depends. What do you think?"

"They're rotten, it's obvious."

"Why?"

I won't answer his why. I'll start thinking about Mamie and Papou and then I'll ask, "Has the cottage got a soul?"

"Hard to say. Why do you ask?"

"It's got a soul—yes or no?"

"Depends."

"On Mamie and Papou?"

"And you."

"And Chanoine too?"

"Maybe, yes."

"I and Chanoine haven't got a soul."

"Why?"

Finally I'll spit as far as possible and just drop the whole business.

"The cottage has got the soul of a boat!"

The sky is reflected in one of the cottage windows and the sparrow crap on the glass seems to be floating in the clouds. Beneath the protective helmet of the Flying Scot, world champion in sixty-three and sixty-five, the single-seaters are jostling with ideas in a kind of Noah's Ark filled with people who don't have souls, like dogs, Chanoine, raccoons, black panthers, tigers and Puss in Boots.

Mamie, her arms still folded, makes up her mind and says, "Would you like some coffee?"

"We woke you up," the Commodore apologizes.

Smiling, she opens the door.

"Come in!"

"I'll let you twist my arm."

When the Commodore walks past Mamie he lifts his cap. One thing I like about the Commodore, he'll lift his cap but he never takes it off. The Flying Scot goes behind him and Papou, holding his book, comes in last.

"Have a seat," Mamie says.

She goes into the kitchen. Papou in his yellow bathrobe and the Commodore with his Indian heads sit at either end of the table.

"What are you reading?" the Commodore asks politely.

"Across the River and Into the Trees."

Jimmy hangs around in the room for a while before taking off his driver's coverall, his silk handkerchief and his protective helmet with the goggles pushed up over the visor.

"Do you know Hemingway?" Papou asked.

"I know the face."

"Didn't you read *The Old Man and the Sea*?"

"I saw the movie."

"I'm writing a book about Hemingway," Papou explains.

The racing driver crawls under the table on his hands and knees and sits down in the middle; the red checked tablecloth falls on either side. Mamie comes in from the kitchen, puts some things on the table and goes back.

The Commodore crosses his legs. "You're writing a book?" he asks.

"A study."

Papou's legs are as hairy as Chanoine's. Mamie comes back once more and says, "It's instant, sorry."

You can hear the water pouring into the cups and the sounds of the spoons. Papou scratches his knee with a fingernail. "I suppose you liked old Santiago."

"It's one of the most beautiful cities in Chile, if you ask me, and the old palace at La Monedad is magnificent!"

"Of course. But what did you think of the old fisherman in *The Old Man and the Sea*?"

Mamie comes and sits between them, her legs folded under her chair. The Commodore takes his time, then replies: "Very good sailor and no complaints about the kind of fisherman he was either."

"Yes, but. . . ."

"The old man knew where to find the fish, how to catch it, play it. Nobody could have done any better; sharks are terribly voracious."

I'm going to have to ask the Commodore to tell me everything from the start and how the story ended; we'll take the time to sit down and talk about the whole business. He knows a lot about the history of boats and sailors because he used to be a boat pilot himself.

"It's symbolic," Papou said, "don't you think?"

"Sorry?"

Jim Clark has been stealthily attacked from the rear; Far West bandits slammed him on the skull with the butt of a revolver, stuffed a handkerchief into his mouth, tied his wrists and ankles and threw him under the table. Jimmy was about to suffocate at any moment.

Papou scratches his other knee; his knees are like the knots on an old tree trunk.

"The story means that we spend our lives looking for happiness but if we find it we can't hold onto it. Do you know Hemingway?"

"No, but he must know his way around boats and fish."

"He liked hunting too, and swimming, boxing, baseball, horses, dogs . . ."

". . . cats," Mamie adds.

"But the most important," Papou begins.

Jimmy Clark is about to have a fit.

"Did you know that for several days Hemingway was impotent?"

The racing driver suddenly has the feeling that the pilings aren't really sunk into the sand but that they're sunk into his stomach, as deep as Mamie's song in his memory.

Jimmy snaps the cords that bind his wrists and ankles and grabs a fold of the tablecloth. All the dishes come crashing to the floor. He runs to the door at full speed. The yellow flags with red stripes are down: there's no more oil on the track. The Flying Scot leaps into his Lotus, turns on the motor, and presses the accelerator to the floor, one eye on the tachometer and the other on the side of the track so he can steer out of the skids. The tachometer needle was in the red zone, the driver stepped on the clutch without lifting the accelerator one hair and dropped into second gear; the motor howled and the single-seater sprang ahead.

Jimmy turns his head and in a glance he takes in the red Ferrari, the green and bronze Brabham and the midnight blue Eagle, all breathing down his neck, noses to the ground like hunting dogs. He slips his glasses, which he'd forgotten on the visor of his helmet, back down over his eyes, abandons the accelerator, steps firmly on the brake and shifts back into first just as he enters a hairpin curve. As he comes out of the turn he opens the throttle out full, a little too abruptly; the Lotus skids; he straightens it out with one turn of the wheel, grazing the bales of hay lined up along the sidewalk, lets out the clutch and slams into second gear, but the goddamn Ferrari has gained during that wasted moment. Faster on the straight, the Ferrari clings to the rear of the Lotus, taking advantage of the suction like a goddamn leech, lets himself be carried along and waits for some awkwardness or sign of mechanical failure. Jimmy negotiates each turn at the outer limit of adherence and pushes the single-seater as far as he can on the straightaway.

The first cars from the back appear: the world champion starts weaving between the slow cars; slipping to left and right, passing even the dawdlers on the curves, he gradually makes gains on the Ferrari, which lacks flexibility. Jim Clark forces the speed, pushes the accelerator to the floor on the second last straightaway, then slams on the brake for a tenth of a second before placing the Lotus inside the last curve, shifts into second, accelerates as he goes into the turn, steadily increasing his speed; the Lotus skids but the tires grip well and the single-seater comes out of the curve at full speed, passes in third and crosses the finish line at the peak of its power. They wave the checkered flag; it's the first victory for the Flying Scot in the Grand Prix de Monaco! Jimmy comes back to the pit and makes the victor's circuit with the famous checkered flag, pulls the Lotus to the side of the track and turns off the engine.

The driver takes off his glasses and helmet, unties the white handkerchief protecting his mouth and nose. A blonde girl with very short hair drapes a wreath of flowers around his neck and kisses him on the cheeks. Dead tired but proud of his Lotus and himself, the driver thinks of a nice warm bath and tells himself that all the same, he and the Commodore should take the time to sit down on a rock and have a good talk about the Hemingway business and all that stuff about impotence.

The Commodore goes back home to split logs before the arrival of Thiers and all his daughters. As Papou goes up to the attic with his book he asks Mamie if Jimmy's still taking his pills and everything. Mamie doesn't answer but says she's going to change and go swimming in the river: it's high tide. She goes into her room.

The driver decides to go swimming with her.

Sitting on the air mattress I put up no resistance. Mamie, who's in the water up to the two buoys, plunges the soap into the river and covers me all over with suds. Sometimes I resist. but, I mean, after the Grand Prix de Monaco you don't mind taking it easy and letting somebody else wash off the goddamn oil and dust.

Before Mamie went to the Hôtel-Dieu, Papou was a racing car expert and he wasn't interested in Hemingway or anything. He wasn't really an expert, but. I mean, he never missed a race at Mont-Tremblant; he'd take us there, me and Mamie, and he'd talk to us. For a Sunday race, like the Labatt Indy, you get there on Friday afternoon with the tent-trailer so you don't miss the trials and the qualifying runs. You decide to set up camp on the other side of the Labatt bridge, at the top of the cliff and close to the fence that's under the trees, and from there you get a good view of the exit from the first curve, a very dangerous one because the cars rush into it in a tight group and then farther on there are four or five slow or fast turns with straight stretches that are either level or on a slope. It's the best observation post and if you're lucky enough to find it empty you don't hesitate for a second, that's where you put up the tent. Afterwards you can take your time, arrange the sleeping bags and the supplies and everything, gather wood, get your water supply, take a look at the cars that are making reconnaissance runs, go to the pits to examine the mechanics' work, study the programme for the race, read technical studies on the new cars. To tell you the truth, you can do whatever you want. I mean, catshit, the important thing is to talk to each other.

At night Papou would make a fire and we'd talk. He could explain how the Tiger was a direct descendant of the Ford and the Cobra, how the Cobra was born of an English chassis and an American motor and he could tell the whole story about Carroll Shelby. We'd drink coffee—I drank real coffee too—and then we'd roll up in our blankets so we wouldn't freeze like turds and the way you'd feel, to tell you the truth, it was as if you were listening to a story about the Far West, fighting against the Indians, How the West was Won with Buffalo Bill, Davey Crockett and the rest of them, or some even older story like the discovery of America and everything. I and Mamie, we'd ask all the questions at the right time and after the story about Carroll Shelby, Papou could talk some more about the drivers in the Labatt Indy, like A.J. Foyt or Mario Andretti, or about Indianapolis-type cars, the ones with their center of gravity shifted to the left and the others that didn't, and he was quite capable of talking until the mountains across from us started to be lit up, like when you drive in the car at night and you can guess that there's a light from another car coming from behind a hill. He wasn't really an expert but he used to talk to us.

All of a sudden Mamie got up and sat on the other end of the air mattress. It tilted and I flipped into the water! The water came in my mouth and nose, my memory was all drowned, I coughed and spat and kicked at the bottom, and then I bobbed up on the other side of the mattress. All the soap suds were floating on the surface in a rosary of little white bubbles. I yelled:

"Man overboard!"

Mamie was lying on the air mattress, eyes closed. Her hands were beside her body, her legs were apart and she was pretending to be asleep, so you wouldn't think she'd tipped the air mattress or anything. But catshit! If it wasn't her it was the sirens.

I rested my elbows on the edge of the air mattress, between her bare feet, to make a motor. You make a motor by kicking the way you do for the crawl, but with your legs on the surface. You can't go all the way out to sea to tell you the truth, because of the Sargasso Sea. You have to tack skilfully in between the banks of seaweed and kelp and different kinds of algae that drift across from the cottage. Those goddamn sea grasses grab you by the legs like maniacs and they can even get tangled in your propeller.

It seems as though Mamie's been asleep for ever and I've gone beyond the Sargasso Sea a long time ago. It's cooler now, the wind's come up and there are waves, but it isn't a storm; you've never heard of a real sailor getting caught in a storm. It's always just a squall and it isn't serious. All the same I slow down the motor so it won't get tired and so I can pay attention to the propeller. I mean, there are logs everywhere. The schooners coming down from the North Shore drop their logs in the river and if you run into one of those goddamn half-submerged logs you'll dent your propeller. And when you've got a dented propeller you look zouave. You have to move cautiously, with your motor slow and an eye on the logs.

You cut your motor to save gas and let it rest for a minute. The sea's changed colour, the wind has fallen and there are no more waves or logs. You aren't really tired but the motor needs a little gas. The way you feel, it's as though you're on a desert island in the South Seas or somewhere. You rest your cheek on your wrists in between Mamie's feet. She doesn't move a hair; she's sleeping. All you can see in between her feet is the water and the sky around the island. Gulls are soaring overhead, letting out little shrieks of fear. The island drifts slowly. You have to watch out for sharks, to tell you the truth. For sharks, you watch for the dorsal fin; if you see one of those fins heading for the island and disappearing, you stick your head underwater, just long enough to let out a tremendous yell without suffocating. Sharks are voracious but they're scared to death of any sound except when they've caught the scent of blood. I mean if you've been hurt and you're bleeding into the water or something. But there's also eels and rays that can give you quite an electric shock, and barracudas and giant octopus. You can always get rid of sharks, but not the others.

I hoist myself onto our desert island: I don't feel like spending one more second in the water. The island tilts; Mamie's waking up. I reassure her, "There's no sharks."

"What?"

"No dorsal fins on the horizon."

She straightens up, leans on her elbows, scrutinizes the horizon and everything.

"Where are we?"

"Lost. Desert island."

"I was asleep," she explained. "You haven't the slightest idea . . ."

"The South Seas, somewhere like that."

"I wonder how . . ."

"With the motor. We crossed the Sargasso Sea."

I spin the motor two or three times so she can get some idea of the whole business; she's impressed.

"What time is it?"

I look at the sky all around us: no sun.

"Have to ask the Commodore."

I swear, sun or no sun the Commodore can really tell you the time by putting the tip of his dagger on the head of an axe and he says my hunting knife works just as well as a dagger. I show Mamie the whole business, explaining with both hands so she can understand it all, how you have to put the tip of your knife or your dagger right in the middle of the cheek of your axe, study the shadow and everything. Then she says, "Maybe Thierry's arrived."

Something I'd like to see every now and then is a cow without any skin. I mean, a real cow but you'd be able to see the whole skeleton with the bones moving when it walked and the cow would do exactly what any goddamn cow does except that it wouldn't have any skin. Another thing I'd like is to sleep with a real girl in my sleeping bag and you'd be as careful as you could not to touch her or anything, because I mean, catshit, if you slept with a real flower you'd be as careful as you could not to crush it.

No time to daydream. I summarize the situation.

"We're lost on a desert island in the South Seas."

"That's no joke!"

She really looks worried. I try again to reassure her.

"They're going to come looking for us."

"You think so?"

"They'll send airplanes or boats with a helicopter. There's a helicopter on the icebreaker 'd'Iberville.' Have to wait, and survive. We can eat raw fish."

"Ugh!"

"Whenever people are shipwrecked that's what they eat. You should have brought your bathrobe."

"Why?"

"To signal to the planes."

I and Mamie haven't got a rocket gun to send a distress signal, no hunting knife to carve a harpoon, no gun to shoot a bird, no line to fish with, no ship's biscuits, nothing. We've got just one chance: if a flying fish happens to land on our island we could pounce on it and eat it raw. I explain the whole situation to Mamie, keeping the business about the flying fish for the end so she won't get too upset. Flying fish are curious, they come close and if one wants to jump over your island it'll land on your head without doing it on purpose.

Suddenly Mamie protects herself.

"Ouch!"

I look in the air, all around: I don't see a thing, not one goddamn flying fish. She bursts out laughing. Catshit! she got me. She laughs like a loony. It sounds like a log tumbling off a woodpile and she slaps her thighs. If I had a blanket I'd put it around her shoulders because of the flu and everything. Finally I start laughing too and I give my thighs a few slaps. We're sitting face to face. Then she gets worried again.

"Are you sure you're taking your. . . ."

"What about you?"

"The little red ones?"

"The little red ones and the big white ones. You?"

"Me too."

"It's nice here, isn't it?"

"Very nice."

I give it a little push.

"Don't you think it's too small?"

"No, just right."

"If it was any bigger the flying fish wouldn't dare jump. Do you need a blanket?"

"No thanks, I'm fine."

"You aren't bored? I mean you really aren't bored, swear it?"

"I swear."

She can get bored and not say so. That was why when she was in the Hôtel-Dieu we started all the fantastic stuff about the cars, the old Jags and the little Lotuses and the Aston-Martins and everything.

What's really funny is a person's eyes. For instance you're sitting face to face with Mamie on this desert island. Mamie's eyes are green and you're looking into them. I mean, the water in the sea around the island's exactly the same colour, but. It doesn't give the same effect, looking at the water, not at all. Another funny thing, you stop looking at the water and you'd swear the water's still there; but you stop looking in Mamie's eyes and all of a sudden it's as if she's gone away.

"You want me to tell you a story?"

"What kind?"

"A story about an island."

"If you want."

"If *you* want."

"Of course I do."

"Good. Once upon a time there was an island. Not an ordinary island, to tell you the truth; a volcanic island. You keep looking at me or I'll stop the story."

"What kind of island?"

She keeps looking to see if a plane or a helicopter or a boat's coming close, or maybe she doesn't want to miss any flying fish. Just try and tell a story to somebody who keeps looking all around!

"VOLCANIC!"

"You don't have to shout!"

"I'm not shouting! You've got ordinary islands and volcanic islands, that's how it is. We're on a volcanic island. If a flying fish landed on our volcanic island, I mean we're going to see it, catshit! Do I go on with the story or not?"

"Go on."

"Volcanic islands appear and disappear. You don't see any island at all at first, then there's a kind of underwater eruption with geysers and steam bubbling, and then real flames, with lava and everything; finally it all cools off and an island appears on the surface. But that isn't all!"

"No?"

She really seems to be worried about being on a volcanic island; she gets up, looks all around the island. I let her have her way for a while. She shields her eyes, using her hand like the visor of my driver's helmet; the sun's come out again. Finally she sits down across from me again, calm now, and starts to smile. We're sitting with our legs folded under us, like Indians; I think of Hawk Eye and Sitting Bull. Another thing that's funny is her smile. I must look zouave with my mouth open like a fish. Then I ask, "Is it better now?"

She nods.

"You aren't afraid any more?"

She shakes her head.

You begin an ordinary story, then all of a sudden you start drifting and you don't know where you'll end up, to tell you the truth, and the story gets scary like a volcanic island or something.

There's a sort of warm breeze; she doesn't need a blanket or anything now.

"Were you afraid of the volcanic island?"

"Yes," she says, still smiling.

"Afraid the volcano would erupt?"

"Can that happen?"

"Well catshit! a volcano's a volcano! Volcanic islands can just up and erupt and disappear under the water. But you don't have to worry."

"Do they warn us at least?"

"There's vapours and rumbling and earthquakes."

"That's reassuring!" She's fantastic. I mean, I and Mamie are stuck on a volcanic island in the middle of the South Seas and she bursts out laughing like a loony. Her eyes sparkle and she's grinning from ear to ear.

"You're going to swallow your ears!"

"Look!"

I look at the tip of her finger. "I don't see a thing."

"Farther!"

I turn around: it's a boat! A destroyer escort or a mine sweeper, hard to tell. Mamie stands up and waves her arms. The boat's heading straight for our island and Mamie speeds up her semaphore. It's an ordinary rowboat, to tell you the truth, a plain ordinary rowboat. "It's Thierry!" Mamie shouts.

They've seen us, they're gesturing, they're coming closer, they're here. I take a look around the island: not a single flying fish in the neighborhood. They're afraid of Thiers's motor. And on the volcanic island there isn't one bit of vapour, no rumbling or earthquake or anything. The volcano's asleep.

The motorboat draws up abruptly and there's a kind of deluge: everybody starts yelling hello over everybody else's head except me and the dogs. Thiers has brought the six girls: Patsy, Ingrid, Kathy, Mary, Lucy and Jenny, and the three dogs: Trixie, Dixie and Flixie. All that's missing is the long-distance swimmer and the Commodore. The island moved back three feet when they landed and I and Mamie nearly fell in the water.

Thiers begins: "You coming on board?"

"Please," says Mamie in a strange little voice. She's really scared of falling in the water, to tell you the truth. She holds the edge of the rowboat with one hand, puts one leg over and then Thiers grabs her by the elbow and helps her with the rest. One of the dogs start to bark.

"Flixie!" the pilot says severely.

Mamie sits on the little bench in the front of the rowboat. I ask, "How about the raft?"

"We're towing it," Thiers says. And he throws me a cable. You stretch out your arm, you run out the cable and at exactly the right time you bend your arm, just like the sailors in the harbour at Anse aux Foulons. I mean, when the liner's close enough to the wharf a man on deck lets out a yell and throws out a cable which unwinds as it falls; the sailors on the wharf do exactly the same as me, pulling on the cable to haul in the moorings and tie them up; then they unfasten the little cable, roll it up and throw it onto the bridge of the liner with all their might.

I lie down flat on my stomach and fasten Thiers's cable to the ring in the rubber raft. I make a very complicated Boy Scout knot like the Commodore showed me. Thiers and the others have got lots of time to see that I'm making them a real double bowline knot. I straighten up and board their bloody motorboat and they know very well that I can get on without any help from anybody.

The knot expert sits on the middle seat next to Mary. Mary asks me something in English. To tell you the truth you haven't got any idea if she's saying "How are you?" or "How old are you?" but you answer her in English too, without a moment's hesitation.

"Eleven!"

Mary starts to laugh as though you were tickling the soles of her feet. I obviously speak English very well and Mary doesn't know one goddamn word of French, as I said; neither do the two younger girls. It's a weird family, to tell the truth; you've got the three oldest girls, the two littlest ones and Mary in the middle. She's the same age as me.

They've got a very good twenty-five horse Johnson, white with red arrows on the side. The motor starts up right away and the boat turns. Trixie, Dixie and Flixie are crouching across from me, and they're examining me with their tongues hanging out. They don't even look at Mary. All three of them look at me with their bloody tongues hanging out. They're hunting dogs and once they've smelled you they'll recognize you anywhere. I mean it doesn't matter if you're disguised to the teeth in your pilot's costume with the helmet and the gloves and the aviator's boots and everything, and flying over them in your helicopter. They're quite capable of recognizing you now in your bathing suit. All three of them recognize you by your smell and they keep an eye on you.

Thiers takes off his black sweater. He throws it over me and Mary; the sweater lands on Mamie's knees. She yells, "Thanks!"

You have to yell because of the motor.

Thiers shrugs and smiles, like when you want to say you didn't do something. Mamie puts the black sweater around her shoulders and ties the sleeves in an overhand knot under her chin. It's the simplest knot you can make, to tell you the truth. You don't have to be an expert in Boy Scout knots. The way you feel is that the pilot, in the back of the boat, is hanging from Mamie's neck; but then you look a little longer and the feeling goes away.

I take a look at the back. Because of the motor you haven't heard a thing but there was an eruption with an earthquake and smoke and flames and lava and everything; our volcanic island disappeared in the water.

"Where were you?" Papou asks.

He's sitting in the middle of the stairs with a book and a Molson. Mamie closes the door; I always forget to close the door, but not Mamie.

"Out in the boat. You must be hungry!"

"What time is it?"

The Commodore isn't there with his axe and his dagger. Papou answers himself: "It must be past noon. I heard a motor."

"Thierry's here. I'm going to make lunch. Didn't he come here?"

"All I heard was . . . Thiers is here?"

"He came and rescued us."

"How? What are you talking about?"

Mamie's talking in her weird little voice again, the same as when she was in the Hôtel-Dieu. Papou starts getting worked up. I help Mamie explain the whole business to him.

"We were stuck on an island."

"Volcanic," Mamie adds.

"In the South Seas or somewhere."

Papou takes a long drink of Molson. He says in a disapproving way, "The South Seas!"

"It's my fault," I say.

"Would you like to explain to me how?"

"Yes, but Thiers came and rescued us with his motorboat."

"How wonderful of him," Papou comments.

"Eventually," Mamie says, "we would have caught one."

"One what?"

"Flying fish," I say.

"How did Thiers find you?"

"Mamie did a very good semaphore; I couldn't have done better myself, I swear."

Papou looks at Mamie. He sighs and says, "You know, I'm really very hungry."

"You look tired; were you working hard?"

"Yes, I was."

"I'll cook you a steak."

"Good idea."

"How's your book coming?"

Mamie's disappeared into the kitchen but she's still talking in that weird voice; it's very soft and you can't hear it if you're very far away.

"What did you say?" Papou asks.

"How's your Hemingway coming along?"

"Not bad, thanks!" he shouts.

"Will you finish this summer?"

"Sorry, what did you say?"

Papou cups his hand around his ear but he stays right in the middle of the stairs with his book and his Molson. I transmit the message.

"She wants to know if you'll finish your book this summer."

"This fall!" Papou shouts.

One morning you're sitting quietly in front of the fireplace talking softly to Chanoine and then all of a sudden old Hemingway himself, with his famous grey beard and his rifle and everything, starts coming down the stairs instead of Papou. You're sitting there with Chanoine and old Hemingway walks past you, close enough so you can hear him breathing; he says hello by lifting the end of the barrel slightly and then he opens the door to go out hunting. I'm the biggest liar in the whole city of Quebec.

You aren't allowed to pour gas or something unless you're zouave.

You're flat on your stomach across from a breathing hole, you strike a match on a rock, you put your hand in between the two logs until the flame licks at the paper or the birchbark, then you remove your hand immediately and crawl to the other three corners to do the same thing without putting out the match or anything.

The three biggest girls—Patsy, Ingrid and Kathy—come together, then the Commodore with Trixie, Dixie and Flixie, then the long-distance swimmer holding the two little ones, Lucy and Jenny, by the hand, and finally, on Thiers's shoulders, smiling, Mary. They sit in the sand around the fire.

I've put on my jeans, my grey sweatshirt with the hood, my moccasins and everything, but.

The girls are quite a sight. To tell you the truth, they're fantastic. I mean all the girls are wearing this kind of long white nightgown that comes right down to their ankles, with lace around the cuffs and everything and white nightcaps on their heads too.

The three biggest ones are running around the fire in their bare feet, carrying flaming branches. You pick a branch that's long enough so you won't burn your fingers, you stick it in the fire for a minute and then you start to run, waving the flame: it's as if you were writing something in the night in letters of fire, and when the flame goes out you can still write your name on the concrete wall in black letters.

The two little ones are playing in the sand with the long-distance swimmer.

But what really hits you in the eye is Mary. Little Mary's wearing a nightgown and nightcap too, but hers have little red and blue flowers on them, exactly like inside my sleeping bag. It really hits you in the eye when you see that.

Mary comes over to me and puts a branch in my hands as she says in English, "If you please!"

She means to put her branch in the fire, leave it there for a minute, then take it out when there's a nice flame at the end and give it back to her so she can do like the big girls; she's afraid of getting burned or something. You don't have to or anything, but you do what she wants. To tell you the truth, you're a little bit zouave.

Lucy, Jenny and the long-distance swimmer are building a whole village with houses, roads, a bridge, a garage, a church and everything. On the other side of the fire Papou and the Commodore are discussing something, the cottage or a boat: it's hard to hear what they're talking about because the three big girls are laughing like loonies as they write on the wall and the three dogs are yapping as they run around the girls. Closer, Mamie and Thiers are talking but you don't hear a thing because Mamie's still talking in her weird little voice.

On the South Shore, at Saint-Nicolas or somewhere, there's another fire on the beach and it's reflected in the water.

The Commodore takes a branch from the fire to light his pipe.

An ember falls in the sand. "Would you bury that for me, young mate?" You pick up a handful of sand, as big as you can, and throw it on the ember so little Mary or one of the other girls won't burn their feet. Mary comes back with her branch.

"If you please!"

"That's enough, Mary," says the long-distance swimmer. She's very tall, with very long blonde hair down to her shoulders and she's very very beautiful, to tell you the truth. You look at her and you can't help seeing her swimming for hours and hours in South Africa where the Atlantic Ocean and the Indian Ocean meet, with her head out of the water to watch for sharks.

I get up and take care of Mary's branch. Little Mary has green eyes, like Mamie.

"Merci," says Mary.

"You're speaking French!"

"Un peu," she says, showing me with her fingers.

"She's changed schools," Thiers explains.

I feel relieved, to tell you the truth. I couldn't care less if Lucy and Jenny can't speak one goddamn word of French, but not Mary. I mean, we're the same age and she's got green eyes and everything. Obviously we could always talk English because I speak as well . . . anyway, I'm relieved; she can ask me to take care of her branch as often as she wants.

The long-distance swimmer takes two bags of marshmallows, pink ones and white ones, from her pockets. Patsy, Ingrid and Kathy calm down and come back to the fire; they choose white marshmallows. You stick a marshmallow on the tip of your branch, get down on your hands and knees at a corner of the fire where there's just coals and you toast your marshmallow, changing hands often because the fire's too hot and you have to be careful your marshmallow doesn't catch fire and turn as black as the devil.

Mary takes a pink marshmallow and then holds out her branch to me without a word in either French or English.

"Mary!" says the swimmer, absolutely despondent.

"What do you say?" Thiers intervenes.

"If you please."

"Et en français?"

"S'il vous plait!"

I toast her marshmallow over the coals exactly the way you're supposed to, I mean just right, without burning it or anything. I give her back her branch. Little Mary! She takes the marshmallow off the tip of her branch with her thumb and index finger, without squashing it one bit, she gestures to me with her mouth to tell me to open mine and then she puts her marshmallow on my tongue, pushing it in a little, very delicately, with her finger. She doesn't really push the way you push something into your own mouth; she pushes with the tip of her finger, just a little, I swear. Then she licks her thumb and her index finger, lapping at them very daintily too, with a serious look, her green eyes shining a little. She really could have eaten the marshmallow herself, that's what I would have done to tell you the truth, but not Mary. You toast a pink marshmallow in the coals on the end of a branch and it melts in your mouth like honey, I swear.

"Another five minutes," says Thiers.

He holds up five fingers to the girls. Patsy, Ingrid and Kathy let out hopeless little cries and hurry to toast the last marshmallows. They run like loonies around the fire which is very low now, with lots of embers all around—just right. They're in too much of a hurry and they walk right into the village which the little ones and the long-distance swimmer built; they demolish the bridge and the church and the little girls start to cry. I get down on my hands and knees to rebuild the whole business exactly the way it was, a whole village with all the houses, the roads, the bridge, the garage and the church with its steeple. The swimmer tells me Thank you so much and the little girls stop crying at the same time. Mary makes me eat another marshmallow; she can toast them herself now that the fire's just right.

"Good night! Good night!"

The long-distance swimmer makes the two little ones say Good night and takes them by the hand; you can see the two little white silhouettes on their way to bed gradually being extinguished.

"Bonne nuit!"

Mary's decided to go home all by herself; you look at her silhouette disappearing into the night and what you see disappear first, to tell you the truth, is the little red and blue flowers like the ones inside my sleeping bag.

"Bonne nuit! bonne nuit! bonne nuit!"

The five minutes are up and there aren't any marshmallows left anyway. The three big girls say good night, get down on their knees to stick their branches in the flames one last time and go back to the Commodore's cottage tracing letters of fire against the black sky.

"Would you like a blanket?" Papou asks.

"No thanks, I'm not cold," Mamie replies.

The other fire's gone out, the one on the South Shore near Saint-Nicolas or somewhere, but the moon's risen over there and you'd think the whole Milky Way was reflected in the water.

Papou asks me, "You want to go?"

She says she isn't cold, but. Ever since she's come back from the Hôtel-Dieu you look after her. She says she isn't cold or anything but all the same you go and get her a blanket or a sweater or something. It's as if you were thinking: she can't take care of herself, but you don't think that and you do what you have to do.

"And how would you like to bring three Molsons?"

I get up, turn my back to the campfire. The problem, well, catshit, it isn't bringing three Molsons and a blanket all at once; you turn your back to the campfire and everything's as black as if you'd gone blind all of a sudden. To tell the truth the problem's telling the difference between the tree trunks and the crocodiles, the ends of branches and the snakes, the seaweed and the dead rats. You use radar for walking, you send off waves and wait for them to come back so you can see the whole business on your screen before you take a step. You use your radar till you get used to the dark. Eventually you can distinguish the outline of the cottage fairly well, on its twelve pilings with the iron ladder in front that's sunk into the sand, and you can't help thinking about Mamie's song.

Chanoine appears out of nowhere, running between my legs at a hundred miles an hour. He did it on purpose, I swear, to show that his radar's better than mine. All I saw, to tell you the truth, was a black ball with two stones gleaming in the moonlight. He climbs up the iron ladder ahead of me, barely touching the rungs, then he slips inside. He comes and rubs against my jeans and drags me over to the fridge. I take out the tin of Puss 'n Boots, fill his pink dish and then pour some milk into his yellow bowl. He devours it like a castaway. Then I take three beers out of the fridge and go into Mamie's room.

There are blankets all over the cottage, to tell you the truth, but you always go into Mamie's room. You switch on the light and then as though by magic you see the row of bottles, jars, tubes and everything appear, all in a nice straight line; then there's the series of bottles of multi-coloured pills, then the great collection of dolls, big and little, displayed on every piece of furniture, with their eyes open if they're sitting up, closed if they're lying down, and you could even think they've been drugged by the smell of perfume that fills the room, the way Mamie was herself at the beginning when I went to see her at the Hôtel-Dieu.

I take the grey blanket from her bed and switch off the light. Chanoine goes out of the cottage at the same time as me, he jumps off the iron ladder in one leap and then I lose him in the fog.

Papou's putting three or four logs on the fire and replacing the ones that were half burned. I pass the three Molsons. The Commodore finishes his story about a boat, a very old one because it talks about the old channel.

With the new logs it's a good fire and it's warm under the blanket. I mean, I and Mamie have each taken our half, we're sitting side by side, we've pulled the blanket up over our knees and the blanket's got a kind of perfumey smell, I swear. Something I like is wool that has a perfumey smell and when Chanoine lies on the bed he seems to like it too. The Commodore's just finished his old story about the boat and I'm starting quite openly to fall asleep. Mamie puts her knee over mine. What's funny, when you look in the air, is her blonde head sticking out of the blanket, with the short hair: Thiers has longer hair than she does, to tell the truth. If I wasn't falling asleep so fast I could take off my grey sweatshirt with the hood. I and Mamie, with our blanket, we're in a kind of wigwam, like the campfire before it was lit; she's the squaw and I'm the papoose. There's three Indian chiefs beside us, drinking beer; the oldest one's smoking the peace pipe.

"How are your pilings?"

"They're rotting, they're rotting."

"All pilings rot."

Long canoes filled with Indians and furs are on the river, gently slipping into the Milky Way. The papoose closes his eyes and the wigwam starts to lean a little on one side.

"Are they really rotten?"

"We'll have to wait."

"Wait for the high autumn tides."

The papoose can't even open his eyes now he's getting heavier and heavier someone's hands are pressing against the eyes of the little papoose big red hands around him the wigwam's started to turn more and more the tide's rising the high autumn tide surrounds the wigwam it's turning faster and faster and the papoose drifts away.

"She's taking a seaweed bath."

"What?"

I was watching Capitaine Bonhomme. He'd just told the

children: "I'll count to forty-eight and we'll start on three!" when there was a knock at the door. I said come in, shouting louder than the Captain. Thiers opened the door. He said he didn't want to bother me or anything, that he just wanted to see Mamie. Without getting up from the real Australian wool rug I told him Mamie was taking her seaweed bath; he looked surprised. Capitaine Bonhomme declared that all the boats were beautiful, that everybody had won the drawing contest at the same time and he handed out prizes to everyone, to tell you the truth.

Thiers insisted, "A seaweed bath?"

"Of course."

Mamie calls him Thierry and he really does look like Thierry la Fronde, but. What I like is that he's a pilot. When somebody's a pilot you can't see them any other way. Like a long-distance swimmer: you can't see her any other way either. I mean, even the Commodore, you don't think of him as just a pilings expert or a boat stories expert; you think of him as a pilot. Once you're a pilot you're a pilot for life; it's like once you're a man you're a man for life.

The pilot sits down on the rug. He asks, "Are you watching Capitaine Bonhomme?"

He's talking to the deaf. Finally he adds, "You like it?"

"No."

"But you're still watching it?"

"Yes."

"All right."

I don't want it to look as if I'm babbling at anybody, but. Anyway, there's some things that you don't like or anything, but you still do them. Thiers seems to understand that.

"A seaweed bath?"

"That's the second time you've asked."

"In the river?"

"Catshit! In the bathtub!"

Thiers is the best pilot in the whole city when it comes to taking boats from Quebec to Les Escoumins and back, but. I guess the long-distance swimmer doesn't take seaweed baths very often. I cross my legs on the rug, exactly like the pilot's legs, and I start to explain the whole business to him, without even one glance at Capitaine Bonhomme.

"You know the Sargasso Sea?"

"Yes, why?"

"You ever been there?"

"No. How about you?"

"Of course."

I'm the best liar in the whole city of Quebec. You start telling some ordinary story, like Mamie taking her seaweed bath, but you don't really know where you're going to end up. Without even looking at Capitaine Bonhomme I explain the whole thing to the pilot. You can always get your seaweed from the beach if it strikes your fancy, but. The best thing to do is, you take your bath and you sail to the Sargasso Sea, you pick up the long brown seaweed that has come in on the currents, you fill up your boat in five minutes, start your motor (in the Sargasso Sea it's always as smooth as a mirror so you can't use sail) and bring your cargo of seaweed back to the cottage. Then you borrow the Commodore's old tobacco chopper to cut the seaweed into little pieces and you scatter them in your bath. Mamie likes the smell of seaweed that spreads in the steam from the hot water and she says seaweed's very good for the skin and everything.

Thiers looks surprised. You've got the best pilot who takes boats from Quebec to Les Escoumins and back, and he doesn't know a thing about seaweed baths. "I came to talk to your mother," Thiers says.

"She's still in the bathtub."

"I'll wait."

"It can last a long time."

"Yes?"

"A seaweed bath lasts a long time. You can talk to her through the keyhole."

"I'd rather not. Do you do that?"

"Sure. Why didn't you come and see Mamie at the Hôtel-Dieu?"

"Isn't your father in the cottage?"

"Why didn't you come and see Mamie?"

"I was out on the boats."

"You could have sent her some flowers. Other people sent flowers. I brought her some too."

"I didn't think of it. Isn't your father here?"

"Yes and no."

"That isn't very clear."

"He's here and he isn't here."

"All right, I won't say anything else, I'll wait for you to explain."

The pilot folds his arms and waits. I mean, he honestly looks as if he's made up his mind to wait for a week, sitting there on the real Australian wool rug. So I explain.

"Papou's in the attic."

"Is he writing a book?"

"Did the Commodore tell you that?"

"Yes."

"Catshit!"

I can't hold back the question any longer.

"Could I be a good boat pilot?"

"Have to go to the Ecole de Marine at Rimouski. What grade are you in?"

"Six."

"You go to high school, then the Ecole de Marine."

"Is that what you did?"

"No, I took an apprenticeship in deep-sea navigation. I got a place on a cargo ship that was going to Japan and we spent five months at sea. I was eighteen."

"That's what I'll do too. I don't want to go to any cat-shitty Ecole de Marine."

"Just what is it that your father's writing?"

"Catshit! What was the last boat you worked on?"

"A laker."

"Where'd it come from?"

"The Great Lakes. It was taking grain up to Baie Comeau."

"And then?"

"And then the barges go back to the Great Lakes with iron ore for the steel mills in Cleveland."

"And then?"

"And then what?"

"Are they hard to pilot?"

"No, barges have a shallow draught. You take a barge that's seven hundred and thirty feet long and sixty-five feet wide. It can carry twenty-five thousand tons of ore but it only draws twenty-five feet."

"And then?"

"Do you know what that means, draw?"

"Obviously. And then?"

"You might find yourself with an old barge, a smoker. They're as slow as molasses in January; it can take you seventeen hours to get to Les Escoumins and a good boat does that distance in eight. Besides, they aren't safe. They can break in two. It's happened on the Great Lakes."

"Could they break in two between Quebec and Les Escoumins?"

"No, the sea's too choppy."

"Are there bad storms on the St. Lawrence?"

"No, not really."

The pilot takes a cigarette from his package. He smokes the same kind as Mamie. He takes out a lighter, lights up. He asks, "Will your father be down soon?"

"No. Is there a channel the whole way?"

"I think I should be going now."

"The channel! Is there a channel the whole way?"

"Just from Pointe Saint-Jean to Cap Tourmente; the rest is deep water."

"And then?"

"And then what?"

"Are some stretches harder?"

"Yes, at Cap Brûlé or Petite Rivière Saint-François, but the hardest is still the Channel around Ile Madame. Between Ile Madame and Ile aux Ruaux there's three feet of water at low tide; you could walk there!"

"Catshit! How about the boats?"

"They go in the channel! The channel's thirty feet deep at low tide."

"You were scaring me for nothing."

"Wait a minute, sometimes the channel's only twenty-seven feet deep because of the sand banks."

"All right, let's say it's twenty-seven feet deep. Then what?"

"You've got a forty-ton tanker, loaded to a forty-foot draught."

"So you can't get through."

"Obviously."

"Throw it in the fireplace," I say. "And then?"

No question of getting up to find him an ashtray, he just has to throw his ashes in the fireplace. Out of the question to stop his story. I'm serving my time as an apprentice pilot so he can throw his cigarette ashes in the fireplace and nobody will have to get up and he can get the hell on with his story. I summarize the whole business: "Shit! you've got a forty-ton tanker with a forty-foot draught and the channel's only twenty-seven feet deep off Ile Madame."

The pilot takes his time. You feel like yelling, but. Papou'll come down from the attic where he's writing his goddamn book about Hemingway, he'll come down like a zouave to see what's going on; Mamie'll come out of the bathroom at a hundred miles an hour with seaweed all over her back and her head and everything. So you just sit on the real Australian wool rug and don't say a word or move an inch, with your legs folded like the pilot's across from you and without looking to see what's happening to Capitaine Bonhomme. A good pilot takes his time before he decides exactly what he has to do and not make a mistake. He's just passed Pointe Saint-Jean with his forty-ton tanker and he's in his pilot's cabin along with the captain, the duty officer and the two sailors, thinking. The tanker's slowing down.

The apprentice pilot bites his tongue. At last the pilot throws his cigarette into the fireplace and decides: "We'll have to wait for the tide."

"Fine. Will you have to wait a long time?"

"Two hours. When it's risen for two hours I'll have around forty feet of water."

"Is that enough?" Isn't it a little close?"

"The tide keeps rising; I'll go slowly and use the sound."

"Catshit! I'd forgotten the sound!"

"I use the sound but I don't trust it."

"Why not?"

"Let's say there's two feet of mud. The waves cross the mud, strike rock and come back up; it seems as if there's forty feet of water but there's only thirty-eight. Understand?"

"So do you use the sound or not?"

"I use it, but mostly I rely on my experience."

"Just what is that, experience?"

"I only came to have a word with your mother."

"She's taking a seaweed bath, I already told you. A seaweed bath lasts a long time, I said that too. It's very good for the skin; when she comes out she'll be more beautiful than ever. What's experience?"

"That's something I'll have to see!"

"What's experience?"

"Something you do for a long time, something you do well."

"Can you see experience?"

"You can see if a pilot's got experience by the way he gets on board a boat. The launch takes the pilot from the wharf at Quebec to the boat, it comes up alongside of the boat, the pilot gets up on the deck of the launch and holds onto the ramp in the middle with one hand. The pilot has to calculate exactly how the wave is going to move and let go of the ramp at exactly the right time, then get a good grip on the rope ladder so he won't be thrown in the water. It's even harder in the winter; the rope ladder's covered with ice but an experienced pilot grabs his rope ladder without getting all worked up, not like a shipwreck victim grabbing hold of a life-buoy. You understand?"

"I've got experience driving Formula Ones."

"You interested in car racing?"

"I know all the racing cars there are and I'm an expert at Formula Ones. Do you know the difference between a Formula One and a Formula Two?"

"No."

"A Formula Two and a Formula Three?"

"Don't know that either."

"Doesn't matter, you can learn."

"You do any driving recently?"

"I won the Grand Prix de Monaco."

"You could say that we're both pilots."

"You could, but."

"But what?"

"I have to tell you something: I'm going to become a boat pilot."

"You giving up car racing?"

"No, but. It's hard to explain, wait a second."

I move a little closer to him on the real Australian wool rug and sit directly opposite him to tell him the whole business. I talk very softly.

"It's hard to explain. One thing for sure, I'm going to become a boat pilot because of the goddamn pilings."

"The pilings?"

"They're rotten. The Commodore didn't want to come right out and say so but I could tell from his eyes. The pilings are completely rotten, I swear."

"I don't understand."

"Is there such a thing as high tides?"

"Of course."

"When do they come?"

"When there's a full moon."

"Yes, but. Besides the full moon there's even higher tides, aren't there?"

"In the spring and fall."

"That's what I mean: the high tides in the fall! You understand?"

"I'm not sure."

"Catshit!"

"Explain what you're trying to tell me."

"It's hard."

I moved a little closer to the pilot. Suddenly Mamie comes out of her seaweed bath. It really hits you in the eye. I mean the two pilots sitting across from each other on the white rug made of real Australian wool, talking about the whole business in a low voice, and all of a sudden Mamie comes out of her seaweed bath, wearing her long bathrobe with the belt that forms a knot on her thigh, her head wrapped in a white towel like a Hindu turban, in a cloud of perfume and her face all shining.

The pilots rise before the Hindu princess. The boat pilot bows deeply. "My compliments, Madame."

Mamie looks very serious. She holds her hand out in a funny way, a little to the side. I mean not a bit like a great lady when she wants you to kiss her hand, but more like when you hold out your hand to help somebody. The pilot takes her hand, holds it in his for a while, then drops it gently.

"Please accept my apologies for keeping you waiting," Mamie says in a slow voice.

"Not at all," says the pilot.

"I'm really sorry."

"Please, I just got here."

"He just got here," I say.

The two of us are the biggest liars in the whole city of Quebec.

"I beg you, please be seated," says Mamie with a ceremonial gesture.

"You're too kind."

The pilots remain standing; the boat pilot doesn't take his eyes off Mamie for one second. The long-distance swimmer never takes seaweed baths. He looks very impressed, and as though he's out of breath. Mamie offers: "Will you have some coffee, or something else to drink?"

"No, thank you very much. I just came to invite you somewhere."

"Invite me?"

"To invite all of you for supper at our place tonight."

"That's very kind of you," says Mamie, bowing her head with the Hindu turban. "Just a moment, if you will."

Mamie's speaking in the same slow, serious voice she sometimes used when she came home from the Hôtel-Dieu, when she was talking on the phone.

"Please excuse me," Mamie says. Very slowly she climbs up the stairs and knocks three times on the trap-door to the attic. The telephone hadn't rung or anything but she'd answer it and spend hours talking with people I didn't know at all and neither did Papou.

Papou comes out of the attic, climbs down two steps and Mamie transmits the pilot's invitation. He looks down the stairs where the two pilots are still standing, then turns his face back to Mamie. He takes his time before he speaks. Slowly she slips her hand up to his cheek and says: "You know, nobody's seen you all day long."

"What time is it?"

Mamie doesn't answer but the boat pilot, down below, says, "Five o'clock."

"Is your work going well?" Mamie asks.

"Five o'clock already?"

"You work far too much, my friend," she says in the same serious voice that she uses to talk to strangers on the telephone.

"Hello," says Papou, as though he's just noticed the two pilots.

"Hello."

"Would you like a beer?"

"No thanks, I just dropped in for a minute."

"There's none left upstairs, but I think there's some in the fridge. You won't change your mind?"

"No, really, thanks. I have to be going."

"You should eat something my friend," says Mamie. "I'm sure you haven't had a thing since this morning."

"I think you're right," says Papou.

Then Mamie slowly comes down the stairs, stops at the last step, half turns towards the two pilots, opens her arms slightly and in the same voice says:

"We accept your invitation with pleasure."

The way you feel is as though you've stepped on board Noah's Ark.

We're eating outside and the dogs are absolutely out of their minds, running all over the place and diving under the table at a hundred miles an hour. I ate three honey doughnuts and so did Mary; she's sitting next to me and eating exactly the same thing as me. If you want to say anything you have to yell as though you were in a helicopter; the two little girls keep howling and fighting, the three biggest ones laugh like logs tumbling off a woodpile and Papou's burying everybody. Mamie and the pilot are talking in low voices but they seem to understand each other. I don't know how they do it.

Five empty Molson bottles are lined up in front of Papou's

plate. He's finishing a big glass of cognac as he talks to the Commodore. The only thing the Commodore's got time to do is smoke his pipe and nod his head with his eyes half closed, while Papou talks about Hemingway. Papou hasn't said a word for a week or something; now he's overflowing. He's finished telling the whole story about the old fisherman even though the Commodore said that he knew it and everything, and without wasting a second he's started on a war story that happened up in the mountains, with all kinds of soldiers, an old woman who makes you think of a man and a very sweet young girl with her hair cut shorter than Mamie's; I didn't understand why. The long-distance swimmer offered me a fourth honey doughnut; I said yes and Mary asked for another one too.

Papou raises his glass of cognac.

"To the health of old Hemingway!"

The girls applaud and laugh like loonies. The long-distance swimmer tells them in English that it's time to put on their nightgowns. They dive under the table, pop up between Papou and the Commodore and do a three-legged race to the cottage except that their legs aren't tied together. Mary comes fourth. The swimmer starts to clear the table. Mamie and the pilot get up and head for the beach.

"Eighty-six?" Mamie asks.

"Eighty-six pilots and last year each of us made a hundred and twenty trips. There's going to be a strike and it could. . . ."

Then you don't hear what they're saying. Papou sets up a battle for the Commodore, between the glasses and the bottles. He puts a fork in between the two groups of soldiers.

"Here you've got the bridge," he says.

"Sorry," says the long-distance swimmer.

In one move she takes away the bridge and captures half the soldiers by sticking a finger into the mouth of each bottle. Then she turns to me and begins: "Mary is. . . ."

"Pardon?" I say in French.

"Mary is your friend?"

"Yes, Madame."

Then she asks another question in English and this time I don't ask her to repeat it or anything.

"Yes, Madame."

Papou stopped short when the swimmer took away the bridge and started helping her take the dishes into the cottage. The Commodore looks sad. During the story about Hemingway he couldn't get one goddamn word in. He's just lit his pipe. When you see the Commodore's pipe you always think about the signals the Indians make with smoke and a blanket and you want to do the same thing with your two hands. I ask the Commodore, "Something wrong?"

"What do you mean?"

"Something's wrong; you can't get a word in."

"No, no, nothing's wrong."

"But you look sad."

"No, I'm not."

"Yes you are!"

"No I'm not."

"Is it because of Papou?"

"No."

"Because of our cottage?"

"Yes and no."

"Because the pilings are rotten."

"No."

You start to get tired of asking questions. You shut your trap and wait. He's making smoke signals without knowing it. Eventually he makes up his mind.

"I think it's sad when a house hasn't got a foundation. Do you understand?"

"Of course."

I said of course so he wouldn't look so sad. But he still looks sad, to tell you the truth. He adds, "A house without a foundation's like a man who didn't have a childhood."

"Of course."

He runs his hand through my hair and sighs, "Poor little mate."

I'd give the Commodore my agates, I swear. I mean the agates I collected at Anse à Beaufils when we took that great trip to the Gaspé, when we went along the North Shore to the end of the road, at Moisie, and then crossed over from Baie Comeau to Sainte-Anne des Monts on the "Gaspésien." I'd give them to the Commodore. I'd really give him all my agates, at a hundred miles an hour.

It's a real obsession. I'm always saying "at a hundred miles an hour" and "I mean." I've got obsessions like some kind of zouave. What you feel like, to tell the truth, is that everything's happening at a hundred miles an hour like when you're driving a Formula One. Another feeling is that everything's starting to drift away. You haven't got time to name all the things: they've taken off at a hundred miles an hour, or they're drifting. I mean, you haven't got time to talk like people or anything.

Mary's back already.

One thing I'd like would be to go out on the air mattress with Mary. I'd start the motor and we'd travel very slowly to the other side of the Sargasso Sea; she'd stay in the middle of the raft so it wouldn't tip and I'd be careful not to splash her too much with the motor. We'd go slowly because of the waves and take time to watch the flying fish jump over the raft, and the schools of dolphin running in circles around us and the whales spouting when they come to the surface to breathe. We'd hardly talk except when I'd tell little Mary if it was a white whale or a blue whale, a sea bream or a tuna, a killer whale or a porpoise, and when I talked to her about hammerfish and sawfish and swordfish. I could lend her my grey sweatshirt with the hood; she'd say no I'm not cold and everything, but. I'd tell her gently to put it on anyway so she wouldn't catch cold or something. One thing for sure, we wouldn't talk too much; I'd just explain the things she wanted to know and I'd ask her first to be more sure. We wouldn't go a hundred miles an hour and things wouldn't drift away either. If we found a starfish we'd make a detour to take it on board. I'd hold Mary's feet while she leaned over to pick it up. She's got small feet, to tell the truth. With a lot of blue veins that you can see right through the skin. We'd come back to the cottage slowly, but not dawdling, so the long-distance swimmer wouldn't get worried. The swimmer does her washing in the river. I mean, she really goes right into the water with her skirt hitched up above her knees and in the river water she scrubs away at the sheets and the girls' clothes while the basket floats beside her. Then Mary and I would slowly come ashore and the swimmer would be doing her washing as she sang an English song and we'd show her our starfish and I'd tell Mary to keep it and hang it up over her bed.

Mary didn't take time to wash her ears or anything; she rushed like a loony so she could be out before the other girls. She's standing there in front of me, hands behind her back, stiff as a fence-post with the little red and blue flowers on her nightgown and her cap. You can't get used to it. It hits you in the eye every time you notice those little flowers exactly like the ones inside your sleeping bag. The way you feel is like in the winter when you fall down to make an angel in the snow. I mean, one fine day you'd fall down in the soft snow with your arms out and when you got up to see the angel the snow would have melted and there'd be little red and blue flowers everywhere.

She takes her hands from behind her back and holds out a doll.

"Mary," she says.

"Her name's the same as yours?"

"Yes. You can take Mary."

I take the doll. She's all naked and her skin's as soft as real skin, except that it's cold like when you get out of the water.

"Can your doll talk?"

"No."

Mary shakes her head and sticks out her tongue, a little pink tongue like Chanoine's. She says, "How do you say broken?"

"Brisée."

"That's it," she says, "brisée."

"You got any other dolls?"

"A teddy bear."

She spreads her arms to show me how long her teddy bear is. Her arms are just long enough to show me the exact length, to tell you the truth. Then she puts her hands behind her back again and asks, "Have you got a teddy bear?"

"Yes, but."

"But what?"

"I lost it in my helicopter."

"Bad luck! Have you got a helicopter?"

"I was flying over the jungle in a helicopter, one of those goddamn helicopters without a door. You understand? No door," I repeated in English. "The teddy bear fell out of the opening, just when I was flying over a swamp. When there's a swamp in the jungle it's always crawling with crocodiles. The teddy bear fell out right in the middle of the swamp, I swear it, and I saw tree trunks turn into crocodiles all along the shore, and they threw themselves in the water at a hundred miles an hour, heading for the teddy bear."

"Was he eaten?"

"Eaten up! Très probablement. Probably."

"Sorry," said Mary.

The little red and blue flowers shuddered. Mary looked as sad as though she'd lost her own teddy bear in the swamp filled with crocodiles. In a moment she said, "I've never been in a helicopter in my whole life."

"No, but your father's a boat pilot."

"Yes."

"And your mother's a long-distance swimmer."

"What?"

"She swam all the way to the other side of the river, didn't she?"

"To Saint-Nicolas? No. My father says no. My father sounds funny when he talks about swimming."

She traces the edge of the beach with her finger. Mamie and the pilot are sitting on a big rock.

"Is your father a pilot too?"

"No. I'm going to be a pilot but I don't want to go to any cat-shitty Ecole de Marine."

"What does he do?"

"Papou? Catshit, he's writing a book! But usually he listens to stories. Wait a minute."

I lie down in the sand and start explaining the whole business to her.

"People lie on the couch like that, at the clinic in the Hôtel-Dieu, and they tell stories. The last one I heard was Puss in Boots. Do you know it?"

"No."

"Papou's behind his desk, a sort of half-moon shaped desk, and he writes down the story. You want me to tell you about Puss in Boots?"

"Yes!"

"Sit down there."

Mary sits close to me. I draw a half moon in the sand in front of her.

"There was once upon a time a Miller. . . ."

I start with that great sentence and Mary draws the whole story in the sand as the characters appear. She's bending over the sand in her nightgown and she's really drawing the whole thing, even the hardest part, when the Cat stops the carriage and persuades the King that his master's going to drown, so he'll send for royal garments for the Marquis de Carabas. Puss in Boots goes ahead of the carriage to the Ogre's palace and he asks the Ogre to turn into a lion and then a mouse; he falls on the Ogre and eats him up and persuades the King that the Ogre's palace belongs to his master. The Marquis de Carabas shyly offers his arm to the Princess to help her down from the carriage, while the King murmurs in the ear of the Princess, "That's how shy I was when I was courting your mother." Little Mary begins to look shy too as she draws the scene, then the banquet that follows, with the most exquisite wines and everything. Finally the Marquis de Carabas dares to ask for the hand of the Princess and the whole business ends up with a great wedding.

Mary still looks shy.

"Have you got a pussy cat?"

"Of course. You're a real drawing champion."

"Can I see the pussy cat?"

"Have to go to the cottage."

"In a helicopter?"

"On foot. I broke my propeller."

"Bad luck!"

"You'll have to see Mamie's dolls too."

"Yes."

We take the beach road. The tide's low. In the distance, Mamie and the pilot seem to be leaning against each other. The tide's left logs and seaweed and old bottles and rotten fish on the beach; you can't have a tide without finding some goddamn rotten fish. And every time you turn up a rotten fish you can't help thinking about the business of the fetus.

I'm the biggest liar in the whole city of Quebec. Mamie wasn't just convalescing or something: she was in the Hôtel-Dieu because of some business with a fetus. I know all about what a fetus is and how babies are born and everything. Mamie explained it to me. But what I wonder is, when the fetus comes out too soon and it's dead, what do they do with it? I mean, they can throw it in a garbage can or they can have a ceremony. To tell you the truth, I'd rather they had some kind of ceremony or something. Not necessarily a whole service with a mass and a burial and everything, but they could find some kind of ceremony. I hope that's what they do; what I really don't like is to think they might just throw it in the garbage can.

"Ouch!" Mary shouts.

"What is it?"

"I cut my foot!"

"Let me see."

"No!"

"Come on! Sit down, I'm just going to look."

"Catshit!"

"Don't say that."

"*You* say it."

"All right, whatever you want. Show me your foot so I can examine it."

She sits down in the sand and I lift her foot in the air so I can see the bottom.

"I can't see a single thing."

"Catshit! I didn't cut my foot then."

Mary bursts out laughing, like when you've just played a good trick on somebody, with her foot in the air. She rolls around in the sand.

"Come here!"

I hold out my hand to help her; she gives me her foot. I tickle the bottom of her foot. She laughs like a loony. Finally she calms down, takes my hand and we start off for the cottage.

We're three steps from the iron ladder. I put my arm around Mary's neck.

"The river's a hundred and twenty feet deep," I say.

"Oh!"

"It isn't really dangerous."

"Have you got a good grip on me?"

"Yes. Now you do exactly as I say. We're on the little launch and it's coming up to the ship. Watch out for the waves! You have to hold the railing really tight with one hand. Are you holding it properly now?"

"Yes."

"You have to wait till the launch is right against the side of the boat. It's coming in slowly. The boat seems to be ten times as high as we are. The waves are moving us up and down. Being seasick's out of the question."

"My father never gets seasick."

"The boat doesn't stop, it just slows down. The launch is coming even closer. You see the ship's ladder?"

"Yes!"

"It doesn't look like a good ladder. Catshit!"

"You said catshit again."

"It's an iron ladder, never saw such a thing in my whole career. An iron ladder!"

"Bad luck!"

"You still holding the railing?"

"Yes."

"Never saw that in my whole career as a pilot. A boat with an iron ladder! We're going to go on strike or something."

"My father's going to go on strike."

"Catshit. Boats always have rope ladders."

"Why?"

"Less dangerous, don't you understand?"

"No."

"Say yes. I'll explain the whole business after."

"Yes."

"Look at the iron ladder; can't you see that it rolls with the boat? Rope ladders don't sway nearly as much. You understand?"

"Yes."

"Really, or are you just saying yes?"

"I really understand. Are we getting close to the boat?"

"Yes, but. Just a minute, I didn't explain the whole business; boats have two ladders. You go up the rope ladder and then you come to a diagonal iron ladder."

"What's that?"

I trace the ladder with my hand, still holding on to the railing on the launch, then I put my arm around her neck again. The launch keeps coming closer.

"Watch out when you get on board, it'll give you a jolt. You still holding onto the railing?"

"Yes!"

"Good. We've just come up to the boat; the waves are going to get smaller and we'll be able to climb up. Ready?"

"Yes."

"I'll count to forty-eight and we'll start on three. You let go of the railing, take two quick steps onto the deck of the launch, get a good trip on the ladder and then put your left foot on the first rung. Are you scared?"

"No. How deep is the river did you say?"

"A hundred and twenty feet or something."

"I don't know how to swim. My mother swims very well."

"Do exactly what I do. One, two three!"

We do things together, the two steps, grabbing the ladder and everything, except that I keep my arm around her neck because of the iron ladder. Catshit! Never seen such a thing in my whole career! You want to board a boat to do your pilot's work between Quebec and Les Escoumins and you land on a goddamn iron ladder that sways with the rolling of the boat.

The boat's deserted.

I mean, when you get on a boat there's at least a duty officer and two sailors, and most of the time there's somebody to welcome you at the top of the ladder, but here there's nothing.

We go looking for Chanoine.

There's nobody in the living room, but. There's a fire in the fireplace as though somebody was there. You can't say that the fire itself is somebody: that's zouave and everything. The way you feel is as if you'd found a lighted cigarette, not in an ashtray but floating in the air. Or a cup of coffee that wasn't on a table but up in the air too. I mean, you really see those things in the air and you wouldn't be surprised or anything. I'm the biggest liar in the whole city of Quebec.

Mamie's room is open.

I take Mary's hand. We tiptoe into Mamie's room because of the sleeping dolls. Mary stops, looks all around.

"Count them, Mary."

". . . eight, nine, ten!"

When Mamie came back from the Hôtel-Dieu she brought a new doll home every week and you thought she'd never stop. Papou would see her arrive and unwrap her parcel; he'd shake his head gently, like when you say no without talking, and then slowly climb up to the attic. All Mamie did was lie down on the bed beside her favorite doll, the one in the long white dress and transparent veil, like a bride.

I'm an expert at stories and racing cars and helicopters and boats. But not dolls. Mary's an expert at dolls, you can see it in her face. She's got round eyes that shine like my agates from Anse à Beaufils and it's as if that shining thing was overflowing and spreading right across her face or something. You don't want to look at it for too long, to tell you the truth. It's like when somebody starts to cry and you see the tears: you watch for two seconds, something tells you not to watch for too long, and then you start looking off to the side. I'd give her my teddy bear, I swear I would. If my teddy bear hadn't been devoured by the crocodiles when I was flying over the jungle in a helicopter I'd really give it to Mary.

I give her hand a little tug.

"You coming?"

"Yes."

"Chanoine must be in my room."

"Is that you?"

With one finger on her other hand Mary points to the little figure hanging over Mamie's bed.

"No, catshit!"

But I give Mary time to look at the painting.

It's a boy my age in blue jeans like mine, except he isn't wearing a grey sweatshirt with a hood but a kind of old shirt, blue or grey, you can't decide which. The boy's holding a rose in his right hand, almost under his chin, and his head's turned towards his left shoulder, just a little, to tell you the truth. In his left hand he's holding a little branch across his legs. The flower's all right, he wants to give it to somebody. His head's down and everything. But what's funny is the little branch. It's too short to make a helicopter rotor or even a small propeller blade, and you can't imagine what the boy would be doing with a branch like that.

I tug at Mary's hand again.

"Are you coming in my room?"

"Yes."

I raise both hands in the air.

It's Eliot Ness. I take one big white pill and one little red one in the morning, but. To tell you the truth, I never know when it's going to start. I mean, you feel as if you're doing something ordinary, for instance you invite Mary into your room to see Chanoine and then Eliot Ness jabs you in the ribs with his revolver. You never know ahead of time when he's going to do it. He doesn't say a word, "Federal Police" or anything; all he does is jab you in the back with his revolver and you stick your hands up without looking or anything.

Mary asks in a low voice, "What are you doing?"

"Nothing. Eliot Ness."

She considers this for a moment, then puts her hands up too. One thing I like about Mary, you don't have to explain things to her for half an hour.

All you can do is keep your hands as high as possible and wait. You can still see Ness's revolver in your back, exactly in between the shoulder blades. Mary, in her nightgown with the red and blue flowers, keeps her hands in the air too. Eliot Ness never shoots first. Some policemen get all worked up but not Eliot. All the same, when he's there with his revolver in your back you can't think about anything else. You see him in his office in Chicago with his two assistants. He's taken off his jacket and he's wearing some kind of vest. He's unbuttoned his collar and pushed his hat back on his head. You can see his revolver in the holster he wears under his left arm. He's sitting on the corner of his desk. The telephone rings; an assistant answers, "Eliot Ness's office—one moment please."

He holds out the phone to Ness. Eliot places the receiver against his ear, puts the phone on his knee and says, "Ness!"

He says his name and that's all! You can tell he's a man just by hearing him say his name on the phone in his office in Chicago. He doesn't say anything else, he just writes an address or something on a piece of paper, hangs up, walks to the door and picks up his jacket as he goes out. The two assistants do exactly the same thing without saying a word and they follow him like zouaves.

Eliot Ness has gone.

I lower my hands and so does Mary.

We go into my room.

Thiers says there aren't any real storms on the St Lawrence, but. You always put your things away carefully and when you come back unexpectedly there's a kind of storm: the aircraft carrier has capsized and all the planes have fallen into the water; the ferry's gone aground at Ile d'Orléans and the cars have come clattering to the ground. There's been a general shipwreck and there's débris everywhere: flotsam, shoes, socks, car wheels, books, cookies and everything.

Mary walks cautiously through the débris. Suddenly she points at something. On the wall there's that great big huge picture of the Lotus, the green one with yellow stripes and the number six on the nose, and Jim Clark at the wheel with his helmet; under the picture there's my bed, which is the same length, with my sleeping bag on it. Mary's seen the bump in the sleeping bag.

"The pussy cat," Mary whispers. "Sshhh."

She puts a finger to her lips.

"I wasn't saying anything," I say.

"Sshhh!"

"SSSHHHH!"

The bump has moved a little.

I pull down the zipper, just to the middle, because of Chanoine. I slip inside the sleeping bag and push myself down to the bottom. Mary comes over. She sits on the bed, lifts her legs in the air; I pick up the edge of the bag so she can slide her legs in and then slip inside like a kind of snake.

Chanoine starts to purr.

You can do up your sleeping bag from the inside or the outside. From the inside, you press one foot against the bottom, you reach across little Mary and then you pull the zipper up to the top without too much difficulty. From the outside, you have to stretch yourself out like a zouave and almost get out of the bag; Chanoine would go running out at a hundred miles an hour. I reach across little Mary and close the bag from the inside.

Chanoine stretches out between our legs and purrs louder.

"You hear the motor?" Mary asks.

"Of course."

"The pussy cat's warm."

"Say 'Chanoine.'"

"Sanoine. Is that right?"

"Yes."

It isn't, but. You close your eyes and you feel good. To tell you the truth I always feel good in a sleeping bag. In the summer you can undo your zipper as far as the last corner, for ventilation and everything. I mean, you always feel really good in it and you're proud because Papou bought it from Latulippe Surplus de Guerre. Even with your eyes shut you'd swear that little Mary's still there, in her great nightgown with the little red and blue flowers like the inside of your sleeping bag. The way you feel with Mary and Chanoine, it's as if the warmth is slowly making us melt so we become one person in a big nightgown that's slowly drifting to the other side of the Sargasso Sea. Without opening my eyes or anything I say to Mary, "You hear that?"

"Sanoine?"

"No, don't you hear the. . . ."

"Sanoine's got a motor like my father's boat."

"Yes, but. Listen, can't you hear the sound of the waves?"

"Yes, Sanoine's boat's in the water."

"Yes, but."

"What?"

"There's a full moon."

Mary's a little bit scared. I didn't do it on purpose, I swear. She asks, "Is the full moon dangerous?"

"Listen, Mary, the full moon means high tides. Understand?"

"No."

So I tell her the whole story about the tides and the moon, exactly the way the pilot explained it to me. At the end I ask her, "Did you understand?"

"Catshit!"

"Why?"

"I'm scared. Are they really rotten?"

"Who?"

"The pilings, catshit! Are they rotten?"

"Don't say catshit. They're rotten, but."

"But what?" Mary asks.

"I'm thinking about Papou and Mamie. I've got one of your hairs in my mouth, can you see it?" I open my mouth and stick out my tongue. Mary looks.

"Yes, I've got it."

"Thanks. I'll tell you one thing—promise not to tell anybody?"

"Yes. No!"

"The pilings are rotten and so are Papou and Mamie. I'll have to talk to the Commodore about it again."

"When my doll got broken I talked to the Commodore about it too."

"You aren't listening to what I'm saying."

"Yes. I'm listening to what you're saying but I'm scared. When I'm scared I think about my doll. Have you got another one of my hairs on your tongue?"

"No."

"I'd have taken it off with my fingers too."

"Thanks. Can you hear the sound of the waves?"

"You asked me that before."

"Listen, the water's under the cottage now."

"Is that dangerous?"

"Not yet, it isn't the high tides that come in the fall. Did you move?"

"No, it's Sanoine."

"He must be dreaming."

"Does a Sanoine dream?"

"He's having a nightmare because of the water under the cottage. He's turned off his motor and he's drifting."

I'll have to have a serious talk with the Commodore. I mean, with all this business about the full moon and the high tides and the rotten pilings and everything, we're going to have to take some time and sit on a rock, I and the Commodore, and really have a talk about it all.

III

Rain. All day long.

It was coming down like some kind of flood in the days of Noah's Ark and I phoned the Commodore to ask him if the autumn had arrived or what. He told me not to get my boots in an uproar, that we'd sit on a rock and talk about the whole business whenever I wanted.

It's evening. The rain's stopped. I put on my grey sweatshirt with the hood and go outside with Chanoine. You haven't seen Papou all day long. I mean, usually he at least comes down for breakfast and tells you your feet are dirty or something and he asks Mamie if she slept well. But not this morning. He must have slept in the attic with his case of Molson and old Hemingway. It doesn't really matter, to tell you the truth.

It's clear in between the clouds; you can see the moon and the stars from time to time. The Commodore said he'd come after the girls were in bed. I'm sitting on a rock. The tide's out.

When you say it doesn't really matter, to tell you the truth, it's because you're mostly thinking about Mamie. I and Chanoine had to get dinner and supper all by ourselves, like zouaves. Mamie spent the day in her room; she was talking to somebody. I mean, there was just me and Chanoine in the cottage and Papou up in the attic, and every now and then you could hear Mamie in her room talking with somebody. Things like this:

"Will you close the window?"

"Of course, if you insist."

"You're going to think I don't like the rain."

"Not at all."

"Look, there's water on my pillow. The wind's blowing this way now."

"It's turned."

"I'm sure there's water all over the floor. Shall I tell you? I used to love running barefoot through the water. He'd hold my hand and I'd run through the puddles till I was out of breath. Are you listening?"

"Go on, please."

"We'd run for hours. He was very gentle and he never lost his temper. You're very gentle too, aren't you?"

"Of course."

"When I was exhausted he'd carry me on his shoulders. Shall I tell you? I'd put my hands over his eyes so he couldn't find the way back to the house. . . . I'm really sure there's water all over the floor. Will you go and look?"

"Yes."

"Is there any water?"

"A little."

"Will I be able to go out this afternoon?"

"If you want."

"I don't like being closed in. I don't want to hurt you but. . . ."

"But?"

"Nothing."

"Do you feel closed in?"

"A prisoner. You know those playgrounds with bars? Look, there's rain all over my dolls too. I really must go out, I can't take this."

"Aren't you comfortable in here?"

"I like you very much, you're very patient, you listen to everything I say. Can you hear the wind now?"

"Yes."

"He had a big black sweater and he'd wrap me up in it to shelter me from the wind. He'd take me in his arms and rock me till the wind died down. I'd close my eyes and pray that the wind would never die down. You see, I'm closing my eyes like that now and the pipe smell that the wool gave off is still there and it's still intoxicating. And when he wanted to see if I was asleep he'd move a little or I'd murmur something and he'd go on rocking me in his arms."

That's what I and Chanoine heard, the rain on the pillow, running through puddles, the wind, the black sweater and the whole zouave story.

It doesn't really matter either, to tell you the truth. I mean, I and Chanoine wouldn't writhe around on the white wool rug and we wouldn't pull out our hair or anything. But you can't help thinking there was nobody in the cottage except I and Chanoine and Papou up in the attic and Mamie in her room and that's all.

The moon's hidden now.

You're sitting quietly on a rock at low tide, thinking about Mamie and the whole business while you wait for the Commodore and then all of a sudden the beach is covered with sea elephants; all around you and as far as you can see there's this great herd of sea elephants, all stuck against one another, slowly flicking their tails back and forth, rolling over on their backs with a moan like someone in pain, and they're looking at you stupidly with their eyes wide open.

You pull up your hood and tie it under your chin.

You close your eyes.

First you smell the pipe and then: "Are you cold?"

You hear voices and you either like them or you don't. The ones you like build themselves a nest in your ear, a little at a time, with blades of grass and moss and everything. The feeling you get whenever you hear that voice, is as if a bird was returning to its nest. I'm the biggest liar in the whole city of Quebec.

The Commodore says, "The dampness goes right through you."

I open my eyes. He's sitting on my rock. I ask him, "Did you see the sea elephants?"

"I wasn't paying attention."

What I like about the Commodore is he never gets upset. I mean, some people might get really upset, tell you we aren't at the ocean, that sea elephants don't come up the St Lawrence or something. But not the Commodore; he says he wasn't paying attention, that's all. So I explain the whole thing to him, man to man: the rain like some kind of flood, Papou who doesn't even come downstairs any more to tell me my feet are dirty, Mamie talking in her room and finally the sea elephants.

He has to think about it.

The moon's come back.

I ask the Commodore, "Is it autumn?"

"In a few days."

"High tides soon?"

"There's a full moon."

In the moonlight you can see that the Commodore's wearing his sweater with Hawk Eye and Sitting Bull and the big totem pole on the back and his Commodore's cap. He takes out his pipe and spits. You can hear very clearly the little wet sound of the spit coming out and you'd swear it was going to land really far away; you don't see it but you can guess.

"You feel like talking?" the Commodore asks.

"Yes and no. Catshit!"

"What do you mean?"

"You start to explain something and you don't know where to land."

"Say the first thing that occurs to you."

"The pilings are rotten."

"Let's assume they are. Then what?"

"Before, I used to tell myself the pilings are rotten and that's all."

"And now?"

"Now it's rotten all over the place, catshit! You know what I mean?"

"Of course."

I pucker up my mouth so its round like a hen's behind and I spit as far as I can. At night it's as though you'd spit two miles.

The Commodore says, "You can talk if you want."

"Is it true about the smokers?"

"Who told you about that?"

"Thiers. Is it true or not?"

"Yes," the Commodore admits.

"Were you ever a pilot on a smoker?"

"Yup."

"What's it like?"

"They're slow, they drag, you're there on the edge of the channel with your big cloud of black smoke, you let everybody pass you."

"Yes, but. Catshit! I mean on the Great Lakes?"

The Commodore thought for a moment, turned his pipe upside down and knocked it several times against the rock.

"We should go inside; don't you think it's damp?"

He gets up, pulls down the zipper between Hawk Eye and Sitting Bull and sticks his pipe in his shirt pocket. Then in one breath I come out with: "Thiers says the smokers can break in two on the Great Lakes!"

The Commodore sits down again abruptly. It's easy to see the wet sea elephants moving slowly in the moonlight and from time to time you can hear them moan, I swear you can.

The Commodore picks up his pipe again and takes out his package of tobacco which has a kind of red flower on it: Rose Quesnel or something. He presses down the tobacco with his finger and you can see that he's taking his time. He lights up slowly. His lighter makes a huge flame that can stand up to any storm on any sea in the world. The way you feel when you look at the Commodore's flame is that those old lake barges are quite capable of lasting all the way from Baie Comeau to Cleveland, with their iron ore, and that you're getting your boots in an uproar for nothing.

Suddenly, across from us, it's like a beacon being lit and then going out: the door to our cottage is opened, then closed right away, and you can make out a thin white silhouette going down the iron ladder.

I say to the Commodore, "Did you see that?"

"Yes."

"It's a ghost."

"Of course."

His voice sounds funny. The Commodore always talks with his pipe in his teeth, but not now. He's stuck it in his mouth all the way back to the place where they take out your tonsils, I swear it.

In the moonlight you can see the white silhouette motionless at the foot of the iron ladder and behind it, vaguely, the rotten pilings. Up above, floating in the night as though it was on the mast of a ship, is the little light in the attic where Papou's working with Hemingway like some kind of zouave. You look at the light, the pilings and the ghost and you can't help thinking of Mamie's song.

Now the white silhouette slips onto the beach towards the Commodore's cottage; it drifts slowly among the wet sea elephants that are sparkling in the moonlight.

I ask the Commodore: "Is the long-distance swimmer there?"

"She's asleep."

"And the girls?"

"Sleeping too."

"Yes, but Mary?"

"Listen, the swimmer put the girls to bed after supper and she went to bed too. Is that clear?"

The Commodore's rammed his pipe in past his tonsils again and he's in a bad mood.

"You said we'd talk about the whole business together man to man sitting on a rock."

"Yup."

"Did you say it or didn't you?"

"I said it."

"Good. Does the long-distance swimmer sleep soundly?"

"Like a log."

"Does Mary sleep like a log too?"

"Mary too."

"Is Thierry La Fronde at your place?"

"Of course."

"Mamie's the one who calls him Thierry la Fronde. Is he asleep?"

"No, he was playing with the dogs when I. . . ."

"Look, did you see that?"

Another light came on for two seconds, then went out. I and the Commodore got a good look at the light over the herd of sea elephants, far off to the right where the Commodore's cottage is, with the swimmer and the girls who sleep like logs and Thierry la Fronde who's playing with the dogs. The Commodore lights his pipe again with the flame that can stand up to any storm on any sea in the world, then he turns directly towards me.

"Now listen. It'd be a good idea for the two of us to have a serious talk."

I spit for two miles.

"Man to man?"

"That's right."

"Pilot to pilot."

"Whatever you want. I have to explain something to you."

"About Mamie?"

"That's it."

"If it's about the fetus I know all about that. What I wonder is if they throw it in the garbage or if they have some kind of ceremony or something."

"Mamie was very sick. There are some women who . . . who . . . go back. . . . Are you listening to me?"

"Yes, but."

"But what?"

"I'm thinking about Noah's Ark."

"You aren't listening to me."

"I'm listening, but. When I think about Mamie I think that the pilings are rotten; when I think about the rotten pilings I think about the high tides; when I think about the high tides I think about Noah's Ark. Did you feel any rain? A drop landed right on my forehead."

"The rain's starting again. The moon's hidden. It's going to be a real downpour I think. We should go in. What you're going to do is go straight home, get into your sleeping bag with Chanoine, pull the zipper all the way up and sleep like a log. I'll take care of everything."

"How about the ghost?"

"I'll look after it. Night!"

"One thing you could do, you could. . . ."

The Commodore didn't understand, he's already gone; you can see that he's drifting a little to the left as he walks, because of the sea elephants or the tide that's coming in.

I wanted to say to the Commodore:

"You could lend her your sweater with Hawk Eye and Sitting Bull."

I go up the stairs.

Soon the dawn will break.

I climb the stairs to the attic cautiously. You watch where you put your feet and you skip the fifth and the thirteenth steps because they creak.

Gently, I open the trap door.

It jabs you right in the heart. The lamp's still on and Papou's slumped at his table, in the midst of loose sheets of paper and bottles of Molson, with his hair all rumpled and his beard long, his face resting on his wrists; and what really jabs you in the heart is when you see, beside his head, on a half-written sheet of paper, this sort of yellowish puke mixed in with spilled beer and Chanoine's nose in it.

The first thing you do, you pick up Chanoine by the scruff of his neck and send him flying. Then you go and open the window because of the smell; you open it as wide as you can. If you had a good boxing glove you'd break the bottom panes with two punches and then climb up on the radiator for the two top ones. Anyway, you open the window as wide as you can, you unhook the screen and let it down. Then the fresh air starts coming in. It's still raining outside like some kind of flood, the air's wet obviously, but it's the freshest air you've ever breathed since you were born.

At the sound of the window Papou stops snoring like a helicopter.

I stay at the window because of the fresh air.

Slowly, Papou raises his head.

". . . what you're doing there?"

"Breathing the fresh air."

Papou clears his throat; you hear a kind of rattling. He picks up the half-spilled bottle of beer, drains it in one gulp, then he wipes his mouth on the sleeve of his bathrobe.

"Nobody's allowed in here, have you forgotten?"

"No, but."

"Are you spying on me?"

"I wanted to talk to you a little."

"What?"

"You don't come downstairs any more. I came up to talk to you a little."

He takes a blank sheet of paper and puts it on the desk on top of the puke. Then I ask, "Was Hemingway sick?"

He stares at the blank sheet of paper.

I ask him again: "Did Hemingway get seasick?"

Papou turns his head and starts to look at me. He's wearing his yellow bathrobe with the C over his heart. The way you feel is, it's as though his eyes were looking right through you, getting lost out the window and filling up with rain; they're red and wet as though they were full of rain.

Papou starts talking in a subdued voice. "They want to send Hemingway to the Mayo Clinic again. They all think the same thing, it's written all over their faces. Even Mary—every now and then she takes a look at the guns in the rack in the living room. Hemingway starts talking about F.B.I. agents and all their faces become sad; they think the old man's going off the rails. The only thing they can think of is to send Hemingway back to the clinic and have him undergo shock therapy. They think the old man's finished."

Papou grimaces. He rests his head on his wrists. He starts to cough. I mean, you don't know exactly what's happening, he's lying across the desk with his head in his arms; you can see his shoulders shaking and you hear something like a motor that's choking. The first thing you think of is the dampness. I turn around, take the goddamn window in both hands and, pulling it down with all my strength, I make it bang like a rifle shot. I didn't exactly want to make a noise like a rifle shot, but. To tell you the truth, I just wanted to close the goddamn window as fast as hell so Papou'd stop coughing or something.

He stopped. Chanoine jumped higher than the desk and there he is on his four feet with his fur standing up, and drooling. They look at me as though I was a Martian who'd just landed in the attic in a flying saucer. Papou's staring and he looks dazed; Chanoine's growling and spitting. I kick at a ball of paper to distract Chanoine; he starts running to the other end of the attic. Then, without getting upset, I say to Papou, "I just wanted to talk to you a little."

He looks at me, still staring, not saying a word.

I say again, softly, "I wanted to talk to you a little about Mamie."

"Who?"

"Mamie."

"Mary?"

"Mamie! Catshit! MAMIE!!!"

I shout it with all my might, like a pilot who's just noticed a reef in the fog, right in front of the boat. Chanoine clears the site at a hundred miles an hour and you can hear him tumbling down the stairs with his ass on fire.

Papou gets up, his finger on his lips.

"Ssshhhh!"

He's standing there in his yellow bathrobe with the letter C over his heart, his eyes filled with rain. He's swaying from side to side like on the "Gaspésien" between Sept-Iles and Sainte-Anne des Monts. He says in a very low voice:

"Ssh! The microphones! The F.B.I. agents have planted them in the walls, all over. You won't believe it but they put one in the car. They think old Hemingway doesn't know. They're spying on us, so we have to talk very quietly. You want to talk about Mamie? Of course, of course; we'll talk about her, very quietly. Come a little closer and we'll talk about Mamie very quietly."

"I like it better when you're sitting down."

"All right. Talk a little more quietly."

Papou sits down. I come up to the table.

"Mamie talks to somebody."

"Ah!"

"There's nobody there but she's talking to somebody."

"She's wrong, she shouldn't do that. What else?"

"She shuts herself up in her room and she talks."

"That isn't wise. She shouldn't talk to strangers. Have you seen them? How are they dressed?"

"I haven't seen them, but."

"But what?"

"I saw a ghost."

"Ah!"

"It came out of the cottage at night and headed towards the Commodore's cottage."

"What was it wearing?"

"Long white gown. A nightgown."

"I'll tell the Commodore to look into it."

"A long white nightgown like a woman!"

"Ssh! You're talking too loud. I'll speak to the Commodore and he'll look into it."

"You should talk with Mamie too!"

"Ssh! The microphones!"

Papou gestures with his arms like a gull flapping its wings. All of a sudden I stick my foot on the desk.

I take my bare dirty foot in both hands and put it in the middle of the desk, right under Papou's nose, in the midst of the overturned bottles, on top of the blank sheet of paper that's covering the puke. Papou doesn't say a word. He looks at me and he doesn't say one goddamn word! As if he was seeing my dirty foot for the first time in his life.

I ask him, "Have you ever seen that before?"

". . . ."

"STINKING CAT SHIT! ISN'T IT DIRTY!"

Papou's still looking at my foot as though he's never seen it before in his whole goddamn life. Underneath, I can feel the blank sheet of paper that's sliding a little on top of the puke.

I don't want to talk with anybody any more.

Last time I talked it was with the Commodore, when we discussed the whole business of navigation instruments, sitting on a rock as usual.

He said he'd lend me his radio set. It's an old transmitter-receiver and everything, bought from a captain whose boat had gone aground across from the Ile d'Orléans. The Commodore had just retired and he was bored or something: I didn't really want to hear the whole story. Anyway, I and the Commodore carried the transmitter-receiver from his cottage to my room in the rain.

The people you try to talk with in normal times are Mamie and Papou. I mean, catshit, if there's anybody in this world you should be able to talk with, you feel as if it's Mamie and Papou. Mamie's up to her neck with the pilot; Papou's up to his neck with Hemingway. They're both up to their necks and I won't say another goddamn word to anybody for the rest of my life.

The best talking I've ever done was when Mary and I were in my sleeping bag with Chanoine and Mary had on her great white nightgown with the little red and blue flowers exactly like my sleeping bag. We didn't say anything fantastic, like the kind of things Papou and Mamie and I used to say at Mont-Tremblant when we lit a campfire and spent the whole night talking about racing cars and drivers and all that until the sun came up. I and Mary didn't say anything fantastic, but. I mean, we feel free to talk or not. I mean, cat shit! the important thing is that you feel free to talk or not.

We put the radio on my table and on the other wall we set up the steering wheel. The Commodore got an old spinning wheel from the Demoiselles Ménard in Cap Rouge and we talked about the whole business: the wheel's light, it's easy to attach the handles and everything. Then the Commodore said that the long-distance swimmer wouldn't like it but he'd brought the rolling pin anyway. And I took Mamie's rolling pin. I and the Commodore fastened the four handles to the edge of the wheel with screws. We put the steering wheel on the old broken mop handle: you raise the window one inch or something, you wedge your mop handle under it and you steady the wheel with a nail on either side so it won't slip.

For the radar, the Commodore said he didn't see any solution at all and he was sorry and everything. I told him he didn't have to break his neck to find some gadget or other and I explained how I saw the whole business. He agreed that Papou's TV could do the trick and that you couldn't sail on the river when it was foggy without radar. We set up the radar to the right of the steering wheel.

I and the Commodore had to talk about the compass. With the Commodore's old compass you can't really say you've got a sophisticated apparatus, a gyroscopic compass and everything. I mean you can't brag about telling the difference between geometric north and magnetic north or anything. And you can't make anybody believe you can take your bearings with a sextant and a chronometer, take the longitude from the sun and the latitude from the polar star. To get your bearings you pick up two radio transmissions: you have to know where the transmitter stations are located, then you draw the two lines on the map and the place where those two goddamn lines meet is exactly the place where you are, catshit! Finally we decided the Commodore's old compass could do the job.

We took all the time we needed to talk about the sound. We started by putting some order in the whole business by separating the sound and the sonar: you use the sound to measure how deep the water is; the sonar's just for detecting submarines. With the sound you send a sound-wave to the bottom, you calculate how long it takes to come back to the boat and you write the figure on a piece of paper. Obviously you have to remember the other figure: four thousand eight hundred. That's the speed of sound in water, four thousand eight hundred feet per second, I swear it. Then you take the time to sit down with your pencil and the two figures on the paper and you can start your calculations. The Commodore said in the old days he used a line with a weight; all they had to do was throw the line to the bottom of the water, measure the length and then nobody had to sit down with a pencil and two goddamn figures on a piece of paper to do any calculating. I and the Commodore really did talk about the whole business: you can have the best sound in the whole navy, you can do the calculation without making the slightest mistake and you're still a zouave if there's any sand or mud. In the end, we decided not to break our necks over the whole sound business and rely on the maritime maps instead.

We spread the four maritime maps to the left of the steering wheel, over the giant picture of Jim Clark in his famous Lotus. Side by side they covered the whole width of the wall right to the window, with their names in big black letters: QUEBEC TO GROSSE ILE, GROSSE ILE TO CAP AUX OIES, CAP AUX OIES TO ISLE VERTE, ISLE VERTE TO ILE DU BIC. They're the best maps you'll ever see in your whole career, with the channel drawn between two black lines, the distance in marine miles, the depth in fathoms, the tides, currents, reefs, wrecks, sand banks and everything.

And then I decided not to talk with anybody any more and to let the animals in.

If some zouave starts to say I let the animals in because I felt lonely or something, that zouave is in danger of getting my foot in his behind. You don't feel lonely when you've got a radio transmitter-receiver, a steering-wheel, a radar, a compass and the best maritime maps in the world. To tell you the truth I let the animals in because of the rain.

Chanoine arrived this morning with a little white female cat, both of them soaked to the bones; they'd spent the night outside. I let them in the cottage, gave them half a can of Puss 'n Boots and they ate from the same dish without any squabbling, eyes half closed, till the dish was as clean as when you've just washed it and you put it in the cupboard with the others. When you look at the little white cat you can't help thinking about little Mary and at the same time you feel like a zouave. The best thing to do is try and think about something else. You can always think about the rotten pilings.

Just after supper the two squirrels arrived. It was dusk: the days are getting shorter. I don't want anybody to get the idea that I opened the door and that those two squirrels came right in like a couple of zouaves. No. I had to sprinkle little bits of bread all down the gallery, on the doorstep and right in the middle of the living room like in the story of Tom Thumb and his seven brothers, when he did that in the forest so he could find his way and then the birds came and played a dirty trick on him. You can't really trust birds for anything that really matters and you end up having problems with an ogre. Once the squirrels were in the living room I shut the cottage door and gave them some more bread. They were both soaked to the bones, like Chanoine and the little white cat. You can tell they're squirrels right away by their big tails and their backs, which aren't striped the way chipmunks are.

I was lying in my sleeping bag when the two raccoons arrived. It was midnight and I wasn't asleep, I swear it. When you're expecting something you wait up. You can be lying in your sleeping bag all right, pretending to sleep, with one eye on the navigation instruments. Chanoine and the little white cat started to growl in the living room. I got up without putting on my jeans or my sweatshirt with the hood or my moccasins. I mean, when you've got a sleeping bag that comes from Latulippe Surplus de Guerre, with little red and blue flowers on the inside exactly like Mary's nightgown, you sleep naked in the flowers, like I explained.

Chanoine and the little white cat had climbed up on the back of the sofa, growling like the motor of a schooner that's bringing its cargo of logs from the North Shore to Trois-Rivières. I opened the door: standing on their big back paws, with their noses sticking up in the air, the two raccoons were trying to see in the window. Now I don't want anybody to think the two raccoons just came rushing in right away like a couple of zouaves. To tell you the truth they bolted at a hundred miles an hour without even going down the iron ladder. With raccoons all you have to do is leave the door open, not get upset or anything special like in the story of Tom Thumb. They didn't go far; they were back five minutes later. They came in one behind the other, sniffing around everywhere, noses to the ground, and then I closed the door. Both of them were soaked to the bones like the others, except that they gave off a smell like in Papou's attic before I opened the window. I gave them each half a can of Puss 'n Boots too, but in two different dishes because they were squabbling and they ate till their dishes were clean like I explained.

I went back to bed.

Papou and Mamie don't exist any more, the animals have come in and I'm not talking with anybody.

That sort of Milky Way.

I haven't shut my eyes all night.

The sort of Milky Way that comes in the window.

I've kept an eye on my navigation instruments all night.

Buried up to the neck in my sleeping bag I look at the sort of Milky Way that comes in through the window just over the steering wheel and spreads through the bedroom over the navigation instruments, the maritime maps and everything.

CRACK! YOU'RE ON THE FLOOR.

You look loony, in your sleeping bag on the floor. The bedroom floor is sloping. The crack came from down below, from all over at once, and catshit! the way you feel is as if something's tearing inside your stomach or somewhere. I mean you really feel as if something's broken inside your stomach, the large intestine or one of those pipes. And the sort of Milky Way keeps spreading through the bedroom.

I crawl out of my sleeping bag.

No time to open the zipper, no time to put on my jeans or anything. Naked as a snake I drag myself out of the bedroom and into the living room. I can't see the animals but I hear them breathing, panting as if they'd been running twenty miles with their asses on fire. I open the door and go out on the gallery.

I stand up.

The gallery's sloping with the rest of the cottage and it's as if you've got one leg longer than the other.

I can't see a thing!

Catshit! You look all around and you don't see a thing! You're standing up on the gallery, as naked as a goddamn snake, your eyes are open wider than the Commodore's old compass and you don't see a thing—not the sky or the beach or even the birch trees right near the cottage with the weird-looking little post.

It's the fog! There's fog all over the place, the cottage is wrapped in fog as thick as a sort of Milky Way. You hear the murmur of the waves; it's all mixed up, as though it's coming from everywhere all at once.

CRACK! YOU LAND ON YOUR ASS AGAIN!!!

The cottage is leaning to the other side and once again you've landed with your feet in the air. Abruptly the cottage straightens up, sways a little and then's it's stable. All of a sudden you understand the whole business: the rain, the fog, the high autumn tides, the rotten pilings.

THE GODDAMN PILINGS!!

CAT SHIT! THE COTTAGE IS DRIFTING AWAY!!!

The pilot drops the periscope.

The pilot's landed on his ass, his four feet in the air, naked as a snake, and he's just noticed that he was holding the periscope in his right hand. The raccoons, the squirrels, Chanoine and the little white cat are in a circle around him, looking at him with their eyes wide. Then the pilot drops his periscope.

The pilot starts by inspecting the barge.

No leaks, the hull's intact; reassured, the pilot distributes rations of Puss 'n Boots to everybody, except the squirrels who prefer ship's biscuits, then he closes himself inside the cabin to study the whole business.

You don't feel upset or anything. Maybe because of the animals. I mean, the raccoons could have started running after the cats, the cats after the squirrels, everybody could have got upset, gone running at a hundred miles an hour and messed up the barge; but no. Everybody's calm and the pilot quietly puts on his grey sweatshirt with the hood, his blue jeans and his moccasins. He switches on the radar. In a fog like this you start by switching on the radar: you don't have to go to any cat shitty Ecole de Marine to know that.

The pilot grips the wheel firmly, his hands holding one handle on either side, his feet spread because of the rolling that might start any time and he keeps an eye on the radar because there's nothing to be seen out the window with the goddamn fog. Fog so thick you could cut it with a knife, as the Commodore would say. You could get your hunting knife and cut whatever shape you wanted out of the fog. For instance, you could cut out a shape like little Mary in her nightgown and stand it up in a corner of your cabin. You'd be the biggest liar in the whole city of Quebec. The radar's working well. Nothing to report. N.T.R.

The pilot thinks.

When the radar says N.T.R. you start to think. When that happens you think about people. I mean, the pilot could think about giant tortoises, sea spiders, groupers, sea horses, moonfish, morays, sea otters, porcupine fish, sea iguanas, toadfish, tiger snails; but no. The pilot thinks about people. He's thinking about the Commodore, to tell the truth. The Commodore's stationed two steps behind him, with his Commodore's cap on and his great sweater with Hawk Eye and Sitting Bull; his feet are spread too because of the rolling and he's quietly smoking his pipe, keeping an eye on the radar over the pilot's shoulder and standing ready to say in his firm voice:

"Hard a-port!"

The pilot snaps around: the pilot was daydreaming, catshit!

The rolling increases; the pilot grips the wheel harder, spreads his legs a little wider.

The pilot starts thinking about grandfather Noah. Grandfather Noah has a grey beard like old Hemingway. The animals are investigating the Ark: there's a little cat with a head like Mary, a white sheep with a head like Mamie and a goat with a head like the long-distance swimmer and a horse with a head like Thierry. It's raining buckets and grandfather Noah, dirty and apparently tired, is puking all over the deck. A horrible stench spreads through the Ark, as though everything was rotten. The pilot doesn't feel like thinking about grandfather Noah any more, to tell you the truth.

The pilot stops the wheel with the back of a chair: automatic pilot. The Commodore's old compass indicates forty-five degrees due northeast. The radar's still as white as snow: N.T.R. The pilot goes out on deck to inspect the horizon.

Catshit! There isn't any horizon! Fog everywhere. All you can see is fog. You walk all around the barge, you look in every direction and in every degree between each cardinal point, like on the Commodore's old compass and the only thing you can see's the goddamn cat-shitty fog.

Suddenly the pilot lets out a loud yell: "Ahoyyyy!"

He's let out that yell like some kind of zouave, due northeast. The yell came out all by itself, right out of his stomach like a boat siren that's tearing through the fog. The pilot has a stomach ache. You really feel as if something's broken again; your large intestine or something. The pilot's eyes are wet; he'll have to talk about the whole thing with the Commodore. You've never seen a pilot with his eyes wet except if it's raining or if the waves are splashing him right in the face. What he'll have to talk with the Commodore about man to man is whether a pilot can have wet eyes when he lets out a big yell that comes from his stomach like a boat siren and rips through the fog in the direction of the sea.

There was no echo.

The pilot would like it very much if his voice came back. What he'd really like would be if his voice touched something solid and came back with something changed, somebody's smell, anything.

There wasn't even one little echo or anything.

You yell like some kind of zouave on the river, you let out a yell in the fog, a loud yell that comes from your stomach and rips through the goddamn fog heading right out to sea and you don't even know if anybody's heard it, or even if your voice is reaching Sainte-Pétronille or Ile Madame or Petite Rivière Saint-François or Les Eboulements or Port-au-Persil or somewhere.

The pilot wipes his eyes on the inside of his grey sweatshirt, blows his nose like the Commodore by stopping up one nostril with his finger and blowing out the other one. He goes back to his cabin, unblocks the wheel, has a quick look at the navigation instruments and turns on the radio receiver. Then the pilot consults his maritime maps.

The problem is Ile Madame.

It's easy to get a good grip on the wheel, survey the radar out of the corner of your eye and at the same time study the QUEBEC TO GROSSE ILE map thoroughly.

You're going to have problems with Ile Madame; no need to go to any cat-shitty Ecole de Marine to know that either. You absolutely have to pass through the little channel beside Ile Madame, catshit! The pilot examines the whole business on the map. No problem across from Quebec with a channel fifteen fathoms deep at least, and a good width; all you have to do is look out for the ferry boats and stay on course at 018 degrees. After the Bassin Louise you turn sharply to starboard, direction 049 degrees as far as the tip of Lauzon, then you steer 080 degrees as far as Saint-Laurent and finally you turn to port at 054 degrees to get to Saint-Jean. At Pointe Saint-Jean there's the little channel.

The problem is going alongside Ile Madame, in the little

channel from Pointe Saint-Jean to Cap Tourmente, which is very narrow and shallow; that's where you can tell if you're a real pilot or not.

The pilot isn't afraid of Ile Madame, but. To tell you the truth life's a pretty weird affair; you go through it in a kind of fog. What you shold do is get to Ile Madame in daylight, with the sun and everything, and on the port side you'd see the Ile d'Orléans as far as Saint-François and to starboard you'd see the South Shore, with the church steeples of Saint-Vallier and Berthier. You'd enter the little channel beside Ile Madame, like pilots who've done deep sea navigating, and the sun would give you a kind of blessing or something.

They said on the radio that Jimmy was dead, they said that. They said that old Jim Clark had killed himself in Germany. Jimmy hit a tree at a hundred and seventy-five miles an hour in a Lotus. It jabs you in the heart to hear them say that on the radio about the best racing car driver in the world. The pilot starts rummaging around everywhere; he gropes in all the corners, under his grey sweatshirt with the hood and even down inside his blue jeans to see if he's still got all his parts.

The navigation instruments are working properly, the maritime maps are the best ones in the world, the animals are sleeping peacefully and the pilot's got all his parts. The pilot has everything he needs, but.

When you get to the Ile Madame channel, with that sort of goddamn fog, you can't help thinking. You start thinking about Mamie when she was in the Hôtel-Dieu after that thing with the fetus, when she had permission to go for a walk in the Quartier-Latin with you and she could recognize a Midget and a Sprite at first glance; you start thinking about little Mary, when she had on her nightgown with the little red and blue flowers, when she was lying with you and Chanoine in your sleeping bag that's got the same flowers inside it and she wanted to take another hair off your tongue. I don't mean that the pilot starts remembering what's happened in his goddamn life, catshit! It's just that the pilot can't help thinking about things like that, about Mamie and little Mary.

The pilot feels weird, he feels like some kind of zouave. The fog won't lift and Ile Madame's coming up. The pilot doesn't intend to make a scene or anything; he isn't seasick and he doesn't feel like puking all over the cabin. He holds the wheel firmly, one hand on either side, his feet spread because of the rolling, an eye on the navigation instruments and the maritime map. The pilot feels like some kind of zouave because. . . .

The pilot wants to TALK TO SOMEBODY! Catshit! It's a relief to say that! The way you feel, it's as if Eliot Ness had suddenly pulled his revolver out from between your shoulder blades and put it back in the holster under his left arm and then gone silently out of his office with the other two untouchables, taking his jacket off the rack by the door.

Then the pilot does something at a hundred miles an hour. It's strange, it's like something that's been decided on forever although you haven't known about it, and then at a certain point you notice you're late like some kind of zouave and you rush and do it at a hundred miles an hour.

At full speed the pilot sets the automatic pilot at 54 degrees northeast, sits at the radio, plugs in the transmitter, coughs loudly and sends a message.

"Barge pilot calling Ile Madame. Barge pilot calling Ile Madame. Come in Ile Madame. Over."

You shut your big trap, you plug in the receiver and you listen.

You're lost in the fog out in the middle of the river, sitting at your radio set, earphones on your ears, holding them with your hands, and you're listening with all your might.

Suddenly the pilot hears something. A voice! Not exactly a voice, but. Bits of a voice. Bits of a mechanical, broken, rusted voice.

"This . . . is . . . Madame. This . . . Madame. Over . . . you . . . barge. Over."

Catshit! You can't make up your mind whether the bits of the mechanical voice sound like Mamie's or little Mary's. It's as if Mamie and little Mary were talking at the same time from the other side of the fog. The pilot plugs in the transmitter.

"Barge pilot to Ile Madame. Who's speaking? Over."

"This is Ile Madame. Over."

The two of them are still talking at the same time. The pilot says, "Barge pilot requests direction Ile Madame channel. Over."

"Give present direction. Over."

"054 degrees northeast. Over."

"Turn to port, direction 033 degrees northeast. Ile Madame signing off. Over."

"WAIT, CATSHIT! DON'T SIGN OFF! WAIT A MINUTE!"

"Ile Madame to barge pilot. In distress? Over."

"No."

"Require help? Over."

"Yes and no."

"Ile Madame to barge pilot. Speak clearly. Over."

They're talking at the same time, Mamie and little Mary.

"Barge pilot to Ile Madame. Require . . . affection. Over."

"Ile Madame to barge pilot. Receiving you badly. Repeat last message. Over."

"REQUIRE ATTENTION, CATSHIT! REQUIRE ATTENTION. Over."

The Heart of the Blue Whale

It is correct to say that this operation takes one to the very frontiers of life . . . My journey has brought me closer to you.

Le Père Boulogne

It is within my breast that I write.

Pierre Morency

Le Coeur de la baleine bleue was first published in 1971
in Montréal by Editions du Jour.

The verse passages quoted on pages 164 and 178 are from
"Cage d'oiseau" by Hector de Saint-Denys-Garneau, translated
by John Glassco in *Complete Poems of Saint-Denys-Garneau.*
The quotations have been used by permission of Oberon Press.

"It's a man," Elise said again.

"A woman," I said.

Man or woman: there was no way to tell. The voice came to us through the wall.

My liberty
Long have I held you
Like some rare pearl
My liberty
It's you who have helped me
Cast off my moorings

Then the voice was still. We could only hear it at night, when we were in bed. Our bedroom wall was thin. It was a strange voice, both gentle and strong, always singing the same song. I've always liked songs and ever since the operation I've always had some song in my head.

"I started hearing it when you were in the Hôtel-Dieu," said Elise. A moment later she added, "I'm sure it's a man. I can feel it."

This time I said nothing. I simply thought that it was a beautiful song. I also thought about human warmth. Elise turned onto her stomach, reached over to the bedside table, picked up a Gitane and lit it. Then she rolled onto her back. A pungent odour filled the room.

Doctor Grondin had told us to wait another month. We'd cheated.

"How do you feel?" Elise asked.

"All right, thanks."

"Tired?"

"Not really. As though I didn't have a body."

I was stretched out, with the covers pulled up to my chin. My head was lucid but I couldn't feel the rest. Like a house in the dark, with a light on in the attic.

In a sugary voice Elise said, "Wait, I'm going to listen. . . ."

She got up on her knees, then crouched over me and put her ear against my heart; she closed her eyes and seemed to be meditating. Her mouth was right against mine.

"I can hear it," she said. "Its wings are slowly beating."

"You're not the least bit funny."

Elise would always speak lightly of serious matters and so, in a certain way, she'd taught me how to live. After the operation she asked me what I felt; in the dramatic tone of one who has had a close brush with death I told her about the wounded bird. Ever since, she'd talked about it with a hint of mockery, so I wouldn't take everything tragically.

She opened her eyes.

"I'm not too heavy?"

"No, but you make me feel like smoking."

"Doctor Grondin . . ." she began.

"Making love was forbidden too."

"Forgive me, I couldn't wait another minute. Call me a maniac if you want."

I traced a cross on her mouth.

She brought her cigarette to my lips; I took a long drag and turned my head so I wouldn't blow the smoke in her face. She smoked and said, "I missed you so much it was driving me crazy."

"I missed you too."

"You, with the nurses. . . ."

"Are you jealous?" I asked, not really believing it.

"I need a man. A man just for me. I'm a sex maniac. And besides. . . ."

"Besides what?"

"You allow to be frank?"

"That's an elliptical turn of phrase," I replied.

"Crap."

She rolled over, one and a half turns, to the edge of the bed, stubbed her cigarette in the ashtray on the bedside table and came back to me. She lay her head on my shoulder, draped one knee across my legs and declared, "You didn't want to leave the Hôtel-Dieu."

"Eh?"

"You kept putting off leaving."

"Who told you that?"

"Doctor Grondin. He explained that it was unconscious."

"Eglise!"

She stopped speaking. She didn't like the ecclesiastical nickname I gave her when she became possessive. She had a mother hen quality that went along with an aggressive, almost masculine side. I stroked her blonde hair, which was cut very short like a boy's. I thought of the fox and of what Saint-Exupéry had said about blonde hair and wheatfields, and at the same time I felt that once again time had completely passed me by.

"Are you angry?" she asked.

"Not at all!"

"I hurt you; I'm sorry."

"It's me; I'm too sensitive."

"It's normal, with the heart you've got."

I didn't know if it was normal. I thought of the wounded bird
and I was afraid I'd never be myself again. In her mother hen's
voice, which seemed to be cradling the words, Elise cooed, "You'll
see, you'll see, my friend, my old comrade, you're going to stay nice
and warm in the house and rest and slowly regain your strength
and become your old self; take as long as you need, we're in no
hurry, we'll protect you and watch over you as long as. . . ."

She said "we" as though she'd raised a company of eager,
attentive volunteers, a kind of Salvation Army devoted to my
personal well-being. I was no longer listening to her words but
with my head buried under the pillow and my eyes closed, I let
myself be rocked by the murmur of her voice. I was gently floating
inside myself, on a sort of magic carpet that was sinking, slowly
curving, into an atmosphere of warm quietude. Suddenly the air
seemed cold and I felt faint.

I straightened up.

"What's wrong?" Elise asked, concerned.

"The window," I said.

"But—it's closed. Aren't you feeling well?"

"It isn't serious."

"You're all pale. Are you cold?"

"I'm freezing—inside."

"You were dreaming," said Elise. "You always dream. That's
how you spend all your time."

She looked at me. We sat facing one another in the middle of
the bed, naked, and there was such tenderness in the depths of her
eyes that my anguish was gradually dissipated, and then I felt
overcome by a tremendous feeling of lassitude. Elise said, "Have
to rest now. Lie down."

I obeyed.

She lay down beside me and pulled up the covers. She took my
penis in her hand.

"You're little," she said.

I let her go on; she said that every time we made love. Then as
usual she added, "What are you going to do when you're big?"

I made no reply. I thought of rejection. I couldn't help thinking about it, but I didn't really feel concerned, because by talking
about it—especially with Doctor Grondin—it had become a kind
of familiar creature; or perhaps I was just too tired to feel concerned.
Instead of rejection I sometimes said reflux; I liked that better.

I closed my eyes. We lived on the fifth floor of a tourist house
on rue Terrasse Dufferin. The house was lovely; it overlooked the

Terrasse, the wharves and the St Lawrence and on a clear day you could see, beyond the Ile d'Orléans and its fragile bridge, the distinct outlines of the majestic distant mountains of Charlevoix. Autumn had already arrived and it had snowed. The summer ferries that went back and forth between Quebec and Lévis, trailing their scarves of light slowly through the water at night, would soon give way to the sad winter boats, rigid in their white, frozen carapaces; the ice-breakers would go and collect all the buoys that were strewn along the channel and bring them to the wharf and I wondered how the pilots would get their bearings on the river.

I began to fall asleep. Without opening my eyes I could feel that Elise was bending over me.

"Are you asleep?" she asked.

"Drifting."

"Let yourself go. You're going to sleep."

I said, laboriously, "I'd like . . . talk to me about birds."

"You're dreaming, my friend."

"Tell me the names of the birds you know."

She listed them: "A jay, a thrush, a goldfinch, a swallow, a starling, a warbler, a robin, a lark, a grey gull, a herring gull, a pheasant, a grouse. . . ."

I managed to say again, "You were saying un . . . une . . . un . . . une. . . ."

"There are masculine birds and feminine ones."

"Why?"

"I don't know," she said. "Let yourself go. You're sleeping. You're dreaming."

"Beneath his wing he's losing his blood."

"You're asleep, my friend, you're asleep."

The birds stopped bickering. The one that was wounded smoothed his feathers with his beak. In the distance you could hear only muffled cooing.

This is a love story.

Two eyes.

Two eyes . . . suspended . . . above me.

The fog was beginning to clear and I was clinging with all my strength to those deep, tired, melancholy eyes.

Doctor Grondin was leaning over my bed. I was alive. I looked at the strange head with the skull wrapped in green and the masked nose and mouth; it suddenly seemed irresistibly comic and I began to laugh. The laughter caught in my throat where it shook me and caused me pain. I felt a tear on my cheek. Then I said, in a whisper, "You have eyes like a spaniel, doctor."

"Thanks a lot!" he said merrily.

The warmth of his voice comforted me. Without turning my head I let my gaze wander around the room: white walls, strange equipment, a nurse. I came back to Doctor Grondin.

"The wakening room," he explained.

Wakening . . . wakening. A rather ridiculous song, too military, that used to play on the radio at noon:

Nature now is awakening
All revives in the light of the sun.

I closed my eyes. The two phrases pursued me obsessively, and I let myself go. I moved my limbs a little. I heard the surgeon's voice.

"You have all your parts?"

I blinked and made a sort of grimace to indicate that I did. I was like a child—happy to be alive but very weak, and content at the thought that people were going to look after me. Cautiously I brought my hand to my chest. My fingers touched a thick, tight bandage and beneath it was a dull, vague pain that could have belonged to someone else. The heart was beating peacefully and I let myself be gradually invaded by sleep which seemed to rise from the depths of my being like a spring tide.

A love story between me and old Quebec.

"I've read your books," Doctor Grondin replied.

The surgeon was sitting at the foot of my bed.

He had come into my room with an older doctor and he had attentively followed the complete examination, from feet to head, that the doctor had me undergo. Then he accompanied his colleague to the door, exchanged a few remarks with him in a low voice, and came back and sat down. I'd drawn him out of his reverie by asking him how he thought I was; in reply, he'd made that remark about my books.

I was insistent.

"How do you feel?" he retorted.

"It seems as though I'm coming back to life, am I right?"

"You've come a good way."

"Is there a lot left?"

"The worst is over," he assured me. "I think you're doing very well."

All the same, I was even more insistent.

"You seem concerned."

"Why do you write?" he asked suddenly.

The question caught me by surprise. Before the operation I'd had to answer all kinds of questions, often unexpected ones, about life, death, my wife, my books, and the questions surprised me because for Doctor Grondin a heart transplant is just a simple matter of tissues.

Finally I answered, "So I won't feel guilty."

He smiled feebly, got to his feet, lit a cigarette and walked to the window. With his arms folded and the cigarette in the corner of his mouth he looked out at the landscape. Then without turning around he said, "Why does a man begin to write?"

"Perhaps because life is difficult for him."

The reply had, by itself, opened a path outside and something in the atmosphere of my room had changed. The silence was filled with birds and the fluttering of wings.

Whenever everything is still
You hear the fluttering of his wings.

The rest of the poem wouldn't come to me. I felt as though I were escaping from some obscure danger, as though my memory had rejected into forgetfulness whatever had been threatening me. Eventually the first lines came back to me:

I am the cage of a bird
A cage of bone
Holding a bird

Memories are strange: flowers beside a precipice. For a moment I tried to remember the rest of the poem, then the surgeon asked, "How do your novels start? In the very beginning, I mean, what's there?"

"Usually an image," I said. "But you have to leave it, let it slowly rot."

"Like what?"

"Like the one that's been following me since . . . the operation."

"Tell me about it," he suggested, turning towards me.

"You won't like it very much," I said.

"Tell me anyway."

So I described to him what I saw, somewhere beside the river, at the back of an abandoned garden—the sort of playhouse and inside it, bound to a chair, the little girl with blonde braids and the boy dressed up like a cowboy.

The surgeon turned back to the window, hands in his pockets. I said, hesitantly, "He's decided to rape her."

". . . ."

". . . to get some peace."

Doctor Grondin said nothing more and I added, as though it were an extenuating circumstance, "It's strange, I can hardly make out the landscape around them."

He still said nothing. I went on, "They say in every writer there's a monster."

He opened the window, tossed out his cigarette, came back and sat at the foot of my bed. "I don't believe in monsters," he said, looking at me intensely.

"What do you believe in?"

"In the traces of childhood or something like that."

"I'm not sure I understand."

"It's simple enough," he said, as though to himself.

He remained plunged in his reflections for some time. Finally, speaking almost lightly, "In your opinion, when did your childhood end?"

"Elise says it isn't really over yet," I said.

He spread his arms a little to indicate that this was conclusive. Then he got up, stared at the floor and began to pace back and forth.

"Something wrong?" I asked after several minutes.

"Eh?" he asked.

"You're wracking your brains over something?" I asked.

"No, no, I'm thinking."

"About rejection?"

He kept pacing. I tried to understand. Childhood. Rejection. Childhood. Rejection. Childhood. And if the language wasn't within us? And if it was man who lived inside the language? Finally I took the risk and asked, "Do you think that childhood can be a form of rejection?"

"You're going too fast," he said. "And I've got something else to tell you."

He came over to the bed, bent over me and put his fists on the pillow, on either side of my head. He frowned.

"Listen, man with the young girl's heart," he said in an exaggeratedly rough voice. "I'm the doctor! Diagnosis is my business. You just worry about getting better as fast as you can, that's all we're asking you. Understand?"

Then he was silent, but continued to wither me with his gaze. He put his fist under my chin, then straightened up and burst into loud laughter that filled the room. I started laughing with him.

A little later Doctor Grondin left; he had other calls to make. I was rather tired. And I was beginning to wonder if there was some relationship between gentleness and death.

A love story between me and Old Quebec.

I'm sitting on the steps of the Librairie Garneau, not at the main door but in front of the children's book section.

I'd settled myself on the windowsill.

It was a large window, half-moon shaped and very low, with a broad windowsill you could sit on with your legs stretched out. A heavy autumn rain was falling, lashed against the window by the northeast wind. The lamps on the Terrasse had been lit all day long, as though the day hadn't broken at all. You couldn't see the Lévis shore and at intervals you could hear the wail of a siren on a phantom ship. I had a blanket around my shoulders, on top of my old bathrobe.

That same morning Elise had returned to her old job as secretary in a psychiatric clinic. She'd decided on it all by herself. I was taken by surprise so I couldn't argue. Besides, she was talking in her masculine voice.

The doorbell rang. It was twenty past five.

I went to open the door. Elise was there, rain dripping off her, terribly out of breath, but her face was glowing, lit by a triumphant smile. She was holding her leather briefcase in one hand and a shopping bag in the other. She came towards me, offering her cheek, and I kissed it.

"But—that's *my* raincoat!" I said.

I relieved her of her packages and began to unbutton the coat. It was a very old military raincoat, with a very broad collar and lapels and a large number of buttons and fastenings.

"Will you be an angel and hang it over the bathtub?" she asked.

"Of course."

She took the bag of groceries and went into the kitchen. I'd barely finished hanging the wet raincoat over the shower-head when she came into the bathroom.

"I put a chicken in the oven. Are you hungry?"

Without giving me time to reply she went on: "I'm ravenous! Will you hand me the big blue towel?"

I held out the towel; she wiped her face and began to dry her hair. I asked if she wanted me to help her.

"No thanks," she said. "I'm fine."

"You look happy."

"Yes."

Are you glad to be working?"

There was a muffled growl. Her head had disappeared under the towel.

"Dry me," she said suddenly. "I've changed my mind."

She was sitting on the edge of the bathtub. I stood facing her, between her legs, and began to rub her hair with the towel. She moaned softly. I asked if I was hurting her.

"No, no, it feels good."

She opened my bathrobe, slipped her hands behind my knees, stroked my legs and then higher.

"You must be tired," I said.

"I feel fine."

"You've been working all day."

"I'm ravenous," she said again.

"And you're all wet."

"It was raining buckets."

"You'd better change, you'll catch a cold."

"You're sweet," she said.

"Your voice sounds as though you've already caught cold."

She took the towel from my hands and put it on the edge of the bathtub. She got up and said, as she turned around, "Would you like to help me?"

"What?"

"My zipper, please."

I pulled the zipper down to the small of her back.

"Help me some more," she pleaded.

I helped her free her shoulders of the woollen dress, which she let drop to the floor. She stepped aside and I bent down to pick up the dress.

"Now, undo that," she demanded, pointing to the hooks on her brassiere.

"I'm going to take a look at the chicken," I said stupidly.

"Please," she insisted.

I did as she wanted. She shed her brassiere by bending over, and in the same motion she slipped the remaining garment off her thighs. She stepped out of it and turned towards me. Her expression was troubled, like the stagnant water in a swamp, and for a moment I thought I could see in the depths of her eyes long hairy fingers that were wriggling like insects. I watched her, fascinated; I felt as though I were slipping down the wet sides of a well, irresistibly attracted to its bottom.

Suddenly she thrust out her arms to form a cross.

"Notre-Mère-la-Sainte-Eglise!" she declared grandiloquently.

I burst out laughing, she threw her arms around my neck and I held her affectionately in my arms. The malaise had dissipated. I felt fine, I lifted her and whirled her around. She laughed like a loony. She lay her head on my shoulder and asked, "Were you scared?"

"I don't know," I said.

"You've never seen a naked woman before? You're strange."

She began to laugh again, then announced:

"Eglise is going to take a bath."

"I'll look after supper," I said.

"You really are an angel."

She knelt in the bathtub and began to run the water. I handed her the soap and sponge and went to the kitchen. An old lullaby sung by Paul Robeson was running through my head: "Sometimes I feel like a motherless child."

Elise filled the wooden grinder with Mocha and Java beans and turned the handle until the little shells were reduced to a fine powder; she added a pinch of salt and tipped the powder into the filters on top of the cups; slowly she poured on boiling water and the good smell of freshly ground coffee spread through the room.

She added four cubes of sugar and a drop of cream to my cup. She herself drank coffee very black. She lit a cigarette.

"Weren't you hungry?" she asked.

"Not really."

"What did you do today?"

"I read Bachelard and Henri Bosco."

"What? Together?"

"Of course," I said.

"So you haven't started your novel."

I tried to explain. "It's started now; I can feel it moving inside me."

"You know," she said, "it's a little like a woman who. . . ."

She hesitated. She was holding her cigarette between two fingers, her cup of coffee in the hollow of her curved hands and she looked at me with rather troubled affection, a sort of unpleasant complicity. Prominent cheekbones broke the oval of her face. She looked after things while I looked after dreams. Sometimes she would bring me rather abruptly down to earth and sometimes the footbridge between us broke: an abandoned man on the wharf with an empty suitcase at his feet and a birdcage in his hand.

"I didn't put in any cognac," she said, "because of your heart."

"What?"

"What's the matter?"

"Not a thing."

"It happens often," she said. "All of a sudden you seem far away."

"It might be because of the story that's begun," I said.

"Tell me. Explain it a little. You hardly ever talk any more."

"It's complicated but André Breton once wrote something that's helped me understand. 'To depart for the self's inner pole.' "

She seemed to be pondering what I'd said. I'd have liked to be in her shoes to know how she saw things. On the table, a candle, stuck into an old bottle of orange-flavored cognac, was burning; the bottle's swollen belly was covered by a stalactite of multicolored wax. Elise took a long drag of her cigarette then, in a voice that was suddenly gentle, asked, "Are you unhappy?"

I felt wrapped in her presence, as though enveloped in a warm blanket, and I replied that I felt fine.

"Thank you," I said.

"Do you want me to stop working?" she asked.

"Of course not."

"Are you sure?"

"You need to work. You'd end up being annoyed with me."

"No I wouldn't! I can stop if you want."

"No," I said firmly.

She pondered again, stubbed her cigarette in the saucer and said in a voice that lacked assurance: "I understand very well. It's agreed, then, I'll let you make that journey by yourself. All right,

But I'll be waiting at the end. Will you be there?"

"Is it a date?"

"Precisely."

"I'll be there then."

"Swear?"

"I swear," I said. "But are you sure you'll be waiting?"

"I swear too."

We were both awash in romanticism; it was ridiculous and marvellous, as at the very beginning. Evening surrounded us, the wounded bird had been put to sleep and the old candle was dripping honey.

I'm sitting with my elbows on my knees and my head in my hands, in front of the children's book section. The door to the bookstore is slammed and a moment later I open my eyes: two bare feet beside me, brown, motionless, close together. I look up, not out of curiosity but rather absently.

Elise had just left for the clinic.

She'd prepared a very copious breakfast: freshly-squeezed orange juice, bacon and eggs, toast and jam, coffee. She put on my old raincoat, kissed me and, with ill-concealed satisfaction, left for the day.

I walked cautiously down the five flights of stairs, keeping one hand on the bannister and catching my breath at each landing. At the bottom of the stairs the concierge blocked my way. When I got out of the Hôtel-Dieu she'd mounted guard and like an uncompromising sentinel she had literally thrown the journalists and the curious out on the street, telling them the most unlikely lies.

"Do you need anything?" she inquired, very suspiciously.

"No Madame, thank you."

She stood there, motionless, her head crowned with curlers, feet in worn-out pale blue slippers, arms folded over a pink housecoat with faded flowers, cut very low at the north to reveal a bosom going south. She asked, concerned, "You aren't going out?"

"Just a short walk," I said with a sort of humility.

"A walk!"

"Yes," I said, a little more firmly.

"Al by yourself?" she asked in a panic.

"All by myself."

"Does Madame think you should?"

I answered affirmatively, to get some peace. She stepped aside very unwillingly, then immediately began a counter-attack.

"Wait," she said, "I'm going to ask my husband to go partway with you. Georges!"

"That isn't necessary," I said, raising my voice. "I feel fine, really. Thank you very much for your . . . solicitude. Elise has told me about everything you've done for me and. . . ."

"I did it from my heart," she broke in rather abruptly.

She grumbled as she opened the two heavy doors to the street. I walked past her and said, to reassure her somewhat, "It's Indian summer."

She followed me down a few steps, in silence, and when I reached the United States Consulate I could still feel her eyes, heavy with disapproval, on my back.

I walked diagonally across the small park, pompously named the "Jardin des Gouverneurs": it looked very unnatural with its symmetrical alleys, the red plastic numbers on the trees and the grotesque monument. I took a detour so I could run my hand over an old tree I knew, all twisted and stunted.

At the corner of Mont-Carmel and Haldimand I began to hesitate. A light fog was coming up, there was a warm and gentle wind and scraps of memory were moving vaguely inside me. I took a few steps along rue Mont-Carmel and stopped for a moment in front of number 20. Behind this locked door, these windows masked with wooden bars, the finest years of my student life slept peacefully, divided between Marc, my faithful friend, and Marie—little Marie as we used to say—we who had recreated on the top floor, where we were absolute masters, the atmosphere of a family life where everything was shared and we were unspeakably happy.

For a few moments Old Quebec seemed like a book of old pictures and I let myself slip slowly along rue Haldimand, among the old houses and the memories that I recalled. I greeted the Hôtel du Gouverneur as I went past, and my career as a waiter which had lasted only one summer day; further down was the door that had often opened on the very beautiful Michèle and her strange little dog with his eyes hidden under shaggy hair. At number 9, the Petit Château, where my university friend had lived in the attic and shared with me his meals of potatoes, cretons and honey doughnuts, which we enjoyed on the roof near the Château Frontenac; at the bottom of the hill, the Café des Jardins, formerly called George's Grill, with the old Irish woman who had so often served us pork sausages or minced steak, followed by the inevitable rice pudding.

After rue Saint-Louis, I saw the Café de la Paix, in front of which I had often run into Marie-Claire Blais, who happened to be going that way, with the long braid she wore to one side, and who always said hello with a smile that was both timid and warm; further still, the old and tiny bookshop called Le Bouquiniste where on rainy afternoons I used to come to rummage around and rent books.

I crossed rue Sainte-Anne which still gave off a persistent odour of horse manure, then turned right at the corner of rue Buade. I took a few steps: Giguère's Tabagie, Librairie Garneau, then I slowed down and turned towards her. Rue de la Fabrique.

What I felt didn't come from the fatigue creeping into my limbs and pressing down with all its weight. Nor did it come from my memories, rather lukewarm, like life, with their colours—like those of old houses faded by time—overlapping and blending. I still could have gone down rue des Remparts, towards the old mice-filled apartment with its magnificent view of the Bassin Louise, crossed through the archway onto rue de l'Université, bathed in its glow of beneficent half light, or climbed up to Saint-Denis where the light, reflected off the greenery of the Citadel, was brighter than anywhere else.

I could have gone wherever I wanted but I stayed there, facing rue de la Fabrique where my memories had led me. A few pictures still whirled around me and farther away, much farther, from the depths of my collective memory and my unconscious, other images rose, yellowed like old engravings; they made an Indian fort, a gravel road, a missionaries' school and a large public market loom out of the past.

Slowly I let myself be carried down the sloping street and I gradually realized that the air was softer, that there was a sort of tenderness in the light and a reverse movement had begun, unfurling before my eyes a steady, motley procession of multicolored clothing, fine lace, Chinese porcelain, precious jewels, Eskimo carvings, delicate perfumes, watercolours, woollens and trinkets of all kinds, while the names of the shops resounded stubbornly in my head: Mannequin, Irène Auger, Birks, Symonds, Kerhulu, l'Artisan, Chérie.

In front of the last boutique I sat down on a short staircase and put my head in my hands. I felt some mysterious agitation, I felt relieved, drained of all the images of this street—as though each memory, when it rose to the surface, had truly taken leave of me.

Very slowly the truth took shape in me, unsteady and fragile at first, then suddenly dazzling: my memories had guided me along the streets, like blood through the arteries, as far as rue de la Fabrique which was the heart of Old Quebec. And that heart too was a woman's.

I stood up then and when I retraced my steps to get something hot to drink, the last boutique at the bottom of the street, all painted pink, with its little girls' dresses and laces and jewels, kept repeating its name like a whisper: "Chérie, Chérie, Chérie."

As I raise my head rather absently I notice faded blue jeans turning grey and creased at the knees, a pale blue sweater that is too big, with the sleeves pushed up to the elbow, rather frail shoulders and a young, serious face framed by black hair that curls around the neck. Suddenly I feel a shock inside: is it a boy or a girl? I can't decide. Generally you hesitate for a fraction of a second and then suddenly it's settled, but this time . . . I feel a sort of discomfort, like a door opening on the unknown: mystery, gentleness, the feeling of something forbidden.

For the silent pleasure of taking possession of things I went around the apartment without touching anything. I glanced out the window at the river: the night was bright and steely blue and the boats were tracing broad furrows through the ice. Then I returned to the little round table with the green velvet cloth, to read myself once more.

Jimmy, in a cowboy outfit, was removing the gag from his prisoner's mouth and standing squarely before her.

"Listen," he said. "You're a prisoner because I want to rape you. Now that I've said it I'm relieved. I'll never say it again. I'll look as if I'm thinking about anything at all, but that's what I'll be thinking about all the time. Understand?"

"Yes, but why?"

"To get some peace."

"And . . . what does that mean, rape?"

Jimmy was nonplussed for a few seconds, then he became furious. You fling yourself around like a zouave, you manage to capture a girl just like in the westerns, you want to rape her—and she doesn't even know what it means! Catshit! He hurled invective at his prisoner, shook her by the shoulders, kicked at the furniture, threw to the ground whatever fell into his grasp. Finally he sat on the floor in the midst of the mess, abruptly drained of all his anger.

That's where the story got away from me.

I'd hoped it would burst out, brutal and primitive, and then only at the end a sort of tenderness would set in, like when evening comes and covers the traces of a stormy day. From the outset Jimmy had been thrown into the swift current of an adventure, with unexpected whirlpools and sudden surges, from which he had emerged victorious, carrying with him his victim, bound and gagged, stumbling along paths ill-lit by moonlight, tumbling into the ditch, following the road breathless and exhausted, as far as the playhouse at the back of the garden.

The story had scarcely begun when already the words that came from my pen were gentle, diluted: Jimmy was invaded by a great wave of gentleness that came from I don't know where. My story was escaping me and I couldn't do anything about it. At first I mercilessly scratched out, replacing words, tearing up pages, starting again where I thought I'd lost my touch, but the same feelings, slightly disguised, kept returning, the same phrases, barely transformed, reappeared. I finally abandoned it completely to the stranger who had moved into the depths of my being, who saw everything in a different way, and the only responsibility I still assumed was that of being there, prepared to transcribe whatever wishes came to me. And when nothing surfaced in my consciousness I wrote nothing; I waited, forcing myself to be attentive to signs.

I had learned that a story sometimes curls up on itself, like a cat that lies down and goes to sleep, and that one had to wait; then, snatches of light would abruptly flare out in the inner spaces and clearings, just as a solitary walker in the dark forest might emerge into a sunlit clearing. Then I noticed a few fleeting images, fragments of a décor: a group of houses clustered about a church that looked like a boat, a rocky beach rent by a long haul of eels covered with moss and seaweed, a swarm of white-robed nuns on a rock, like a flock of gulls. It was enough to lead me along to other images, gratuitous and excessive: Jimmy stealing eels to feed to his prisoner, or befriending a very pure nun who would understand him and try to explain, in a strange mixture of tenderness and detachment, the feelings the young girl might be experiencing, the acts he must perform, the words he must choose. I was dreaming. I still could not perceive the entire landscape and I was waiting for the story to begin again by itself.

On the wall opposite my table I had pinned up a big picture of Hemingway, taken when he was around fifty. The contrast was moving—between the black hair, scarcely flecked with grey at the temples, and the beard that was nearly all white. But most astonishing was the eyes: the left one small and crinkled up, staring into the distance, the right one slightly larger, vague and nostalgic. And under the picture I'd put this note, written in my own hand:

You stare into the distance
But still, it's within yourself that
You find the way —
Old Hemingway —
To watch over the oldest man
With a new heart.

It was laughable and it made me smile whenever I looked up and saw the note pinned up crookedly. Because I was writing I was neither happy nor unhappy. I didn't even feel that I was really a writer, since I was alive.

Outside, on the St Lawrence, the chunks of ice were still, as the tide hesitated between high and low. I put down my pen and switched off the lamp.

I gently opened the bedroom door: Elise was already asleep, buried under the covers, and I could hear her agitated breathing growing louder.

I took off all my clothes, folded them carefully over the chair beside the chest of drawers, then cautiously lifted the covers and slipped in beside Elise. She turned over on her stomach and I heard a murmur stifled by the pillow; I thought I heard her say, "Bill."

I repressed a nervous giggle. After all, my name isn't Bill. She must have been dreaming. My name is Noël, obviously. A long gurgling sound rose from my stomach—the coffee I'd just finished. In answer to my rumbling, Elise again murmured something indistinct. I didn't really feel like going to sleep right away so I parted my legs slightly and let the warmth of the bed invade me. Hands folded behind my neck, I felt my arteries throbbing, two short thuds close together, then a longer one. Suddenly there was a harsh light: masked individuals with bloodstained hands were hunched over a bleeding, quivering mass. I pushed aside this too brutal image and closed my eyes; then, lying in the dark beside the sleeping woman, I took pleasure in musing that the city had a woman's heart as I did, that no one else knew about it and that in a way my heart was safe behind the walls of Old Quebec.

Suddenly, an insidious idea: my body accepted a young girl's heart—it had needed one even before the operation—an old story that went back to my childhood and everything. I tried to ponder it, hunting for old memories, but my memory was blocked; the images were muddled and I remembered nothing, only an old wall and lizards scurrying into the stones.

I don't know why but I began to think about Henry Miller, about his prodigious honesty and the statement: "If a neurotic follows his neurosis to the bitter end he'll see a marvellous road opening before him." That was the road he'd tried to take; in his way he'd departed for the inner pole. I wondered if you could be just as honest if you wrote stories instead of sticking strictly to autobiography. I didn't know. And I was too fond of stories; that must come from my childhood, too. A story is like a house. It's strange; you let yourself go and immediately you drift back to childhood or a house. The wall reappeared before my eyes, and the lizards; a chameleon disappeared as though it had evaporated. Elise woke with a start.

"Eh?" she asked.

"Ssh!"

"What's wrong?"

"Nothing."

"Is it you?"

I could think of no answer; when someone wakes up it always makes me laugh. She sat up.

"What's the time?"

"Don't know. Two o'clock maybe."

She took a kleenex from under the pillow and blew her nose.

"You scared me," she said, lying down.

"I'm sorry. Were you dreaming?"

"Yes."

"About what?"

She didn't answer and pulled the covers up to her chin. Her hip grazed my hand.

"You're cold," she said.

"I'm sorry."

"Did you go out again?"

"No, I was working in the living room."

"You work too hard," she said, yawning.

"You're a mother hen," I said.

She sat up.

"What did you say?"

"You're a mother hen."

"I haven't heard that for a long time."

"You seem to like it."

"It's true, I am a mother hen. I need to protect someone. I've always been like that. But. . . ."

"But what?"

"Nothing. Give me a cigarette, will you?"

We had moved in the bed as we spoke; we were sitting face to face now, knees drawn up to our chins, wrapped in the blankets which we held around our shoulders. It was beginning to be pleasantly warm and it felt both sweet and ridiculous to be sitting there in the half light, so close but so far apart. Holding onto the covers I reached out to the bedside table, took a Gitane, lit it and held it out to her.

"Thank you," she said.

I put an ashtray on the bed right beside her.

"Your enamel ashtray," I said, to warn her; it tipped easily.

"Thanks, you're an angel."

She drew on her cigarette and the glow illuminated the lower half of her face. Then she said, "Do you want to talk to your old mother hen?"

"Of course I want to."

"Something bothering you?"

"No, nothing." Every time, the urge for a serious talk left me, for no reason.

"You talk less and less," Elise said.

I took a drag of her cigarette and asked, "Don't you want to tell me what you were dreaming about?"

"I forget," she said. "You know dreams. . . . So you were writing?"

"Yes and no."

"What do you mean?"

"I didn't actually write, but there were some clearings."

". . . ."

"You aren't going to ask me what I mean?"

"What do you mean?"

"You're walking in a forest and you don't see a thing, as though you were blind. And suddenly you emerge into a clearing."

"Then what?"

"And then you see some images, but . . ."

". . . ."

"I don't see the whole landscape," I went on. "I can't make out the whole thing."

"Is that very important to you?"

"Perhaps the landscape frightens me. I don't know why. I feel that it's very important."

"What I feel is that you're moving further and further away from me. I feel that you're very far away right now."

"Be patient for a while," I said. "We only invent old things and it's hard to know yourself. Do you know me? You know my skin, the surface of my skin, but what about my soul? Do you know my soul?"

She looked at me without replying and in the half darkness I guessed at something in the depths of her eyes that resembled a reproach. After a long moment she said, in a low voice, "You're talking too loud. The neighbour's going to hear us."

She tapped her cigarette into the ashtray.

"Listen," she said, "how long has it been since we've made love? Do you know?"

"Two weeks?"

"A month ago tonight!"

"I've been writing for a month," I said. "Sometimes it's hard to do both at the same time. It's complicated; Hemingway talks about it a little and so does Montherlant."

I tried to explain to her but I got tangled up and started drifting.

"You complicate your life, getting yourself upset like that," she said. "Tell me something simple."

"I feel old."

"Old?"

"Sometimes fifty, sometimes twenty," I said.

"What else?"

"I need human warmth."

"Everyone does, but you try to find it inside. It's as though you were devouring yourself."

Then Saint-Denys Garneau's last lines came back to me; they spoke of the bird in his chest and I could hear more clearly than if Elise were reciting to me herself:

He'll not go until he has
Eaten everything there is
My heart
The spring of blood
With life inside.

I noticed that Elise, leaning towards me, was tapping the left side of my chest with her index finger.

"But that's young now, isn't it?" she said.

I began to giggle again, silently at first, like a series of waves that died in my throat, then swelling, growing irresistible. I let myself drop onto my back. Then nervous laughter, hysterical, uncontrollable, burst out in successive waves that would fall back and began the climb again, shaking me from head to foot. I laughed and cried and choked.

Suddenly I received a resounding slap on the face.

At this moment the bare feet turn slightly in my direction. I look up higher and discern, between hands folded over the chest, a large blue and white book; against a sky blue background a white bird in full flight stands out, the wings broadly unfurled, the beak and claws red and a black cap at the crown of the head. I think of what old Marie used to say about birds. But the book moves, is placed under an armpit; and my gaze loses its fulcrum and descends again to the feet. They show signs of nervousness, then begin to walk.

I get up to follow the bare feet of this person who has no sex for the moment, but that's not what I'm really thinking about; rather, I'm thinking about old Marie. Marie has a habit of writing poems of sorts on the white placemats at the Café Buade. She's a waitress. One day she wrote a poem that began like this: "It's got no sex. . . ." So I'm thinking instead about old Marie, but it amounts to the same thing.

I knocked on the door of Doctor Grondin's office: three short, three long, three short—our signal in Morse code. I heard him reply and opened the door.

He was leaning back in his leather armchair, hands folded on top of the green cap that swaddled his skull, feet placed squarely on his desk among the bits of paper, books and magazines. A steaming cup of coffee was balanced on one corner of a drawer.

"Am I disturbing you?"

"Not in the least," he said, gesturing towards a chair with a jerk of his chin. "I've just come out of an operation and I've got peace for an hour if my calculations are correct and there aren't any complications."

"Transplant?" I asked, sitting back in the chair.

"No, a simple valve replacement."

"A routine job."

The comment evoked a feeble smile and a gleam of light in his eyes, as though he were seeing again the work he'd accomplished. He reached for his coffee and took a sip.

"Something wrong?" he asked.

I nodded.

"Do you want a test?"

I shook my head.

"It isn't physiological?"

I nodded agreement. I was silent and quite naked, seated on a mountain peak, and scientists from the world over were coming to examine me in silence.

"Do you want an interview with the psychiatrist?"

"No!"

"Sorry," he said, "I just wanted to hear you say something."

He smiled, drained his cup of coffee and added, "But he's the one who might understand you, isn't he?"

"I don't like the pleasure he gets from asking questions. And besides—how can I say it?"

"Say it however it comes out!"

"It's as though I felt. . . ."

I stopped for a second; one hand was under his chin and he sat perfectly still, patient and attentive.

I dropped the sentence in one breath: "You're responsible for me."

I felt both relieved and uncomfortable. He sat there not moving, his face betraying no emotion of any sort. Finally he took his feet off the desk, pushed up his chair and took a box of matches and a cigar from his desk; he lit up and then, in the warm and strangely harsh voice I liked so much, said, "I usually accept my responsibilities."

He was surrounded by blue smoke. A fragrant aroma spread through the room and I began to feel better. He brought me down to earth abruptly. "You want me to help you but we don't see your heart in the same way!"

"I know. You tell me it's a muscle, a pump."

"I see them on the operating table every day," he said, shrugging slightly.

"And mine?"

"Yours?"

He began to laugh very softly, and even his silent laugh

communicated a sort of warmth. Half seriously, he added, "Listen, the heart I sewed inside your chest seemed normal: no particular marks, perfect tissue compatibility. . . ."

"What about emotional compatibility?"

"Eh?"

"You won't agree but . . . if that young girl's heart was really compatible with mine, her emotions would be too, wouldn't they?"

Doctor Grondin folded his arms and said very calmly, "I'm curious to know what's led you to believe such an extraordinary thing."

"Words!"

He waited for me to go on, so then I began to explain how words bring things to life, how things then begin to seek the power of expression, but I got mixed up. Once again I began to drift, though I tried awkwardly to catch hold of many phrases, such as, "It's only with our hearts that we see properly," and then I cited a great number of popular images that express a quantity of wisdom accumulated since the beginning of the world, but I lost my footing; ultimately, I wanted to show that poets, who are closer to things, perceive forms of reality unknown to common mortals, and I quoted Saint-Denys Garneau. I stopped then, out of breath, my heart pounding.

Doctor Grondin, who had remained in control of his reactions throughout my laborious exposition, seemed sunk in endless reflections.

"Would you like a cup of coffee?" he asked suddenly.

"No, thank you," I said, surprised.

"You've earned it," he said, smiling rather ironically.

I changed my mind then and he ordered coffee on the intercom, taking time to tease his secretary. I closed my eyes. Something inside me felt like a spring that was unwinding, endlessly unwinding.

"Roll up your sleeve!" the surgeon's voice commanded.

I opened my eyes: Doctor Grondin was standing there holding a blood pressure gauge. He repeated the order, his voice gentler but still imperious. I obeyed without a word. His face was impassive. He wrapped the cuff above my elbow, asked me to clench my fist, squeezed the bulb to fill it with air, closely watched the movement of the needle. He began again, then removed the device. Just then someone knocked twice at the door; the secretary came in, put two cups on a corner of the desk and went back out without a word.

The surgeon walked behind me. Suddenly the back of my

chair tilted, the cushion rose and a sort of stool was slipped under my extended feet.

"Are you all right?" he asked.

"Yes, but. . . ."

"Let yourself go."

"What happened?"

"Nothing serious. Rest. Relax completely."

He took a small bottle from a drawer, sat on the corner of his desk, then inquired, "You've nothing against Rémy-Martin?"

"No."

He opened the bottle of cognac and poured a few drops into each cup; I smelled the fine aroma as it spread. He put my cup on a small wheeled tray and pushed it until I could reach it.

"Drink it slowly," he said. "It's hot."

He went back and sat down on the corner of his desk across from me, looking pensively at me while the coffee, which I was taking in small sips, spread its warmth to every part of my body. I thought of my father, who used to pour me one finger of liquor and wrap me in an old woollen blanket when I came shivering out of the icy water of the lake where we used to swim. I felt an urge to tell Doctor Grondin that he reminded me of my father, because with the new heart he had given me a new life; but he would have laughed at me and said, in his rather harsh way, that I was pushing his responsibilities rather far. In spite of myself I smiled at the thought.

The surgeon smiled too as he looked at me. He drank his coffee in small sips, as though he wanted to share my slow recovery. Finally he remarked: "You seem better now."

"Yes, I even feel a little warm."

"The cognac," he said simply.

"What happened?"

"Nothing serious, you're just a little excited."

"But this isn't the first time I've talked about. . . ."

He put his hand up to interrupt me and then said, choosing his words carefully, "You were talking about something that . . . touched you deeply." Then he added immediately: "I haven't changed my mind, but I'm beginning to think that you believe yourself."

I reflected on this for a moment and took the last sip of coffee, then asked if it didn't amount to the same thing.

"I'm afraid it does," Doctor Grondin replied.

"Something about his voice was different: there was that sort of respect you feel when you're facing the unknown.

I asked again, "So, Doctor, what do we do?"

He crumpled the cardboard cup which he was still holding and adroitly tossed it into the waste basket.

"When you came in," he said, "you used our alarm signal."

"Yes."

"You wanted a serious talk?"

"Of course."

"Let's get down to it then. Perhaps I took things too lightly, and I apologize."

"No, I'm the one who's complicating your life."

He stubbed his cigar, folded his arm as he often did to begin a new discussion.

"May I ask you some questions as I used to do?"

"Of course."

"You'll answer as coolly as possible and you won't get upset."

"Excuse me, but here I am lying down and you're sitting beside me. The only thing that's missing is a notebook, a pencil and a little beard."

"Now you're the one who isn't being serious," he observed gently.

"I am, but. . . ."

"It's the way you express anxiety," he said, smiling.

"You see! You're already playing psychologist!"

"Try to relax instead," he said without picking up the reference.

He began pacing back and forth, hands behind his back, then stopped at the window where he seemed to be contemplating the landscape. The window looked out onto the Bassin Louise where a row of boats was held prisoner in the ice near the grain elevators. With my eyes closed I had the peculiar impression that external time had stopped but that inside me it had speeded up; I felt as though things were becoming clear of their own accord.

Finally I heard him ask, "Are you afraid of your young girl's heart?"

"Yes."

"Afraid of the emotions it arouses?"

"Exactly."

"Does it really do that?"

I told him everything then: rue de la Fabrique, the landscape that was escaping me, my strange attitude toward Elise. I could feel him without even opening my eyes, truly present and attentive as though I were touching him with my fingertips. He let me speak without saying a word.

"What's troubling you in all this?" he asked at the end.

"The sort of gentleness I'm possessed with now. And . . ."

He waited.

". . . the need for warmth," I said.

I stopped. He turned around.

"Nothing abnormal so far," he remarked coldly. "Particularly for someone who hasn't got his strength back yet."

"Is gentleness normal nowadays?"

"Don't you feel normal?"

"I don't feel American!"

"In what sense?"

"In the sense of knowing Tchaikovsky through Walt Disney. Or rather, in the sense of having the wild hope in my heart that everything can be accomplished by force. I don't feel like a citizen of America."

"Stay calm," he said.

I began again, more slowly.

"There's no place for gentleness any more. Even women should have men's hearts transplanted into them."

He let me talk.

"The worst thing," I said, "is that there's no way out. The first road to take is gentleness; but it doesn't lead anywhere."

"And the other?" he asked in a voice that sounded concerned.

"The other one is rejection, you know that very well. The business about gentleness doesn't sound all that serious to you, and anyway you think it will all work out in time. But what you fear is rejection; you know as well as I do that once I'm on that path nothing can prevent me from going to the very end."

Doctor Grondin appeared to have aged. He turned his spaniel's eyes towards me and looked at me for a long time, pensively. Finally he said, "Everything's in the will to live. You know Hemingway. You must know how much he loved being alive and how. . . ."

"And how he died?" I asked.

The bare feet of the person without a sex are heading towards rue du Fort, and I follow them at a respectful distance. They stop for a long time in front of Darlington's window, which is filled with beautiful, brightly-colored wool scarves, then decide to turn back; I pretend to be looking at the menu of the restaurant Aux Délices and I resume my shadowing just as the feet turn the corner at rue du Trésor. They stop for a moment in front of Louisa Nicol's small ink drawings, in which you always see children and horses; then, as though there wasn't a single painting left to look at, they weave quickly through the artists and the on-lookers, cross rue Saint-Anne diagonally and go into the park at Place d'Armes. The young person sits on the grass, back against a tree and the bird book open on the knees. The park is filled with people sitting on benches or on the grass, around the fountain and along the sidewalks, where calèches and victorias are parked. I'm looking for a convenient spot to sit and watch when I notice the person gesturing to me.

I go over.

"Sit down, if you want."

"Thank you very much," I say, as I sit facing the person, very close to the feet.

"You were following me?"

"Yes, I was."

"I thought so. I've had a tremendous experience."

The wind was cold and I'd walked too far. I stopped at the florist shop at the bottom of Côte de la Fabrique and asked the salesgirl to make me a bouquet of red and white carnations. She told me the price, removed the flowers from the glass case and took them to the back of the shop.

A man came forward; his *soigné* appearance, his assurance identified him as the owner. He greeted me, then went on: "Cold, isn't it?"

"It's winter," I replied.

I was sitting on a stool near a counter where there were greeting cards and a pen, which was fastened to the wall by a chain. For something to say, I asked a question about a large plant standing near me; the owner told me its name and its properties, why the lower leaves were a darker colour. He was chattering. I listened absently. The plants made me think of animals. A crocodile in a bathroom. I suddenly realized that he'd just said:

"Luckily I don't have a dog any more."

"Pardon me?"

"Can you see me walking a dog in weather like this? I sold him at the beginning of the winter."

"I prefer cats," I said.

With no transition he began telling me that he'd spent his childhood in Lévis, at the edge of the cliff; he raised pigeons in a sort of hut; when he needed twenty-five cents he'd catch a pigeon and sell it to a Chinaman who would roast it and eat it. He'd finally sold all his pigeons to the Chinaman.

The salesgirl came back with a box. She handed me the bill. I paid and left, happy.

I walked back along rue de la Fabrique, Desjardins and the Côte Haldimand. At the corner of Mont-Carmel a gust of wind from the northeast snatched at me brutally; I pulled up my hood and then, bent over and clutching the florist's box under my arm, I walked with difficulty around the park that was buried under the snow. It was impossible to chase away the repulsive image of the Chinaman and the roasted pigeons. Never eat Chinese food again.

I climbed the stairs very slowly, thinking of Doctor Grondin. He had advised me to move and I'd replied that seeing the St Lawrence was as important to me as life, that I preferred to take the risk. He told me I was wrong, insisted, spoke of scales of values; using a vulgar pun on scale and stairs I managed to extract a smile from him, and his consent.

I turned the key in the lock; the door opened part way, then jammed: the security chain. The little barricaded house at the bottom of the garden. It was something past four and I was glad that Elise had come home earlier than usual.

Surely she had heard.

No sound from inside.

I rang the bell.

She didn't come. She must be taking a bath. I rang again: two short rings. Naked, she was getting up, briskly drying herself with the big blue towel, putting her feet into slippers, slipping on her bathrobe, tying the belt, coming, opening the door . . . But no, she hadn't heard me. I put my head near the doorframe and whistled softly, twice. I listened carefully: nothing. I wanted to sit down and rest; I was becoming impatient. I pressed the doorbell and counted to ten. The whole house must have heard! Then I sat on the top step, the box of flowers beside me, and lit a cigarette.

Sound of the chain. The door opened. I turned around.

"Is it you?" Elise asked.

She was on the doorstep, wearing her bathrobe and slippers, exactly as I'd imagined her. All my impatience vanished at once.

"It's Père Noël," I said.

She laughed and said, "I thought you were somewhere in Old Quebec."

"I *am* somewhere in Old Quebec."

"You're pale," she said. "Are you all right?"

"Tired. Didn't you hear the bell?"

"No."

"Were you in the bath?"

"You brought me flowers! Don't just sit there."

"Were you taking a bath?"

"Yes."

I got up. She kissed me on the nose, took the box and walked in. I followed her and closed the door. In a loud voice she said, "He brings me flowers and I let him vegetate outside. That's unforgivable."

She put down the box and turned to me. "Give me your parka and you go and rest. Do you want your sheepskin slippers? You really look tired. Know what darling? I've got company."

There was a man in the living room. He got up. He was very tall and he stooped slightly. His hair was in a brushcut and one arm was in a cast. Elise said, "Darling, this is Bill."

The name reminded me of something. He moved towards me and held out his left hand.

"My husband, Noël," Elise said.

"Very glad to meet you," Bill said. "I've seen your picture in the papers." His voice was familiar too. It was strangely veiled and seemed as though it didn't belong to him.

"How do you do?" I said. "You hurt yourself?"

Elise explained, "He has a broken wrist. Bill's a hockey player."

"Which league?"

"American," Bill replied.

"Are you in Quebec for the Carnival?"

"I've been playing for the Aces since November. I was traded to Quebec by the Philadelphia Flyers. You don't like hockey?"

"Of course I do."

"Noël hasn't been following it because of his operation," Elise said. "He's usually a real hockey nut."

"That's true," I said in all sincerity.

"He brought me some flowers," she said. "I'm going to put them in water."

The hockey player smiled. Elise disappeared into the kitchen. I invited the visitor to sit down.

"Thanks," he said, "but I have to be going." He sat down anyway and the sofa cushion sank. Again he said, "I've seen your picture in the paper."

"In Philadelphia?"

"Yes. Everybody was taking about 'the man with the young

girl's heart.' "

I sat at the other end of the sofa. The cushion rose because of the heavy weight at the other end and I felt as though I was going to roll towards the middle. I was exhausted and afraid I'd have a fit of nervous giggling. So I asked, "How did you break your wrist?"

"In a fight," he replied, tapping the cast on his wrist.

"Have the Aces got a better team this year?"

He seemed to ponder the question seriously. Then he replied, "No, but don't tell anybody!"

He threw his head back and burst out in a clear, almost crystalline laughter. I would have laughed too but I felt the beginning of an attack of dizziness, and pains in my left arm. Elise came back, put the bouquet on the little table in front of us and sat in the armchair.

"Looks lovely," said the hockey player.

"Thanks very much," she said.

She was saying it to him or to me. If she had sat between us she would have rolled towards the hockey player; the cushion was tilting in that direction. My head was spinning more and more.

"I like flowers," Bill said, "but I can never remember their names."

"It isn't serious for a hockey player," Elise said.

I completely disagree. Everyone should know the names of flowers and trees and birds. There's a priest in a pulpit and he announces that it's obligatory for everyone, on pain of mortal sin, and there's a multicolored parrot on his shoulder and the church is filled with flowers and birds and trees and there's a very tall man above the high altar, wearing a long robe, and he has very long hair like a woman's and his head is crowned with thorns and on his chest you can clearly see his heart, split open, with blood flowing from it.

I opened my eyes.

Elise was sitting on the bed.

"What are you doing?" I asked.

"You have to take this."

"Eh?"

I sat up. She was holding a pill and a glass of water.

"Why?"

"The doctor said to wake you up at nine o'clock to take this. It's nine o'clock."

"Was he here?"

"You gave us an awful scare: you fell asleep in the living room."

"Who brought me in here?"

"Swallow this," she said.

"The hockey player?"

"His name is Bill," Elise said softly.

I took the pill and swallowed some water.

"What did he say?"

"That you weren't heavy at all. He put you over his shoulder with just one arm."

"No, I mean the doctor. What did he say?"

"That it wasn't serious. Just fatigue."

"And then?"

"He said your heart was fine. He gave you an injection and asked me to wake you up in four hours for the pill. That's all."

"But I'm undressed!"

"Of course."

"The hockey player?"

"No, no, I did it. Relax now. You're wearing yourself out for nothing."

"You swear?"

"Come on now, darling, you're worse than a child!"

I lay down again and she pulled up the covers. I already felt numb and my eyelids were very heavy. Elise bent over me.

"How do you feel?"

"As though I were drifting away."

"That's the pill. Close your eyes."

I closed my eyes and said, with difficulty: "As though you . . . you were drifting away too."

"Don't worry," she said, "you're going to sleep."

Then I heard her murmur, with a smile in her voice, "You see, darling, I was right."

" . . . ."

"The voice we heard on the other side of the wall was Bill's."

She added, as though for herself, "You said it was a woman."

Sleep lay more and more heavily on my eyelids. I could still hear Elise's voice, coming from very far away:

"You can see now that he's a man."

I heard nothing more. I tumbled down a hill.

I'm a little surprised.

"You think people your age have a lot of experience?" I ask.

She doesn't reply. I try to explain to her.

"I was following you because of the book. I mean—because of what old Marie used to say about birds. But you don't know old Marie."

She says nothing.

"You know what?" I say again.

"What?"

"I was wondering if you were a boy or a girl!"

"That isn't important."

"One can tell you're a girl right away because of your feet."

"The small blue veins?"

"Of course," I say. "I didn't notice them at first."

"People don't always notice," she says steadily. "My name's Charlie."

"Isn't that a boy's name?"

"What does that matter."

She doesn't say it like a question, but clearly as a declaration. I told her my name.

"That's a nice name," she says. "When you turn it around it's Léon."

"I'd really rather you didn't turn it around," I say, somewhat irritated.

"They call me the Blue Whale, too," she says, as though trying to console me.

"Why?"

"Because of the way I breathe. Apparently I breathe very loud."

"I don't think you do," I say, listening carefully.

"It's just when I'm lying down. It's an old story and I can't tell you about it now."

Suddenly I think of Doctor Grondin and I feel as though I've been hit inside.

"Something to do with a man?" I ask.

"Eh? Who told you that? Simon?"

"I don't know Simon. Excuse me, but I'd like to know how old you are. It's important."

"Simon wouldn't have done that," she murmurs. "But except for him there's nobody who. . . ."

"Who's Simon?"

"Simon's Simon," she says. "Simon the calèche driver."

"Eh?"

"Now listen."

Through the splashing of the fountain, the purring of automobiles and the confused clamour of people, you can hear the jerky cadence of a horse walking along the pavement; a red calèche is turning onto rue Sainte-Anne.

"I can always recognize the horse," she says without even turning her head. "He has a slight limp."

The calèche moves rapidly away and I watch the man holding the reins disappear: a broad back and hair turning grey at the back of his neck.

"Is he your father?" I ask.

"What difference does it make?" she asks in the same tone as before.

She is looking at me and I can't tell whether I've made a mistake; you can't really read in someone's eyes, but you can imagine things.

Little by little I entered my story.

As the inner fog dissipated I was able to distinguish my characters. Jimmy's hair was unkempt and his cowboy outfit, faded and patched, was too small for him. His prisoner had blonde hair that fell to her shoulders, a face that still had its childlike roundness, and green eyes; she wore a very short skirt and a white blouse with lace around the collar and cuffs.

She was very naive, with large, astonished eyes, yet she had a certain curiosity and a taste for adventure. The boy was just as naive, but he put on airs. He had a package of Alouette tobacco and Vogue papers in his shirt pocket and from time to time, with studied nonchalance, he would roll a cigarette, crack a match on his thumbnail and spread clouds of smoke all around him. He took himself for an authentic cowboy: he'd begun this business to assume some importance in his prisoner's eyes, but in the end he couldn't distinguish the true from the false: he shamelessly declared that his horse was tied up under a tree at the top of the cliff and went out several times a day on the pretext of feeding it or riding it into the village. She was very concrete, asking precise questions, discussing his replies, stating her objections, and thereby forcing him deeper into his imaginary world.

She said to him, "You don't even smell of horses!"

"Horses only smell when they sweat."

"Why doesn't your horse sweat?"

"The village isn't very far away."

"So why do you go on horseback?"

"I always travel on horseback. When I was young, out West. . ."

And he invented vast plains for himself, at the foot of the Rockies, which he crossed every day on horseback when his father and the cowboys on the ranch rounded up the cattle beneath a blazing sun, a shotgun across his saddle to defend himself against the Indians whose troubling silhouettes could be seen up above. He also spoke of the sound of tomtoms and of smoke signals.

She asked, "Why didn't you stay out West?"

"My father was killed. My grandfather sold the ranch and we took the train."

"How was he killed? Indians?"

"An arrow in the back. He'd stopped at a river to drink. But he would have died in any case."

"Why?"

"The water was poisoned."

"Who told you?"

"There were animal carcasses on the shores. That's a sign. When there are animal carcasses you can be sure the water's poisoned."

"Didn't your father see them?"

"He saw them, but he always did what he wanted to do. A man always does that, do you understand?"

"And your mother didn't say anything?"

"You must be hungry now."

"Your mother?"

"MY MOTHER? LEAVE MY MOTHER ALONE! I DON'T WANT YOU TO TALK ABOUT MY MOTHER! UNDERSTAND?"

"You don't have to yell so loud."

"I'M NOT YELLING! BUT I MIGHT GET MAD IF YOU GO ON LIKE THIS!"

"All right, all right, I won't talk about it any more. I swear."

"On your grandmother's head?"

"I swear, on my grandmother's head."

She bit her lips.

"I think I'm hungry now," she said.

"I'll make some Nestlé's Quik."

And he thought: "I'm a heavy drinker of Nestlé's Quik." It was as though he'd just kicked open both doors of the saloon in a town in the Far West: all the cowboys, sitting at tables or standing at the bar, would shut their big yaps and turn in his direction; he'd stand erect and motionless, frozen in silence, his hands beside him, ready to shoot the first man who moved.

In a rather husky voice he said, "We can make you some hot chocolate if you prefer."

"No thanks."

"We're perfectly capable of heating up the milk and everything, exactly the way you're supposed to."

"No thanks, that's fine."

He poured the milk, took the can of Nestlé's Quik from the cupboard and added two spoonfuls to each glass; he stirred the liquid for a long time so there wouldn't be any lumps. Then he offered her a glass.

"Can you help me drink it?" she asked.

"Why?"

"My hands!"

He'd forgotten. He apologized and considered it for a moment.

"I'll untie one hand," he decided.

He went behind her chair and untied one hand, making sure the other hand and the ankles were still in place. She rubbed her sore wrist against her lips, took the glass which he held out to her and drained it in one gulp.

"If you want some cookies you can have maple or chocolate."

"No thanks."

She smiled at him, her eyes sparkling; something brown was dribbling from the corner of her mouth.

"That was very good," she said, handing him the glass.

"You're going to get your blouse dirty."

"You can wipe my mouth if you want."

"Eh?"

"With a kleenex or a damp washcloth."

He drank some Nestlé's Quik, then declared: "I'm going to untie you, but. . . ."

"But what?"

"You have to swear you won't try to escape."

"I swear on my grandmother's head."

"If you run away I'll rape you before you can say boo."

"You said you'd never say that word again."

"Excuse me, you're right."

"I always keep my promises," she said proudly.

He didn't reply, but knelt beside her and untied her completely.

"Thank you," she said simply.

She stretched her arms and legs and went to the tap to wash her face. Jimmy was watching her. Suddenly he asked, "What's your sign?"

"Libra," she replied, wiping her face with a towel.

No luck, he told himself. You want to rape a girl and then you have to end up with a goddamn Libra. They never know what they want, never make up their minds, never want to go all the way. And the worst thing is, they're faithful. What rotten luck: there's twelve signs and you end up with a goddamn Libra. Brigitte Bardot's a Libra too. I'm not saying I would have minded ending up with Brigitte Bardot. Not necessarily. I mean, she isn't serious enough, if you ask me. All right, so she's terribly sexy and all that, but she isn't serious enough. Just try and think for a second that you're going to rape Brigitte Bardot: it isn't the least bit serious. You're dreaming. Now let's suppose you explain things to her, that you want to do it to get some peace and everything: ninety-nine chances out of a hundred she'll burst out laughing like a loony, shaking her hair and telling you to go and play cowboy somewhere else. And if by chance she doesn't laugh in your face she'll pretend to go along with you and understand everything, but basically she'll be playing a role; and you'll be lucky if she doesn't start laughing just at the very moment you're about to take out your diploma.

Needless to say I was the one who was born under that sign and who had the hesitant nature and even the double personality. As I traced the thread of the story, I'd set off without knowing it in search of myself, going back to the sources, and I suspected these two young characters, for whom I wanted a brutal experience but who had quickly come to treat one another as brother and sister, to be nothing but the double reflection of the person the newspapers had shamelessly called "the man with the young girl's heart."

I wasn't naive enough to find that explanation satisfactory; ever since the operation nothing that happened inside me had been so clear; everything seemed somewhat foggy and I was less and less lucid. I began to believe that when we write we invent nothing more than images that have been sleeping within us.

Besides, I was finding it hard to write. I mean: I was writing timidly, as though there were something disturbing at the end of the words; as though at the turn of a phrase I would suddenly find myself facing something indescribably threatening and irremediable. But still I went on, I felt pushed to do so. I wasn't a real writer, moved by some irrepressible need to create, to express or communicate; it was more like an *idée fixe*. It was as though words constituted both the only possible way out, a kind of initiation and a rite of passage of the kind certain primitive tribes require adolescents to undergo when they claim that they're becoming men.

"How old are you?" I ask Charlie the Blue Whale a second time, near the fountain.

"I have no age," she says, with a tinge of melancholy.

She raises one shoulder rather high, then bends her head to one side and rubs her cheek against her shoulder. Suddenly she says, "Did you hear that?"

"Eh?"

"The bird," she says.

"The sparrow?"

"Chick-a-dee-dee-dee," she says, imitating the bird. "Not a sparrow! A black-capped chickadee!"

She points to a birch tree whose branches stick through the iron grille, behind the old Protestant church.

"I don't see anything at all," I say.

"It's a male."

" . . . . "

"Because of its bright colours and its song," she explains patiently. "The females are dull and they have only a cry of alarm."

"Usually it's women who like colours and who. . . ."

She smiles; she disagrees but I would have stopped in any case because of the way she smiles. With a motion of her head she invites me to turn around: before the fountain a dozen young people form a circle around an old man who is scraping at a guitar. They're all wearing beads and brightly coloured clothes.

"People don't dress like that," I say. "Those are exceptions."

"The calèche-driver says you must seek the truth among the exceptions," she says, without relinquishing her calm.

"He could be mistaken."

I'm sorry I said that; I think again of the concern I felt when I hesitated a while ago between masculine and feminine: truth may come into the world in any manner, even in the form of an emotion. "Excuse me," I say.

She looks at the table of contents in her book, opens it to the place indicated. "Look," she says.

She points to a color plate showing the black-capped chickadee.

"It's beautiful," I say.

"All birds are beautiful, you know."

"They fascinate me, but they frighten me too."

"I know."

"You can't know," I say.

"It's simple, we're afraid of the things that are inside us."

"Are you a student?" I ask.

"No."

"You work then?"

"No."

She laughs.

"I look after birds. Someone has to do it."

She laughs again. Then she remarks, "You follow people, you ask questions."

"I'm searching," I say, a little embarrassed.

She doesn't say anything.

"I'm looking for what is at the end," I say, once again taking refuge in the ridiculous. She closes the book, places it against her chest and crosses her arms over it. She examines me for a moment.

"You always seem to be coming back from somewhere far away," she says, smiling.

Absently I take out a cigarette.

"One for Charlie," she says.

"Sorry."

I hold out the package, give her a light, then light my own cigarette.

"You aren't worried?" I ask.

"I look after the birds and Simon looks after me."

"I mean: you don't feel sometimes as though life's a burden? That it's crushing you?"

"You don't know Simon," she says.

She smokes silently. I ask, "Do you read books?"

"I'm very hungry," she says suddenly.

"Didn't you eat lunch?"

"No. Or breakfast either."

"Do you want to go to a restaurant?"

She gets up.

"I'm going to see some friends."

"Where?"

"Don't know. I'll go and look. . . . I haven't any money or anything."

"If you wouldn't mind," I say, "you could come to my place."

"Is it very far?"

"Very close. On the other side of the Château."

"All right," she says. "I eat less than a bird, but I have to eat something anyway, otherwise. . . ."

She places her clasped hands against her cheek and bends her head like a child who has fallen asleep for the night. She didn't answer my question about books. She doesn't always answer.

"So you've played in the NHL, have you?"

"Oh yes!"

He was very proud of it.

Tenth time I'd asked him that question, at least. Bill came to our place every day. At first, Elise would call him. She'd knock on the wall a certain number of times; they had a code. Eventually he'd come by himself. We had long conversations about hockey. I'd ask, "What position do you play?"

"Left wing."

"Who's the hardest player to cover?"

"Gordie Howe, obviously."

He swallowed some Molson, then added, "He's always been my idol. When I was very young. . . ."

He stopped and looked at Elise. I don't know if he was really looking at her or if he was lost somewhere in his childhood. I'd always thought that hockey players had no childhood. I mean: that they didn't live with their childhood, except for a very few, like Frank Mahovlich and Bob Rousseau, who still carried part of their childhood onto the ice. I had an urge to talk with Bill about it, but a sort of reticence held me back.

"Have you played against Howe this year?"

"Yes, twice."

He looked at Elise as he answered me. He went on: "He scored five goals against me and I didn't get a single assist! Maybe that's why I'm back in the American League. . . ."

"Is he as rough as they say?"

"There's a souvenir of him!" he said, showing me a scar above his left eye. He explained: "He elbowed me and I went into the boards head first. When I picked myself up, the fight broke out. I don't remember the rest: I left the ice on a stretcher."

He laughed with slightly exaggerated pride. Elise said, "You could have been seriously hurt."

He smiled at her without saying a word. When he didn't speak he smiled. Elise sometimes called him "vous," sometimes "tu"; you couldn't tell in advance and it spread an impression of warmth through the room, as though all three of us had drunk hot gin with lemon and a spoonful of honey. I asked the hockey player again, "Is Gordie Howe better than Maurice Richard?"

He considered this question intently; at least four deep furrows crossed his forehead and he held his glass of beer in both hands. He began by saying, "You know, I was fairly young when Richard was at his peak. So it's not easy."

Then, after a long moment of hesitation, "Richard was more spectacular. Gordie Howe's a more all-round player. The two greatest players in the world."

"And Bobby Hull?"

"Wait, let's see in five years. He's already talking about retirement. I'm not sure he's got the sacred fire."

I thought his judgment was accurate and I enjoyed talking with him. I offered him another beer and he accepted, after glancing at Elise.

"Don't you drink at all?" he asked me.

"Hardly ever."

"Because of your. . . ."

"That's it."

I asked Elise to make me a coffee and immediately brought the conversation back to Richard and Howe. Every time I spoke of Richard, heard his name, I felt something ancient move within me, like a beast that had been sleeping since the operation and now was stirring in its sleep. I was listening to the hockey player but I felt like talking to him about the dazzling breakaways Richard would set up as he skated around the net, of the famous goal he'd scored with a player on his back, of his legendary battles, of the riot at the Forum and on rue Sainte-Catherine after President Campbell suspended him, of the sadness we felt at the sight of him dragging his leg at the end of his prodigious career. I wanted Bill to understand to what extent Richard's image was alive in the hearts of people my age, and how remembering him stirred up such profound emotions they touched our deepest roots, back to the common heritage of our race. I had a lump in my throat and I could feel all those things churning inside me, but I couldn't explain them; on the surface there was a layer of gentleness, a sea of oil that blocked out everything.

Elise brought my coffee.

"I put a drop of cognac in it," she murmured with a wink of complicity.

"Thank you."

I took a sip and asked Bill what he thought of young Cournoyer.

"He's the most like Richard. At least between the blue line and the goal."

"Who's the sneakiest player?"

"Mikita."

"He's rough?"

"Not exactly. He hits from below," he said with a certain disgust.

"Who's the roughest?"

He took his time. You could see that the question interested him; this was his domain.

"You're thinking of John Ferguson or Eddie Shack?" he asked.

"Yes."

"Because they cross the ice to throw somebody into the boards?"

"Of course."

"That isn't very dangerous; you can avoid them. But if you show up at the blue line just once with your head down when Bobby Baun's on the ice you'll wake up in the hospital!"

"What do you think of Robert Rousseau?"

"Very bright for a player his size, but he plays too often sitting on the ice. You're a Canadiens fan?"

"Of course. Doesn't it show?"

"Fairly well," he said, laughing.

He drained his glass of beer and I asked, "Have you ever played against Jean Béliveau?"

"Yes," he said, wiping his lips with the back of his hand.

"And what's he like?"

"He's the most intelligent player. Always uses his head. The spectators think hockey players aren't very bright but I think they judge too quickly. Anyway, Béliveau's game is pure intelligence."

"You've got a degree in political science," Elise interrupted.

"Just a B.A."

"Like Dick Duff," I said.

"That's true."

"There's a Quebec poet who said. . . ."

I stopped.

"What did he say?" Bill asked.

They were both looking at me. I went on hesitantly.

"He's a very good poet. He won the Prix France-Québec. I don't mean he's a good poet just because he won. . . ."

"What did he say?" Elise repeated.

"He said that a breakaway by Béliveau was. . . ."

I felt uncomfortable.

"He said that a breakaway by Béliveau was as pure and beautiful as a poem."

Elise was sitting on the sill of the half-moon shaped window, her face impassive. There was a gleam of pity in the hockey player's eyes; he was looking at me the way people did just after the operation. I fell back into my own thoughts.

"Must be going," said Bill.

"It isn't late," said Elise.

"I usually go to bed early."

He got up and left. Elise followed him. I heard them speaking very quietly in the corridor, then I heard nothing more.

Elise didn't come back immediately, but when you live within yourself you sometimes forget that time is passing. I decided to go to bed. I was very thin; usually I didn't think about it, but there were times too when I became acutely aware of it. I wondered if it was life that was in movement or movement that was in life. And I wondered too if a clown could be as fine a thing to look at as a tree.

Charlie and I are walking towards the Château. It's hard for me to keep step with her because she walks like a free person. There are all sorts of things in my head: she holds the bird book against her chest; departing for the self's inner pole; there's a bird inside my chest, I want to know it and I'm afraid; either you live like everyone else or you seek the key to the mysteries; the beginning of her name sounds like cat; my childhood resembles an old ruined castle, inhabited by cats; cats dream a great deal, birds hardly ever; I mistrust creatures that are incapable of dreaming.

"I've got a room here," she says as we walk under the arcades of the Château, "but I never go to it."

"Of course," I say. "But what's the use of dreams?"

"They're useful for the anima. Simon says that's very important."

"Why?"

She doesn't answer.

Beside the park on the other side of the Château she stops before the obelisk commemorating Montcalm and Wolfe and attempts to decipher the Latin inscription.

MORTEM. VIRTUS. COMMUNEM.
FAMAM. HISTORIA.
MONUMENTUN. POSTERITAS. DEDIT.

"Simon'll have to translate it," she says finally.

"He knows Latin?"

"Of course. When he doesn't want me to understand something he speaks Latin."

"Why?"

She turns her head towards me and says calmly: "You're like a child, always asking why."

"That's true," I say.

"It's better to find out yourself."

"I've tried."

"And it didn't work," she says.

"It's funny, it's as though my experience diminishes every day. What are you thinking about?"

"Simon," she says.

"You have a mother?" I ask abruptly.

"No, but I had a mother hen."

"I'm very fond of mother hens. Where was she?"

"On the North Shore. I'd rather not talk about it."

Across from the tourist house I show Charlie my window on the fifth floor; I suggest she walk quickly and quietly past the concierge's apartment so we'll have peace.

From the window Charlie the Blue Whale spent a long time looking at the river and the boats, and bent over to see, on her left, the bridge to the Island and the distant mountains of Charlevoix, for it was a bright clear day. She also glanced at my painting—the tree in the fog with the sun behind it—and she smiled enigmatically. I asked no questions.

She had something to eat, then lay down on the sofa, saying nothing, and closed her eyes. She breathes hard, as she said; she seems to be asleep.

Honestly, I haven't asked any questions since she's been here, not about the painting and what Doctor Grondin said about it or about gentleness and what old Marie wrote on the tablecloths at the Café Buade, or even about birds and the senseless hope that they'd aroused in me.

She's breathing very hard.

I sit by her and she opens her eyes.

"I didn't want to wake you up," I say.

"You know what?" she asks.

"No," I say, wondering what secrets make her eyes so black.

"There's a dream I have often. A pack of wolves turning the corner of the street, heading for the house; they'd come closer, their mouths open and tongues hanging out between their pointed teeth. Then just when they got to the door I'd wake up, screaming."

"And your parents came to see what was going on?"

"My father would come into my room and tell my mother to go back to sleep. He'd sit on my bed and talk to me softly. Then he'd turn on all the lights in the house and take me into every room, even the cellar. He'd hold my hand and with him in pyjamas and me in my long blue nightgown we'd walk to the corner of the street where there was a lamp post and then come back to the house together. He'd take me up to my room and tell me something to put me back to sleep."

"I like your memories very much," I say. "I've always liked memories."

"Come a little closer then."

"Wait."

I go to get a pillow. I slip it under her head and lie down beside her. She's breathing very loud.

"You're a real Blue Whale," I say.

"That's true."

"I wonder. . . ."

"What?" she asks, eyes half closed.

What I wonder is whether you can become a friend of a very young girl who likes birds, but that isn't easy to ask. And then there's a question I can't hold back.

"The painting of the tree, did you. . . ."

"I wonder what's become of. . . ."

"The painting?"

"No, a man. It must be five years now and I still think about him," she said pensively.

"What man?"

"The man who was beside me. I was going over to Lévis on the Louis-Jolliet. It was summer. Suddenly, in the middle of the river, he straddled the railing and jumped in the water."

"What did he look like?"

"Old, wearing a black suit and a black hat. I think of him often, you see."

"Of course."

"I feel responsible, you understand."

"I understand. Don't think about it now."

"I'll try," she said, "if you'll hold me in your arms the way Simon does."

"Like this?" I ask.

It was Sunday.

Elise had gone out with Bill, to the canoe race. I'd stayed home to write.

From my window you could see the Terrasse swarming with a motley crowd of people, gaily spotting the snow with colour. They walked about with their arms around one another's waists, dancing and drinking to warm themselves and from time to time blowing noisily into colored plastic trumpets. Near the Château, pairs of skaters were turning to the strains of a Strauss waltz, around the little skating rink edged with translucent sculptures; in the middle of the Terrasse, toboggans with their passengers leaning forward and clinging delightedly to one another were hurtling down the slide three at a time; on the St Lawrence the two winter ferries, heavily laden with official spectators, were motionless in the midst of the ice as helicopters whirled overhead.

I was glad Elise and Bill had gone out. Elise needed some distraction and besides, if they'd stayed I would have had to write in Bill's room; he let me use it so I could work in peace. He came to our place almost constantly, which I didn't like very much. I had trouble getting used to his room, as the window didn't look out on the river and you could hear the murmur of their voices through the wall.

For some time I had only to close the window, sit at my table, light a cigarette, pick up my pen and effortlessly I'd be back in the midst of my imaginary world.

It was beginning to be inhabited, even though the landscape as a whole still eluded me. At the top of a very sheer cliff there was a vast country house where a community of nuns lived; on sunny afternoons (it was the middle of summer in my story) you could see the sisters walking down the path in a long white line and going to sit on the rocks that jutted out into the water. The riverbank, which undulated in a series of coves of varying depths, was composed of a mixture of gravel and sand; at the bottom of the coves the sand became very fine and soft underfoot. Here and there large fish cages had been put up, subdivided into several sections; they had been battered by the winter ice and fishermen came down to the beach to repair them; later, towards the end of July, they would set them on the sandbanks for fishing eels until the arrival of winter. When it was very hot and the tide was high, the young people from the village came there to swim. You would also see cats hunting for food. I felt as though I were reconstituting, one piece at a time, some enormous jigsaw puzzle.

Whenever I returned to this imaginary world I felt more comfortable than the time before. It was all around me like a shelter, a refuge. Some days I didn't write at all, simply for the pleasure of feeling well and doing nothing as I sat on the big rock—the one that was farthest out in the river, with gulls soaring around it, lost in this universe where the sun shone, the wind was a gentle breath and the time a great, still, reassuring gentleness.

What troubled me a little and brought me back to reality was the increasingly frequent thought that there might be some secret relationship between gentleness and death.

Even with the window closed you could hear garbled voices and the purring of helicopters as they flew over the house. I put my nose against the window: hundreds of curious people were leaning over the balustrade on the Terrasse or standing in groups on the wharves, as far as the Bassin Louise; the ice was drifting rapidly, small fragmented floes that left only one channel of open water on the Quebec side. At Lévis a swarming mass of spectators darkened the large wharf the canoes had to touch before making a half turn to cross the river. The race hadn't yet begun. I recognized Elise and Bill, leaning on the green fence on either side of the slide, turning their heads together as the toboggans went past. The hockey player was wearing my raccoon hat and my *ceinture fléchée*. He lifted his white plastic cane and brought the spout to his mouth; it was filled with gin and orange juice. He passed it to Elise who also took a long swig. From time to time they danced comically. It seemed to be very cold.

I returned to my landscape.

Summer. Gentleness.

I started.

Two knocks at the door.

The apartment was dark.

More knocking, louder this time.

I got up, regained my balance with a little difficulty and switched on a lamp, turning my head so it wouldn't dazzle me. I glanced at the old cuckoo clock—it was past midnight. I must have fallen asleep at my table. My neck was stiff. I lit another lamp and opened the door.

The hockey player was standing there, muffled up in my raccoon cap, with the *ceinture fléchée*, the red tuque and the aviator boots and he was holding his white cane; he'd knocked on the door with it. Mouth open, his expression uncertain, he swayed slightly back and forth; he was drunk as a skunk.

"You're drunk," I said gently.

He waved his plastic cane under my nose and shook his head negatively.

"Not drunk!"

He clutched the door handle and mumbled, "Tut! Tut! Hockey player . . . never drunk . . . not allowed! Big Bill . . . not drunk . . . just tired because. . . ." He pointed his cane awkwardly over his shoulder, towards the stairs.

"E-gli-se," he articulated the name.

"Eh?"

"Eglise. Bottom of the stairs."

"Her name's Elise," I said.

"That's right," he said. "My friend Elise. I dragged her to the bottom of the stairs. Tired because of my arm. Understand?"

His voice became pleading. I heard myself ask, "Is she sick?"

"Not sick," he said. "Tired." His eyes were attempting unsuccessfully to connect with mine. Drops of sweat pearled his forehead. He tried to place his hand on my shoulder but it landed in the air. "Need help," he said with difficulty.

"All right, I'll try to help you. Then everybody's going to bed."

He started laughing and turned around, staggering towards the stairs.

"Thanks a lot," he said as he cautiously moved one foot towards the first step. "Everybody's very tired. Everybody's going to bed."

"Wait!" I said.

He was frozen in a comical posture, one hand on the bannister and his foot in the air.

"Have to take that off," I said, pointing to his outfit.

"Have to take that off," he repeated.

I untied the *ceinture fléchée* and after several minutes' effort managed to take off the heavy raccoon cap, then the aviator boots. He let me proceed, but stubbornly refused to let go of his red tuque or his plastic cane. I went slowly down the stairs ahead of him. At each landing I turned around to keep an eye on him and encourage him. With the cane under his broken arm, he clutched the bannister with his good hand; he moved his leg forward, explored the terrain at length, then put down his foot as though the staircase were strewn with mines.

Elise was lying on the last step.

She was lying across the staircase, her head to one side, leaning against the wall, with the eyes closed and a smile on her face that made her look like a little girl. Standing near her was the concierge, wearing a long white nightgown, her arms folded and her head crowned with the eternal rollers, her face a mask of total disapproval.

"Bonsoir, Madame," I said weakly.

She paid no attention to me but kept an eye on the hockey player who, having reached the last steps without mishap, was now taking an exaggeratedly long step to get over the considerable obstacle represented by Elise's body. When he had accomplished this feat he bowed deeply to the concierge, took off his tuque as a sign of respect and began to babble a long, confused story from which it finally emerged that everyone was very tired and wanted to go to bed. Before the supreme contempt that was painted on the old lady's scowling face, he was finally completely silent and then—stupefied, open-mouthed—he began to observe her in the uncertain manner of someone contemplating an exotic statue. Before he touched her to check whether she was real, I took him by the arm and brought him back close to Elise, who had just opened her eyes.

"Feeling better?" I asked her.

She couldn't focus her eyes on me. I patted her cheek and I could hear a feeble moan. The hockey player grabbed my hand; he gently pushed me away.

"You're hurting her," he protested. Then added immediately: "Big Bill knows what to do. Just a minute."

Cautiously he got to his knees, bent over and kissed her delicately on the cheek. She looked at him and smiled, and I began to think of Sleeping Beauty. I knew it was stupid. The concierge was burning the back of my neck with her gaze but that's what I was thinking about. More precisely, of the Walt Disney movie.

She asked, "Are you there?"

"Of course," Bill replied.

Exactly what I would have answered. He was on his knees, the cane under his arm, the tuque crooked, eyes moist; and he was smiling sanctimoniously.

"You've abandoned me," Elise said, her voice charged with emotion.

The hockey player gestured that he hadn't. He kept shaking his head for a good while, then he stammered, "Everybody's going to bed."

He bent towards her then and said in a somewhat firmer tone, "I've brought help."

She'd just closed her eyes again. He touched her shoulder.

"Noël's here," he went on.

She seemed to have fallen asleep again. Her head was leaning against the wall and flung to one side as it had been earlier. The cheek you could see was moist.

"She didn't see you," Bill said. "Just a minute."

And he was about to bend over her once again. I stopped him by putting my hand on his shoulder.

"Don't wake her up," I said.

"No?"

"No!"

"She's very tired."

"You carry her and I'll take her legs."

Rather curtly, I showed him how to proceed: we seemed to be dividing Elise into two pieces. I held her legs by wedging them under my folded arms. The hockey player put his hands under her armpits and tried to lift her.

"Too tired," he said. "Going to have a drink."

He tried to get a grip on his cane which he'd stuck into his belt. It took me several minutes to dissuade him. Suddenly I realized that he couldn't lift Elise because of his broken wrist. I explained the situation to him.

"I'll take your place," he suggested, rubbing his wrist.

"Impossible," I said.

The thought of him taking my place was depressing. He didn't seem to understand that I couldn't make any strenuous effort. I showed him what to do: bend down, put his arms under Elise's shoulders, support the weight on his forearms. He repeated my actions, muttering words of encouragement to himself. He managed to lift her without too much difficulty, and without wasting a moment I was about to pick up her legs, which were trailing two steps behind. With one boot clamped under each arm I turned my head to give the starting signal: the hockey player had both hands firmly against Elise's chest and her head was in the hollow of his shoulder. Her face, rather red, was split by a broad smile.

"I could climb as high as the sky!" he said joyously.

Under the incensed eye of the concierge we set off and almost immediately I heard Elise's voice.

"Are you rocking me?" she murmured.

"Of course," Bill replied.

She whispered unintelligible words and Bill answered her very softly. At times it seemed as though she were moaning. I could feel my legs growing weak and I was afraid I wouldn't be able to hold out till the fifth floor. Then I heard the still plaintive voice.

"Are you still rocking me?"

"Yes."

"Sing me a song."

"What one?"

"Any song. The Carnival song."

He began to sing the refrain in a rather hoarse voice, interrupted by panting, but always in tune. Elise was humming too and without really wanting to I mentally sang along with them. At the third floor the hockey player stopped and drank his gin in one gulp; it was impossible to make him change his mind.

When we reached the fifth floor we lay Elise on the sofa. She'd fallen asleep again. I turned around to pick up the raccoon cap, the *ceinture fléchée* and the aviator's boots from the landing, closed the door and slumped into an armchair. The hockey player, a little less drunk now but still staggering, was coming back from the kitchen with a beer. My heart still hadn't calmed down. I took my emergency flask from my pocket and swallowed a pill. In a few moments my breathing became calm, my limbs grew numb and my eyelids heavy.

I heard a sort of moan.

I opened my eyes.

Through a haze I made out the hockey player's back; he seemed to be bending over Elise. I couldn't see what he was doing but I could hear Elise's voice and she was moaning.

I cleared my throat. Bill turned around suddenly.

"You weren't asleep?" he asked.

"I was."

"I need help."

He seemed much less drunk. I got up. My legs felt like lead.

"Something wrong?" I asked.

"Yes."

"Is she sick?"

"She's very hot. She's suffocating."

I approached the sofa.

"Put your hand there," he said.

And he placed his own hand on Elise's forehead, then removed it, wet with perspiration. He undid the buttons of her suede coat, then made me kneel on the edge of the sofa and said, "Take her in your arms."

He helped me raise her shoulders and I held her against me.

"Hold her carefully."

He slipped off her coat, pulling off one sleeve at a time, then with an abrupt jerk removed it completely. The shock made me lose my balance and I found myself lying beside Elise.

"Are you tired too?" he asked.

"I'm tired and I'm very sleepy. What time is it?"

I looked at the cuckoo clock but there was still too much haze and the hands of the clock danced before my eyes.

"You can go to sleep now," the hockey player said.

"No, I have to help you."

"I think it's all right now."

"No."

I knelt on the sofa again and began to lift up Elise's sweater.

"That isn't necessary," he said feebly.

"She's very warm."

I pulled the sweater over her head, then asked Bill to help me complete the task and he did, to the very end, muttering things I didn't understand.

My fingers were growing numb so I hurried, afraid of becoming weak before I'd finished. In the end, Bill suddenly stopped talking and we spread a flannel sheet over Elise. She was breathing more easily and she'd stopped moaning. She seemed to be sleeping soundly.

"Thanks very much," I said to the hockey player.

He didn't reply.

"I couldn't have done it by myself," I said.

"You look very tired," he said softly.

"That's true."

I sat on the sill of the half-moon shaped window and stretched out my legs. Bill went into my room and came back with two pillows; he placed one under Elise's head and slipped the other behind my back. I stretched out a little more and felt quite comfortable.

"Are you all right?" he asked.

"Just fine, really. Thanks."

"That's good."

"Have another beer," I said. "You know where it is."

"All right, but this is the last one."

He went to get a Molson from the fridge, then came back and sat in the armchair I'd abandoned. I felt very weary and very gentle at the same time, without being able to distinguish one from the other. I was also thinking of Doctor Grondin.

"What are you thinking about?" Bill asked.

"Hockey," I said to make him happy.

"I don't believe you."

"I'm sorry. As a matter of fact I was thinking about Doctor Grondin."

"You're lucky to know him."

"That's true, I am."

"What's he like?"

"Very good, very human."

He poured half the beer into his glass and said, "You're like that too."

When I was very small I was already wild about hockey and so was my father. Elise was breathing deeply. My numb body was closing around me and my memories, like a nest around the wounded bird. Among the chunks of floating ice the lights of Lévis swayed in the river water.

"Are you falling asleep?" the hockey player asked.

"Of course not," I said.

"I won't say anything more."

"Talk if you want to."

"You need some sleep."

"You're a good guy."

"Don't say that."

"Why not? You took care of Elise as well as I'd have done."

"Not at all."

"What do you think of her?"

"She's very beautiful," he said, "if you don't mind me saying it."

"I meant morally."

"She has no faults."

"Don't you think she's sometimes . . . a bit of a mother hen?"

"No. Perhaps a little . . . more like a little girl. Excuse me."

"That's strange."

He was silent for a few moments.

"Sometimes I find it hard to understand you," he began again.

"I don't understand you right away. I've never met anyone like you."

"No?"

"You never get angry," he said.

He took a long swallow of beer.

"Have you always been like that?"

"Of course not," I said, holding back a yawn.

"When did it begin?"

"I think I'm going to sleep now."

"I'd like to know how you feel with your. . . ."

I tried to chase the fog from my head.

"With my wife?"

"No, no. With your young girl's heart. Excuse me."

"It isn't easy," I said.

"Don't you feel comfortable?"

He poured the second half of his bottle. He was talking too loud. I was afraid he was getting drunk again.

"Listen," he said, becoming animated, "I think you're great. I'd like to have a young girl's heart myself!"

I nearly laughed; it was quite funny to see him. But I was afraid of waking Elise.

"Excuse me," said the hockey player. "I think I've had too much to drink. Sincerely, that's what I think."

"It doesn't matter. You're a good guy," I said once again.

"No, don't say that. I don't like it when you say that."

He slowly emptied his glass, then suggested:

"Do you want to talk about hockey?"

I didn't answer.

"We could talk about Jean Béliveau if you want."

I said nothing. I took one last look out the window: on the winter ferry that had just left Quebec, the broad face of Bonhomme Carnival, all illuminated, stood out. I had no idea what time it was, but it was very late, the next day was the eve of Mardi Gras and the Carnival was going away like the boat.

The Blue Whale raises herself, I slip one arm between her neck and the pillow and the other around her waist. She puts her arms around my neck.

"A little harder," she says.

I squeeze her against me; she's breathing very loud, very close to my ear.

"I feel all right now," she says.

"You're breathing very hard, Charlie the Blue Whale."

"So are you."

"That's because of my heart."

"With me it's because of my experience."

"I remember, you said you're very experienced."

"That isn't what I said. I said a tremendous experience. It isn't the same."

"I understand."

"You know," she says, "whales are very affectionate."

"I didn't know."

"When fishermen harpoon a whale and drag it behind the boat, do you know what happens?"

"No."

"The other whales follow the boat and rest their heads against the belly of the wounded whale and keep it company till it's breathed its last."

Eyes closed, I rub my nose against her cheek, close to her ear, where the skin is very soft and slightly perfumed.

"Are you all right too?" she asks.

"Yes"

"I'm not crushing your arm?"

"No. I'm fine."

"Now I can tell you why I breathe so hard," she says.

"I'm not asking you anything."

"No, but you hold me as well as Simon does. So now I can tell you: it has to do with a man."

"I know."

"One night when I was little he came into my room. He was one of my uncles. He tried to. . . ."

She stops for a moment, then says rather sadly, "You understand, I thought he was entitled to do it beause he was my uncle."

"I understand; don't say anything more."

"Now whenever I'm lying down I breathe hard."

"Don't say anything more."

"That's why Simon calls me the Blue Whale," she goes on, to complete her explanation.

I kiss her neck, my lips making no sound. Then she asks, "But what about you, why do you breathe hard too?"

"It's too complicated," I say. "It's as though I were coming to the end of a journey . . . as though I were about to discover something very old and. . . ."

"Unbearable?"

"Yes. And I wonder if there's a relationship between gentleness and death."

"Gentleness is you," she says.

I kiss her neck again, soundlessly, and she says, "That's hard, the relationships between things. Have to ask Simon; he's very gentle too."

"Where does he live, your friend Simon?" I ask.

"At Saint-Nicolas. It's very beautiful there."

"I've never been there."

"You know what I'd like?" she asks.

"No."

"What I'd really like is for our parents to be standing in the doorway, all four of them, looking at us; and your mother would be there, for instance, nudging your father with her elbow."

"Now it's as though they were there."

She says I talk like the calèche driver and her breath sends gusts of warmth onto my neck. I'm still holding her close, but I've put my arms around her back, under her capacious blue sweater. She wears nothing under it and beneath my fingers I can feel that her ribs and vertebrae are very close to the surface and under the palm of my hand her skin is soft everywhere. The sweater is really too big. She guesses and says:

"It floats around me and I feel as though I'm taking shelter under a blanket. Do you understand?"

"Of course."

"And you know what I'm thinking about?"

"No."

"I'm thinking about my aunt."

". . . ."

"My aunt the nun," she says. "She's leaving the convent forever next Saturday. She's spent her whole life not knowing you could be happy like that."

"Perhaps she's going to spend the rest of her life wanting to be 'happy like that.'"

"I hope so," she says. "It was nice of you to say that."

She is silent. She seems always to be thinking of something specific.

"There's a nun at Saint-Nicolas," she says.

"Of course," I say, rather concerned.

"She's very pretty. Her name's Soeur Claire."

"Eh?"

"Do you know her?"

"Not exactly, but. . . ."

"It's a beautiful name," she says. "Doesn't it make you think of a spring?"

"Of course."

"You always say 'Of course' and your voice is sad. Are you all right?"

"I'm fine."

It's true and not true. I feel fine because of the warmth given off by childhood like a roaring fire in the fireplace; I'm worried because of the confused business about gentleness and death and because of reflux and because of this Soeur Claire. I don't have the gift of understanding, just that of walking in the dark, guided by a hand that's young and. . . .

"She's like you," says Charlie, "except that she's always cheerful and you aren't."

"That's the way it is and I don't know why."

"But you haven't been extinguished inside," she says. "I know some people who are."

I feel a cold hand on my shoulder.

"Eh?"

I was closed up in a cage with a hundred exotic birds, in the Zoo at Orsainville, and Doctor Grondin was looking at me from the other side of the bars. I heard a muffled moan.

I awoke with a start.

"What's going on?" I asked.

"Nothing. It's only me."

Elise was sitting on the edge of the bed.

"What's that noise?" I asked, still hazy with sleep.

"The rain," she said. "Were you dreaming?"

"Is it raining hard?"

"Pouring."

It was spring, then. The first spring rain. It would turn the grass green in the Jardin des Gouverneurs, and on the talus near the Terrasse. The day before had been Easter; the weather was splendid, very mild, and the three of us had taken a long walk.

"What time is it?"

"Seven o'clock."

"I'm going to sleep some more," I said. "I'm cold."

I lay down again and pulled the covers over my head. Then I sat up suddenly.

"What are you doing with my raincoat?"

"Listen. . . ."

"I'll buy you one exactly like it, with wide lapels and shoulder straps and fastenings around the wrists. From J.M. Clément on rue Saint-Jean. It's the only place where you can find raincoats imported from England. Now I'm going back to sleep."

And once again I buried my head under the covers.

"Listen for a second."

"What?"

"I'm going away," Elise said gently.

"Today's a holiday. Easter Monday."

She persisted.

"Listen, Noël."

"Eh?"

Basically, I didn't mind at all being wakened up: it was early and I could sleep some more; it was pleasant just to think. Elise's voice, heard under the covers, was far away and rather melancholy. She said, "You don't understand."

"You aren't going out in this rain!"

I wondered whether my voice sounded different to her too.

"Take an umbrella then, and ask Bill to go with you," I said.

"You don't understand."

"This is the second time you've said that."

I was huddled with my knees to my chin, head bent, hands between my thighs; ever since the operation I'd slept curled up like a fetus. Cats are the best dreamers; in my childhood there were always cats; it was in the country; Jimmy would get up with the sun, walk on the beach, go and sit on the big rock. The tide was high and a wisp of fog would dissipate over the river.

"Are you asleep?"

She pulled down the covers.

"Are you asleep?" she repeated.

I opened my eyes.

"What are you doing?" I asked.

"You were sleeping," Elise said, patiently.

"I was on the rock."

"The rock?"

"You wouldn't understand, it's my story. I'll explain if you want."

She looked at her watch and said, "Some other time, if it's all right."

"Whatever you want. Why did you wake me up?"

"I have to talk to you," she said.

"You should let people dream. But you can talk to me now. I won't go back to sleep."

"No. Get up."

"Why?"

"Please, just get up and don't ask any questions."

"No. I'm comfortable here. Unless you tell me why."

"Listen," she said, "there's some things you just don't say to a man who's lying naked in a bed."

I shivered and that made me think of *The Old Man and the Sea*: the old fisherman, when he got up at dawn, used to tell himself he'd shiver himself warm. I didn't know shivering could make a person warm.

"Hand me a bathrobe then," I asked.

"No."

I was sitting up in bed, the covers over my legs, and I looked at her, rather astonished.

"You said no?"

"Listen," she said, "get dressed."

"Why do you start every sentence with 'listen'?"

She looked at me calmly, without replying. She took my clothes from the chair and put them at the foot of the bed. Without getting up I put on first my grey sweater, then my glasses, which were on the bedside table. The old wool felt good against my skin and warmed my heart.

"Sorry for being impatient. You can start your sentences however you want. I take back what I said."

I threw back the covers. Elise turned around very ostentatiously.

"Why did you turn your back?"

"Because you're putting on your trousers."

"First of all they aren't trousers, they're my jeans!"

In a single sustained movement, as in a slow motion film, I lifted my legs in the air, slipped on my jeans and then, pivoting on my behind, stood up by the bed as I buckled my leather belt. It had taken long training and usually Elise enjoyed admiring my exploit. I'd kept all sorts of old habits: I wondered whether everyone was like that, but I really didn't care if I found out or not. I still felt impatient.

I tapped Elise's shoulder.

"Mind if I'm barefoot?"

She looked at my feet and indicated that she had no objection.

"Will you speak to me now?" I asked.

"You can go in there," she said, pointing to the bathroom. She looked at her watch again.

"Why do you keep looking at the time?"

"I'm going to wait for you in the living room" she said.

"You could take off my raincoat, couldn't you?"

She shrugged and headed for the living room. I went into the bathroom. I urinated for a long time, then flushed the toilet.

I got on the scale and looked between my feet: one hundred and ten pounds. Four limbs and a waterway and I was as thin as a rail. The toilet stopped its roaring and once again I heard the rain: an army of Lilliputians was dancing on the roof. From time to time I could hear the sparrows chirping. I opened the window. It was just big enough for someone to pass through, and outside there was a small iron ladder that went up to the roof.

I washed my face and started to shave and two things were bothering me: the bottles and flasks that usually cluttered the toilet tank had disappeared and the whole house could probably hear the sound of my damn Remington. Libras often think of two things at once.

I put the razor back in its box. This rain would mean the end of spring skiing. I wasn't saying that for myself; I was thinking of Elise and Bill, who went to Lac Beauport every weekend. But perhaps it was still snowing in the Laurentians. The hockey player's wrist had completely healed. He'd soon be going back to Philadelphia for the playoffs. The Flyers had recalled him. They'd finished the season in second place. Obviously, they had two good goalies. What they lacked was a couple of good scorers. I'd have to talk to Bill about that so he could suggest it to his coach: trade one of their goalies for someone who could score.

I used to play a trick: you close your eyes and put your face a few inches from the mirror, then suddenly open your eyes; or, with your back turned, you walk backwards towards the mirror and then turn around abruptly: with luck, you'll see another face for two seconds. I saw Nana Mouskouri, or something like that. Maybe because of the glasses and the hair hanging down my neck. Or some other reason. And I'd seen Jimmy. I'd tried to see Bill; obviously you don't see what you want. I repeated the trick in different ways, but it didn't work.

What I had in my head when I came out of the bathroom was *High Noon*. The song from the movie. It's an old tune that makes you feel like whistling. If I owned a house I'd have bought an old jukebox. I'd have put it in the basement. I didn't feel like going into the living room. There aren't many objects I like as much as jukeboxes. Even sculptures. Obviously I'd make an exception for Rodin's *Cathedral*. I thought of these stupid things because they kept my mind off others. One thing I didn't like about jukeboxes was the hit parade: most of the songs were worthless, even if some of them were very pretty. I'd have filled my jukebox with the songs of Léo Ferré. I didn't feel like going into the living room because I was beginning to understand. Léo Ferré wrote the most beautiful ones. Or rather I was beginning to admit that I understand. The one I liked most of all was "La mélancolie." The sound of the rain on the roof gave me a heavy heart. Léo Ferré said of melancholy: "It's an impoverished kind of despair." I opened the door to the living room.

Suitcases. Five of them. Four that I recognized and another. They were near the vestibule. Elise and the hockey player were sitting at either end of the sofa.

I gestured discreetly to Elise to let her know I understood everything and I saw the corners of her mouth droop imperceptibly. You had to be very attentive to realize that it was a smile. I felt empty inside, except for the wounded bird, and there was a great deal of room for what was happening on the outside. A Gitane butt was smoking in the ashtray. The rain was drumming against the window; the wind was from the northeast then, spring hadn't really arrived, there was still a risk of snow. You think something's over and it isn't true.

I sat in the armchair, facing them, and tucked my bare feet under me. I didn't really feel sad; only a little melancholy, because of the suitcases and the rain and the fear, still a vague one, of having to live all by myself. The silence was growing heavier, so I asked:

"Are you taking the bus from the Central Station?"

They began to look at me in a peculiar way. Eventually I understood: it was my voice. In the morning the first time I try to talk to several people my voice is foggy, and all you can hear is a sort of growl. I cleared my throat carefully and repeated the question.

"We're taking the train," said Elise.

She seemed relieved and Bill stopped staring at his shoes. She turned to him.

"It's at half past eight, isn't it?"

He nodded several times.

"Have you had breakfast?" Elise asked me.

"No."

It was good for her to talk. She knew very well that I hadn't had time to eat.

"Shall I make you something?"

"Maybe some orange juice, if you don't mind?"

"Of course not."

She hadn't looked at her watch or the cuckoo clock. She got up and I closed my eyes to imagine what she was doing: she'd open the fridge, take out two oranges, close the door, take the blue plastic juice squeezer from the cupboard.

"WITH SUGAR?" she shouted.

"PLEASE!"

For a few seconds I felt submerged by a wave of sorrow, because of a silly question about sugar, then the wave passed and calm returned. Elise came out of the kitchen and handed me the glass.

"Thanks very much," I said.

It was full. She'd used three oranges. The sugar was beginning to form a deposit in the bottom; it never dissolves completely in real orange juice. I said very softly to Elise, "Maybe he'd like a coffee or a beer."

She looked at Bill; he'd heard and was beginning to smile.

"Perhaps a coffee," he said.

"All right."

She went back to the kitchen. I heard the sound of dishes and in a few minutes she'd come back with a steaming cup of coffee.

"Thanks a lot," he said.

"Careful you don't burn yourself."

"Thanks."

His eyes were like those of a dog that's just been given a bone. He sipped his coffee and grimaced.

"Is it hot?" I asked.

"Very," he admitted sheepishly.

"You're drinking too fast."

"I don't feel well this morning."

"He has indigestion," Elise explained.

"How come?"

"I don't know what's wrong," he said. "It's like before a hockey game. I often get indigestion just before I jump on the ice."

"Nerves," I said. "Several good players have the same thing."

"Oh yes?"

"Glen Hall, for instance. It often happens to him."

"It helps to hear you say that. I didn't dare talk about it."

"There's Ralph Backstrom too, but I can't swear to that. Anyway, he's the most nervous player on the Canadiens."

"Is that so?"

"And as soon as he jumps on the ice everything's normal again."

"Same with me."

He took another sip, cautiously, and said, "You know more about hockey than I do."

"Just theoretical knowledge," I said, with the feeling that the sentence was out of place.

Elise looked at me with a sort of warmth in her eyes and she wasn't thinking at all of looking at the time.

"You've never played?" Bill asked.

"Yes," I said, "in school."

"What did you play?"

"Right defence."

"You weren't a little . . . on the light side to play defence?"

"The first time I tried to check a player into the boards I had a shoulder separation for months."

"Shoulder separation?"

"Something like that."

When you write you always feel as though you're outside everything; to find out what's going on you tell yourself stories. When I was a child the maid was called Marie-Ange; she was as gentle as her name and to put us to sleep she used to tell us extraordinary stories, very old ones, like the many adventures of Little John and the Giants.

"What are you thinking about?" asked the hockey player.

"Nothing important," I said.

"Excuse me."

He looked at Elise and for several seconds they seemed to be speaking silently. I left them alone for a while, then asked, "Are you going to play in the playoffs?"

"It isn't definite. They recalled me in case anybody gets hurt."

"Are there any injuries?"

"Not yet."

Suddenly I didn't feel like talking about hockey any more. I drank the rest of the orange juice, holding the glass so the sugar would slip onto my tongue. At that very moment I was thinking about Vincent Van Gogh's brother, and I thought that I too might have had a brother Theo, or someone like that. Elise and I had never really talked to one another. Suddenly I heard myself telling her, "You said you'd wait for me."

"Eh?" she asked.

I began again, more softly:

"Didn't you say you'd be waiting for me at the end of the journey?"

She seemed to be hunting in her memory. Once again I wished I were in her shoes, so I'd know how she saw things.

"What journey?" Bill asked.

She kept trying to remember. I said nothing. No one answered him.

"Excuse me," he said.

"It doesn't matter," I said, to his confusion.

"I remember," said Elise. "The journey to the north pole."

"The self's inner pole," I said.

"Ah yes! That beautiful expression of André Malraux."

I unfolded my legs and placed my bare feet on the rug.

"It was André Breton," I said, rather impatiently.

"That's right. I'm sorry, you know I don't know a thing about literature."

That hurt, what she just said. For her birthday I'd given her *l'Arrache-coeur*. And I'd bought *L'Attrape-coeur* to read at the same time. We'd read slowly and taken time to talk about our books. Then we traded and in the end we felt as though Boris Vian and Holden Caulfield knew one another.

I waited for a minute, then said, "We'd said that I'd go part of the way by myself and that you'd be waiting for me at the end of the journey."

"I remember," she said. "Now I remember very clearly."

Her face lit up.

"I'm very glad you remember," I said.

"I'm very glad too."

Bill smiled, not understanding. The drumming of the rain on the roof had abated. I wondered once again if it was snowing in the Laurentians. Elise looked at her watch and stood up. The hockey player got up too and stood as he drank the rest of his coffee. I went to sit on the sill of the half-moon shaped window.

Elise moved close to me. She looked outside.

"Still raining?" she asked.

"Yes, still raining."

Then she went to telephone and called a taxi.

One December twenty-fifth in the morning, when I was small, I found my cat lying stiff under the Christmas tree and it was dead. It was a black cat, a small cat, but it seemed bigger because it was stiff. It just fit into the shoebox where we'd put it to be buried. I hunted through my memories. Perhaps behind the house, where there was an abandoned garden. I couldn't recall exactly where we'd buried it. Christmas is my birthday and that's why my name is Noël.

The Blue Whale is breathing heavily against my neck and I'm beginning to understand certain things: birds, Jimmy's story, Doctor Grondin's questions. But the time has started to pass more quickly.

Charlie slips one knee between my legs, lifts her head a little and, half bending over me, begins by moistening all around my lips with her tongue; she kisses me slowly, little pecks, the way you might taste something. I feel well and warm all over and inside too; I'd like time to stand still.

"You can kiss me too," she says finally.

I kiss her in turn, on the eyes. I hold her very tight against me and I'm breathing as hard as she is. She's fragile, trembling all over, it's moving to find her there and almost unbearable to have her so close.

The notion of reflux brushes against me for a second, then it goes away by itself and I begin to feel well and warm inside again. Charlie murmurs, "I feel good with you. Do you?"

"I feel fine."

"Near our house there was a swing under a big willow tree. The cords were tied around the first branch and it bent right down to the ground. Can you see it?"

"Yes, I can."

"And can I tell you something?"

"Yes."

"In a while we'll have to leave for Saint-Nicolas."

"I know," I said rather sadly.

"Because of Simon and everything you're looking for."

"I've known ever since you talked about Soeur Claire."

"I won't always be there, you understand."

"I understand."

"And you'll have to go to the very end," she adds.

"Of course," I say, thinking of the song that goes "There's so little time to go to the end of myself." The words are by Aragon and Léo Ferré sings them from his heart.

"There's no great hurry," Charlie says.

"I want to stay a little longer."

Under Charlie's sweater I bring my hands up to her chest, into the little hollow.

"For the warmth," I say.

"Of course," she agrees, pressing her forehead against mine.

"You're very small here."

"I've always wanted to be a boy."

"Do you think sex and all those things are important?" I ask.

"I don't think so."

"Why?"

"Life's too large," she says.

She makes a broad gesture, then puts her arms around my neck and again suddenly squeezes me hard enough to choke me.

"You know what?" she asks.

"What?"

"At this very moment I'm in love with you."

I say nothing. It hits me and keeps me from speaking.

"But still," she says, "I don't have a heart."

"No?"

"I gave it to someone."

"Eh?"

"I gave it to Simon."

She moves her head away, looks at me.

"Something wrong?"

"It's nothing," I say. "I was thinking about something but it's gone now."

"What about you?" she asks.

"What?"

"Are you in love with me?"

"I'm not sure but I think so."

"But only right now?" she insists.

"Of course, don't worry."

"That way we remain free."

"Of course."

"And what would you do with a Blue Whale like me?"

"That's true," I say, rather sadly.

"Why are you so gentle?" she asks, closing her black eyes.

"Don't say that. Don't."

I close my eyes too.

We slept for a few moments, her arms knotted around my neck, my hands nestling in the hollow of her chest.

Before she fell asleep she talked about a path that went down the cliff between the village of Saint-Nicolas and the beach, and I felt that it fit into my story well. Then I understood that gentleness was the path that leads to death and also that death was like a river going to the sea. Words most certainly have a soul. My stomach was upset and I suddenly felt like vomiting. I wondered if the reflux had begun, very gently, without my knowledge. I don't think things over much, hardly ever; words make their way through me, finally emerging into the light. Another thing that I understood: the greatest gentleness is death. And then we went to sleep together, as I said.

Then I began to get excited.

I mean: she was a woman, I was excited, she was in my arms, the warmth was overflowing, we were rolling from side to side, breathing like two blue whales.

Suddenly Charlie straightens up, sitting on her heels.

"We woke up the cat," she says.

"Eh?"

"We woke up the cat."

"But . . ."

"What difference does it make? It's as if there was a cat. You should never get worked up and wake up the cat."

"Of course."

She bends over and buries her nose in my old grey sweater.

"It smells like under the bark of a tree."

She straightens up again and says, "There's a cat in Saint-Nicolas. Simon calls it Chanoine."

"We can go there now, if you want," I say, sitting close to her on the sofa.

"If you find it in your heart to leave," she said.

"If you find it in your heart."

"One cigarette and we're off. Just one for the two of us."

The cigarette is slightly crushed; I light it, take a long drag and give it to her.

"It's a little black cat," she says.

"Of course. And the house is like a playhouse?"

"Mustn't talk about it now."

"And it's hidden behind a row of trees at the back of the garden?"

"You'll see."

"And on the sandbar there are cages for catching eels? And a big rock that juts out past the shore?"

"Your voice sounds funny," she says.

"And that's where Soeur Claire comes to sit in her white outfit that comes down to the ground?"

She says nothing more. I think of an old American film, *River of No Return*, with Marilyn Monroe. I see the man, the woman and the child on a big raft, carried along by the river's swift current. When you journey within yourself, the currents draw you inevitably back to your childhood and there, among the old landscapes of your memory, you run a great risk of finding once again memories that will cause you to lose the way back. It's hard to say why, so I'm silent and Charlie, as though out of respect, doesn't speak either.

I opened the door and looked around inside Le Buade: my place was empty. I opened the second door into the restaurant. I was walking rapidly down the right side when the manager burst out from behind the counter and blocked my way.

"Monsieur?" he began.

Arms folded, he held a stack of menus against his chest. I followed his disapproving look, which was taking in my moccasins, my jeans, my old sweater and my long hair.

"Monsieur?" he repeated curtly. "This way."

He led me into the space between the tables on the left and stopped at a small table for one person, on which he placed a menu.

"Voilà, Monsieur," he said.

Staring at the floor, I muttered that I was waiting for someone.

"Ah! Monsieur is expecting someone?"

He emphasized the first syllable when he said "Monsieur." He was beginning not to like me very much. I turned abruptly and went towards the right, to my usual table.

Aside from Le Buade I also knew Wong's, which was less expensive; the restaurant Aux Délices, a little further away; the Grenada, at the bottom of the Côte de la Fabrique, which was almost always deserted; La Cloche d'Or, on rue Saint-Jean, which was filled with a peculiar odour of rotten wood; old George's Grill, on rue Saint-Louis, ugly since the beginning of time; and the Alouette snackbar, for people in a hurry. I preferred Le Buade because of old Marie.

She came towards me.

"Bonjour, Monsieur," she said.

"Bonjour, Mademoiselle."

We called each other "vous" and when I called her "Mademoiselle" it always made me think of a dragonfly; a very old story.

Old Marie was short, with red hair, and freckles all over her face. She said she was the same age as Old Quebec.

"Excuse me, Mademoiselle," I said. "I'm waiting for someone."

"Of course, Monsieur," said Marie in her strange voice that was almost as rusty as her face.

She gave me a menu and put another on the placemat on the other side of the table. She took a pad from her apron pocket, then a yellow pencil and put the point in her mouth. I pretended to look at the *menu du jour* and in a moment I said, "I believe I'll wait."

"If you wish."

"It shouldn't be long."

"Would you like an apéritif?"

"No, thank you."

"I can keep you company."

"You're very kind. Better not though, because of the manager."

"That's true. I'll be back in a while then."

We had to say the same words every time, without a mistake, and if each of us played his part properly then luck was with us for a while. It was the kind of ceremony you find in families.

Marie never smiled; she simply hadn't got in the habit: everything took place in her eyes, if you went to the trouble to look. But she had another habit: she would write things on the placemats. One evening when luck didn't come, she bent over the small white placemat where Elise sat, wrote something and went into the kitchen. I read:

It has no sex, it has no age
Sometimes it looks like a cat
It's the reverse of contempt
It's name is tenderness.

Old Marie was an accomplice of all the habitués of Le Buade, those who arrived at a set time and always sat in the same places. But there were the Americans too. It wasn't quite summer but they were already invading Old Quebec. When they turned up you began feeling lonely and Marie served them in silence.

She returned.

She waited, pad and pencil in hand, her eyes questioning me.

"I'm not ready," I said.

"She isn't coming?"

"I haven't succeeded. She's late."

"It's because of the Americans," Marie said. "With the Americans you feel lonely."

"That's exactly what I was telling myself, but I think there's another reason."

"You think so?"

"Yes. Eventually it becomes more difficult. I'm beginning to wonder if I have enough respect for time."

"That's a good question," Marie admitted. "Have to think it over."

She put the tip of her pencil in her mouth.

"I'm going to try again," I said.

"Take as much time as you want."

"The manager isn't getting impatient?"

"No. I'll take care of him."

"You're really kind."

Her eyes began to gleam.

"Do you want me to write something to help you?"

"I'll try by myself for another little while."

"Close your eyes," she said.

She moved away. I closed my eyes to forget the Americans. I saw the walls of Old Quebec. On rue des Remparts, at the level of the former Grand Séminaire, someone had written on the grey wall—once in red and once in black—REVOLUTION. I like it when people write on walls, on houses, on sidewalks, in the street, everywhere. In any case, I like words. What escaped me was the relationships between things. Léo Ferré said that poets wrote out their rebellion with the claws of birds; there was a new thing living in my chest, a thing Saint-Denys Garneau had described as a bird; Goethe said that ideas have doves' claws. Although I couldn't understand, I guessed that the poets sometimes leave us behind them, on an ill-lit road like the one I'd borrowed to write my story, a road that led infallibly to rejection and. . . .

I no longer heard the Americans.

"Is it better now?" asked the hoarse voice of Old Marie.

"Yes," I said, bravely.

"Luck has arrived?"

"I think so."

I opened my eyes.

"I think it's all right now," I said.

"I'm going to help you," said Marie.

"Of course."

I could do nothing without old Marie; I'd have told her that to warm her heart, some gloomy day.

She asked, "What would you like?"

"Just a second," I said.

It was the critical moment.

"The same thing as Elise?" Marie prompted me.

"Yes."

"Two pea soups, then," she said, writing on her pad, "and two Spanish omelets."

And she added immediately:

"And french fries for Madame, of course. And you?"

"Mashed potatoes," I said, almost joyously.

"Mashed potatoes for Monsieur," Marie wrote down, her face impassive and her eyes gleaming.

She picked up the two menus.

"Thank you," she said.

She always said thank you as though you'd just done her a favour, and it was pleasant to hear her strange voice that scratched at her throat. She went back to the kitchen.

Elise took off her shoes; in the summer she did that everywhere. Some people weren't too fond of seeing her do so, especially in restaurants, but I let her do as she wished. To tell you the truth I'd probably put my moccasin on one of the table legs and not on Elise's foot, and I'd apologized just for something to say.

"What's wrong?" asked Marie, who had come back and was holding, like a juggler, the two bowls of soup, the basket of bread and crackers and two saucers containing pats of butter.

"I stepped on her foot," I said.

"She doesn't seem angry."

"She's very gentle."

"You're very gentle too. That's what I like most about you."

"You remind me of a song."

She put the plates on the table, beginning with Elise. She placed the various things so precisely that we never had to rearrange them. Some people, though, moved things just to take possession of them; I could understand that. Elise and I never touched things and that's what Marie liked most, even though she didn't say so.

"A song by Guy Béart," I said.

And I hummed the tune. Marie helped me with the last words, which were more difficult. One day she'd written on the placemat that musicians are the most important people in the world. At the end of the song she said, looking at Elise, "He always has a song in his head."

"I'm not really gentle," I said. "It's just my heart."

They both looked at me, seeming not to understand.

"I mean it doesn't depend on me," I said, attempting to be a little more clear.

"It's difficult to live and be happy," said Marie rather brusquely.

"I'm happy because I write and because Elise is with me," I said, looking straight ahead.

"I'm very fond of you," said Marie.

She began again: "I'm very fond of both of you. Now your pea soup's going to get cold and the Americans are trying to get my attention. See you later."

I began to eat, slowly and without a sound; at the first moment of inattention, at the slightest abrupt gesture, luck might very well take leave of me. I buttered some soda biscuits for Elise. And at the same time I talked. She said nothing. Some days, all she did was listen and old Marie, who spoke very softly to her, was the only one who could elicit a few words from her. I didn't mind; I kept on talking. I said, "It's for you that I write."

I had enough to go on talking for a good while. When you write you seem completely selfish, but basically you write for someone else. You can even write for someone you don't know. It's hard to explain but I really tried.

Old Marie came and replaced the soup with the Spanish omelet. She put the plate with the french fries in front of Elise, the one with mashed potatoes in front of me, without making the slightest sound.

I'd come to the end of my explanation. Not the very end, as a matter of fact, but as far as I was able to go. Just looking at Elise, examining her even, you couldn't tell what she thought about it. I still wanted to be in her shoes for a few moments, just to know. I let her consider things for a few minutes, then, attacking the omelet, I asked, "You know what?"

And without giving her time to reply I went on:

"When I'm asleep I have the feeling that all my parts are together. And when I wake up all alone in my bed that feeling persists, but gradually it's as though the parts were separating."

She didn't seem to be following me, so I tried to explain some more. The explanation was a long one and besides that, I took my time so she wouldn't lose the thread. When she lost the thread she'd stop looking at me, with her green eyes and her strange hair that was cut short like a boy's. Marie came back when the omelet was finished, and suggested dessert: we both ordered *pudding au chomeur* and coffee. And when Marie brought our orders I was far from having finished my explanation, Elise was following the thread very well, it was as though there were no more Americans in Old Quebec and I felt warm inside and even beneath the old scar.

Old Marie brought the two bills, slipped the first one under my saucer and the second under Elise's, saying thank you each time.

"Something wrong?" she asked.

"No."

"You aren't holding out?"

"I felt weak all of a sudden. I was speaking just fine and then I couldn't find the words. I mean, I couldn't find the exact words at all."

"That can happen to anyone," said Marie.

"Of course."

"It's my fault."

"No it isn't."

"I shouldn't have left you."

"Don't say that. I just had a moment of weakness."

She asked, "Did you enjoy your lunch?"

"Very much," I said. "It was good for both of us."

"Madame didn't eat very much."

"She doesn't have a big appetite. Right?"

Elise took forever to reply. Finally, she nodded; a tiny sign, imperceptible, but I was glad she'd answered.

Marie's eyes began to shine.

"Another coffee? It's on the house."

"Thanks, you're too kind. Only. . . ."

"Only what?" she asked.

"Stay with us for a few moments, please."

"Of course."

What would happen when we left Le Buade: Elise would get lost in the crowd. You walk along the sidewalk, watching her out of the corner of your eye. You stop for a second in front of the windows of the Librairie Garneau to take a look at the illustrated book about Jean-Paul Lemieux and then, seized by a foreboding, you suddenly turn around: Elise has gone. You run down rue Buade, through the artists on rue du Trésor, onto Place d'Armes with its fountain and calèches and up to the Terrasse, looking on all sides. You can climb up the long flight of stairs, cover the Promenade des Gouverneurs as far as the Citadelle which is located at the beginning of the Plains of Abraham, if you find it in your heart. You could go on to the end of the world.

"What are you thinking about?" asked old Marie in that hoarse voice that always surprises you.

"The end of the world," I said in all honesty.

"Is your book coming along?" she continued.

"Yes. I'm not writing but I'm working a lot. It's coming along."

"It's the work that counts."

"I don't like work," I said. "But it helps me make some inner progress."

"Of course."

She often said "of course." I've always liked people who said it.

She said, hesitantly, "If you need. . . ."

"I still have some," I said. "Enough to last till the end of summer."

"And after that?"

"You know the song, 'Il n'y a plus d'après'?"

"Of course. I especially like it when Yves Montand sings it."

"You're an old romantic," I said, "and you warm my heart."

"I'm an old woman and an old fool," she said.

"That's true."

I began to laugh very softly. She wasn't laughing but her eyes were wrinkled up.

"I like old women very much," I said. "It's because of their human warmth and gentleness."

"You're really a maniac about human warmth, and about gentleness too," she said.

"That's true."

"But I'm still fond of you."

She put out her hand and began to stroke the hair on the back of my neck.

"I like your hair very much."

"Because it's long?"

"Long and soft. I hope Elise isn't jealous."

"She isn't. Not enough."

Elise said nothing.

"I like to feel it move against my neck when I turn my head," I said.

"I understand," she said, still playing with my hair.

"At the same time, it worries me a little."

"What you are in the very depths of yourself is more solid than your emotions and ideas."

"Thank you," I said.

She looked at Elise, then turned her wrinkled face towards me. Her eyes had the same expression as Doctor Grondin's spaniel's eyes.

"I'm going to help you hold out," she said finally.

There was a silence, then she added, "Really, don't you want another coffee?"

"No thanks. I think Elise would like to go now."

She glanced at Elise and removed her hand.

"As you wish."

"Are you coming to our place this evening?"

"I work tonight, but perhaps. . . ."

She hesitated.

"Evenings are difficult," I said.

"I understand."

"It's harder to hold out when it's dark."

"Of course."

She considered for a moment, then said, "Go and see a movie. I'll come to your place afterwards."

"Which film?"

"Go to the Empire," she said. *"Les Oiseaux vont mourir au Pérou.* If Elise agrees, of course."

Elise was smiling mysteriously.

I'd never explained to old Marie how Elise got lost in the crowd when we left Le Buade; there's no need to make people unhappy.

"That might be all right," I said so as not to complicate things. "But why the Empire?"

"Because of the birds, obviously."

"You're thinking of the Saint-Denys Garneau poem too?"

"Of course."

"I'm beginning to understand then."

She didn't say so, but she seemed to be thinking that it wasn't a minute too soon.

"Everything all right now?" she asked.

"Yes. We're going to leave."

"Do you want me to write something on the placemat?"

"No, thanks very much. We're leaving."

"Good luck. I'll see you this evening."

"See you later."

I waited for Elise to get up, then I left my tip. She walked ahead of me. At the cash register I put our bills on the counter. The manager examined them as though they contained some coded message and looked me right in the eye as he gave me my change. I held the first door open for Elise, then opened the outer one, which gave onto the street. An old American woman came in and said "Thank you" in English.

On the sidewalk I let Elise choose; she took the left and I began to walk beside her, matching my steps to hers. Her right hand was resting inside my elbow. People turned around as we passed them. The sky was slate grey and gentle to look at. We could hear pigeons cooing somewhere on the roof of the old Basilica. In front of the second window at Garneau's I glanced at the Jean-Paul Lemieux book. I couldn't help myself.

Finally, Charlie hands me the cigarette.

"I'm ready for Saint-Nicholas," she says. "Take the last puff."

"Just a minute."

I take the cigarette, sit at my work table near the window and open my writing pad.

"What are you doing?"

"I'm going to leave a note for old Marie."

"Is she an old friend?"

"A very old friend."

"Write gently, then, and take as much time as you want."

"You can watch the boats if you find it in your heart to do that."

"I'd rather watch you write, if I may."

"Of course."

She sits across from me, on the other side of the table between the Petit Robert and the etymological dictionary. She switches on the extensible lamp, which always makes me think of a long arm with bones and muscles and a luminous hand at the end, then folds her arms on the table and rests her chin on her wrists.

"I can read upside down," she says, "but I don't want to see. I just want to watch you write."

"Of course."

"But write gently if she's a very old friend," she says again.

At the top of the page I write: "My dear Marie, my dear old comrade."

I contemplate it for a moment, then I go on.

"Before I leave I'll switch on the lamp; you won't feel so lonely when you come. Thank you for making me understand the importance of birds; I'd like to say it aloud but I don't have time now. Everything's started to go very quickly, the reflux has begun, but there are still so many things to do. When you see Elise again, tell her my journey is nearly over and that she can still wait for me at the end.

"If you open the drawer you'll find the manuscript of an unfinished story. It would warm my heart to think that you had read it. I haven't put a title on it but it's called 'The Heavy Drinker of Nestlé's Quik.' Burn it afterwards so it won't fall into anyone else's hands.

"I'd like you to look after my painting; it will be safe with you. Also the big picture of Hemingway. And the Léo Ferré records too; you can leave the others if you wish. I'll have to ask you to take all the books; there's a lot, but I'm trying to be honest with myself. Soon I'm going to meet someone called Simon. He could help you; he has everything you'll need for carrying them and I'll talk to him about it."

Charlie says nothing more, so I go on.

"Marie, dear heart, everything's started to go so quickly, as I was telling you, and my soul is not at peace. It's hard to explain; certain things seem completely unimportant but yet . . . I know I'm going to complicate your life. I feel morally obliged to do so, to finish the rest of the journey in peace and reach the inner pole.

"Do you remember the time I went to Tewksbury? I parked the Tiger on the side of the road that overlooks the village; I looked at the church standing all alone on its raised platform and down at the very bottom, in the hollow of the valley, at a row of houses along the river that seemed so small, and then the beautiful wooded mountains, the oldest ones in the world, the Laurentians, enclosing it all like a sort of jewel case. It takes your breath away when you look at it from above, from a certain spot on the road, just before the church. I looked, but I feel guilty because I didn't really contemplate it; it's as though I hadn't shown someone the proper respect. Do you understand? And then on the way back I felt as though the church seemed to be keeping a vigil; I thought of the importance of the one who keeps a vigil and of what Saint-Exupéry said about it in his last book. Since then, carelessly, I've left all that to chance, which is a place where things get lost. Do you understand?

"Something similar happened to me in Port-au-Persil, a village on the North Shore not very far from Saint-Siméon. To be absolutely honest, my conscience isn't at peace either when I remember Baie-Trinité, much further north; but I can hold out if that's too far away for you, because I spent a good night there in a tent, right on the sand beside the river, and I got up very early to see the sun rise and awaken the village.

"Marie, dear heart, I've never been able to find a song Yves Montand used to sing very long ago, that was called, if I remember correctly, 'Le Chant des partisans.' It's very old, maybe Russian originally, I'm not sure. It's extremely important; it's the very first song I ever heard on a record, at my grandfather's house when I was very small. It talks about crows and grenades; it's a revolutionary song and I remember a few words:

On the main roads tomorrow black blood will dry in the sun. It's impressive, very solemn and beautiful, and sometimes the music would stop and all you could hear was the irregular pounding of footsteps along the road. Raoul Roy could give you a hand. On an old Yves Montand record, as a matter of fact, he discovered another old military song, a very beautiful one too, that's called 'La Butte rouge.' He lives at Saint-Fabien-sur-Mer but he comes to Quebec every now and then; even if he can't help you, you'll see: it will warm your heart, all the songs he knows. You could ask him to sing 'Freddie' too and he'll sing it if he's at peace with himself.

"When you have time—and only when you have time—listen to Léo Ferré's song 'Mon Camarade' for me; it's the record in the bright red jacket; it's the most gentle of his songs and I haven't taken the time to listen to it often enough. And another one too, if you don't mind, an old Louis Armstrong song: 'A Kiss to Build A Dream On.' I feel guilty for the same reasons."

Charlie doesn't move at all and I go on writing my letter.

"Marie, dear heart, there are some questions that you leave behind unanswered. You know how much old Hemingway liked to hunt, yet he became very attached to a white owl that he'd wounded; he took care of it, caught a mouse for it every morning, and he was unhappy when the time came to set it free. How could someone like hunting and do a thing like that? It happened in 1958, at Ketchum in Idaho, a small village in the mountains near the Sun Valley ski station. Do you understand? I haven't had time to understand it. Time is the most precious thing we have and mine is drifting away.

"Now I have to talk to you about F. Scott Fitzgerald and his novel *The Great Gatsby.* I fell in love with this book from the very beginning, when I was studying literature, and then like a coward I gave it up. Afterwards, when I read Hemingway's Paris memoirs, I learned how difficult it must have been for Fitzgerald to write, because of Zelda who was nearly crazy and very jealous of his work. But I still didn't take the trouble to reread the novel and I feel terribly guilty about my cowardliness. Hemingway said you had to be good to Fitzgerald, and understanding.

"I should have reread Bachelard from start to finish too, especially for what he says about fire and candles, and Henri Bosco at the same time. And Rilke's *Letters to a Young Poet*, for their gravity. And all of Van Gogh's correspondence with his brother Theo, for its human warmth.

"Perhaps I sound unhappy, but it isn't true. I only feel guilty. And I know I'm asking you for far too much. At the same time, I'd like you to start to forget me, beginning now, very gently, a little more each day; I mean, for you to begin to transform me in your memory.

"Marie dear heart, I would have liked to have a long conversation with you about cats, because they're affectionate and never servile and because true freedom must be something like them. It's too late for me, but you could talk about it with a very young girl who's often to be found around Place d'Armes; she goes barefoot, she looks like a boy and when it pleases her she answers to the name Charlie the Blue Whale. I don't know if I'm right: I've never trusted anyone who doesn't like cats. And we could have talked about Old Quebec, tried to find out why we feel safe there, whether it comes from the old walls, the old houses, or the soul.

"We haven't talked enough. We could have talked as we strolled on the new ferry, the 'Radisson,' between Quebec and Lévis. Or on the 'Duc d'Orléans,' near the Quebec bridge or on the Sainte-Pétronille side. I've never taken the time in the summer for those boatrides on the St Lawrence.

"Something else I forgot to tell you about Bachelard was that he dreamed about words when he was a child, that later on he continued to dream about them and then toward the end he got in the habit of looking for a masculine word to correspond with a feminine one and the reverse, so the words wouldn't feel lonely.

"You won't believe me, but I've never gone into the English bookstore on rue Saint-Jean to see if I could find Salinger in the original, and even worse, for ten years I haven't set foot in the Bouquiniste's little shop on rue Desjardins.

"I'm concerned about the paintings; I mean paintings in general. At exhibitions, aren't they too close together? What if they were shown one at a time? I know that's a ridiculous thing to say and I can't really explain myself; the important thing, perhaps, is to be able to contemplate each one without being distracted. And it's sad to think that we didn't take the time to talk about Vlaminck. I'm hurrying now and I must say something else about a painter from Roberval; when there's no snow he can't work. He goes and sits at the foot of a tree and says that his soul breathes better there.

"I'll close with a message for you to give Doctor Grondin. He often comes to the Institut de Cardiologie. Just tell him that it's intuition that will lead to truth, because intuition comes from the anima, but don't say it so pretentiously. And tell him too that I'm completely responsible for myself now. That's all. But you can also tell him, if you want, that he has beautiful hands. I didn't have time.

"That's it; I'll leave the lamp on for you as I said. The worst thing is to feel that you're alone. I don't because I'm with Charlie the Blue Whale for what remains to be done.

"Affectionately,

"Noël."

"We hadn't heard from you," Doctor Grondin said. "I was passing by so I stopped."

"Come in, I'll put on the lights."

I switched on the lamp by the door and stepped aside to let him pass.

"You live very high!" he said.

"Close to Heaven."

"Because you're disheartened?"

I could think of nothing to say in reply. He began to laugh very softly, then stuck his hands in his pockets and looked around.

"You don't even seem out of breath," I said.

"I'm in good condition. What about you?"

"Would you like to sit down?"

He continued to walk around the room.

"You were sitting in the dark?"

"I was watching the boats."

"It's a magnificent view," he said, stopping at the half-moon shaped window.

"You can see the bridge to the Ile d'Orléans," I said.

"So you can."

"In the daytime you can see the mountains of Charlevoix. That's where I'd have liked to live."

"Me too," he said.

"And when it's clear you feel as though you can see as far as the

North Shore. Do you know Vigneault's song 'Le Nord du nord'?"

"Of course."

And he began to walk again, then stopped in front of the painting. It was a tree shrouded in fog. The painting was unframed.

"I like that very much," he said.

"So do I," I said. "But you aren't seeing it properly."

"Why not?"

"It's a wash drawing. You should look at it in daylight."

"What happens?"

"Take a good look at the fog around the tree."

He came closer.

"There are spots of colour," he said. "Red and yellow."

"In daylight it's as though the sun were shining through the fog."

"I understand."

"That's why the tree trunk stands out so clearly."

"It's a birch, isn't it?" he asked.

"Yes."

With his fingertip he absentmindedly stroked the old scar on his neck, on the right side.

"I'm sure it was done by a woman and that she was having trouble with a man. I've read quite a lot about trees. I'd even say it was a young girl, a very young girl. Am I mistaken?"

"I don't know," I said.

He scrutinized the bottom of the painting.

"I can't make out the signature," he said. "What's her name?"

"I don't remember. Don't you want to sit down? I'll bring you something to drink."

He stepped back two paces and said very softly, as though to himself, "I'm sure she was having trouble with a man. You were saying?"

"Won't you sit down for a few minutes?"

"Gladly."

He sat on the sofa and crossed his feet on a stool.

"What would you like? Coffee? Cognac?"

"Cognac."

"I'll make myself a coffee at the same time."

"Not allowed. At this hour of the night nothing stronger than hot chocolate."

"You remind me of my father," I said.

"Thank you," he replied in the same tone.

I poured him a cognac, then went to the kitchen; it was hard not to think of "The Heavy Drinker of Nestlé's Quik." I came back to the living room and sat on the windowsill so I could see the lights of the summer ferry glide across the water.

"Is Elise in bed already?" Doctor Grondin asked.

"No."

"She isn't here?"

"No."

I took a long swallow of hot chocolate.

"Has she gone out?" he asked.

"Not exactly."

You could hear, very softly, a whistle, then immediately afterwards a muffled sound. You had to listen carefully because of the murmuring of people on the Terrasse. I knew without looking that the Quebec ferry had given the order to raise the bridge, and that it had struck against the hull of the boat; they were casting off.

"So she's gone, has she?" he asked.

"That's right."

"I'm sorry. How did it happen?"

"Two a.m. A black Cadillac. Three masked men armed with machine guns. The car disappeared at full speed."

The surgeon sipped his drink; he let the cognac warm in his mouth before swallowing it.

"And they're asking for a ransom," he added.

"She went away with the hockey player," I said.

He reflected for a moment, then asked, "How did you react?"

"Are you thinking about rejection?"

"Answer," he said gently.

"Didn't react at all. Does that reassure you?"

He lit a cigarette. I looked at the other boat that was slowly approaching Quebec.

"Excuse me," he said. "I'm just trying to understand you. You're an intelligent man, you'll come out of it."

"Intelligence, you know. . . ."

"The sky's most beautiful after the sun has set, have you ever noticed?"

He was silent for a long moment. Finally I ventured to say to him, "During the winter several of your patients . . ."

His glass stopped halfway to his lips.

". . . haven't held out," I said.

"That's true."

"Life isn't easy for you either."

He sipped his drink.

"It's as though part of me died every time."

"It's hard to accept?"

"Yes, but there are all the others, the people who die every day because I don't have a new heart for them. That's even harder."

"Listen," I said, "are you sometimes tempted to take yourself for God?"

"Yes."

And he began to laugh. A moment later I said, "Now I'm your longest surviving patient, isn't that right?"

"That's correct."

He gave me an artificially severe look and went on, biting off each syllable: "It gives you a sort of moral responsibility."

"I do my best," I said.

"There's a whole team of researchers behind you. And our new serum's much more effective."

"I know. I'm sorry, but I still feel all alone."

"Why?"

"Don't know. Perhaps because death is personal. Everyone dies, but the details are personal. Basically, it's a question of details."

"You're not very cheerful," he said. "May I pour myself another cognac?"

"Of course."

He stood, took the bottle from the table and poured a finger of cognac. Then he came and sat across from me, at the other end of the window.

"You're very fond of Quebec City?" he asked, looking at the river and the lights reflected in the water.

"It's a love story," I said.

He smiled in the half-light. I said abruptly, "Can I tell you something stupid?"

"If you want."

"I don't know why, but when I see you I always feel as though you're going to help me understand everything. I wait for the phrase that will shed light on everything, exactly like. . . ."

". . . like the sun that lights up the fog in your painting?" he asked.

"Yes."

"I can understand that."

"I suppose it's very infantile."

"You know, everyone is looking for a father. To love or to kill. And how's your story coming along?"

"I'm not making any progress at all."

"Why?"

"It happened a few days after Elise left. I suddenly realized there was no more distance."

"Distance?"

"The distance between the writer and the narrator," I said. "Usually you can feel it, it's a reassuring presence. It allows the author to be himself, to go on. You understand?"

"And then what?"

"That's all. Now there's no more distance."

He looked pensively at the river. "Writing is a strange adventure," he said. "I wonder. . . ."

"What?"

"I wonder if what you feel just comes from the fact that you're writing."

"Writing means having a young girl's heart," I said ironically.

"You don't mean that," he said reproachfully.

"I only said it because it was a fine phrase."

He ran the back of his hand across his forehead.

"Since we're on the subject," I said, "may I ask you a strange question?"

"As long as we're on the subject."

"Did you know the girl?"

"The girl?"

"The one whose heart I have."

"I knew her slightly," he said. "Your question doesn't surprise me. What does surprise me is the fact that you've waited so long."

"I'm unhinged," I said. "I mean, I never think of things at the proper time. What was her name?"

"Absolutely secret. The family insists. I can tell you that they're fine people."

"Can you tell me her first name?"

"Her name was Charlotte," he said after hesitating for a second.

"How old was she?"

"Just fifteen?"

"That's very young. Half my age."

"Of course, but her . . . excuse me, her tissues were perfectly compatible with yours, you know."

"Isn't that rather surprising?"

"No, it really has nothing to do with age. There's no age for giving your heart," he added with a smile.

It was beating too hard inside my chest and I had to wait a moment, long enough to calm down. The surgeon was watching me from the corner of his eye.

"Take things gently," he recommended.

"Yes, Doctor," I said with a hint of disrespect.

I slowly drank my Nestlé's Quik. Then I asked:

"How did she die?"

"Motorcycle accident."

He'd taken his time before he answered. He added, "She was very fond of motorcycles."

"So am I," I said."It's strange."

"What's strange?"

"I can tell that it affects you, talking about the accident. But for me it's almost as though she weren't really dead."

"I'd rather you didn't say that," said the surgeon.

"Why not?"

"No reason. I'd rather, that's all."

"What's wrong?"

"Nothing. It's just the way you say things."

I didn't really understand, but I kept quiet. You think people are invulnerable beneath their carapaces, and they're not.

"I can tell you some more about her if you want," he began.

"Of course."

"I wanted to talk to you about her but I didn't dare admit it to myself. I was waiting for your questions."

"I'm unhinged," I said. "Was she pretty?"

"Very. Especially her eyes. Very big and. . . ."

He was searching for a word, or perhaps he was drifting among his memories. He took his time describing the young girl, in a voice that had lost its usual firmness; a voice like white wine that's too old. His reassurance came back at the end.

"Your cognac's very effective," he laughed nervously by way of apology.

"You're tired."

"I'm in perfect condition."

He drained his glass. Then he looked at his wrist to see what time it was.

"I must be off to Montreal."

"It's eleven o'clock," I said, after consulting the cuckoo clock.

"Already? I must be going."

"Just a minute. I wanted to ask you something else."

He folded his arms and looked at me with infinite patience.

"You want to know what her personality was like?" he asked.

"Yes," I said, a little surprised.

He slowly lit another cigarette. His lighter flame didn't tremble.

"She was gentleness personified. You'd have got along very well with her, in spite. . . ."

"In spite of the difference in age?"

"Excuse me," he said.

"You forget that I haven't always been gentle," I said.

"No?"

"I've become what she was, haven't I?"

He looked at me without replying. I was beginning to have doubts about some very old things, and an old question came back to the surface.

"Doctor Grondin."

". . . ."

"Before you decided that this young girl's heart suited me you asked me a lot of questions, do you remember?"

"Yes."

"In particular about what I was writing, didn't you?"

"Of course. What of it?"

"You weren't, by chance, trying to take into account the compatibility of our personalities?"

He got up.

"Listen," he said. "I've already explained that the heart is simply a muscle, a sort of pump."

"You explained it, but. . . ."

"Very well, then. I haven't changed my mind."

"Excuse me," I said.

In a gentler voice he added, "Let's say that I ask myself certain questions." And once again he said, as though he were answering me, "Yes, particularly because of you. Now I really must go. Thank you for the cognac."

He bent down to put out his cigarette in the ashtray, then went towards the door.

"One last question," I said. "A stupid question."

"Yes?" he asked, hand on the doorknob.

"During the transplant, did you hold the heart in your hand?"

"Obviously."

"Did you feel as though you were holding a bird?"

He opened the door part way, turned towards me; he seemed to hesitate, then went out without saying anything.

Charlie has watched me write the entire letter, her chin resting on her wrists.

"It'll take her her whole lifetime," she says.

"Eh?"

"To do all that."

"You read it upside down?"

"I didn't intend to but you were talking about birds at the beginning. It's going to take her whole lifetime," she repeats.

"You're right. I'll write her to forget it all, except Bachelard and the cats."

"No, that would be dishonest."

"Do you think so?"

"I'm sure. You're a writer?"

"An apprentice."

"Why do you write?"

"So I won't feel guilty."

"But you feel guilty all the same?" asks Charlie, pointing to the letter to old Marie.

"Of course."

"I understand," she says gently.

"I don't."

"I've had a tremendous experience," she says. "And I have Simon."

"You're very lucky then."

"You have old Marie, don't you?"

"Of course. Don't you sometimes wish you had a family?"

"A real family?" she asks pensively.

"Yes."

"A family's useful mostly when you're old."

She hadn't said that to hurt me and I don't feel hurt either.

"We must go now," I say.

"Do you have a car?"

"Yes."

"What kind?"

"Do you know a lot about cars?"

"All except the American ones. I'm a car expert. What kind?"

"Why did you use the masculine form of expert?"

"What does it matter," she says.

She didn't pose it as a question.

"Sunbeam Tiger."

"Why are you looking at me like that? I didn't tell you I wanted to be a boy."

"You did tell me that. We must go now."

"Can I drive the Tiger?"

"If you want."

"Listen."

"You can hear the purring of a motor."

"It's a helicopter," she says. "It must be taking off from the icebreaker 'd'Iberville.' "

She is leaning out the window. If the sun isn't shining on her hair it's because it's already on the other side of the Château. The day is ending. She turns around, smiles, and we decide to go. I leave the lamp on. I take nothing with me.

Charlie stops the Tiger at the edge of the cliff. She's driving the car far better than I would have done, not touching the brake and using the gears to the maximum on the curves of the old Chemin Saint-Louis and along the sinuous road to Saint-Nicolas.

She gets out, her face glowing, and hands me the key.

"Simon's here," she says.

She points to the calèche, half-hidden in the tree.

"Look," she says again.

"What?"

"Over there, near the calèche, a redwinged blackbird."

"I don't see a thing," I say in a low voice.

"What's wrong with you?"

"Nothing."

"Don't you think the air is mild?"

"Very mild."

"And don't you think it's beautiful?"

"Very beautiful."

"The tide's going out," she says.

It's true that the tide's going out. From the top of the cliff we see part of the beach, the big rock and the cages of eels that are half submerged. Towards Saint-Augustin, on the other side of the river, the sun is nearly at the horizon and it is beginning to turn the wet sandbank pink. Of course the air is mild, and it's beautiful to look at, but I can't forget the slight nausea that hasn't left me since morning. And then there are some things I'm beginning to understand and others that escape me. I can already see, through the trees, the narrow path that will take us to the bottom of the cliff where, behind the row of trees, at the back of the abandoned garden, we will find the playhouse. Stories are complicated when hearts are involved. The landscape that's inhabited me forever, which I soon will see in its entirety, is nothing other than childhood itself. I know it now: the inner pole was childhood. And so I understand that Charlie, who lives very close to hers, could have helped me pass the final stage; essentially, each person's childhood is like all the others. And of course the road had to be the road of gentleness. I'm not late for the appointment, but I'll never be able to live in this landscape because life is aggression. Finally, it's my own childhood that's rejecting me; it's funny, just now I feel as though I've always known it. That's what I understand. It's all rather unclear, but stories where hearts are involved are too complicated for me, I no longer have my own, I have only that other one which doesn't suit me, or which suits me only too well. I think too that life begins to reject us from the very moment of our birth and that we're satisfied to grope for our personal way of dying.

"You coming?" Charlie asks. "We're going to miss the sunset."

She pulls me gently by the hand. I resist.

"Wait a bit," I say with difficulty.

I am shaken within. My chest and stomach hurt. I lie in the grass. The only sound that reaches the outside is a very gentle laugh that is slowly extinguished. Then I sit up.

Charlie is kneeling close to me.

"You were sad and now you're laughing," she says.

"It's nothing. Stupid ideas. I was taking myself seriously."

She puts her arms around my neck.

"I like you very much; you're like Simon."

"My old Blue Whale," I say, very gently, into her ear.

"Come now, because of the sun," she says.

She takes my hand again and leads me to the path; to please her, I pretend to be lost. At the entrance, which is partly masked by two blue spruce trees, she drops my hand and starts climbing down. I follow her, a step at a time. The path is narrow, tortuous, slippery.

Immediately I am out of breath. I stop. She turns around. My breathing is loud. I walk over to her and sit down on a large root that obstructs the path. She sits too, her elbows on the knees of her jeans, face raised up towards the crown of the trees, and she begins to whistle the cantata "Jesu Joy of Man's Desiring." She's not winded at all, she whistles the cantata right to the end, with perfect mastery. Afterwards I put my hand on her shoulder to tell her I'm ready. She points towards the bottom of the path.

"Look," she murmurs.

"Where?"

"Just where the path disappears from sight."

"Yes."

"The ray of sunlight, can you see it?"

"Of course."

"A little to the left," she says. "There's a bluejay."

"I can't see it."

"Look at the tip of my finger."

I bend over to follow the direction precisely.

"I don't see a thing," I say, rather sadly.

"Doesn't matter," Charlie says. "You don't see birds at first. It's as though you were blind."

"Tell me what it looks like."

"Don't be sad, it's very beautiful. His back is as blue as a winter sky, his belly's grey white, there's a beautiful blue crest on his head and a black necklace around his neck. There are black streaks and white spots on the wings and on the long tail."

"That's very pretty."

"Yes, but you're still sad."

"It doesn't matter now."

"I'm going to help you. I'm going to tell you about the dream I had. I've only told it to Simon. Do you want to hear it?"

"Of course, but the sun. . . ."

"It doesn't matter, the sky's more beautiful after the sun has set."

"That's what I always say."

"I saw a big white bird soaring over the river between Quebec and Lévis. It was an Arctic tern, my very favorite bird. It has broad wings, a black cap and dark blood-red beak and claws. It's a bird from the far north and it never comes down past James Bay but it was still the bird I saw in my dream. It was wounded and there was blood flowing over its white chest. Have you ever seen an Arctic tern?"

"Never."

"It's the bird on the cover of the book I left at your place. You aren't listening."

"I was thinking about Doctor Grondin. Excuse me."

"That's the first time you've called me 'tu.' You think too

much, but I'm still fond of you. You're always asking questions and you think too much, you're like a child. And you're gentle too and you made me think of a cat."

When someone says they're fond of you, you want them to understand everything.

"I was thinking of the doctor because of gentleness and death."

"I'm not asking you anything," says Charlie.

"Of course, but death is the final stage of gentleness. Death is absolute gentleness. It's rest and calm. It's the absence of movement, and peace."

I was speaking slowly, taking the time to explain properly. Now Charlie says nothing more, but for a moment her head rested on my shoulder. Then, to please her:

"It's a very beautiful dream and only a Blue Whale could dream it."

"I was lucky," she says, her voice sounding as though she has a cold.

She coughs several times to clear her throat and says again, "I've always been very lucky."

"You can go now, my Blue Whale."

We walk down the rest of the path, slowly but without stopping, and Charlie doesn't notice the bluejay or another bird. At the bottom we step abruptly onto the beach. The tide is already out and the long sandbank, torn by the rock, is still purple in the last rays of the sun.

Charlie pulls me onto the sandy beach. I could walk with my eyes closed; it's as though I were going home after a long absence. It's just that the nausea is getting worse and I don't know if I'll be able to go to the end. She leads me to a cove where the cliff recedes before a small woods. We walk through the first row of birches, cross an abandoned garden, walk around a spruce tree and a birch and then fifty feet away, the house appears.

Simon is standing in front of the open door, and from here he seems to be nearly as tall as the house. He's tanned, with a high forehead and black hair, a beard that's turning grey, very broad shoulders; he's wearing a black shirt and velvet trousers, with boots that come up to his knees. He is looking at us.

Charlie lets go of my hand, rushes over to him and, resting the tips of her bare toes on the calèche driver's boots, she throws her arms around his neck. She seems to be whispering in his ear. I've stayed where I was, out of breath, heart pounding. I feel old and young at the same time, like someone who all at once has lost all that he had experienced. It's hard to explain. I'm glad to see the house; it's made of brown wood, turned a little more brown by age and it's a little smaller than I'd thought.

Charlie turns around and gestures to me to come closer.

"Welcome," says Simon in a rough voice, shaking my hand.

"Thank you."

"The Blue Whale says you've taken a journey and that you're tired."

"That's true."

He and Charlie have the same eyes.

"Come in then, and rest," he says.

He holds the door open. He resembles the photograph of Hemingway I used to have in Quebec, but he reminds me of someone else too, a man I've met and forgotten along the way.

I bend down to go inside. The house has only one room. In the middle there's a very low table and four small chairs; in a corner, the narrow beds stacked on top of one another, with a short ladder between them; Chanoine is sleeping on the bottom bed; in the opposite corner stands a child's piano with a rag doll sitting on it, its disproportionately long legs dangling onto the keyboard.

"That's Jimmy," says Charlie, who was following my gaze.

"I know," I say softly.

And books. Books everywhere. But on one wall, hanging from nails, there are shotguns and revolvers. Simon has closed the door without a sound and is leaning against the wall near the entrance. There were no firearms in my daydreams. And under the bed I see again the two wooden boxes. I look at Charlie.

"You're surprised?" she asks.

"No."

"That's a case of dynamite and the other one has grenades in it."

I'm not really surprised; my throat is dry and I'm too tired to ask questions.

"The Blue Whale tells me you're a writer," the calèche driver says calmly.

"Apprentice," I say very softly.

"I've chosen the other way, you see."

"I understand."

After a moment I say, not really knowing why:

"You like books. . . ."

"He's very gentle too," says Charlie, as though she were speaking to herself.

"You can also write with the feathers of birds," I say.

"I'm too old and I don't much like ideas any more," says Simon.

"Neither do I."

"Go and rest on the bed," he says.

"Yes."

"Tomorrow the house will be empty."

"You're going away?" I ask as I lie down on the bottom bed.

"You must keep moving. So if there's anything you need. . . ."

"I have everything."

"Rest in peace," says the Blue Whale.

Simon opens the door and they prepare to go out. Then Charlie turns around.

"I'm leaving it open so you can hear the tide."

And she puts her hand in Simon's big hand and they go out. I still wonder if the calèche driver is her father or not. I call weakly: "Blue Whale!"

She turns around a second time.

"If you see old Marie some day. . . ."

"Yes?"

"No . . . nothing."

She makes a small gesture with her hand, then I see her disappear behind the trees with Simon. Chanoine follows them. It's true that you can hear the river; the tide has likely started to come in. I feel as though I'm late. I'd forgotten to tell old Marie not to stop writing: when you stop you do harm to all the others. And I'd have liked to tell the Blue Whale that I liked her heart very much.

I get up with difficulty. I go to get Jimmy from the piano, I lay him down on the bed. Then I lift the lid of one of the boxes and take out a grenade. I remove the pin. I slip my hand, which is clutching the grenade, under my old grey sweater. I lie on my side, head bent, knees raised and my other hand between my legs. The nausea has passed and I feel well. There's a song in my head but I can't think of the title. No, it's more like the song of a bird. A bird that's been set free.

30,687